THE SECRET JOURNALS OF ADOLF HITLER

VOLUME 2

A. G. MOGAN

A NOVEL

THE STRUGGLE

Copyright © 2018 by **A. G. Mogan**

The Secret Journals of Adolf Hitler, Volume 2 – The Struggle/ A. G. Mogan, 1st Edition

Note: This is a work of fiction. Names, characters, places, and incidents either are the product of the author's imagination or are used fictitiously. Any resemblance to actual people, living or dead, or to businesses, companies, events, institutions, or locales is completely coincidental.

Book Cover © 2018 by BookCoverMall

For future releases and promotions, or to connect on social media, please visit the author's website at:

www.AGMogan.com

DISCLAIMER

Although based on real characters and circumstances, this is a
work of fiction and of the author's imagination.

For David,
our ray of sunshine

CONTENTS

Beware that, when fighting monsters, you yourself do not become a monster, for when you gaze long into the abyss, the abyss gazes also into you.

Friedrich Nietzsche

GHOSTS OF THE PAST

I always thought that, except for our sun, stars don't shine in full daylight. But Hanussen's do. They shine bright and flicker, blinding me with their kind, generous light. More so on a cloudy dreary winter day, 20 December 1924, when less than nine months as an official prisoner between damp walls, I am released from prison.

My photographer awaits me at the fortress gates in a brand-new, supercharged Mercedes.

"It is time," I say, pointing toward the ever-present camera in his hands. His eyes fill with strange dancing lights. His hands shake as he prepares the camera for the long-awaited snap.

"The best propagandistic picture I have ever been graced to take," he boasts.

"Not here!" A coarse voice behind us pushes into the moment. "Move away, no pictures allowed here." The bald, massive security guard steps toward us, waving his hand.

"Well, I guess your day is not as lucky as mine, Hoffmann," I say, and jump into the car.

"I shall make it my lucky day," he declares.

As we drive off, I turn to face the fortress one last time. A feeling of profound relief invades me. With my eyes on the little barred window, my only connection to the outside world for almost a year, I hear myself whispering: *Thank you. My university education at state expense.*

After travelling north for a few miles, Hoffmann pulls over.

"Here," he says, pointing at the dark massive medieval gateway, the elegant late-Gothic Bayertor, and southernmost entrance to the old town of Landsberg. "Even better than uninteresting Landsberg prison. This shall excite people's imagination. We could use the picture alongside a monumental newspaper headline, such as: *'The Fortress Gate has Opened!'* or *'No Fortress Can Retain Our Savior Forever!'* Something along those lines."

I laugh at my friend's perseverance and quite surprising propagandistic mindset. Ironing my trench coat with my hands, I finally pose for him. It is the first of a long set of pictures that will make my friend truly rich. He knows it already, as do I, by the satisfied, joyful look in his eyes.

I ask Hoffmann to drive to Hanfstaengl's fancy new house in Munich, where a quiet celebration dinner awaits me.

As he does so, I suddenly remember Hanussen's prediction: *'The dawn of Christmas shall find you dining among friends.'* I smile, and then sigh in relief, for I do not want to go home yet. My Thierschstrasse apartment, which I moved into upon leaving the barracks in April 1920, would give me the same dreadful feeling of emptiness that has brutally plagued me for the last nine months.

When we arrive, I am greeted at the door by Hanfstaengl's wife, Helene. I lean forward to kiss her hand and turn red in the face at the memory of our last encounter. She smiles as I enter, and then her gaze pauses on my bloated stomach.

"Your suit is pulled quite tightly, Herr Hitler. I am happy the idea of starving yourself to death has left you in good time."

"Well, Helene, you saw my prison cell; always full of culinary temptations. Pretty difficult to resist."

"And that is because people love you."

"Indeed. It is for them I go on. I realized this in my lonely moments this past year."

A soothing aria reaches my ears, and entering Hanfstaengl's living room I see my friend hammering out music on the piano. It is his way of welcoming me, of celebrating my release. I close my eyes and begin to hum the notes, deeply penetrated by the music.

"Hanfstaengl, play for me the 'Liebestod'!"

"Still Wagner?"

"Forever, Wagner..."

As he teases the piano keys in my favorite *Tristan and Isolde* aria, tears burst from my eyes. My thoughts fly back to Linz, to my long-lost love for Stefanie, and to Mother. It is strange how Wagner gives birth to such opposite feelings in me...of love and of hatred. My tears are not sorrowful but bring comfort and relief in their fall. Yet they seem to make my friend uncomfortable, as he suddenly changes the tune into lively, but strange, music.

I wipe my tears away with the sleeve of my blue suit. "What is it?"

"Football marches. One of the many things I learned at Harvard," he says, winking at me. I like the sound of it. The beat is engaging, energizing, full of rhythm. My friend's fingers move faster and faster, changing from a low beat to a higher one in a matter of seconds, sending shivers traveling up and down my back. I close my eyes again and imagine the SA men marching on a similar tune.

"This is what I need!" I blurt out. "This is exactly what I need for the movement!"

"Yes, you should include the American beat in your German marches."

I move up and down the room, erect as a soldier, marching to my friend's music.

"Write some for me, Hanfstaengl!" I plead. "Write some of these marches for Germany!"

"Rah! Rah! Rah!" he shouts boisterously, with the last keystrokes.

I parade diagonally now, unable to stand still.

"Marvelous! Simply beautiful! How could we transmute that into a German shout?"

After a few moments of silence, he pounds the keys again, shouting: "Sieg Heil! Sieg Heil! Sieg Heil!"

I am enthralled. Tears again fall down my face. I can now finally picture my movement as a Wagnerian opera; the same grandeur, the same force, the same soaring climaxes. I see, with my mind's eye, the uniformed troops marching through the streets of Germany, carrying swastika flags and shouting: *Sieg Heil! Sieg Heil! Sieg Heil!*

"Hanfstaengl," I whisper, "we've just breathed new life into my movement."

The reality of the movement, as it was before I was taken to prison, no longer exists. Being dissolved by government decree had sent members into trifling bickering. I wanted nothing of that and resigned from the party. Let them see what they will become without me! I could not have allowed my strength, balance, and mission to be tainted by such petty trivialities. The best course of action was to take my leave from politics for a time. Relax, reform, and regroup for the coming time when I would start from scratch again.

This proved to be one of the best decisions I have ever made.

After the meal and the Austrian pastries, served by Helene, I proceed to inspect my friend's new art-cluttered home. As a rich man and the owner of an art publishing house, it is only natural that his home be adorned with beautiful pieces of art.

He offers me a glass of brandy, which I refuse, and then lights up a cigar.

"What do you feel, Herr Hitler, about what went on during your absence? I mean the movement...falling apart?" he asks, puffing on the cigar like a steam locomotive.

"My feelings are...ambivalent. But again, maybe not."

"How do you mean?"

"Well...if destiny wanted this course, it certainly had to be this course. It would be destiny's way of allowing me to recognize the vipers I had nursed at my breast for what they really are. Wouldn't you agree?"

He nods his head resolutely. "I do. I went to their secret meetings a couple of times and soon realized it was all over. All they did was fight with each other. So, I wasted my time no longer."

"You did well. You realize I did exactly the same. I did not want to be associated with a gang of swine, biting each other."

"Indeed. They are now quite divided. They split up and formed several other parties. Will you join any of them?"

"You already know the answer to your question, Hanfstaengl. I will join no one and no thing. I am done being the drummer for others' pursuits. I will rise, like a phoenix, from my own ashes – this time, as sole leader. Joining is for them, not me."

"They have placed a ban on your newspaper, too," he says, matter-of-factly.

"True. And that pig faggot Röhm, and even Ludendorff, whom I praised like no other at my trial, cliqued under the National Socialist Freedom Party! The swine! How dare they use National Socialism – a term I invented? I, and poor old Eckart! He would turn over in his grave!"

"Eckart...what a loss, especially for you."

"A great, irremediable loss. He was the only true friend I had..." I approach the window for air, painful memories of him still troubling me.

"Umm..."

"What?" I stare without focusing through the window.

"Well..."

"What? Spit it out, Hanfstaengl!"

"He wasn't always your loyal friend, you know..."

"What do you mean?"

"Well, I heard that shortly before he passed away he started complaining about you suffering from a dangerous Messiah complex, and that your delusions of grandeur would lead Germany to its ruin. '*When a man gets to a point of identifying himself with Jesus Christ, then he is ripe for an insane asylum*' is what he allegedly said."

I pull out Eckart's last letter ever written and hand it to my friend. He reads it aloud, pausing only for gulps of brandy.

"Well, maybe the prospect of death changed his heart."

"Or maybe what you've heard is nothing but crap – petty

nonsense spread among the envious party members. You mustn't believe everything you hear, dear friend."

"Didn't cross my mind."

"That is because you do not have a political mind. You are an artist and should remain as such."

His eyes crinkle at the corners while taking another greedy sip of the brown liquor. "And what will you do now?"

I burst into laughter. "Ah! That good old question! I used to hate it and just to hear someone ask it of me was to fly into an exhausting rage. Yet now, for some reason, action is all I can think of. Action is what I breathe. *Divide et impera*, as great Philip II of Macedonia would say. This is what I will do."

"Divide and rule," my friend translates proudly. "A wise man, who fathered an even wiser one."

"Alexander the Great!" we exclaim in unison.

I smile and nod. "Well, I like to translate it a bit differently... Divide and impose your will. Your will only."

He narrows his eyes in an inquisitive gaze.

"This means only one thing," he says. "You kept silent and purposefully let the party erode from discord and bickering. I might not have a political mind, but I can sense the genius in this," he concludes, looking satisfied by his discovery.

"There are no serious rivals left; well, except for Röhm. He still rules the SA and the fighters love him."

"Yet he is still your friend, is he not?"

"You say friend; I say there are no friends on the political chessboard. Only pawns to be moved around until you win. I know this – and Röhm knows it just as well."

He puffs some more on his never-ending cigar, making little smoke circles.

"You know, I met him a couple of weeks ago. He said you might strike a deal with the government to facilitate your early release from prison. '*Siding up with the enemy*', he said."

"And you still think he is my friend? The last time I made a deal with the government, I ended up in a fortress!"

"Right."

"I do intend to meet with the Bavarian Prime Minister, but only to ask for the removal of the ban from my public speaking and Völkischer Beobachter. Plus, my policy has changed. While in the quiet of Landsberg, the Goddess of History spoke to me."

"Oh?"

I sigh and look into his inquisitive eyes.

"I am not to waste my energy and resources to achieve power through another putsch. I grew up, Hanfstaengl. I am to do it the right way, by letting the people to vote for me. They must choose me, above all others. I shall enter the Reichstag against Catholic and Marxist deputies."

He nods with slow movements, as if weighing my words. "That will take an awfully long time. You know that, don't you?"

"I do, only too well. Time is indeed my greatest enemy. Yet my mind is set. This is how it is going to be. Mussolini-type power-grabbing is no longer for me." I step from the window, give him a brief sharp glance, and add, "And that's that." He seems to get the hint and pours another glass of brandy, while extinguishing that dreadful cigar.

Over his shoulder, I look at Helene, so smartly dressed, so elegant in her demeanor, and so beautiful without even a trace of makeup. She raises in me a painful longing, so I avert my gaze from her sweet figure to the thousands of books Hanfstaengl owns.

"I am afraid I have nothing of Wagner that would worth your attention," he says.

"That's too bad."

"Is there any other artist you prefer?"

"Franz von Stuck? Do you have anything of him?"

He sets his brandy aside on a table and climbs a ladder to the top shelf of his home library.

"Here," he says, pulling out a thick volume, which he hands over to me.

Glossy, colorful pages transport me back in time, as if I am standing again in the large rooms at the Hof Museum. One by one, the glossy sheets of paper reveal my favorite artist's paintings. I surrender to the feelings of pleasure *Sensuality* raises in me...the voluptuous woman, the feminine ideal of a long-past Renaissance era, who smiles seductively at the onlooker, while an enormous black snake slides through her thighs. The same snake I see again in *Depravity* as it moves through the legs of a similar beauty, who laughs with satisfaction while one hand holds her breast.

I flip the pages excitedly, gasping for more. *Sorcery and Sanctity* depicts Orpheus playing on his lyre, thus seducing the most ferocious beasts, a crocodile and a lion with his lioness, all bowing to him in obedience. I again remember Hanussen's words: '*With Orpheus' Lyre, your voice is touched with a drop of magic and a divine spell. It is full of charisma and talks of one who has been touched by the other world.*' I imagine the most ferocious beasts of men will bow under my strong will.

And then, there is *Pursuit,* in which a black centaur chases a blonde woman, and beyond that is *Scherzo,* where a black creature, the Devil himself, enjoys a blonde, white girl.

My blood raises to my temples and I tap the picture forcibly. "Look, Hanfstaengl! This is the bloody Jew! Always spying to defile the racially pure young women! I tell you this! Germany shall die of Jewish blood poisoning!" My blood reaches the boiling point. "Did you know that on Berlin's Friedrichstrasse every Jew has a blonde German girl on his arm?"

"Yeah."

"And what is his final goal, mind you?"

"No idea."

"I tell you what his final goal is: denationalization!" I shout. I can no longer remain stagnantly standing and slam the book shut, pacing to and past the window with it under my arm. "He has no country and he hates the white race! So, what does he do? He bastardizes the other nations! And he does it to lower their racial level, so he can then dominate the retarded outcome! He ruins young women! He brings inferior races, like the Negroes, into the Rhineland! And why does he do that? To destroy the white race and raise himself as a crowned head of humanity! This world is at an end!" I stop mid-step and give my friend a piercing look. "Mark my words! Study the history of mankind and you shall come to my conclusion. Yet always – always – in times of tribulations, a savior is sent. And we may perish, perhaps, but we shall take a world with us."

My heart is furiously pumping as I trot back and forth through his living room.

"This sounds rather apocalyptic, Herr Hitler. I must agree with you on maybe ninety-five percent, yet—"

"You say apocalyptic and I shall not contradict you," I say as I near my friend. "You see, Hanfstaengl, the earth is like a chalice passed from hand to hand, which explains the efforts to always get it into the hands of the strongest."

"The 'survival of the fittest' concept. I am quite familiar with it."

"That is why you will understand why we must create a Master Race. A Master Race! Well, not exactly creating it, but multiplying the best specimens of an already existing one; one ever in more danger of extinction by blood poisoning. And who else is more entitled to that honor than the Germanic folk, the followers of the Teutonic gods, the first human souls to walk this earth? Who else?"

My friend smiles. "Look, I will not even pretend to know much about—"

"Just look at nature! Is nature immoral because it permits the cat to eat the mouse? One being drinks the blood of another. By dying, the one furnishes food for the other."

"But what about our humanity? We distinguish ourselves from animals just because of that, because of the humanity in us."

"The humanity creates the morality of slaves! We should not blather about it, for it is only a tool of man's weakness, and thus, in actuality, the cruelest destroyer of his existence. We should instead respect and revere the divine laws of existence. What proof other than what nature, hence God, is showing us do you need? The titmouse seeks the titmouse, the finch the finch, the stork the stork, the field mouse the field mouse. Blood mixture and the resulting drop in the racial level is the sole cause of the dying out of old cultures; for men do not perish as a result of lost wars, but by the loss of that force of resistance, which is contained only in true blood. All who are not of good race in this world are chaff! There is no humanity, dear friend, only an eternal struggle – a struggle that is the prerequisite for the development of all humanity. We see before us the Aryan race, which is manifestly the bearer of all culture. Our entire industrial science is, without exception, the work of the Nordics. All great composers from

Beethoven to Wagner were Aryans, even though they were born in Italy or France."

"But, maybe the culture of their birth country rubbed itself on —" he starts, but I cannot have it.

"No, no! Do not say art is international! The tango, the shimmy, and the jazz band are international, but they are not art. Take away the Nordic Germans and nothing remains but the dance of apes!"

"Or merely the evolution. The universe is chaos and humans cannot be any different. In the midst of chaos there is always opportunity for variety."

"And the Jew saw it!" I bark. "What you see as evolution is nothing but the inferior races' rebellion against nature! Against what he perceived as superior, and thus, resented! And in his attempt to defile the noble Aryan, the Jew spread with lashing tongue those humanitarian phrases, which you, too, believe. Thus, his way was clear to create a capitalistic system, to destroy the old culture with his modern art, to spread his cursed syphilis across the whole earth. To me, Hanfstaengl, this is not evolution, but involution."

"And yet the Jewish people are—"

"Responsible! For all of these! The Jew is the first and oldest seed of Evil. He is a growth, the Lord of the Anti-world, the pestilence of the world. The Jews are undoubtedly a race, but not human. They cannot be human in the sense of being the image of God the Eternal. They are the image of the Devil. Jewry means the racial tuberculosis of the nations. And our responsibility is that of respecting the laws of nature, which order us to take action against and finally destroy the parasites, the eternal leeches and vampires upon other peoples. This is the logic of nature, Hanfstaengl, and if the Jew did not exist, we would have had to invent him. A visible enemy, not just an invisible one, is what is needed."

My friend follows my words with a straight face, but I sense he is barely able to retain his words. I reopen the glossy book and flip through its pages again. There, halfway through the book, I see her. I drop into a chair, muted, my hands trembling.

"Herr Hitler? Are you all right?" asks Helene, approaching

me. "Do something, Putzi!" she barks at her husband. "He looks as if he is about to faint!"

"Rather as if he had just seen a ghost." He squats and places a protective hand on my shoulder. "What happened, my friend?"

"A memory...an old memory...my mother...she has the eyes of my mother..." My words barely escape my lips.

In silence, I grab the glossy book, ignoring the astonished look on my friends' faces, and run out into the night.

2

THE ABYSS GAZES BACK

The agonizing nights that follow instill in me an urgent need to see Doctor K again. With all my hate for doctors and hospitals, I somehow trust this one. He might as well be the only person who could cure me.

It is the early morning of a January day. Dawn is just breaking and I open the tall window of my small Munich apartment, the biting cold storming in as soon as I do so. I close my eyes and make no effort to remove myself from it, as somehow, the severe low temperature serves to chase away my dreadful feelings of despondency.

Yet terrifying images from my earlier nightmare willfully persist. I slam shut the window, pull on my blue suit, and exit into the cold.

For two long hours, I walk the streets of Munich lost in thoughts. I remember Linz; how I walked for several days through knee-length snow, pondering the hostile world around me and all the abandoning people and loneliness. Munich has little snow this January, but I still ponder the same truths.

At 9 o'clock sharp, I knock on the door of Doctor K's home clinic.

"Good morning, Doctor," I say, shaking his hand. "It has been a long time."

"Good morning to you, too, Herr..."

"Hitler," I say, sensing the futility of still using Father's old last name. "I gather you already know that by now?"

"I do. Just wasn't sure if you'd still prefer to be called by the other name. It is indeed a long time since our last discussion."

"Yes. Many things have happened since then."

The doctor rubs his sleepy eyes. "Indeed...and I must admit that I looked into the unfolding of events quite keenly. It was fascinating entertainment for me, even though I wasn't surprised in the least."

"And why not?"

"Because I had expected it. I am still expectant of things that are even more fascinating. The greater the imagination, the grander the idealized self."

I raise an eyebrow. "I am afraid I don't follow."

He smiles, his perfectly white teeth contrasting with his tanned skin. Is he traveling even in January?

"Well, we psychotherapists can sometimes have a knack of predicting the course of someone's future life. That is, of course, if the person in question is not willing to respond to therapy."

"And you can do that based on...what?"

He gestures me to sit down and takes his place in front of me.

"Based on the events that took place in one's childhood and based on how those particular events affect one's growth and psychological development."

"I see. So, I disclosed some truths about my mother and father, and that made you expect a failed putsch and an imprisonment? Is that what you are saying?"

"No. Not like that. I can predict your psychological disposition, not particular events. I can tell you, sometimes with astonishing accuracy, what motivates you to do what you do, what stops you from doing things that would be good for you, what frightens you, and so on."

"You know, Doctor, an astrologer would point to the influence of certain planets, while you would point to the influence of childhood events – and the list could probably go on. So, I ask you: where does that leave me? My will, my choices, my premeditated actions?"

"It is you who chooses, and then acts on those choices. But

again, these things depend entirely on your power of creativity, on the power of your imagination. As I mentioned before...the greater the imagination, the grander the idealized self."

I roll my eyes angrily. "And as I mentioned before, I still don't follow. Is this guessing game supposed to reveal some new things about me?" I take in one breath, then add, "Because, frankly, I find you quite arrogant this morning."

He pauses and slightly furrows his eyebrows. "You are right. I am sorry. I was indeed quite arrogant in my enthusiasm. What brings you here today, Herr Hitler?"

"A dreadful nightmare I've been having for the past few months, almost every other night," I say, and notice my hands beginning to tremble.

"I am all ears. Please, proceed."

I sigh deeply and stand up. I need to pace the room, as it can calm me down.

"It always starts with me being a child," I commence, an invisible claw raking at my stomach. "I am quite happy and joyful. My mother places me in a trough of pleasantly warm water. I wriggle my hands enthusiastically, hitting the water and splashing it all over. I look at her, somehow searching for her approval of my behavior. She is nothing but smiles and her eyes exude the infinite love I know she feels for me. I continue to splash the water vigorously, still eager to make her happy and receive more of that soothing love. When I tire of my game, she stands me up, and taking soap in her hands, rubs it all over my body, making foam and bubbles. This action tickles me and we laugh together while she washes my hair, my hands, my torso, and my legs. She then..." I pause, heaving a sigh.

"She then...?"

"Then, as she reaches my private parts, her expression becomes sad, pensive, almost...angry."

"What do you think is the reason for her change in mood?"

"I do not know for certain, but I sense it has something to do with my defected body, my missing parts."

"Do you remember such an incident happening in real life, as well? When you were a child?"

"I am not too sure...it could have been...it is like a faded memory, but I am not sure if it is real or yet another nightmare."

"All right. And then?"

"Then, the embarrassment I feel and the overwhelming pain of having disappointed her tear me away from that scene, only to throw me into another painful one."

"Which is?"

"I am standing naked in front of a mirror. I am a grown-up now. The mirror I am staring into is the only thing adorning my childhood bedroom," I recount, twisting my fingers.

"And what do you see in the mirror?"

"I told you, Doctor. I see myself." *Is this idiot even listening to me?*

"I got that," he says, as calm as usual, his attention on jotting something in the notebook he holds. "What I meant was...what do you see when you look at yourself?"

"Oh. Well, I see an ugly person – a hollow-chested, disgusting person with a large torso and short skinny legs. My hips look wider than my shoulders, and my muscles are soft and flaccid. My face is equally repulsive with big bulging eyes, broad cheekbones, a hideous nose with large nostrils, and a small mouth full of rotten, brown teeth." I sit, suddenly tired, and lean my forehead against his desk. "Still looking in the mirror, my face twisted in disgust, I open my mouth and smell my foul breath. Above all else, I sense my handicap, my missing parts again, yet I cannot look at that spot. It is as if an invisible force renders me blind as soon as I look toward that part of my body. I continue to look in the mirror until my mounting hate impels me to break it into pieces."

"And this is how your nightmare ends?"

"Far from it," I say, raising my head. "After shattering the mirror, I somehow still see myself in it, yet in tiny broken pieces. It makes me even more aware of my distorted, deficient, incomplete body and I crash to the floor, wailing. At that moment, through my bitter tears, I see someone standing behind me. Startled, I turn around and see a mighty knight dressed in armor and holding a sword. I look into his eyes and he looks into mine, and I realize I am him and he is…Parsifal, the great knight of the Holy Grail."

I pause to inspect the Doctor's expression to see if my words amuse him. But his face is unchanged, only his eyes look alive and expectant.

"Go on…" he urges.

"All of the sudden, I am now that knight and look at the repulsive body that's wailing on the floor. As Parsifal, I know I am there to kill that despicable being, yet I *am* that despicable being. I now see Parsifal raising his armed hand and striking me down. 'Jew!' he yells. 'Jew!' Agonizing in the pain, I close my eyes, expecting to die. Yet I hear my executioner laughing. '*Ha Ha! Bist du keusch? Ha Ha! Are you chaste?*' he asks, pointing his sword toward my face. I look instinctively between my legs and I see…he has castrated me! He has cut off my private parts! I scream! And I scream! Kundry! Kundry! And I scream again, so loud that I awake in my room, soaking wet, agonizing like a half-dead, stabbed animal, still screaming … Kundry! Kundry!"

Little drops of sweat invade my forehead and I stand up again, reaching into my pocket for a handkerchief. The doctor offers me a glass of water, which I accept. As I gulp it down, I look at him, seemingly lost in thoughts, staring at a pencil he twirls between his fingers.

"Quite hard to decipher, eh?"

"Do you like Wagner, Herr Hitler?"

"Very much so. I know all his operas by heart."

"I see. I know Parsifal as being one of Wagner's heroes, but I am not familiar with Kundry. Who is this person…also from Wagner's opera?"

"Yes. She is an alluring sorceress, a redeemed wandering Jew. She calls Parsifal by his name and he asks how is it that she knows his name. She replies, '*Ich sah das kind an seiner mutter brust. I saw the child on his mother's breast,*' and tells him she came to know his name from his mother, who had loved him and tried to shield him from his father. The mother he abandoned and who had finally died of grief. Kundry then reveals to Parsifal many parts of his history and he is stricken with remorse, blaming himself for his mother's death."

I pause, remembering the master's beautiful opera, and then blurt out, "He thinks himself very stupid to have forgotten her. Kundry says this realization is a first sign of understanding, and that with a kiss she can help him understand his mother's love. As they kiss, Parsifal suddenly recoils in pain, shrieking, and cries out: *Die Wunde! Die Wunde! The wound! The wound!*" Inhaling sharply, I continue, "So, what do you make of it, Doctor? Upon my soul, I'd do anything to get rid of this frightful nightmare!"

He taps his notebook with his pencil a few times, then throws both onto the table and stands up. "Your nightmare is so revealing to me, Herr Hitler, I don't even know where to start!" I watch him taking his turn in marching the room. This unexpected action amuses me.

"You can start with the beginning, or the middle, or the end, I don't care, as long as you shed some light on what has been torturing me for so long!"

"Okay, then...I mentioned to you before that under severe stress and suffering, in your particular case the abuse you suffered from your father, the child develops a defense mechanism. Which is what you did. You could not eliminate your father, of course, and so, being sensitive and vulnerable, you proceeded to eliminate – yourself. You did that by alienating yourself from your true identity – unconsciously, of course – and this was your defense mechanism. You did something else, as well. Eliminating your real self demanded the creation of a new self, in psychology this is known as the *idealized self.*"

"Yes, Doctor, I remember you mentioning this the last time I was here, but is it relevant to my nightmare?" I ask, anxiously.

"It has everything to do with your nightmare, but I must give you an unhurried explanation, so you can understand it deeply and properly. Otherwise, we are just wasting time."

I wring my hands quietly for a while, and then, bending slightly forward, I place them on his desk, my fingers intertwined. "Very well, then. I am listening."

"You shifted your energy from finding a way to eliminate your father to the task of molding *yourself* into a being of absolute perfection, because nothing short of godlike perfection could manage to fulfill the task of eliminating your pain. The attitudes resulting from your unconscious transformation were determined by your temperament. Some children try to comply; hence, they to cling to the dominant parent. Others turn toward aggressiveness, rebelling and fighting, while some move toward aloofness, withdrawing emotionally. Stepping toward one of the three 'moves' entails certain changes in the whole personality."

I look at him impatiently, eager to get to the part that interests me.

"Given your compulsive behavior," he resumes, "your childhood history, and the recent events in your life, which I keenly kept track of, I am certain that in creating your particular idealized self, you turned toward aggressiveness."

Compulsive behavior, recent events, aggressiveness...this doctor is so negative. I almost feel scolded.

"I didn't realize I have a compulsive behavior. I am not even sure what it means, exactly, and what makes you say I have it, but it does not sound very flattering."

"Well, I am not here to flatter you, Herr Hitler, but to shed light into your agony of not knowing what torments you through these dreams. Your compulsive behavior is made obvious by things you do repeatedly, without even being aware you are doing them." His voice is as calm as ever.

"What things?" His frankness and know-it-all attitude is becoming infuriating.

"Biting your nails, picking the hair off your body, scratching your skin, wiping your face and hands off almost uninterruptedly. I also sense you have difficulty listening, becoming impatient when I speak, as if you wish to interrupt me and do the talking yourself."

His words make me glow bright red. "I didn't realize these things have such significance, but I suppose you are right. I do bite my nails and I am very impatient. Please, go on."

"Thank you. As I was saying, I am certain that you have turned toward aggressiveness when creating yourself anew. You began by placing value on strength and on the capacity to endure and fight. But, the transformation was very gradual, with a lot of inner conflict between the old self and the new. Self-confidence could not exist in the early stages of development, but it, or at least a substitute, was desperately needed. Because of the inner conflict and its pain, and because of your isolation and hostility toward the world, you could only develop an urgent need to lift yourself above others."

"Interesting. Is there more?"

"We've barely scratched the surface..."

"Go on, go on."

"You needed something that gave you a feeling of identity, so as to feel meaningful to yourself and give you a feeling of power and significance. And the only way you could fulfill this need was through your imagination."

"Ha! I was and am very imaginative!"

"I know. I remember you selected imagination as the most preeminent quality you possessed since early childhood."

"Indeed!"

"Gradually and unconsciously your imagination created the idealized image of yourself. In the process, you endowed yourself with unlimited powers and exalted aptitudes. You became a hero, a genius, a god. This gave you the significance you so craved and the feeling of superiority over others. You imagined yourself with the capacities of strength, leadership, heroism, omnipotence, and made all of these parts of your new reality. This idealized image became your idealized self as you started to identify with it. I am sure you can now better follow my dictum: *the greater the imagination, the grander the idealized self?*"

"It makes sense now, yes."

"Yet the struggle isn't over and the inner conflict continues."

"Of course...as though it ever ends," I coo to myself.

"Love became an inadmissible softness as you began to perceive yourself as a knight in shining armor, oblivious to softness."

I jump to my feet. "The Knight in my nightmare! Is it related, Doctor? Is it?"

"Of course, it is. I have used the term purposefully for a better understanding. But I am not finished, and we will get to your nightmare shortly. Please, sit down, Herr Hitler," he demands. Lucky for him that he is calm and soft-spoken.

"Good, good."

"Your idealized self becomes more and more real as it answers all your strict needs. It somehow seems to end your pain; and in your passionate need to stick to this newly-found solution, you become *compulsive* and cling to it for life." He looks at me, smiling a foxy smile. I smile back, embarrassed, as he continues. "The process cannot merely remain an inward struggle, so you yearn to express it in *action*, to reassure yourself that the idealized self is indeed the real you. You now start to reach out for glory. Your new needs are for perfection, neurotic ambition and vindictive triumph."

He pauses to look at me and I know his thoughts. My struggle to grab power. My putsch.

"Some ways to achieve that triumph," he resumes, "is through putting others to shame and defeating them through your own successes, or attaining power by rising to prominence; and once you have acquired that power over others, to inflict suffering upon them, mostly of a humiliating kind. The motivating force stems from impulses to take revenge for the humiliation you suffered in childhood."

He is silent again and his words get me thinking. I feel most awkward and out of place.

"Your words make me uncomfortable."

"I know. My words shed light, yet you perceive that light as a threat and are afraid that the truth will make you see through your imagination into the *real* you. You are afraid for the *survival of your idealized image*; and because you cling to who you are now I can predict something very easily..."

"And what might that be?"

"You will continue to come to see me but will never take my words seriously."

I smirk. "Well, a prediction is a prediction and remains only that until proven accurate. And it somehow contradicts itself, because if I am not going to follow your discoveries, why would I want to continue to come to see you?"

"Because here is the only place in the world where you feel your true self is accepted, and I am the only person who might get to know the real you. It might be uncomfortable to have someone blow your cover, but at the same time it is the very thing that attracts you to keep returning. And you will not follow my advice because that would mean *giving up who you are right now*, and that you are not willing to do. It would mean your death, the death of your idealized self, and thus, you would have to give up your vindictive pursuits. You will probably leave no stone unturned until you have had your revenge though."

"This is quite hilarious, Doctor! It feels...forgive me...but it feels like a load of crap. You say that because I hated my father for the suffering he inflicted upon me, I want revenge. You are correct to that point, but you forget one little detail: he is dead and there is no way I can have my revenge."

"Right, I know that. But being compulsive, even fanatic, about payback for all your suffering, your imagination created a *new* enemy. And for now, I believe that new enemy is *the entire world around you*. Later, or maybe even already, you will imagine, even invent, a more specific enemy, who could give you the *opportunity of real action toward revenge*."

His last words render me mute; and for some reason, my last conversation with Hanfstaengl rings in my head: "*This is the logic of Nature, Hanfstaengl, and if the Jew did not exist, we would have had to invent him. A visible enemy, not just an invisible one, is what is needed.*"

I suddenly feel sick to my stomach and am afraid I'm about to throw up. I excuse myself and ask for a few moments alone. I exit into the cold and search for a curbstone on which to sit. The nausea, the snow and the biting cold remind me of the little ground window I stared through at Mother and Father fighting, three decades ago. The same biting cold brings me round and I return inside.

"Forgive me, Doctor, but could we concentrate on the reason that brought me here in the first place? My nightmare?" I ask, struggling to push away other bothering thoughts.

"Certainly. You now have sufficient information to be able to understand what your nightmare means and let us hope it will no longer bother you. Peace comes with the understanding of things."

"Or it troubles you even greater," I mutter under my breath.

"Your connection to your mother was very strong and

continues to be, since she is the only person in your imagination that you allow yourself to feel love toward. You will hang on to the memory of her for the rest of your life. And because you do not allow yourself to feel love in real life, you experience it in dreams. Your nightmare starts as a beautiful dream, with you experiencing that blissful connection of love with your mother. If it wasn't for the many implications of your mental processes, it would have continued to be a beautiful dream."

"I turned it into a nightmare?"

"Yes and no. Your mind did, your subconscious mind, which will never forget who you really are."

"And I suppose that is not a very good thing?"

"If you use it to move toward your real self, it can be a good thing. If not...well, let's say that you will lose your soul, so to speak, which will lead to a permanent inner hell of self-contempt and self-torment."

"I see. Go on with the nightmare, please."

"Now, it is not entirely certain that you ever saw your mother's frustration at your monorchism, but I believe it did happen. It is also possible that she may have been worried, rather than angry, and being afraid that you had disappointed her, you misinterpreted her reaction as anger and frustration. What *is* certain is that it affected you deeply enough to have repercussions ever after. And it is of extreme importance for us to drill on this issue, as it might well be the cause and, finally, the answer to your perceived impotence."

"The cause of my impotence is the bloody Jewish affliction, as I told you before!" I snap, irritated.

"Syphilis?"

"Yes!"

"You still believe you have it, even though your Wassermann came back negative?"

"Yes!"

"But why?"

"That Jewish test can fail. And, who knows, maybe it is *meant* to fail! One can never be completely certain about it."

"Just because the test happened to be invented by a Jewish doctor, doesn't make it a Jewish test, per se."

"*Happened* to be invented? Nothing is left to fate when it comes to those apes."

He looks at me quizzically but resolves to go on. "The person you stare at in the mirror is your real self, or at least the way you perceived yourself through the eyes of your mother and father. Your father's behavior – his lack of love, his aggressiveness, beatings, humiliations, the overall negative attitude he had toward you – made you hate yourself and see yourself as a despicable human being. Yet it is not your father's behavior that continues to haunt you, at least not entirely."

"It's not?"

"No. You dealt with that years ago when, unable to cope with the pain and hate, you created your idealized self. That allowed you to shift the hate from yourself toward your father. And then, having endowed yourself with unlimited powers, you found solace in the idea of revenge, you found peace in the idea that one day your sufferings and humiliations would be avenged. Hence, it is not your father that haunts you, it is not your father that continues to make you hate yourself and see yourself as despicable, but your mother."

My eyes almost come out of my head.

"What in the world do you mean? This whole thing is too complicated!" I blurt, furiously throwing my arms about. "Aren't there simpler answers? What do you mean by my mother haunts me and makes me hate myself?"

"When you perceived your mother's displeasure at your monorchism or at least your deeply instilled fear of her being displeased at it, it was such a blow to you that it broke your soul into pieces. You wanted her to be nothing but happy and proud of you, yet you started to see yourself as incomplete, undeserving, despicable, because you thought you disappointed her. You started hating yourself because you thought you let her down by being incomplete. However, this time, you could not shift your hate toward her, because she was the only person you loved. The love you had for her rendered your vengeful god-like-self null, in at least one respect: you could not get rid of your self-hate by hating your mother."

His words bring to the surface such hateful memories, such

painful feelings that I strain not to exit the room again. I wipe my forehead dry and nod as he continues.

"You tried to compensate for the feeling of incompleteness by blowing out of proportion the creation of your idealized self. You did not become a mere hero, but the hero of all heroes. You did not become just a god, but the master of all gods. An *anointed* person. You, Herr Hitler, are no simple idealized self. To you, it will never end. The flight of your imagination will go from fantastic to fanatic and into the realm of unlimited power, as only to God are all things possible. To you, the search for glory becomes a demonical obsession, almost like a monster swallowing up its creator."

I look at my doctor speaking with such conviction and, on the one hand, imagine slapping his face for being so bold, yet on the other, I cannot help but be...proud of myself. I don't even know if what I feel makes sense or if I should feel embarrassed by it, but I urge him to go on. It is like watching a hilarious, stupid movie.

"In your failings, no matter how small, your reaction of rage will be completely out of proportion to the actual importance of the occasion. You will hate time, because it is something definite, something out of your power to change, and it constricts your plans."

My words burst out, unrestrained. "Dear lord, I hate time! I never have enough! I can predict I will not have enough to carry on with all I've set my mind to do. What else?"

"Well, you might be suspicious of others, for having lost your truth, you will have difficulty seeing truth in others. You will never allow room for others' opinions or criticism – or of you being doubted. Most of all, power-ridden as you have proved to be from your recent actions, you will feel entitled to blind obedience. You have already developed claims of being anointed, you said as much at our last meeting. Plus, Parsifal is the Son of God, according to his creator, Richard Wagner. So, in your mind, nothing could ever happen to you."

Power-ridden...I immediately hate the sound of it. Even if I were power-ridden, I am because I need to save my people. I don't want power for anything else and yet he makes it sound like a sin. For some unknown reason, these two words trigger my anger.

The doctor continues on like a broken machine.

"You will surround yourself with 'weird' people, people with handicaps and shortcomings, just to reinforce your own idea of superiority, of Godliness. You believe that with the magic of your willpower, nothing is impossible. You will find no peace until you put this Self into action. And when you do...may God have mercy on your created enemy."

"What is wrong with you, Doctor? You sound like a failed prophet and I am not sure I like this," I snap, angered by his display of apocalyptic prophecy.

"Failed prophet...that is an interesting choice of words. Everything I am telling you is true. It is a psychological pattern."

"Psychological pattern!" I spit. "Your pattern applies to everyone now?"

"Of course not. In fact, to tell the truth, in my entire career, you are one of the very few I have come across who molds so perfectly on this pattern."

"Right. You seem strangely enthusiastic about it."

"Enthusiastic, yes. But not happy or arrogant, as you might perceive me. Any doctor would be enthusiastic to have found the cause of his patient's affliction, wouldn't you agree?"

I say nothing, just stare at the wall.

"I believe by now you know the meaning of your nightmare?" he asked quietly.

"No, I don't. If I did, I would have been out that door a long time ago," I say, pointing at the entrance door.

"The warrior, the knight in armor, that splendid being, is your *idealized self* personified as Parsifal, who looks down on your true self and sees it as a weak, fearful, vulnerable being. It is your internal conflict between the true self – the weak man on the floor – and the idealized self, Parsifal, who hates the vulnerable being and wants to eliminate it. I do not yet know the reason he calls you 'Jew'... do you?"

"I am afraid not," I answer instinctively. But I *do* know – and the nightmare begins to make sense. It is the fear that my grandmother's story might be true. And if it is...

"Yet he does not eliminate you altogether and instead,

castrates you. Are you familiar with the terms such as *Castration anxiety* and *Oedipus complex*, Herr Hitler?"

I roll my eyes again. "I'm not, but I am sure you will explain."

"Oedipus complex is a child's unconscious desire to have sexual relations with the parent of the opposite sex. The boy's attachment to his mother is the main characteristic of infant sexuality. There, the father figure appears as a disturbing object. A male child from this moment considers his father as his rival in achieving his sexual object, his mother. The Oedipus complex, therefore, is the peak of the first stage of infantile sexuality. If I remember correctly, last time you said that your predominant feeling regarding the relationship between your parents was injustice. You felt it was unfair that your mother's affection went to your father and not you, affection you thought was rightfully yours. It that correct?"

"I suppose I said that...yes."

"Okay. Just wanted to clear that out. Now, the boy is simultaneously afraid of being punished by his father for this aggressive desire toward his mother and for his daring rivalry. The boy now thinks his punishment could be castration, depriving him of an avenue to sexual pleasure. His Oedipus complex is thus destroyed by the Castration anxiety."

"What a load of crap." I need to pace.

"It isn't really. You were afraid of your father punishing you, but you also carried the guilt of having been, unconsciously of course, sexually attracted to your mother. That is why you hate your true self and why Parsifal, your idealized self, punishes you as he does and asks: *are you chaste now?* Meaning: *did you give up being sexually attracted to your mother?*" The doctor pauses to shift in his chair. "You call for Kundry not for her to help you, but to damn her, because her kiss helped you understand your mother's love. She created in you a forbidden sexual desire as well as a fear of being castrated for that desire. Bottom line, Herr Hitler, your hate is not only for your father, but for yourself."

I strain to remember where else I've heard these words and am about to tell my doctor to stop speaking from books, when the memory lights up in my head. *My dear cub, he is your father, therefore half of you. Hating him would only make you hate yourself.*

The doctor goes on.

"You also feel disappointed and cannot forgive *your mother* for submitting to your father's pleasure; thus, betraying your love; Hence, you hate yourself to death, for you cannot hate her, and the memory of her displeasure and betrayal will always feed your self-hatred and shape your romantic and sexual relationships forever more. Herr Hitler, we are very close to discovering the origin of your impotence!"

"Abominable!" I shout angrily, but he ignores me and continues with his jabbering.

"And the cause of your self-hatred doesn't end there. I will explain."

"I am sure you will."

"In your search for glory, of implementing your idealized self into the world, you neglected your personal life, the things that make life worth living – love, family life, creative pursuits – because they would force you see yourself as a mere mortal; thus, in great danger of losing everything. You tell yourself, actually demand, that you should be above pleasures, always control your feelings, and be able to live without close personal relationships. You put your feelings under a dictatorial regime. And then, realizing you could not possibly measure up to these inner-edicts, you began to hate and despise yourself greater still, for you perceived yourself as weak."

"I can measure up to anything!" I exclaim, but he would not be interrupted and raises his finger to quiet me while continuing his monologue. *What in heaven's name! Aren't psychotherapists supposed to give questions and ask for answers?*

"As a child, you despised your mother's compliance, interpreting it as weakness, and you now despise your own perceived weakness. However, in truth, irritability against others is an externalization of our self-rage. And because you must *externalize* your self-hate, you *project it onto the world around you*, drawing a feeling of relief from the belief that the world is at fault for everything. Your punitive and condemnatory attitudes toward others feels justified. The truth is that there is no fault.

Most of us, including your parents, act unconsciously throughout our lives. You unconsciously believe that this vicious circle will be dissolved once you have your revenge and you will be free, at last. Yet that will not be a true healing, a true freedom, for you do not yet see the underlying cause with a clear mind."

"Are you done?" My voice mirrors his calm, while my fists and jaw begin to clench. "You are obnoxious and offensive, you know that? Saying I was sexually attracted to my mother? Are you out of you goddamned mind? Your mind is putrid and your words sickening! I could strike you senseless right now! I could have you murdered!" At this point my words come out as a roar, my head tilted back, eyes bulging and mouth covered in spittle.

"Herr Hitler, I am not the enemy!" I hear him shout as I storm from his office.

Once in the street, I sit again on a curbstone in a desperate attempt to collect myself. My hands are trembling, my head is spinning, and my whole body is drenched in sweat. I pull out a handkerchief and wipe my face, then notice the two portraits I have been carrying for the past few days. As I pick them up, tears invade my eyes.

Mother's bright blue eyes fix me with a stare from one portrait, penetrating me with a force that pierces my heart, the only force that could ever reach my heart. I close my eyes for a moment and ask her forgiveness for the slanderous words spoken earlier, for tarnishing her memory.

From the other portrait, the one I ripped from Hanfstaengl's glossy book, another pair of eyes stare at me. Those of Franz von Stuck's painting, *Medusa*. She looks like Mother. She has Mother's eyes. The resemblance is so exceptional it blows my mind. Franz von Stuck... paints me in *Wild Chase*, then paints Mother in *Medusa*.

I had every intention to show these treasures to Doctor K, to ask him if he believed there could be some significance, some message hidden in that resemblance, but his ridiculous jabber made me forget to do so. I now believe my forgetfulness was fortunate, since Medusa's story of turning men to impotent stone would surely have sparked my doctor's interpretation in only one way. He would have noted the undeniable resemblance, then proclaimed the connection made in my mind was another extension of my Oedipus complex or my Castration anxiety, or a goddamned connection to my wanting to kill the entire world.

What a bedeviled endeavor – psychotherapy – what a misleading, bloody, cursed Jewish invention.

3

THE HALL OF MIRRORS GIVES
BIRTH TO DICTATORS

The phantasmagorical ranting of my doctor throws me into an aggravated, angered mood for weeks. Bits and pieces of his defamatory monologue return to stand the judgement of my consciousness and the more frequently they do, the more I feel my anger and disgust rising in rebellion. At those times, I throw myself into work, into the struggle of rebuilding what others destroyed after my incarceration: the party.

The first, most important course of action is my meeting with the Bavarian Prime Minister, where I ask for the ban on my newspaper to be lifted. The meeting proves fruitful. On 26 February, exactly one year after my trial at Landsberg, my party relaunches with the first issue of Völkischer Beobachter since the gory November putsch.

This calls for a celebration, and I do so by buying myself a beautiful leather riding crop, which now completes my attire in a most magnificent and imposing way. No one will question my resolves now; especially if they do not wish this beautiful object of discipline to meet their cheeks. I am so excited by my new acquisition that I carry it wherever I go.

My German shepherd, Prinz, also follows me everywhere. A gift from a dear friend from the busy pre-putsch time, I had to give him to a family who had the necessary time to look after him.

Yet what did he do, my loyal little prince? He ran back to me! He deserves to be by my side.

The first issue of my newspaper announces my first speech after the uprising, to occur the following day at the Bürgerbräu Beer Hall. This site gave birth to the putsch. The putsch also died nearby, so it is only natural and appropriate to revive my party at the same place.

As I think of the movement's revival, the image of the swastika symbol enters my mind. It is no mere coincidence that I chose it as the party emblem, for it embodies death and continuous rebirth. This is what marks my spirit in golden letters. No matter how many people want us dead, we will always resolve to be born over and over again.

At dusk on the day of my speech, lashing my thigh with my magnificent leather crop, I enter the beer hall. No trace of Röhm or Ludendorff.

I speak like an entranced being before thousands of people gathered to welcome me back. Their ovations, their stomping feet and shouts of *Heil Hitler* interrupt my speech frequently.

"If anyone comes and wants to set me conditions, I tell him: My friend, wait awhile until you hear the conditions I am setting you. I am not wooing the masses, you know. After a year has passed, you be the judges, my party comrades. If I have not acted rightly, then I shall return my office to your hands. But until then, this is the rule: I and I alone shall lead the movement and no one sets me conditions as long as I personally bear the responsibility. And I, on the other hand, bear all the responsibility for everything that happens in the movement."

This is how I conclude. When the audience climbs on the tables and clink their beer mugs, I know I am back – and I know I am sole leader.

With my uniform drenched in sweat and my hair falling over my brow, I make my way from the beer hall, walking erect through the people. Men flock to shake my hand or touch my body; while women fall to the floor at my feet screaming incredible things. *Make me yours,* shouts one. *I want to have your baby,* cries yet another. A bolder one even rips her blouse open, exposing her breasts in full view.

I signal my bodyguards to clear the way, as I deeply hate being touched by strangers. I am moved to the core by their loyalty and truly love them, yet when they try to touch me something twists inside and I become deeply defensive, as if transported to the battlefield trenches where I must counterattack.

When I finally jump onto the front seat of my Mercedes, I sense that, other than my driver, I am not alone.

"Great to see you, old friend!" I hear a familiar voice.

I turn to see Röhm, hand outstretched to shake mine. Giving his hand a single shake, I glare at Schreck, my chauffeur.

"Not his fault," Röhm says, seeing my angered face. "I mistook him for you and jumped into the car before he could make a single move."

"If anyone can jump into my car at will, then maybe I should replace my incompetent chauffeur," I say, still glaring at the flush-faced Schreck.

"That wouldn't be a smart move. He could save your life one day. Plus, I am head of the SA; hence, his boss. I would expect myself to be better than others at certain things, like breaking into a car, without my subordinates objecting to it."

"If you are his boss, then I am yours, so he should have known whom to obey first."

I remain filled with aggravation; however, Röhm is right in one respect. My chauffeur got his present job due to our astounding resemblance, which could save my life indeed, should a less-friendly fellow try to force himself into my car.

My anger subsides and I pat Schreck on the shoulder.

"Why weren't you inside?" I ask Röhm.

"We had a brawl with the Reds up north, in Schwabing. The police came and we fought them, too. Just got here. How did the speech go?"

I clench my teeth so hard that they make a significant cracking sound.

"Forget about the speech! Goddamn it, Röhm! Was I not clear enough when I said: *No more fighting*? What does it take for you screwballs to get it?"

My face is burning, feeling as if it just caught fire. I hear a tsk-ing sound and a sneer.

"I don't even know who the fuck you are since you came out of that damned prison!" he shouts at the back of my head. "You had nothing against aggression before, you craved it! It was you who ordered the intimidation of the communists!"

I turn around in my seat to face him. "That was before! I no longer want brawls! Get it through your chump head already! I am not fooling around, Röhm! This is my wish and you are bound to obey it! I want to do it the legal way – so, no more brawls! Do you hear me?"

"Tell that to the troops! They live to fight! If I order *no fighting* now they will either leave or turn even more violent. They might even rise against me, against us! They are brutish soldiers and we trained them to be even more so ourselves! They want rebellions, brawls, and putsches! And now you want me to order them to sit around and help old ladies cross the street?"

"I don't care! I do not want to disrupt my relations with the Government! I am still on probation! I barely managed to have the ban removed from my public speaking and newspaper. I can't have violence for now! Can't live in fear that I might get deported to Austria!"

"Pacting with Rome..." he whispers, but I hear him.

"Pacting with your stupid head! I want to enter the Reichstag the right way, like a politician. I'm done with the uprisings! And I need you, Röhm. You alone can control the SA. Don't give up on me just now!" I plead with him, torn by the situation.

"I really don't want us to come to that. I care about you, old friend, I really do," he declares, pounding his fist against his chest.

"Then, prove it! Are you on my side? Are you, Röhm?"

Dropping his hand from his breast, he looks pensively through the car's window.

"I think the SA should be disconnected from the National Socialist Party," he says curtly.

I look at him in disbelief and feel like smashing his bulldog head. "And do what with it? Make it swear allegiance to the National Socialist Freedom Movement? You are bound to perish! You'll push up daisies without me!"

"Baloney!"

"Really? What have you done while I was rotting away at Landsberg? You won thirty-two seats in the Reichstag, only to lose more than half of them in a few months! You, hand-in-hand with mighty Ludendorff, could not do in one year what I have succeeded in doing tonight in one hour! You need me more than you need the air you breathe!"

He moves closer to my seat and places his hand on my shoulder.

"Then come join us, and we shall be a force to be reckoned with!"

"You are a fool. Had you not missed my speech tonight, you would have known I needn't join anyone. You would have heard what Count Ernst von Reventlow declared after my speech: *I subordinate myself without further ado to Adolf Hitler. Why? He demonstrated that he can lead!* How many men can say that about you, Röhm?"

He draws back in his seat. "Each and every member of the SA."

"Ha! Those members will soon be loyal to *me* only! Mark my words! Flocks follow leaders, not losers!"

"Then I shall make the SA a non-political private army and become its leader," he retorts angrily, his ego bruised.

I glare at him once more. "And do what with it? Make all its members fags and screw them in the ass with your big, hard, leader cock?"

"An uncalled-for low blow!" he snaps, pointing his finger at my face.

"Then what? An army without politics? Selling yourself to the highest bidder? Have you no patriotic ambition?"

"Is that so dreadful? Not everyone gives a damn about avenging their ancestors or the damned masses!"

"Maybe not. But as sure as hell we all give a damn about power. Don't we, Röhm?"

He says nothing, just stares silently through the window.

"Do what you must. From this moment on, I shall consider that you have betrayed our friendship," I say, and turning my back to him, I motion at Schreck to turn on the car's engine.

"I wish you would consider..." he insists, ignoring my hint.

"Get out of my car, Röhm."

Lingering a few moments more, he finally exits the car, slamming its door behind him.

I sigh and turn toward Schreck. "I need an elite guard of men. A fighting force that swears loyalty to me personally, not the Party."

He nods. "That would be a smart move, Herr Hitler."

"How many bodyguards do I have?"

"Around thirty."

"Good. Schreck, you are in charge. Gather them all. I need them in uniforms by the end of the week."

"What color?"

"Huh?"

"The uniforms. What color?"

"Black. I want them to wear black. Devise an oath, and then arrange the swearing-in ceremony."

"Absolutely."

"And let the Party members know that we are searching for volunteers."

"Yes."

"Good."

"Herr Hitler, what should we call it? The elite guard?"

"Well...it is a protection squad, so we might as well name it as such. Schutzstaffel. We will name it Schutzstaffel. SS."

"SA's biggest rival. Genius."

"Not yet, but soon. Divide et Impera, my friend," I say, patting him on the shoulder.

He smiles a conspiratorial smile. "Smart man!" he replies, "Smart man..."

The next morning, I receive a note from Röhm, together with his letter of resignation from the leadership of the SA.

I take this opportunity, in memory of the great and the trying times we have been through together, to thank you warmly for your comradeship and to ask you not to deprive me of your personal friendship.

Although moved by his decision and deed, I resolve to remain quiet and order for his letter of resignation to be printed in Völkischer Beobachter with no other supplementary comments. If this was nothing but a tactical move meant to soften me and if he thought that with it, he would make me beg him to stay, he was going to be in for a great surprise.

Resolving to forget about Röhm for the time being, I return to other pressing matters. The past night was a small triumph on the long road ahead. A road that will soon prove to be sprinkled with numerous obstacles.

It does not take long for the Government to also notice that I am truly back and equipped with more strength than ever. Thus, only ten days later, I find myself banned again; not only in Bavaria, but soon also Prussia, Saxony, Hamburg, and Baden.

In late April, only a few days after my 36th birthday, Field Marshal Paul von Hindenburg, a seventy-eight-year-old traditionalist, becomes President of the Republic.

The beginning of a new political era begins.

The numerous setbacks scattered over the following months urge me to search for the peace and quiet of the Obersalzberg, a mountainside retreat located above the town of Berchtesgaden, about seventy-five miles southeast of Munich and near the border of my home country, Austria.

I had first laid eyes on this magnificent area two years before while visiting my dear friend Eckart, who was staying at Pension Moritz boarding house. I developed an extreme fondness for the sweeping mountain views, which persuade your senses to believe that you are no less than a god, sitting near the clouds, admiring your creations.

The owners of the same boarding house install me in a small

annex, where I can have the privacy and quiet I need. Here, I can consistently wear my favorite outfit: leather shorts and shoes, with knee-length stockings; even at a temperature of ten below zero. The feeling of freedom they give is wonderful. Having to wear long trousers is always a misery to me.

Hess, released from prison ten days after me, joins me in Obersalzberg and we begin to work on the second volume of *Mein Kampf*; me dictating, him typing on the small black Remington typewriter like a dutiful secretary. In the meantime, I assign Max Amann, my trenches comrade and business manager of the party's publishing house, *Eher Verlag*, as editor.

On 18 June 1925, the first volume of my political autobiography sees its birth in print.

And yet another friend, Erik Jan Hanussen, comes to visit me at around this time in response to my invitation made earlier in the months. He enters my annex wearing a long face – a fed-up sort of expression. My warm reception startles him, never suspecting I know about his 36th birthday, today. His expression mellows and he even goes for a shy smile.

I stand up to welcome him properly with a hefty handshake and a manly embrace.

"I wish you a very happy birthday, dear friend!"

Visibly touched, his shoulders drop. "Thank you!"

"We are the same age, Herr Hanussen, less than two months apart," I say, and hand him a glass of ice-cold water.

He drinks down the clear liquid, then says, "And of the same blood."

That awkward statement again! I am just about to ask what he means, when just like the last time, he swiftly changes the subject.

"I have been traveling all year. I am indeed exhausted. Thank you for the water." His style of speaking in short, clipped sentences hasn't changed.

"Oh, really? Is this the reason you could not visit me at Landsberg? Hess has been trying to reach you for many months, but obviously was unsuccessful." I point to Hess, who nods in agreement.

"Yes. Shows across the country. Every other day, for almost a year. I've been twice to Vienna."

The simple allusion to that city proves powerful enough to bring back my stomach cramps.

"I am glad that the actual cause of your absence was the lack of time," I say, loosening the collar of my shirt. "I was afraid my bad temper had soured our good and possibly mutually fruitful alliance."

He smiles wearily. "No, not at all. I have a very thick skin. Others, before you, have turned against me for what I've told them. You shall not be the last."

"I am sorry about that and about my mistrust in you, as to your prediction about the putsch. You deserve a proper apology." With a wink, I signal Hess to bring out the gift I bought for this occasion.

"There is no need to apologize. I understood your reasons."

"Yes, there is, and I beg you to forgive me for being such a bully," I say, while pointing to the nicely-wrapped box Hess brings into the room. "This is for you, to forgive me and also to celebrate your birthday."

He stands up, embarrassed, takes my gift, and then sits again to open it.

"It...it is quite heavy..." he says. After tearing the paper off, his hands go to his face and he shakes his head in disbelief. "My dear God! A telescope?" His expression is worth all my effort.

"All the better for you to observe your stars. It is Dutch, the best of the best."

"I know, but...dear Lord! This is too much!"

"Mere pittance. You ought to show me my own stars one of these days!" I demand, pointing at the golden telescope.

"It's a promise. On a clear night, it will be my pleasure."

"Good, good. Now, let us get to more serious things," I say resolutely. Turning our backs to Hess, I point the way with my hand.

I guide Hanussen to the adjoining room and invite him to sit. I take my usual habit of pacing the room far and wide.

He sits with a thud; no doubt about it, the man is exhausted.

"Do you have faith, Herr Hitler?" His question takes me by surprise and I look at him quizzically.

"That's a strange question. If you ask me if I am a religious man, then my answer is a definite no."

"I don't care about religion, either. But are you a man who has faith?"

"Faith in what?"

"I shall ask you differently then. In what do you believe, Herr Hitler?"

"Well...I believe in destiny and in myself. I believe the Goddess of History has something of great significance in store for me."

"Like what?"

"Like leading my beloved country to the highest peak under the sun."

"So there...you have faith in your political movement."

"Ah! Yes! In that I do. I have great faith in my movement and in my destiny!"

"Good."

I am still puzzled by his question. "But why do you ask?"

"Because, Herr Hitler, the intensity of a leader's faith gives great power of suggestion to his words. Without faith, a leader is no leader. Without faith, his words cannot reach the hearts of his listeners."

"I suppose that is true."

"A leader fascinates a crowd only after he is fascinated by a creed. Only then is he able to call up in the souls of his fellows that formidable force known as fate, which renders a man the absolute slave of his dream."

"Interesting..."

"Do you recall a moment in your life when you felt ready to put your soul entirely in the service of an idea or person?"

I pause for a moment. "Yes. 1 August 1914. I knelt down and thanked the heavens for the war." Tears stream from my eyes now, as they did then. He avoids looking at me, saving me from my own embarrassment.

"Despotism is yet another condition in obtaining your followers. Crowds want to be obedient."

"Yes! I learned this quite early. I was watching my followers' eagerness to put themselves entirely at my disposal – mind, body and soul. No questions asked."

"Yet they must first be fascinated. This demands a charismatic leader. In the smoky atmosphere of the inn or beer hall, this leader slowly fascinates his comrades. Ceaselessly, he drums into their ears set phrases that, according to him, must surely bring about the realization of all dreams and every hope."

"You mean, if I believe in what I am saying, they will believe it?"

"Yes. Faith is what you need. The sheer force of your conviction will fascinate a crowd."

"And a fascinated crowd is an obedient crowd," I add, dreamily.

"Precisely. It is not the need of liberty, but of servitude that resonates deep within the souls of crowds. They are so bent on obedience, they instinctively submit to whomever declares themselves master."

He reaches for his glass of cold water. "Herr Hitler, do you like music?"

His question puzzles me. "I do, oh, I like nothing better than music. Back in Linz, I never missed a Wagnerian opera. For six hours, I would uninterruptedly have goosebumps all over my body. I would go from motionless to pacing. I would laugh, then cry. Music gives me such deep feelings. It connects me to my core and gives hope and motivation. There is nothing quite like music."

"You could be music for your crowds."

His simple yet stark, almost poetical words reach my inner being with tremendous speed, transforming my inner smoldering fire into a great burning flame.

"Speak to them as if your words had just sprung from your bottomless being," he resumes. "Make your speech an aria, with voices pitched high and low, with soaring verbal climaxes and delivered in imposing surroundings. Encite them stand and sit, cry and laugh, love and fear."

I pour myself a glass of water, needing to tame the embers spreading through my blood, and then head for the window. The view is so breathtaking, it forces a connection to one's inner being. My enthusiasm mounts as I imagine being a political Wagner, a political Messiah. I am struck with the need to talk to my men. I feel I...miss them.

"Herr Hanussen," I ask, continuing to look through the window, "how do I fascinate my masses further?"

I need to know all the means, tricks, and shortcuts. I must become them.

"Well, there are some other powerful tools you could use. The first being your stare."

I smile. "Indeed. You taught me this lesson even before we were officially introduced," I confide.

"How so?"

"When we first met a few years ago at the Thule Society, you subdued me with your stare. I never thought that could be possible...I mean, I never thought that another human being could have such power over me, even for a fleeting moment."

"It takes practice to achieve power through the stare. You must shield yourself from what you perceive as coming from the other person and not allow yourself be influenced by it."

"This is deep knowledge...knowledge into men's psyches."

He shrugged. "I am a mentalist. I am expected to know the human psych. It is my job."

"Right."

"But remember, it takes practice. You might be overwhelmed at first, especially in front of a crowd with all eyes staring back at you, trying to scrutinize you, expecting something from you, asking you for things, for words...shield yourself from that, then turn your stare on them. It is you who wants, you who demands, you who asks for. You will catch on fast and soon will be amazed at how humble, obedient, and ready to sacrifice your crowd will be. From the stage above them, they look up at you staring deep into their souls with an unflinching will. You have then reversed their needs and demands into compliant offering. Always place yourself higher. Whoever stares down at you, owns you."

A shiver runs through my body. "Astounding! *Whoever stares down at you, owns you.* I might quote you on that."

He smiles. "If it pleases you..."

"What else should I know? Don't hold anything back."

"Another powerful tool you could use is *affirmation*," he resumes. "Affirmation pure and simple, kept free of all reasoning and proof, is one of the surest means of making an idea enter the mind of a crowd. The more concise an affirmation, the more destitute of every appearance of proof and demonstration, the more weight it carries. Can you think of an example where masses were swayed in this way?"

"Let's see...the proclamation of war?"

"Think on a larger scale, think of the Bible, of religion altogether."

"Yes! Yes!" I shout, the flame inside me escalating once again. "The Bible! That blasted book erased people's capacity of discernment, resorting to simple affirmations that could never be proven or demonstrated! God created the world in seven days. God had a son with a virgin. God laid down the Ten Commandments and He will punish you if not obeyed, and so on. It produced fascination, and then instilled fear. Despotism, just as you mentioned. The bloody smart Jew! He always had it! He always knew it...how to conquer and destroy!" I roar these last words, violently punctuating each with a swift, sharp sweep of my whip.

Hanussen patiently waits for me to cool off before he resumes. "But affirmation has no power without *repetition*, which is the second tool you must use."

"Repetition," I echo and nod.

"Affirmation must be repeated as much as possible and using the same terms. This way, the thing affirmed becomes fixated in the mind as a demonstrated truth. Then, the powerful mechanism of contagion intervenes. Ideas, sentiments, emotions and beliefs, when presented to crowds as affirmations converted to truths, possess a contagious power as intense as that of microbes."

"Microbes, indeed! Like the Jews!"

"You can use it within your slogans. Another powerful method you must adopt. The creation of slogans."

"Explain!" I urge him.

"Crowds are stupid, Herr Hitler," he says, grimacing. "Men joining a crowd do not possess great intelligence. They need unity with others to feel worthy. They need a leader. They beg for a courageous, more intelligent man to command them. And because crowds are stupid, they need no justifications or explanations. They need slogans to shout that drill your affirmations into their heads; until the last member of that crowd understands what you want them to understand."

"Marvelous! Wonderful idea!"

"Now, can you think of a slogan that can affirm your message until it spreads like a microbe in the hearts of the people?"

I approach the window again, drinking in the splendid view. The power it gives to my imagination is astounding. I look at the mountain peaks covered in snow, close my eyes, and hear the cry of my ancestors and of the long dead warriors of this holy land, who have been cruelly stripped of their rights for supremacy.

"Down with the Diktat of Versailles traitors!" I shout at the top of my lungs.

"Perfect. You will repeat this slogan over and over, then wait and marvel at how powerful it is. It will make your followers hate those traitors. It will remind the crowds of our defeat and instill in them the will to fight."

"No, Herr Hanussen, not defeat! We are not defeated. It will instill in them the need for revenge, to take what is rightfully theirs. To take back their army! Versailles prohibited our army! Can you imagine Germany without her army? Army is what we are! Army is what we always have been!" I shout, livid.

"See the forests on those mountains, Herr Hanussen?" I point at the window.

"Yes."

"There! My ancestors and your ancestors co-existed as a unified army! We were born on this planet as warriors! Take the army away from its warriors and what do you have left? Stupid crowds! Versailles knew this, of course! The Jew also knew this when he stabbed the poor soldiers in their back and sold my country in 1918!" I stride toward him. "These crowds might be stupid – but watch me! Just watch how I will turn my stupid crowds into crowds of warriors! Mark my words, Herr Hanussen! Mark my words!" I am howling now and wipe the spittle from around my mouth.

"Good. This is all the faith you need."

In my fervor, I continue. "It is not only my faith. It is my duty! It is the religious duty of every German, man, woman, and child, to restore their Motherland to her sacred place. I could never forget that cursed day, the day Germany was stabbed in the back! I was out of that dreadful hospital at Pasewalk, recovering from blindness and just beginning to distinguish the writing in the newspapers. I will never forget the words!" I halt my renewed pacing and raise an arm skyward. "'*Vengeance! German people! Today the shameful peace has been signed in the Hall of Mirrors at Versailles. Forget it not! In the year 1871, the glorious German Reich was reborn in its ancient splendor, there the German honor is today interred. Forget it not! By labor without relaxation and without flagging, the German people will re-conquer the place which is their due among the nations! Therefore, revenge for the ignominy of 1919!*' And I vowed to forget it not."

Silence fills the room. I take the opportunity to use it as a moment of silence for my ancestors. Hanussen breaks it first.

"I noticed you used the word 'diktat' instead of 'treaty'. Is this for the reason I suspect?"

"I do not know what you suspect, but 'treaty' is an agreement, as you surely know. Did we, the Germans, agree to give our army away? Did we?"

"Well, yes. Germany signed it."

"Then, you are a fool. It was not the true Germans who signed it – it was the bloody Jewish vermin who stabbed us in the back, who sold us! So, no! I shall not tell my men about a treaty that does not exist! I shall tell them about the betrayal, about how the fungus thinks it can command us, order us! Diktat! This is the true word! The Versailles murderers think they can dictate us and watch us standing with our arms crossed? If so, then they are the stupid crowds for failing to remember that German blood was, is, and always will be, the blood of warriors! They shall be defeated once more! For when I shall cry out, *Versailles!* my men will remember! They will remember that Versailles is the place where Bismarck founded the Second Reich! In the name of Bismarck and in the name of our holy fathers, Versailles shall sound in the heads of my men not as defeat, but as victory! If there is going to be defeat, it is Versailles that shall burn in flames!"

I can contain myself no longer and start marching the room, fiercely cracking my whip, hitting my thighs, my boots, the walls, the table and chairs. My body is shaking, possessed by the Goddess of Redemption and Retribution. Tears stream down my cheeks, burning my skin.

Hanussen stands up and applauds spiritedly. "Bravo!" he shouts. "Bravo!"

I turn about furiously. "Are you mocking me?"

"Of course not. This is what I wanted to see. This is what will enslave your crowds."

"Meaning?"

"Waving your arms violently, cracking your whip, shouting, roaring. Emphasizing certain words: *holy, revenge, blood, fire* and slogans: 'Versailles is victory not defeat!', 'Sieg Heil!', 'The Third Reich is approaching!' These are the things that will make your music. And listening to that music, they will fall under your spell, trembling with excitement and fear."

His words bring tears to my eyes and I fall into the chair exhausted, dropping my arms and unclenching my fists.

"The last slogan you mentioned..." I say, catching my breath. "I like it."

"Which one?"

"The Third Reich..."

"Yes, it's powerful."

"Surely. But, maybe..." I look at the mountains again. "Maybe...The Thousand Year Reich...yes, this is better. For we shall not die when we die, our legacy will continue to live and expand beyond imagining."

"Indeed...for we are living in memorable times. Germany's economic crisis demands a powerful leader. If my crowd pays me thousands of Reichsmarks just to entertain them a bit, your followers would pay with their hearts and souls – if you give them hope and meaning. The time is ripe, Herr Hitler...the time is ripe..."

Indeed, it seems the time is ripe. Yet the Goddess of Time proves sorely obstinate by laying at my feet a further eight-year-long struggle with setbacks, delays, and wishful expectations.

4

LOVELY YOUTH

"Kundry! Kundry! God damn you! Kundry!!!"

"Mein Führer! Wake up! Mein Führer!"

I open my eyes and realize someone is shaking me by the shoulders.

"God damn you!" I scream.

"Wake up! You are dreaming, Mein Führer!"

I rub my eyes. "Hess? Is that you?" I point to one corner of the room. "Did you see him?"

"See who? There is no one here but me."

I go about the room, hysterically inspecting every corner. "I was sure he was here..."

"Who??"

"The knight!" Panting heavily, I pass my fingers through my sweat-soaked hair. Hess looks at me quizzically. "No matter. What time is it?"

He looks at the watch hanging from his gray vest. "Almost eleven."

I rush to the bathroom and stare into the mirror. The dark circles under my eyes, the sweaty hair, the pallid skin, and the sweat beading on my face all conspire to make me look hideous. I furiously splash water over my face, hoping it will cleanse my mounting disgust at what I see.

Returning to the living room I now inhabit at the Deutsches

Haus Hotel, I stare through its' large, open window. It is a wonderful September day in 1925, with a soft wind blowing through the dry heat of a struggling summer.

The changing seasons always held a special meaning for me. I remember Mother and her autumnal equinox celebrations, when she spoiled us with her cinnamon plumcakes. Closing my eyes, I can almost smell the luscious scent that would come from her kitchen.

Pension Moritz had just been sold to a scurvy man with awful managing abilities and even worse cooking skills. Prolonging my stay there proved beyond unbearable and I left Obersalzberg to move down a few miles to the beautiful town of Berchtesgaden. It is the place where my dear Eckart took his last breath.

One of the Deutsches Haus Hotel's suites proves a comfortable enough place to call home. With its large living room and two bedrooms, it offers the natural space of a real home and plenty of accommodating areas for visitors.

Hess moves in with me and we are nigh to closing the second volume of *Mein Kampf*. With the first one published and sales speeding up beautifully, I can no longer complain about my personal financial security, but my movement needs substantial funding. My next move is to plan a tour through the country in search of investors.

"Who is *she*?" I ask Hess, still looking out the window. I had noticed the girl yesterday while she took her lunch on a bench in the park across the street. I went weak in my knees, thinking I was hallucinating again. The girl could not possibly be Stefanie; though the resemblance blew me away. For an instant time stopped and I was again the sixteen-year-old lad admiring his Valkyrie. But she couldn't be...as this girl was so young and fresh, so crude and unspoiled.

And, Stefanie must be pushing forty by now.

That unwelcome realization brings me back to reality with an inaudible thud. I imagine her being old, with sagging skin, chopped hair and a broken spirit. Yes, aging seems to do that to us...slowly but steadily extinguishing the youthful spark in our eyes, the exuberance of our spirit.

Hess approaches the window. "She works in the ground floor clothing shop. That's all I know."

I remain silent and watch her every move. The same blond hair parted in the center and worn in two long braids, the same large blue eyes, and the same air of purity arouse painful memories of the elusive, unrequited love of my youth. Could I have been given a second chance? Could the Goddess of Youth be so kind as to place in my path such a young beauty, just to make amends with me? My questions torture me, so I step away from the window.

I ask Hess to take his place at the typewriter. "Let's move on, Rudi. We should be finishing soon. What's the number?"

"Four hundred and sixty-nine pages in all, mein Führer."

"Good, good. Do you think five hundred will be enough?

"Well, I believe you covered everything you wanted to cover. The number of pages is not important, the content is and you did a magnificent job creating it. The people will love it. They aren't waiting for it to come out; a few hundred have already placed orders for it."

I drop onto the couch. "You're right, Rudi, you're right. Let's close it today, then. September is always a good month for me."

For the next twelve hours, interrupted only by a frugal lunch and dinner, I pace the room diagonally, dictating the closing chapter of my political autobiography.

The large wooden clock hanging from the living room wall shows past midnight. Rudi looks exhausted and I allow him to retire. Yet for me, the thought of getting into bed and falling asleep is unbearable.

I grab the finished manuscript and, lying on the sofa, commence re-reading it. With every word, I become more and more aware of my mission, of my duty to live up to my own words.

To my surprise, every hour or so the image of the blond,

beautiful girl I have seen through the window the past couple of days, springs in my mind. I put the book aside and let her play with my thoughts. Soothed by her warm golden light and feeling protected with the light from the living room left on, I fall into a deep, peaceful sleep.

The next morning, I urge Hess to return to Munich, to meet up with the publisher.

After his departure, I hurriedly wash my body, trim my moustache, and jump into my clothes: light brown breeches, grey wind-jacket, and brown high-boots. As a final touch, I put on a grey velour hat.

Staring through the window, my nervousness mounts. *Where is she?* I slash the leather crop against my boot. It is almost noon. *Shouldn't she be out by now?* I shall not repeat the mistake of my youth. I am a grown man now, not afraid of a child – for she is just a child. I will go straight to her and introduce myself.

"Let's go, boy!" I call out to Prinz, who raises his head, then jumps up, waving his bushy tail. We exit the room and take the stairs to the ground floor. I scan through the clothing shop's windows from a safe distance but see no one inside. At the same moment, my dog jumps on the hotel's entrance door, barking and scratching its window. When it opens, he runs outside, with me behind him like a foolish man.

"Prinz!" I shout out, embarrassed. "You bloody dog!" The dog is making a goddamn fool out of me. When I reach him, I hit him with my whip.

"I am sorry, he doesn't always behave. I apologize for any trouble he might have caused you," I say toward the two girls sitting on the bench in the park. The lovely Stefanie-like beauty is one of them. They are both dressed in black. I think how awkward this is for someone who works in a clothing shop, having so many livelier colored outfits at their disposal.

"No need for apologies, sir!" says the woman sitting next to my beauty. "He just wanted to play with Marko here." She pats her dog, an Alsatian.

I doff my hat. "You are too kind. And your kindness just saved him from a hefty thrashing, even if he is the one being I couldn't do without. But training him with violence is necessary."

"If you say so, sir."

"I am Adolf Hitler. With whom do I have the honor of speaking?"

She extends her hand and I bend down to kiss it. "Anny Reiter. I own the clothing shop across the street."

"Marvelous! Then we must definitely become good friends. I live right above your shop."

"Pleased to make your acquaintance, sir."

"Please, call me Adolf."

She smiles, revealing a perfect set of teeth. "Alright, Adolf. Then, I am simply, Anny."

"Very well, Anni. Tell me, please, who is this blonde darling, with such beautiful eyes?" I ask, beaming at the blushing girl sitting next to her. "Will you, please, introduce me?"

"This is Maria, my little sister."

"Maria! What a wonderful name!" The image of the Virgin from Mother's many religious icons springs to my mind. I bend slightly forward to kiss her hand and the smell of her skin shoots a wonderful sensation through me. "I am—"

"I know who you are," she interrupts. "My brother-in-law saw you walking your dog the other day. He called on me and said: 'Look, Mimi, that is Hitler, the politician who has been in prison!'"

Her unaffected, sweet voice makes me smile.

"Really? And what were your first thoughts of me, if I may ask? I really thought myself to be completely unrecognizable around here."

"Well, at first I thought I should be afraid of you, as I ought to be afraid of any man who has been to prison, but then..." She pauses and bursts into a fit of giggles.

"Then what, beautiful flower?" I ask, quite taken with her childish giggle.

"Then I saw your moustache. It looked like a fat, black fly! I thought that if you would kiss a girl, it would tickle her to death! So, I said to myself that there is no way you could be dangerous!"

My smile disappears and I take a step back, adopting an erect posture.

Is she laughing at me?

"I am glad you are not afraid of me, as I could never hurt a fly, not even a black, fat one," I say jovially, trying to save my dignity.

She laughs again, tilting her head back. "You are funny!"

"What about now? What are your thoughts of me now?" I insist, hoping to elicit a more encouraging response from her. Surely, she likes me, she is just afraid of showing it. A well-educated man from the city, a spirited conversationalist, a politician. These are more than enough qualities to captivate a girl, any girl.

She giggles again. "Now, all I can think of saying is that... well...that you smell of cooking oil. Do you use it on your hair?"

"Mimi!" her sister exclaims admonishingly, nudging her sister in the ribs. "You are being rude! Please forgive her, Adolf! She is barely sixteen, only a silly child. She didn't really mean it..."

I wish she would shut up, as her defending of her sister only makes the girl's presumptuous character more evident. My pride is mortally wounded. I stretch my arm out wide in a Nazi salute.

"Heil Hitler!" I shout and hit my boot with the whip to signal Prinz, then turn and head toward the hotel.

Behind me, Maria gives full vent to her laugh.

Once in the room, I wrestle with my anger. What was I thinking? Going and exposing myself to those nameless faces, just to be ridiculed? Do they even know who I am? Who I *really* am and how many men bow to me in utter obedience and adoration?

"Stupid women!" I roar, cracking my whip furiously. There is not a single decent, sweet, loyal and feminine woman left in this world! And her...holding her in such esteem, thinking the world of her only to find her depleted of the sweet innocence a child should still have at such a crude age. She behaved as any woman of my age would; contemptuous, proud, and presumptuous. I think now I did well in not introducing myself to Stefanie those many years ago. For if I had seen in her the same horrible traits I was exposed to just now, I would have unquestionably ended it all.

She was laughing at me! The realization booms again in my

head. "And you, you goddamned stupid dog!" I yell, hitting Prinz repeatedly. "You made a fool out of me! If my own dog cannot take me seriously, what can I expect from a foolish child?" I continue shouting and hitting the yelping dog.

I need to walk, as walking always subsides my anger. Yet before I exit my rooms, I write a note inviting the two girls to attend my next speech, which is going to take place tomorrow afternoon at the hotel. I will show them who I truly am!

It takes me two complete hours to reach the Obersalzberg and I enjoy every minute of it. The brisk air at this high altitude and the rough terrain keep my mind engaged for long enough to forget about my anger entirely. Even with my strength and physical shape to boast about, I feel the need to rest and, dropping to the ground, I inhale the refreshing air deep into my lungs. It is one of my favorite rest stops, as I used to bum around here, in the company of Eckart, talking about politics, eugenics, the wonders of nature, and even the movement of the stars. Often forgetting about time, we lingered in the clutches of nature, hopelessly bewitched by it.

Near to where I sit, a small vacation cottage, House Wachenfeld, built ten years ago, presides over the most magnificent building lot in the world. I might have not seen the world, but my mind cannot imagine a more desirable place in which I would rather be. I have inspected it so many times in the past, scanning through its windows alongside Eckart, marveling at the enormous living room. I remember saying to my friend: "Look, Dietrich, such a spacious living area and only a small window on each wall! To have Paradise itself in front of your eyes and not be able to see it in its entire splendor from your sofa? Isn't it a pity? If the house had been mine, I would have had the entire wall torn down and replaced by an enormous window!" My friend always agreed. Ah! How I wish to be able to look through its windows every morning at the beautiful Berchtesgaden, now several feet below, embraced in the arms of the imposing mountains behind it, like a lover! You truly feel like God here.

Helped by this feeling of almightiness, I vow that one day, in the not too distant future, this house will be mine.

The hall of Deutsches Haus Hotel, where I am about to hold my speech, is filled to the brim and abuzz with voices. As I enter, the room goes quiet for a moment. Flanked by some of my aides, I advance toward the small platform set up for this particular occasion. I ignore the stares, the shouts, the extended hands eager to shake mine, and scan the crowd for a certain pretty blonde head. But there is no sign of her. She must really think me a clown with a funny mustache and cooking oil hair. A ridiculous old man, old enough to be her father, searching for the company of a girl her age.

I mount the platform despairingly, approach the lectern, and place my notes on it. My head spins and sweat invades my forehead. I prop my hands against the lectern and think of my last talk with Hanussen.

You might get overwhelmed at first, especially in front of a crowd with everyone staring back at you, trying to read you, expecting something from you, asking you for things, words... shield yourself from that, then turn your stare on them. It is you who wants, you who demands, you who asks for...

It seems that the entire town has gathered here to see me, to hear me speak. The entire town, but one.

I clear my voice. It is I who demand, I who command. My fright is gone and before I begin speaking, I stare at each and every man comprising the audience. The first few moments seem an uncomfortable eternity and, more than once, I feel a deep urge to break my stare as the closeness produced by it renders me exceedingly nervous.

*Shield yourself from that...*so, I do.

Instantly, my defensiveness is gone, vanished like the orange sun behind the horizon at sunset. My heart fills with incredible strength, my body with so strong a willpower that I can almost feel it tingling in the tips of my fingers.

Ten minutes or so into my harangue, the doors swing open

and the two girls walk in. My excitement at seeing them is so great that I lose my head and step down from the platform, hurrying to welcome them.

"I see you received my invitation..." My voice is slightly shaking and I resent that. "It is an honor to have you here."

"The honor is all ours, sir," says Anni, scanning the room with her eyes. I wish she would stop calling me *sir*. It makes me feel old. Such constraint I impose only to men, for they are the ones needing my whip, so to speak; they are the ones that must be trained obedience.

"Please, follow me!" I urge them and wave my aides from their seats at the table next to the stage, so the duo can sit as close to me as possible. Then, stepping up onto the platform, I find I am unable to stop smiling.

I bend forward to the microphone and point at the two women. "My guests of honor! Please, behave well, so we make a good impression on the ladies. I need it." The hall fills with laughter, which relaxes me further. The women smile, too, yet are visibly embarrassed by all the attention.

I speak to my crowd for an hour straight, but I can only gaze at Maria. I wonder if my stare, if me looking down upon her from the platform could make me own her. *Whoever stares down at you owns you.* I want to own her. I want to possess her entirely and by any means.

The usual clamor, the familiar shouting and applause at the end serve me well, for when I look at my sweetheart's face, I know the clown is gone. My actions prove shrewd and worthwhile and I congratulate myself. No girl can resist such a display of force, determination, and masculinity in a man.

I can barely wait for the hall to empty. I motion for my aides and ask one of them to retain Maria and her sister until the hall empties. I instruct the rest to guide the people out as quickly as they can.

In a quarter of an hour, I am alone with the ladies. Respectable as I am and proving it so just now, it is easy to get rid of Anni, promising that I will release her sister in no time. In turn, she assents to it only if I promise to join them for dinner. I agree and she takes her leave.

It is just the two of us in the big hall, plus the daughter of the hotel's owner, who is clearing the tables.

"Maria, sweet child!" I exclaim, moving my chair closer to her. I notice her fidgeting and her flushed face. "I am so glad you came! Did you have a good time?"

"I did. Unexpectedly so..."

"Unexpectedly?"

"Well, if I must admit...I didn't think much of you before this evening," she whispers, again embarrassed by her words, by me pulling even closer to her, by her own flushed face, probably.

"That's harsh on the ears," I say, but continue to smile at her, encouraging her to keep talking. "Why was that, sweet child?"

She bows her head and stares at the floor. "Well...you...your manner, although very respectful, seemed...womanish, libidinous. And the way you walked away...with dainty little steps...I am sorry, I don't mean to...please, forgive me..."

Her boldness is beyond all stomaching. Had it been one of my men uttering those humiliating words, I would have struck him senseless at once. This young, naive girl will learn soon enough that such boldness is perceived not as a strong quality in our world, but more as a weakness. By being so distinctly honest, you expose yourself to the listener in a way that can render you a helpless victim of treachery and manipulation.

I brush my wounded ego aside and realize that, for me, it is exactly what I need outside my political world. I gaze at her, at her marvelous white skin, her thick blond hair now pulled back in a ponytail, her mesmerizing blue eyes filled with child-like wonder.

"And now?" I demand, finding myself eager for her veneration, anxious for her words to mend my wounded pride.

"Now, I see you in a different light." She rubs her hands and averts her look again. "I see you above all the men that were gathered here earlier. You were on the platform and..."

"Yes?"

"And somehow there was a strange light around you, like an aura." Her face twists strangely, her cheeks redden, and her eyes moisten with tears. The sudden change startles me. I grab her hands in mine and rub them gently.

"What is it, Maria? What happened, my sweet child?"

"It is the same light...I saw the same light as I sat near my mother's dead body two weeks ago. She seemed so peaceful with that aura surrounding her."

"Dear Lord, I did not know! I am so very sorry, Mimi! I truly am!" I cry, then lift her small hands to my mouth and kiss them incessantly. "Poor child, motherless at such age..." Surely, this must be the reason she always wears black clothes. Her sorrow brings back memories of my own grief. "You know, I lost my mother at about the same age as you are now. A child should never have to bury his parent at such a crude age. What did your mother die of?" I immediately regret such a question that might further produce unnecessary heartache.

Her sobs increase. "She died of cancer." Now I hate myself for the stupid, useless question. "And yours?" she asks, her voice intermittent.

"Mine also died of the same scourge. The dreadful scourge that will eat us all alive!" I hit the table with my clenched fist, making her jump in her seat. "I am sorry. I startled you, please, forgive me..."

"Did it go away? The pain? How long before it went away?"

"It never went away, sweet Mimi. I am still mourning her loss." Her expression of desperation shakes me to the core. "But with time, it subsides," I hurry to add. "You will miss her, mourn her, yet the pain will no longer torment you with the same intensity. Trust me, child."

She squeezes my hands back. "I do. For some reason, I do trust you, Herr Hitler."

That *Herr* again. I remove one hand from her clutch and pull out the portrait of Mother from my coat pocket.

"It is the last portrait of her. I made it myself."

She lets go of my hand to blot her tears away with a tissue, then looks at the portrait with curiosity. "She wanted you to draw her with her eyes closed?"

"No. She was dead."

"Then why—"

"I wanted to immortalize her...mortality, lest I forget how fleeting the happy moments in our lives are. It hardened me; it made me realize that there is no one left to lean on but myself. It made me want to go on," I say, no longer able to hold back my tears.

She extends her hand and caresses my face.

"You suffered so much, Herr Hitler, so much..."

Somehow, the roles have changed and she is now the one comforting me.

"You know, Mimi, you have the same eyes as my mother. One day I will show you one of the portraits in which her eyes are open. Then you will see it for yourself."

Her lips draw back in a most beautiful smile, revealing the same impeccably white, little teeth as her sister's. I think of my own brown, rotten teeth and become painfully self-conscious.

"What about your father? Is he still alive?" she asks.

"No."

"Mine still is and I thank God for that. And I thank him for pulling me out of that dreadful Catholic boarding school. I hated it there!" Her face darkens.

"Well, guess what, Mitzerl? We have so many things in common. I hated school, too, and dropped out of it when I was your age. And look at me now! Who says school is the best educational path to undertake? Many of us are better off as self-taught people!"

"Herr Hitler, why don't you marry?" I hear the voice behind me. I look over my shoulder and see the landlord's daughter, who I had completely forgotten about.

I turn my head to look Mimi in the eyes. "Marry? I cannot marry. All I can do is be with the woman I love. A woman I love with all my heart." My words make her giggle and she beams at me full of admiration.

"Let's walk our dogs!" I exclaim. "Surely the fresh air would do us both some good!"

Maria nods, her features animated again. She grabs me by the hand and swings it back and forth, like a carefree, happy child. A happy child – it is the very feeling also possessing me these days. And the more my mind insists on telling me how ridiculous this feeling should seem to a thirty-seven-year-old man, the more determined I am to keep it alive.

We fetch our dogs and exit the hotel. The streets have cleared out and we find ourselves alone here, too. I look at my sweetheart's face, at how the twilight enveloping her frame in its strange glow makes her look enchanted. A sudden image, strange and surreal like taken out of an old movie, enters my head. I walk down the Danube bridge, hand-in-hand with Stefanie. Her honey-colored waves bounce up and down as she walks and a golden sun makes them look aflame.

"You are so very pretty, Stefanie. A very pretty child," I say, toying with my ridding crop. My hands long to touch her face, her silky hair. I must keep them busy.

"Who is Stefanie?" Maria asks, pausing mid-step.

"What?"

"You said: *You are very pretty, Stefanie.*"

"I said no such thing. You must have heard it wrong." I turn my face away to conceal my embarrassment, and we resume our walk. "But what I did say was that you are the most beautiful child in the whole wide world!"

"You are silly, Herr Hitler. I am no child! I am sixteen years old!" She chuckles and pushes me gently with her shoulder.

Is this a hint I should acknowledge? My inexperience with flirting, with seducing a woman, becomes painfully obvious to me. Of all the books I've read, of all that information, there was nothing in them that could save me now. I look at her and she looks back in a strange way. Her eyes are sparkling, her gaze inviting. Yes, surely, this is a sign.

I reach out to pull her closer to me, but sudden growls avert my attention. I turn to see that our dogs have attacked each other and are now fiercely fighting. The noise coming from their clash is frightening.

I let the altercation go on for a while, pondering how every living being instinctually fights for survival, for territory, for supremacy. Human beings are no different, maybe only more cunning in the methods they employ. I wish I could let the altercation go on and on and reward the winner, for only he deserves to live. The same truth applies to humanity. He who would live must fight. He who doesn't wish to fight in this world, where permanent struggle is the law of life, has not the right to exist.

"Do something!" Mimi shouts. Her eyes betray panic and she draws back, clutching her purse to her chest.

I must prove myself. It is now or never.

Tightening my hold on the riding crop, I fly upon the dogs and begin hitting them with all the force I can muster.

"Stupid, ungrateful beasts! I'll show you pain, if pain is what you desire!"

My unexpected attack and the stinging pain force them to loosen their grip on each other, yet the gates to my anger are fully opened and my rage pours from me in rivers.

I grab Prinz by the collar and shake him so forcefully that his yelps become distorted, like the cry of a hunted forest beast. That enrages me further and I whip him again, one vicious lash after another, until warm blood spills through his fur.

"Will you behave? Will you behave now?"

"Enough!" Maria shouts, but that fails to stop me. The dog yelps and whines and barks, but I simply cannot stop. I lash him, again and again, until he falls motionless to the ground.

"Stop it, please! You will kill him!" Mimi screams, grabbing my arm, her fingers digging into my flesh. I feel her touch almost as an electric shock. Then I stop.

"How can you be so brutal? You said this was the one being you couldn't live without, and you nearly killed him! You said you could never hurt a fly!"

"I am sorry. I couldn't help it. It was necessary." It is the only answer I can think of giving, even if it is the most simple, truthful one.

Her expression is of disgust now. Throwing her purse to the ground, she squats to attend to the wounded dog. Her face is turned away from me, but I know that she is crying. How could I have failed so grotesquely in showing my strength, my authority, my prowess?

"His wounds need to be treated. You will have to carry him in your arms."

I find myself fulfilling her command like a well-trained soldier. It is amazing what guilt makes of you. Lifting Prinz in my arms, I cover him with my windbreaker and return to the hotel. Mimi trails behind me and I can hear her light sobs. At the hotel, I place my dog in the care of one of my aides, as I have no idea what to do to him.

"Let's take you home, child! I gave my word to your sister." I search her eyes for the earlier spark. But no, I only see disgust in them. We walk to her sister's home in uncomfortable silence.

Mimi's family greets us royally in the small dining area with the table set as if for Christmas Eve. That relaxes me a little and I think that maybe my war is not completely lost. I still have a chance to impress her, and the cordiality of her sister and brother-in-law will help me. Yet she is quiet during the entire dinner, only Anni chatters away uninterruptedly.

"You know, Herr Hitler, it is such an honor to have you at our table!" she says, as she places food on our plates.

"Thank you, Anni."

"I am no good at politics, never have been and never will be. So, to my shame, I did not recognize you the other day in the park..."

"It doesn't—" I reply, trying to absolve her of her guilt, but she cuts me off as if my answer is of no importance to her.

"...but soon I learned who you were, and not only thanks to your speech tonight, but also from my father. Our father."

"Oh. Is he—"

"He told me everything about you. He knows so much about politics! He is such a learned man!"

"Good for—"

"And also, a politician. Just like you, Herr Hitler."

"Well, I am the founder of—"

"And did you know that this one here is a Nazi sympathizer?" she asks, pointing at her husband, who suddenly raises his look from the plate. I do not give a straw if the entire Berchtesgaden is Nazi right now! My heart is preoccupied with other concerns. I gaze at Maria, who plays with her food.

"Oh, is he, really?" I retort. Knowing that she does not hear what I say, I quit making an effort to be witty or entertaining and continue to look at her sister. Maybe my unflinching stare will make her uncomfortable enough that she will finally look at me?

Somewhere in the background, Anni's chatter sounds like swarming bees. "...and what a lovely day it was...my wedding... mother was there...this one here looked scared..."

I would have, too, I muse.

I can no longer bare Maria's silence and pull my chair closer to her.

"Sweet Mitzerl?" She finally raises her eyes. "Would you, please, play something for me?" I point to the majestic piano in front of the window.

"I play badly."

"Now, now, don't be modest, Mimi," her sister intervenes. "You are an exquisite player. Go on! Indulge Herr Hitler's wish!"

Rolling her eyes, Maria stands up and slowly makes her way to the piano. I follow her with my eyes...her slim, young body seeming to float, her long golden hair swinging as she moves, her delicate, small hands reaching for the piano keys. Turning her head toward me, she asks for my favorite aria.

"Whatever it pleases you to play is fine with me, dear child."

She pauses a few moments, making herself comfortable on the leather stool. When her fingers reach for the keys and begin striking them with confidence, my heart drops to my stomach.

Ride of the Valkyries!

Without thinking, I leave the table and place myself at Maria's feet. Burying my face in my hands, I begin to weep.

This must be a sign. No! This certainly is a sign!

Burning tears wash both my palms while she continues to play, her delicate fingers moving swiftly left and right on the keyboard. I look at her feet...I want...I desire to kiss them. I imagine doing so and I imagine her smiling wickedly, as she kicks me with her shoes.

Embarrassed, I cover my face again.

"Did you like it?" she asks, pulling at my fingers. Seeing my tears, her face twists in anguish. "I am so sorry, Herr Hitler! You hated it? Surely, you hated it. I am so stupid! I told you I play poorly! You must think I'm such a silly, untalented girl now!"

"Maria..." I say, taking her hands into mine. "Do you even realize what you did to me tonight?"

"I am so—"

"You played Wagner! Wagner is my God!"

"Oh?"

"Do you have any idea how difficult it is to play *Die Walküre* solely on the piano, especially the *Ride of the Valkyries* aria, which turns to life only by flutes, oboes, trumpets, horns, and harps? Disappointing me? Hating it?"

"Yes, I thought I—"

"You enslaved me, silly head!" I burst out, forgetting that we are not alone in the room. Nor do I care. But *enslaved* me?

The word rings in my head strangely. Did I mean it as enthrallment at the wonderful display of her talent or as...literally subjugating me, making me the slave of her beauty and charm? A slave being kicked with her shoes? What in the world possessed me? I must immediately cast away such thoughts back to wherever the hell they came from.

Her mouth opens in a bewitching smile. "Really?"

"Really. What made you play Wagner, Mitzerl?"

"Well...I determined to choose my favorite aria, if you decided not to disclose yours."

"Unbelievable! It's unbelievable how many things we have in common!"

Her cheeks redden and she averts her gaze again. My girl is back.

"What makes this particular aria your favorite? It is not a part I would have expected a girl to like, what's more so, to play it!"

"Well...for one, my mother taught me to love Wagner – and every time I play it, I somehow feel her presence around me, as silly as it sounds..." Her face twists in anguish again. "She was the one who taught me so many things, especially artistic things, as she herself was deeply artistically inclined."

"It does not sound silly, Mimi. It sounds of painful longing, which makes it all the more tragic. I have never heard Wagner sound so tragic."

"Really? Was I that good?"

"You weren't good. You were magnificent! You played precisely the way the great master intended his operas to be played." She blushes again and fidgets on the stool.

"And the other reason?" I inquire further.

"Well, as a child I always imagined myself as one of those brave Valkyrie sisters singing their battle-cry while carrying the fallen heroes to Valhalla."

"And now?"

"Now I know Norse mythology is just that...myth. Yet even so, I am still fascinated by these female figures who had the power to decide which soldiers die in battle and which live. There was so much power in these mythological beings, so much magic. I will tell you a secret, Herr Hitler. If I were to live in a myth, this is what I would want to be—a Valkyrie."

I stare at her for the longest time and I see no difference between her and a magic being.

"Maria, listen to me. Myths are not simple inventions. They are stories told by and about our ancestors. If you are fascinated by them, then surely in a past life you have been one of those powerful women."

"You're so silly, Herr Hitler. These were stories my mother told to put me to sleep at night. Every child believes they are real, this is their purpose. Yet I am no longer a child. Rest assured, I do not need you to tell me such nonsense, I sleep quite well." She laughs a strange laugh.

Ah, that unnerving laugh again! Is she really laughing at me? Or is it simply a childish giggle, meant to shake off her painful timidity and embarrassment? Or maybe she really finds me amusing? I do not know. And she is a child for heaven's sake, the very reason that attracted me in the first place.

If a woman my age would have attracted me, then I would have had that mature woman's traits: arrogance, pride, self-sufficiency. But these are faults I cannot stand! No man can. She is a woman-child; I won't have it any other way!

Upon my soul, I feel so old. I remember how much I hated it when others called me a child when I was Maria's age. I must refrain from calling her such. I want her as a woman, to own her, to possess her, to...

"Mimi, why don't you make us all a nice pot of coffee, would you, dear?" Anni asks mirthfully. She was probably eavesdropping on our entire conversation and now she, too, is laughing at me.

I stand up from the floor and straighten my trousers, then follow Maria to the kitchen. Her back is to me as she strains to reach the top cupboard for the coffee jar. I find myself eyeing her small, perfectly-rounded bottom. I approach her and put my hands on her shoulders, slowly turning her to face me.

"You are beautiful, Maria. A beautiful dream." I frame her face with my hands. "I am crazy about you."

"I...I thank you. I think I, too—"

"Shhh, don't speak," I say, placing my finger on her lips. She stands unmoved within my grasp, her body tensing up. Her parted lips draw me closer and closer and I feel her warm, speeding breath on my face. I press my body against hers, my chest against her blooming breasts. Her scent, her golden hair, her child-like expression intoxicates my senses. She looks abashed and uneasy, yet her eyes are filled with desire. My heart leaps in my chest as I lean toward her lips.

"No! Please, I can't!" she cries, gently pushing me away from her. My heart slows down, my judgment returns.

"But why? Why won't you let me kiss you? Don't I mean anything to you? Don't you want the same as I want?" My voice sounds desperate and I immediately detest such weakness.

"I do! Believe me, I do!"

"Then what?"

"My father! He would never allow more than friendship with such an old man!"

I take a step back and pierce her with glare. This is as far as I can take her humiliating me.

"Then, we shall never see each other again. Do you hear me? Never!"

"Herr Hitler, please!"

I turn my back on her and put on my windbreaker. "Heil!" I shout, and with this last word, I exit into the night.

I climb the rough terrain to my rest stop near House Wachenfeld in less than an hour, all the while hearing Maria's words reverberating spitefully in my head...*you are so silly...such an old man*. Not even the pitch-black darkness has the strength to slow my frenzied hike. It is as if I want to run away from her words ringing maddeningly in my head. I let my frazzled body fall slowly to the ground and I lay on my back, arms outstretched.

Lying here like this I can encompass the entire sky and gather all its heavenly bodies to my chest. The brisk night air and the vastness of the sky help my anger to subside, and I dare to think of Maria again. Her rebuff had only bruised my pride, yet it brought to life another feeling in me – admiration. A girl her age must reject impetuous suitors! She must, for in doing so, she will preserve the purity of her heart unspoiled, she will keep the Flame of Life kindling, the sacred love untarnished, the only true love that awakens between two beings who have kept themselves pure, body and soul.

I stare at the starry sky for the longest time, oblivious to the cold damp soil beneath me. I remember how, two decades ago, these very stars helped me realize how powerful I was. I had understood then that I am one of them and all I had to do is to show my brilliance to the world. I remember *Rienzi* playing in my ears and the voice of the Goddess of Fate urging me to go on, to never lose sight of my destiny.

And yet another aria rings in my ears tonight – the *Ride of the Valkyries*.

5

THE STAR OF SUCCESS

The next day, Emil Maurice, now my full-time chauffeur, drives to Berchtesgaden to fetch me and take me back to Munich, as pressing political matters need my immediate attendance back in the Bavarian capital. However, I cannot take my mind off Maria and resolve not to budge until she has consented to meet me again. Deeply ashamed by my past behavior the evening prior, I charge Maurice with the task of securing for me the much-desired second date.

He raises an eyebrow in puzzlement. "And what am I to tell her?"

"Do I have to teach you that, now? Tell her whatever you tell all those women flocking around you all the time!" I say, trying to look and sound confident. In truth, I have no goddamned idea of what I must say to placate an undoubtedly distressed woman.

He grins, raising his chin to display that amusing vanity of his. "I know what to tell my women alright!"

"Bugger off then!" I demand, motioning for him to go away. "I shall wait for you in the car. And be fast! I want to reach Munich by dusk." I throw out the silly details to downplay my inner torment. No one must suspect the soft, weak state I'm in.

As he trails off, I scrutinize him with my gaze, as to ascertain the secret to his self-assurance. He is tall, broad shouldered, and fairly muscular. His long, oval face, short brown hair and that splendid pair of brown eyes make him – well, I believe it all makes him quite a handsome specimen. Still looking at him, I find myself clenching my jaw. He looks so manly and I...*womanish... libidinous...dainty little steps*...I gasp for air. Is this jealousy? Envy? I have no bloody clue. Yet I certainly know that even for an instant while watching him walk away, I hated him.

Ten dreadfully long minutes pass until he returns. When he jumps into the driver's seat, I notice he wears the same stupid, confident grin on his face. He rotates the key clockwise and the engine roars to life. Is he trying to annoy me by prolonging the delivery of the news?

"Well?"

"Well, I worked my magic," he says, snapping his fingers, "and she's all yours, Herr Hitler!"

"Of course, she is. What else did you think?" I yawn audibly in an attempt to seem indifferent. "How did she look?"

"Darn cuddly!"

I smack him on the back of his head.

"You darn horseshit! I didn't mean physically."

He beams again, then places his hands on his face. "Like this when I arrived." He pulls his face downwards. "And like this when I left," he says, pushing upwards so his mouth mimics a smile.

My lips curl up as well in a hefty smile. Emil Maurice, one of the very few people in this universe that can make me laugh.

In less than two years' time, I will very much love strangling him to death with my bare hands.

With Maria's consent to another date ensured, my mind feels at peace again. I can now relax on my way to Munich and spend the entire trip looking dreamily out the car window at the forests we drive past, and at the white fluffy clouds above.

Once in Munich, however, the peace deserts me, making way for the alert, scheming, struggling side of my judgment—the part of my judgement that leaves no room for softness or compromise when dealing with the most critical and pressing matters of my political endeavors.

One such critical matter, which will keep me away from Berchtesgaden for months, is the battle for Berlin. Driven by the golden promise of National Socialism, many pseudo-leaders have risen to prominence in the aftermath of my incarceration at Landsberg. They were all my men, and yet they were not. That is how politics work. You form alliances only for as long as they serve you.

One such rising star is Gregor Strasser. He speaks through The National Socialist Freedom Movement and succeeds in amassing an ever-increasing number of Nazi followers. That bestows on him an alarming amount of power.

He must be removed.

In a shrewd political move, I make him resign from The National Socialist Freedom Movement by offering him the lead of the Nazi Party in the entire north-German area. This sends out the message that he is to obey but one leader: me.

Yet while he is speaking daily to my followers, I am being damned by the ban; hence, condemned to silence. The voice of National Socialism is shouting up north and I am constrained to only listen. Soon enough, that voice is shouting a leftist National Socialism, rather than my rightist one.

Again, he must be removed.

Divide and rule. The slogan that shouted in my head since I left Landsberg, that served me well many times before, must be used again.

I take Strasser's most loyal subordinate, Joseph Goebbels, the awkward little man with a club foot who visited me at Landsberg, bearing news of Eckart's death, and make him the new gauleiter of Berlin.

To Strasser, I offer a new position, that of Reich Propaganda Leader. Yet I also allow Goebbels propagandistic autonomy. The seed of resentment now skillfully planted, all I have to do is wait and watch its growth from the sidelines.

Problem solved.

Another pressing matter suffers little or no delay: the foundation of the Hitler Youth—*Hitler Jugend*—must be proclaimed. The future of Nazi Germany lies in the hands of its children. As I've always said, it is in youth that men lay the essential groundwork of their creative thought. The young must be chiseled away. I want young men and women who can suffer pain. Young men and women who have no concept of their own mortality.

By the summer of 1926, I feel I have made serious progress. I have the SA, which nonetheless I continue to mistrust; the SS, still in its infancy; and now, after proclaiming the foundation of Hitler Youth in July, I have little heads to be shaped as fighters, as future Aryan Overmen. Young boys, aged ten to eighteen, who upon reaching full age will become members of the SS. And young girls, aged ten to eighteen, who upon reaching full age will carry the responsibility of bearing strong German children to the Motherland.

I will give our youth motivation that will enable its joiners, as soldiers, to fight faithfully for their Motherland. For no child should grope through life without purpose, without motivation. That would make for a wasted life. And what is more meaningful to a German, who has combat and war in his blood, than to fight for his beloved Motherland?

The memories of my own youth and of how I first wandered aimlessly through a boring school with a dreadful, monotonous curriculum, then through my years in Vienna where I had to beg repeatedly for a loaf of bread, make my hair stand on end! I will not allow such a fate for my German children! Never! We are Germans! We are fighters! Blood, Sword, and Fire are our watchwords!

A young German must be as swift as a greyhound, as tough as leather, and as hard as Krupp's steel!

In training my youth, I will put more emphasis on physical and military training than on academic study. Intelligence is supra-estimated and I have no intention to breed brilliance in my children. It is the superior physical condition that will enable the young men and women to develop into strong, driven fighters. It will allow them to use, for the benefit of all, those qualities they were born with and allow them to sacrifice themselves for a common good: Germany's revival.

Our superior children have no right to loaf about, to become a nuisance in public streets and in cinemas. The school system is to rid itself of the notion that the training of the body is a task that should be left to the individual. There is no such thing as allowing freedom of choice to sin against posterity, and thus, against the race! The right to personal freedom comes second in importance to the duty of maintaining the race!

It is almost thirty years now that I made a promise to revolutionize education! And I have kept my word.

After the speech I give in honor of the proclamation of Hitler Youth foundation, Maurice drives me to my Munich apartment. During this brief trip, I am bothered by a new feeling taking hold of me. Riding in my car and staring out the windows always puts me in a reflective mood, I notice. I discover that the clamor, the clinking of beer mugs, the applause, no longer quenches my burning spirit. Is it a yearning? Yes, this is the word—nay—the new feeling grappling with my soul. I yearn for the quiet and solitude of Berchtesgaden, for the quiet and peace that my sweetheart brings to my soul. Is it true what they say, then...that financial stability gives birth to a certain predisposition toward laziness, to a bare-of-action fatalism? Or is it just the passing of so many months since I last saw Maria's cheeky face?

As engulfed as I certainly was these past months in the ever-arising problems within the party, within the movement, and on the country's political scene, still, not one day has passed without her being present in my thoughts. Was she also thinking of me all this time? Was she hurt by my absence? Has she moved on?

I picture her in the arms of a youth...less 'libidinous' and 'womanish' perhaps. In the arms of a muscular officer, who toys with a strand of her blond hair and whispers in her ear, making her blush and laugh...just like Stefanie, who blushed and—

"Take me back to Berchtesgaden at once!" I yell at Maurice in the driver's seat, who jolts, startled, at my shouted order.

He rolls his eyes and hits his forehead with his palm. Then, he pulls the car over. "But I can't, Herr Hitler! I am about to have dinner with someone and I must keep my word!"

"Another one of your women?"

"I hope she will be."

"You place a woman above your commander and friend?" He says nothing. "Nevertheless, you must take me back tonight. You can bring your woman friend along, if you want."

"But that might take a while."

"I don't care, as long as in the morning I drink my tea in Berchtesgaden! Now take me to Hoffmann's studio and go fetch your friend."

I am relieved to find the lights still on at my photographer's studio. Once I step from the car, I pause for a while to observe his shop. Its façade is painted in black; above the door the massive golden letters composing his name are thrown into bold relief. The contrast between the black on the outdoor wall and the gold of the letters is spectacular. Hoffmann's attention to detail and his certainty in their assured impact on people, mirror my own.

The entrance door is fancifully encompassed by two large show-windows. In the one on the right, four printed portraits of myself are exposed to passersby's scornful or enchanted gaze. One of the portraits is painted in watercolor and shows me standing behind my lectern, with my hands propped against it, staring at the crowds. They are beautiful indeed, but I cannot escape the thought of me as merchandise. To tell the truth, I am equally enthralled by the prospect of my picture hanging on the walls of every German house.

"Heil, dear friend!" I say as soon as he opens the door. "You are burning the midnight oil." His expression is that of exhilaration and he shakes my hand vigorously.

"Heil, Herr Hitler! Indeed, I am caught up in something extraordinary. What were the odds of you coming to see me at this precise moment?" he asks, and motions for me to get inside.

"Why? What's going on?"

He indicates the back room with his hand and I follow. "I believe you and I have a sort of telepathic connection," he says as I trail behind him.

"You believe in that, too? I always thought I could pass out information to others by the means of intuition only, yet people rushed to think I was mad, so I never mentioned it again to anybody. Until you introduced me to Hanussen, that is."

"Come, come! Look here!" he exclaims enthusiastically, pointing his finger at his work desk. I approach it, curious as to what he is making such a fuss about. A large print of what seems to be a gathering of men rests on his desk.

"Go on, take a look," he urges me again, tapping the print with his forefinger. As I look closer, I notice the white lions flanking the entrance to Feldherrnhalle.

"Is this the...?"

A satisfied smile lights up his face. "A print from that great day in August, 1914, yes. Germany-joins-the-war day. I, myself, took it."

Tears invade my eyes as I remember that fated moment. *Russia has thrown her protective arms around the shoulders of Bosnia! And in doing so, she has become our enemy! We must fight not only for Austria but also for our own existence, for our future freedom! Germany must fight in the name of our German ancestors who shed so much blood in the past! Let there be war! War! War!*

"Isn't it a rarity?" he asks, pulling me back from my painful remembering.

"Indeed, it is. I, too, was right there in that square, you know... more to the back, kneeling down," I confide and pull out my handkerchief to blot my tears away.

"No, you weren't."

I look at him quizzically.

"Take a *closer* look at the print," he urges.

With my mind still quizzical, but with an escalating curiosity, I bend slightly forward to look closer.

"Bless my soul! How the hell did I end up there?" I ask, as I recognize myself between the people in the front rows.

"I put you there. Now there is no doubt where our next Führer was on that glorious day."

I burst into laughter. "Heinrich Hoffmann, you devil! I should give you an office! You are too shrewd to remain a mere photographer! The Ministry of Propaganda should fit you quite perfectly!"

"Nah! I would be a round peg in a square hole. I am happy where I am and certainly most happy with what I do. You are my most distinguished client, and with you I can finally be as creative as I please."

I smile heartily and scrutinize the print further. "It's quite astonishing, Hoffmann! I never thought you could forge pictures in this way."

"I am the father of forgery!"

"Well, maybe not the father, but certainly great at this skill." The dim light of his back room turns his eyes into dark blue jewels and I marvel at their strange blaze.

"Are you displeased with the outcome, Herr Hitler?"

I grab the print with my hand and step nearer to my puzzled friend. His expression amuses me. With his shoulders drooped and slightly bending forward, he looks like a scolded child.

"Look here," I say, holding a magnifying glass I had grabbed from his desk over my skillfully implanted head. "My mustache here is quite narrow. That July, I was consumed by a frightful depression, hence I let the hair on my face grow unbridled. That August day, I was the possessor of a marvelous handlebar moustache. The goatee is a nice touch though, as I indeed had one."

"But who would know? It's not like you've been photographed in those days!"

"Well, I've been snapped a couple of times in the trenches. I wouldn't be surprised if a scoundrel of a journalist would dig deep enough to find those photos. Have you published it already?"

"No, not this one."

"And look here. My face looks as if I have some sort of growth on the left side of it. And the fellow next to me who doffs his hat – look at his hand – his elbow is so unnaturally far away from his head that you might think another person is trying to steal his hat! And if you analyze it even closer, everyone in the crowd looks somewhere to the left-hand side, at a fellow who was addressing us that day, while I am the only one looking straight ahead."

"I thought it was perfect," he whispers, confounded. His expression turns gloomy, his eyes darken further. That amuses me even more and I pat him jovially on the shoulder.

"Not perfect, but exquisite! I want nothing altered. It is just because I know all the details of that day and of the way I looked that I am being so overcritical. No one else will notice."

"You think?"

"Trust me, friend. Crowds are stupid, as our mutual acquaintance would say."

"Hanussen?"

"That's right. We met several times this past year."

I recount everything to Hoffmann, every word spoken, every gesture. In recounting, I feel I am reliving everything that has been spoken and start pacing his back room diagonally, gesticulating wildly, swishing my whip in the air, clenching then slackening my fists over and over again. I notice him taking pictures of me.

"Why are you snapping me?" I shout.

"So you could see yourself in different postures and decide which of them best suit you for when you deliver a speech. I will have them developed for you as soon as possible."

"That's brilliant, Hoffmann."

My friend sets his camera aside on a hook.

Exhausted, I fall wheezing into an armchair and drop my arms to my sides.

"Sometimes I feel so tired, Hoffmann, all these stumbling blocks thrown at my feet. One day I am being banned from public speaking, then I am not, and then I am again once more. And the people! They call themselves Germans! But they have no goddamned notion of what being a German truly means! I, an Austrian, have more German blood flowing through my veins than all of the people stepping on this holy land!"

"Yes, yes," he nods, hanging on every word that exits

my mouth.

"They wouldn't even grant me the citizenship! Can you imagine the hypocrisy? Can you even begin to grasp the worry with which I must live every day, knowing that I might get deported? That old deranged Hindenburg might wake up one morning and decide in his senile mind to get rid of me! One less inconvenience! One less voice crying in the wilderness! And all of this for what, I ask you? For the stupid majority that doesn't even deserve me!"

My friend opens the bottom drawer of his desk and begins rummaging through it.

"Ah! Here it is!" he exclaims, contented, while pulling a tightly-folded sheet of paper from the drawer. He then sits on the floor next to me, crossing his long legs with his feet underneath his thighs.

"What is it?"

Ignoring my question, he unfolds the paper and looks at it in silence.

"Well?" I insist impatiently.

He throws out a single, bizarre word: "Fomalhaut."

"What the hell is it, Hoffmann? You know I hate guessing games!"

"It is the paper on which I wrote down notes when you asked me to," he says and reads the text aloud: '*A Royal star, Fomalhaut, represents a trial or a temptation through which the individual must work before true success can be achieved. It can be in for a rocky road, with many potential pitfalls, or areas where the individual can fall from grace. Yet always, with this star, it will be success.*' Don't you see, Herr Hitler? Even these setbacks were and are supposed to happen! But do they matter, really? Knowing that in the end you will have what has already been ordained from above?"

A shudder runs through me and burning tears stream from my eyes again. The truth in his words, the way they ring, so judiciously at such a right moment. My discomfort, my restlessness, my despondency melts like the last snowflakes in the warmth of a March sun, making way for a precious elixir to wash through my veins: relief. I motion for him to stand up and thank him with a heartfelt embrace.

Muffled voices reach me from the doorway and I know Maurice is here.

"I want nothing altered on that print, Hoffmann, do you hear me?" I demand, pointing toward his desk on my way out. "I have rarely seen such fastidious handicraft. Take it to Völkischer Beobachter in the morning. It will be printed first off."

The journey back to Berchtesgaden feels like a blessing. The swinging produced by the speeding car, the clear starry sky and the brisk wind cutting through my open window serve to transport me to an unknown faraway distance. I shoot a look at the brightest body in the heavens and let my imagination take me over...*always with this star, it will be success.*

6

LIKE A WOLF

We arrive in Berchtesgaden at close to three in the morning. The town is dead quiet, but I can hear a relentless, constant sound—that of my speeding heart. A few years later, rumors of me having a deeply frozen heart, or none at all, shock me with equal intensity each time I hear such whisperings. I have the greatest, warmest heart of all. Yet it pulsates for one thing only: Germany. For a Motherland free of all the weeds suffocating her. Would you judge a farmer who plucks the weeds growing on his land for the prosperity of his crop? Would you think of him as a heartless being? Of course, you wouldn't. For he knows, just as I do, that life is made out of one thing: struggle. A perfect result, in every area of life, is achieved only by struggle, the struggle for supremacy and survival. He who does not want to fight does not deserve to live.

Here, embraced in the sweet clutches of nature, I can finally say that I feel at home. The blessed drive seems to have prolonged the peaceful feeling well into the morning. For the first time in a months-long queue of dreadful nights, I sleep a dreamless sleep. Being able to pass through a night without having a nightmare is in itself a beautiful dream.

I dress quickly and run down to Maria's shop. I have missed her. Oh, how I missed her!

Her face brightens as she sees me and I understand that she

has missed me, too. She runs toward me and I sense she is about to clasp me in her arms, but she doesn't. Yet, I now know that she hasn't moved on.

"Herr Hitler, you are back!"

"I am back for you, Mitzerl. Have you been well? Did you miss me? Would you like to have morning tea with me?" My nervousness makes me throw out questions, as I sway from foot to foot.

"I would, but I can't. I am preparing to go visit my mother's grave."

"Who drives you there?"

"No one. I will walk."

"That's out of the question. I'll fetch my driver and go with you. Would you like that, my child?"

"And how!"

"Ah, my sweet child! I was totally lost these months away from you!" I blurt out.

"You are calling me a child again!"

"I will stop calling you 'child' when you will no longer call me 'Herr Hitler'."

"Sounds fair."

"As fair as your whole self." She glows bright red.

"Then, shall we meet in front of the hotel, say, in half an hour?" I ask.

"Yes, please." I kiss both her hands and return to my room.

"Wake up, lazy head!" I shout out to Maurice, knocking heavily on his bedroom door. "It is almost nine! Wake up!"

Maurice's new girlfriend, Ida Arnold, a beautiful but somewhat stupid girl, pops her head out through the slightly opened door.

"Give us a few more minutes, I beg of you," she pleads, rubbing her sleepy eyes.

"Of course, of course!" I reply embarrassed, drawing back and bending a little forward as in a bow. She gives a wide smile and slams the door in my face.

I start pacing the living room for want of anything better to do. Yet my annoyance mounts. The stupid coward sent his wench to shut my mouth and I have to wait on him while he snuggles under the blankets. *Who works for who, goddamn it?*

I approach the bedroom door and knock on it again. Finally, a disheveled-looking Maurice comes out displaying his trademark grin.

"Dress up! And fast!" I shout, resuming my diagonal march. "We must be downstairs in half an hour!"

Miss Arnold suddenly appears behind Maurice. "Where are we going?" she asks. She is wearing nothing but his unbuttoned shirt. Now I am about to explode at her display of debauchery.

Potiphar's wife!

I glare at her. "You, darling, are going nowhere. I only need Maurice today, so could you be so kind as to return his shirt?" She glares back, her lip trembling. Then, with one swift movement, she turns her back to us and slams shut the bedroom door again.

Maurice chuckles. "You made her mad, you know."

"You should be more concerned about you making *me* mad, you idiot. Now, wash your face and let's move!"

"Where to?"

"I shall accompany Maria to her mother's grave. You will drive us there."

As we go down the stairs, powerful emotions overwhelm me. If they will spring out due to my nervousness of being in Maria's presence again or at the prospect of visiting the grave of her mother, I do not know. Memories of my own mother turn in my head in a sequential fashion: her sweet face staring in the mirror while brushing her silky hair, her echoing warm laughter while soaping my naked body, her bitter tears washing down her face while watching my father's coffin descend into the pit, the suffering in her eyes in the last months of her miserable life, struggling with her cursed illness.

When I see Maria patiently waiting outside the hotel, I do not know if I should be happy or get even sadder. She looks like Mother when still very young, yet dressed as she was at Father's funeral service. Her long, golden braids are now tucked away under a black bonnet, from which hangs an equally dark veil covering her sweet face. Her hunchback-like posture makes her look much older than she really is, as if all the troubles of the world have suddenly decided to rest upon her shoulders. Naturally slim, her body now resembles a beanstalk hiding beneath a black dress. The huge bouquet of red roses she clutches bestows the only vibrant spot of color in her otherwise gloomy countenance.

"You look so pale, my child," I dare to say as we enter the cemetery. "Are you sure it was a good idea to come here today?"

"I look pale every time I come here, so today or any other day, I will be no different."

Her words come out in whispers, as if she does not want to disturb the dead. We advance carefully through the graves, stepping on the weeds that cover the ground like a green rug. I believe that if something was to disturb the dead, it would surely be these weeds.

As we advance through the graves, I look at the tombstones, fascinated, reading the inscriptions on each. How captivating to be in a graveyard! It is as if you are walking through a huge library composed of biographical books only! And how difficult for the relatives of the buried, to be limited to only a few words to describe the many qualities of the departed!

"Here she rests," Mimi says, coming to a halt. Bending forward, she places the flowers onto the grey stone plaque. I get closer to it, eager to read the inscription.

> *A few more steps along life's road,*
> *Perhaps a few more years.*
> *Then, by God's grace we'll meet again,*
> *Beyond the veil of tears.*

I fall to my knees. Propping my head against the cold plaque, I grip its sharp edges until my fingers hurt. *Mother!* I scream in my head. *Why? Why did you leave me here all alone? Mother!* I continue howling inaudibly. Her sunken face, her intermittent voice, her last words hurtle toward me like poisonous arrows out of a dusky void, flooding my entire body with a cold rush of deadness. *I should have put an end to my miserable existence! I should have followed you! To what purpose was I left to live? I should come after you, Mother, and leave this ungrateful and undeserving world behind!* I silently lament, banging my forehead against the plaque.

Maria places her hand on me, gently caressing my neck, and I can hear her muffled sobs. Then suddenly, out of that dark void, I hear a sound, the shout of a trumpet. With great effort, I tune out the other voices in my head, leaving only the cry of the trumpet to shout in my ears.

I remember why I was left to live. The Goddess of Destiny ordained it, for I do not belong to myself anymore, but to the world, to the Motherland, my new Mother. *I am not ready to become dust yet.*

Maria's muffled sobs turn into a loud, almost hysterical cry. I stand up from the grave and grabbing her hands into mine, fold them and press them to my chest.

"I am so very sorry for the pain I caused you in bringing you here," she says, with a falter in her voice. "What just happened?"

"I...I am not ready to...not yet," I repeat, this time out loud.

"Ready for what, Herr Hitler?" I pause to shoot a look at the sun. *As long as you continue to rise, I will, too. I am a star. I am a sun. I must continue to burn like one.*

"My dear, listen. From today I want you to call me Wolf."

"Oh? Well, alright. But why Wolf?"

I grab her by the waist and turn her to face me. "Because, sweet darling, it is the wolves that reign in this world, not the lambs."

Her eyes fill again with child-like wonder. "But our sweet Lord Jesus is symbolized by a lamb. And he was king!"

I burst out laughing and draw her closer to my chest. Why women wouldn't embrace their sole function of childbearing and go on being only sweet and silly, I would never know. Mimi's sudden burst of intelligence is entertaining, like watching a good comedy.

"The uncrowned and unwanted king of the Jews. That equals nothing."

"Still, he—"

"Come, Mitzerl, don't clog your sweet head with such

nonsense," I say pulling her to my side. We sit on a curbstone next to her mother's grave and I take her hands into mine again.

"Promise me something, Mimilein, would you?"

"Anything!" She slips her hands from my clasp and lifts her black veil away from her face, allowing those magnificent blue eyes to stare into mine.

"Promise me that you will always be by my side. I am a man of destiny, little Valkyrie, but I do not want to go on without you."

"I promise." Her voice sounds sincere, warm, and determined. "But what do you mean by 'a man of destiny'? Aren't we all, you know, guided by destiny, by fate?"

"I am not sure how to answer to that. I can only answer for myself. I have been entrusted with a great task, greater than any other man in this land has been."

"What great task?"

I shoot another look at the sun, which now hides behind the branches of the trees in front of us, spreading that magical warmth through its rays.

"Wolf?" she insists in a kind, childish voice.

"My task, sweet face, is to rebuild Germany. Please, be by my side. Together, we will see our Motherland grow in greatness!"

"You are such a special man, Wolf. I knew it from the very moment I saw you." I burst into laughter again, making her fluster. "No, don't laugh! It is true! When I saw you running after your dog you looked a bit ridiculous, I have to admit that. But then, when you approached us, your voice, your smile, your shyness...I saw something in you. And when you asked my sister to introduce you to me, I barely resisted the urge to stand up and run away!"

I grip harder at my riding crop and hit the ground with it.

"But...you mocked me, my mustache. You said I smelled of cooking oil..."

"I was so embarrassed, and sometimes I do that, out of a painful timidity. I guess that, well, if I attack first, then I won't be attacked." Her cheeks burn, her eyes glitter with strange lights. "Forgive me, I don't even know what I am saying..."

"What you've just said is very wise, well beyond your age.

You have a strong survival instinct, child. I wish more German men would have it."

She giggles, then adopts an admonishing look. "I will be seventeen pretty soon. Maybe then you will finally stop calling me a child?"

"You will always be my sweet child, Mimilein. When is it... your birthday?"

"A day before Christmas Eve, on December 23."

I stare at her mother's grave, as painful memories hurtle toward me again. "What a sad day. My mother was buried on that day, nineteen years ago. I was just a child, like you, Mimi. And I was left all alone."

She squeezes my hands. "Poor thing! I wish I knew you then to comfort you," she cries. "But you know what? You are a wolf! And wolves are solitary. You don't need a group to survive or even thrive. You'll do better on your own."

I look at her in admiration. What a sweet serious face, and how deep and cathartic her words – even though wolves live in packs. There are some lone wolves, but they are rare. Very rare.

"It is another sign, Mimi, do you see that? A sign that Fate brought us together! I believe in such signs, such omens, don't you?"

"I don't know. I think so."

"Come, enough sadness for one day," I say as I jump to my feet. "I have an idea! Give me your hand." She complies and I help her stand up.

"What is your idea?"

"An excursion! We will drive to Starnbergersee!"

"But I cannot! Not without Anni. She would never allow it!"

"Then we are going back to fetch her! What do you say, sweet Mimi? Don't refuse me, I want to spend this entire day with you!" My eyes are begging alongside my words and she cannot resist it.

"Well, I suppose we could try."

I wait an irksome half hour before Mimi returns to the car, accompanied by her sister, and I almost go weak in my knees at the metamorphosis unfolding before my eyes. The awful black color disappeared from her countenance as swiftly as a mirage. It is a splendid transformation, like watching a butterfly coming out of its cocoon. No wonder such comparison pops into my head, since her sky-blue, knee-length dress has purple butterflies printed all over it. Also, for the first time, I see her wearing her hair loose. Long waves of honey-colored silk fall to her tiny waist and traces of lipstick stain her sensuous mouth.

"*Stefanie...*" I whisper, my eyes bulging.

I step from the vehicle to hold the door open for the two girls to climb in; it is what every gentleman would do.

"Forgive us for keeping you two waiting," says Anni, and extends her hand to Maurice. I introduce them and he shoots an alarmed look at me.

"Ida's going to eat my nuts!" he whispers.

"I look forward to that," I whisper back.

He beams at the chatty, uninhibited girl. "Delighted to make your acquaintance!"

Under different circumstances, these two would have surely made a great couple.

"Likewise!" Anni says. "I made sandwiches for us all! And all in such a hurry! You should have seen my husband's expression! A thousand words are not enough to describe it! And then, just when I was about to—"

The swarming bees are back and the noise produced spins my head in a whirling vortex. A couple of miles are more than I can take it and I ask Maurice to pull the car over.

"Anni, I believe the two of you have much to talk about, so why don't we switch places?" I say and smile at Maurice's imploring eyes.

With a swift move, I find myself next to Maria again, taking her hands into mine. "You are so very beautiful, Mimi. Those colors on you...you are a child again."

"I thought of your words, Wolf. Of how you said that I will mourn my mother forever, but the pain will eventually subside."

"It is true."

"So, I decided that I shall mourn her within me, but go on with my life. She would have wanted me to lead a happy life." She nods as to convince herself that her decision is the right one and will eventually pay off.

"And are you happy?"

"Happier than I've ever been." I look down at her small, adorable white hands resting in mine.

"I shall hold your hands like this forever," I whisper, and bring them to my lips. The smell of her skin is intoxicating, the feel of it divine. I kiss them over and over again, desperately pressing my lips on them. The warm, pleasant sensation I felt at her house while she was playing at the piano, conquers my entire body again and I willingly surrender to it. I draw her hands closer to my body and press them down on my crotch. Could this wonderful creature make me feel strong again?

A shudder runs through me and I close my eyes to let it spread, yet she pulls her hands so swiftly that it lasts only a moment. The bees are swarming over our heads again and the warm feeling is lost.

After a few more miles on the drive, we come to a clearing and I order Maurice to stop the car. On the right side of the road, a splendid meadow caught my eye and I decide to take Mimi for a walk. The sun has climbed to the middle of the sky and its rays are dancing through the leaves of the fir trees, making the meadow look enchanted.

"You know, Wolf, you can have all of that when I am your wife," she whispers as we advance further into the meadow, cracking the brushwood under out feet. She talks in such a low voice that I strain to understand her words.

"Mimi, darling, I want you to be my wife, believe me, I want it so much! Then we could have blond children with bright, beautiful blue eyes!" She smiles a shy smile and caresses her belly tenderly.

"That would make me so very—"

"Yet my mission is not yet complete. I cannot think of marriage, not now. Not until I have saved Germany."

"What? No!"

I frame her sad face with my hands. "Listen here, I promise you this: when I get my new house, not far from here, I will bring you to live with me. And you will have to stay with me forever! You will not be able to leave me, anymore!"

"I shall never leave you, Wolf, not as long as I live. But—"

"We will choose everything together, Mitzerl, the chairs, the paintings, the carpets! I already can see it all: beautiful, big lounge chairs of violet plush," I say enthusiastically, motioning with my hand in the air as if sketching an invisible drawing of our future home. My artistic imagination will never leave me.

She opens her arms and lifting herself on her toes, she clasps me in her embrace. She seems to have bypassed her sadness. Children are so easily fooled.

"Could we also buy a piano and a round bed? I have seen it in the movies," she says.

"We will spare no expense. But come now, let us be children for a little while longer!" I beg and, grabbing her by the hand, I pull her after me. The sun, the wood, the fresh air has a wonderful effect on me and I suddenly feel transported into a different world; a carefree world in which manipulation, strategy, and political intrigue have lost their significance; a world in which I am being allowed to romp freely, hand in hand with a beautiful girl, far from the condemning gaze of the outside world. I don't feel awkward here, I feel like...myself.

"Come child! Romp with me!" I yell, running across the meadow like a lunatic. "There is no one to see me here, but you!"

She props her hands on her hips and looks at me reprovingly. "And who is the child now?" We both laugh and run holding hands, jumping lightheartedly over the dry logs scattered around the earth under our feet.

"Catch me if you can!" I gain momentum and slalom among the tall fir trees.

"Wait! I can't run this fast!" she cries, trying desperately to reach me.

"Who is the old lady now?" She is giggling and that renders her even slower. "Come on, lazy legs! Catch me! Catch me!" I continue jesting and running, looking at her over my shoulder.

Then, in a split second, I find myself on the ground as if pushed from behind by a tremendous invisible force.

"Bloody log!" I mutter, crawling on four legs like a toddler.

"I caught you!" Mimi screams enthusiastically, then jumping on my back in a riding position, she grabs the collar of my shirt. "You are my Wolf now! Now smooth along, Wolfie! Yeeha!"

"Wolves cannot be ridden, silly head."

"Now, now, don't be disobedient! Move, I say!"

I laugh even louder and slowly start moving on all fours, sustaining both our weight on my palms and knees. I can feel Mimi's warm crotch pressing on my back, as she squeezes me between her tense thighs. When I move she also moves on my back, rubbing me with the warm flesh between her legs. My blood rises to my head.

"Maybe we should stop," I say.

"No way!"

Bending slowly to one side, she extends her arm and swiftly snatches the riding whip from my hand. "Faster! You are a lazy wolf. Faster!" she shouts and hits me with the whip over my legs. A sudden burst of electricity runs wildly through my veins. I speed up as fast as my palms and knees allow me. But the reason is not the fear that I might get whipped again or yelled at. The reason I speed up is the one unthinkable occurrence that shall haunt me, steadily and mercilessly, for the rest of my remaining days.

The slower I move the harder Mimi whips me, and the harder she whips me the more enraptured I become. To her this is all a childish game, yet for me it ceased to be that at the first blow of the whip. My skin breaks out in goosebumps, my blood boils, my cheeks burn. My thighs also burn and sting. Yet my body, through a mysterious chemical transmutation, has translated the pain into pleasure, sending explosive feelings of excitement throughout my entire being. I remove one hand from the ground and reach tentatively for my crotch, as somehow this entire bliss feels undiluted there. A shudder runs through me and my heart almost stops as I touch the bulge in my pants. *Ye gods! It is back!*

"I am back!" I shout, beside myself with excitement. "Sweet Mimi, I am back!" She gets off of me and I jump to my feet.

"What are you screaming? Back from where?" Her confused head keeps her from seeing what I do not want her to see: my erection. But I can feel it! Good grief, how I feel it, both in my pants and in my soul! I am a man again.

I sweep her up in my arms. "Back from the land of...the dead!"

"You are a strange man, Wolf."

"Shush! Don't talk!" I command, setting her down and leaning her against a fir tree. I turn her face to the left then to the right and I arrange her messy hair.

"Just stay here," I say, taking a few steps back. I look at her, gliding my gaze all over her bewitching body. The bewitching body of the Forest Goddess who, with her magic whip, claimed me from the land of the dead. The Dame Meadow who, with her merciless blows, awakened my lurking passion.

She tilts her face skywards. "What should I actually see here under this great fir?"

"Nothing. You should only stop to see how I made you. A celestial picture."

She throws a wicked smile at me. "Come on, Wolf, we are not at the theatre!"

"If only you could stay for the rest of your life as you are now! I wish I had my watercolors with me to paint you."

She chuckles, revealing two beautiful dimples on each cheek. "Then I would have stayed like this forever!"

Shafts of sunlight break through the tree branches as if desperate to reach to her and embrace this otherworldly being in their warmth. They too seem like magical arrows coming out of a magical world. The vision is bewitching.

"You know what you are now? Now, you are my *Waldfee*! My own wood nymph!"

"You don't say! What makes you suddenly think that I was a wood nymph?" she asks, revealing that wicked smile again.

"You will understand much better, later, Mimi, my child." But the truth is that not even I have the slightest clue to what had actually happened. "Run to me, Goddess!" I shout out, stretching my arms wide.

"King Wolfie and Goddess Waldfee! Yeeha!" She laughs and claps her hands in excitement.

"You should never laugh at me, Mitzerl," I say and rush to her side.

"But it does have a funny ring to it, doesn't it?"

"You know what is funny to me? You know what is so strange to me?"

"What?"

"That I cannot resist you any longer! You are doing something to me and I don't know what it is! Close your eyes!" I say, and placing my fingers on her lids, I pull them shut. She continues to giggle, spreading the scent of her skin around. Indeed, I can resist no longer and press my lips against hers. They are so soft, so willing. Her giggles stop and I can feel her body relaxing under my grasp. She has finally relented and I imagine her as a butterfly caught in the nest of a spider.

Are you sure it's not the other way around? Who is actually the butterfly and who the spider? a loud voice in my head mocks.

I look at her face, at her closed eyes, her sensual expression, her parted lips. I place my thumb on her lips and glide it softly over them, smearing her lipstick over her white skin. The image of her deeply sensual face, with the smudged lipstick and eager lips inflames me all the more and I press my body against hers, rubbing my erection against her stomach.

"My darling, I am desperately in love with you," I whisper in her ear. "You are everything to me. I could crush you right now, in this very moment. I want to squeeze you 'til it hurts."

I want you to squeeze me till it hurts!

"Kiss me," she whispers back, her eyes still closed. I ground a hard kiss upon her lips and explore her whole mouth with my tongue. The taste of her is like nothing I have tasted before. The more I kiss her the bigger my erection gets and I feel the burning need to enter her, to possess her, to make her entirely mine. Images of her riding on me earlier, of her whipping me, shuffle in my mind and bring me to a climax. Moaning and shouting her name, I continue to rub myself against her body, faster and faster, nearly choking her with my tongue. Her fingers dig into my flesh, pulling me and crushing me against her body. I no longer feel myself, it is as if I had united with the entire universe around me and giving myself entirely to this entrancing power I explode into a million little pieces.

I remain hanging on Maria's body for a long time. My mystic connection to the universe is gone, making way for a painful, torturous embarrassment.

How could I let myself be seen in such disgusting, humiliating way?

Unable to look Maria in the face, I close my eyes and kiss her cheeks, her forehead, her neck, clenching then slackening my fists over and over again.

She pants softly, still digging in my flesh. "I...I felt strangely... happy," she whispers haltingly, as if searching for the proper words to describe the unknown sensations.

"I must take you home now."

She searches for my eyes with hers. "But you said...you said you wanted to spend the entire day with me! Have I done something wrong?"

How can you explain to a child what just happened, when even a thirty-seven-year-old has not a goddamned clue of what has actually come to pass? How can you explain to a child that the person standing in front of her, declaring his love and admiration can have her only when a whip is present?

Can I have a woman only when a whip is present? I howl desperately in my head.

Mimi grabs me by the arm. "Have I?"

"No!" I shout, startling her. "Have I not told you how perfect you are?" I continue, softening my voice.

Yet I must run away from you. I should like to run away from myself instead, but there is no other place for me to hide; except in this defective body, in this twisted, startling mind. I want to run slaloming through the trees again and punch them until blood spews from my fists, until my knuckles become a loose mass of shattered bones.

I drag Maria after me, ignoring her confused questions, and continue to clench then slacken my fists in joint-popping sounds. On the drive back, she is still whispering maddening questions in my ear and I furiously take my fingers to her lips, clamp-shutting her mouth.

As I drop the two sisters in front of their house, I press Maria tightly to my chest.

"Write to me," I whisper to the bewildered girl, then in a swift movement, I climb into my car and speed away, before she has a chance to ask anything else.

Still up in the sky, the sun looks no longer playful and friendly, but a monstrous torturer, poking me with his burning rays as if to punish me, to burn to ashes this new entity nestling in me.

I do not know now what's worse: to sleep at night and have dreadful nightmares or to be tortured by frightful waking thoughts through the night until the break of dawn. Both ways, I feel I am living in a nightmare. Yet I can still wake from an actual nightmare, but from a wakeful one there is no escape. Not even in sleep.

Dawn's dim light struggles to make its way to me through the shutters. In a way, it is comforting to know that a new day begins, with its fuss and important matters to attend to, chasing these clinging thoughts away.

On the other hand, this very light scares me to death, as the brighter it gets, the more demanding I perceive it. In a subliminal way, I have always perceived sunlight as a strong, unshakable connection to one's honesty, to one's truth. *You can start with the beginning or the middle or the end, I do not care, as long as you shed some light on what is torturing me for so long!* This very sentence rings in my head right now. *Shed light.* As if by bringing light in close, the whole truth comes out, demanding to be dealt with.

I jump from my bed and push the shutters wide open. With bitter tears already burning my flesh, I shout out: "Who am I, goddamn it? What am I? Answer me!"

And I howl, like a wolf to the moon.

Like a Wolf to his unknown God.

7

QUIXOTIC IDEAL

Early November, 1926, and I am back in Munich. The brisk wind whistles through the cracks of my apartment window, producing a frightening sound. When it reaches my nostrils, I can sense the smell of pending winter in it. It smells of snow. It stenches of Linz, of wretchedness, of Christmas trees and cinnamon plumcakes.

Frightening images, as ripped out of some silent horror movie, fast forward before my gazing eyes: Mother clutching her pregnant belly, her bluish sunken flesh, her soaping my privates, Maria snatching the crop from my hand, her blows, my moans and the cursed uncontrolled sounds coming out of my mouth in that moment of weakness...Ah! The shame! The guilt! The blasted blemish on my manliness!

I shake my head in disgust, cursing at Father, at the Jew who poisoned my blood, at the entire world around. *They will pay for this! One day they will all pay for this!* I seethe, repeatedly punching my palm with my fist.

Jumping into my uniform, I resolve there should be no more time for bitter reminiscing now. Only time for action. Action that forwards my plans and brings closer the day of reckoning. Ergo, a matter of great significance for my advancement must be addressed without delay: naming the new leader of the SA.

My choice is Franz von Pfeffer. A brave veteran of the Great War, who had fought fiercely during those four bitter years, making the Prussian Army proud. If I am to confess, his reputation impresses me as much as it makes me envious, as he is one of the few courageous soldiers who did not allow the end of the war to put a stop to his career. He continued to drill, with ambition and perseverance, into matters that gave meaning to his spirit. He had organized resistance groups, eager to put an end to the bloody French occupation of the Ruhr and scourge the Frenchmen out of the holy land for good. The enemy of yesterday cannot be recommended as the ally of tomorrow. Even God participates in stopping France's campaign of plunder. Thus, whoever fights France, our mortal enemy, becomes my friend.

In my instructions to Pfeffer, I make it clear that from now on the SA should and must be used as a Nazi propaganda machine. What we need is not a hundred or two hundred daring conspirators, but a hundred thousand and hundreds of thousands more fanatical fighters for our creed.

We have to teach Marxism, once and for all, that National Socialism is the future master of the streets, just as it will one day be master of the State.

My next move is to begin a tour throughout the country in search of new investors, as the party needs more and more money, with elections coming soon. I deliver speeches in the few areas in which I am still allowed to speak: Essen, Hattingen, Bonn, and Konigswinter. Another means for forwarding my plans is raising money through the new *Illustrierter Beobachter,* an illustrated propaganda magazine founded by Hoffmann, my photographer, and Amann, my editor. It provides me with large sums of money for my contribution to it: a monthly editorial.

In mid-December, the second volume of my political autobiography, subtitled *The National Socialist Movement* is published. *Mein Kampf* is now complete. I cannot complain about the sales, yet it will take another few years until it will be raised at the standard it deserves: Germany's bible. Sometimes, when I hear people complaining about my ways of handling things or the Party's objective, when I see my own Germans denying me, cowardly evading our mutual informal agreement, eschewing our meeting of minds in a desperate attempt to escape their own guilty consciences, I send them to read *Mein Kampf* again. For I have hidden none of my intentions, everything was displayed out in the open for everyone to see. I've always said what luck it is for rulers that men don't think. Yet beware when they are no longer on your side. Then, danger is imminent.

In the midst of my struggle with politics and raising money, my thoughts obstinately fly back to Maria. They are always conflicting thoughts, pushing and pulling my mind in opposite directions, instilling in me an insufferable feeling of wretchedness. Her two letters, both written on the day of my departure, do nothing to alleviate my despondency. Rather, they increase it all the more. Their reproachful content, her questions and demand of explanations are deeply bothersome, for I am not used to explaining myself, nor do I know how. And even if I knew how, I would not know why. Why did I leave in such a hurry, why did I react the way I did, why did all those distressing things happen to me? So many questions, for which I have no reasonable answers.

Yet, I realize I must write back to her. And because Christmas is coming, as well as her birthday, I send one of my aides—better equipped than myself in matters of women—to buy her a present. I also have the two volumes of my book wrapped in beautiful festive paper, ready to be sent to her.

When I gain the composure I need for replying to her, I sit down at my desk at the party headquarters.

My dear child,

You don't know what you have come to mean to me. I would so much love to have your sweet face in front of me so that I could tell you personally, what your dear friend can only write. December 23 is your birthday. Now I beg of you take my greeting, which comes from the depth of my heart. From my present, you should see how pleased I was that my sweet love is writing to me. You have no idea how happy a sweet little letter from you can make me. Out of it your lovely voice speaks to me. And then I am always taken by the desire for you as if it was for the first time. Are you also sometimes thinking of me?

You know, if I sometimes have troubles and sorrows, then I would like so much to be with you and to be able to look into your eyes in order to forget these things. Yes, child, you recall, don't you, what you mean to me and how much I love you. But read the books! Then you will be able to understand me.

Now again, my sincerest best wishes for your birthday and also for Christmas.

From your Wolf

It takes me two full hours to complete such an apparently easy letter. I can write one of my long speeches in less than a quarter of an hour, yet somehow, writing letters of love are tremendously difficult. *Sweet.* Have I used this word too often, and now I am being in danger of sounding womanish and libidinous? *Ah! Those two cursed words! I shall never be able to fully forget them!* I stand up from my desk to head toward the window.

There is no wind whistling through the great window of my office here in Schellingstrasse. But there is snow. It is on the windowsill, the lamppost in front of the building, and everywhere else, for it snowed for two long days and nights in the first week of December, gluing me to Munich.

Should I re-write the letter in a more formal manner, then?

As I pace the room, pondering on the question, unbearable stomach cramps take hold of me unexpectedly. I clutch my belly with both my hands and squat down near my working desk, instinctively knowing that position would alleviate the pain. Yet the longer I wait for it to go away the more agonizing it gets. I stretch my arm to grab the chair in a desperate attempt to get up and call for help, yet I realize I cannot trust my eyes either, as they suddenly play tricks on me, making me see double...two chairs instead of one...maybe three, even four. Stubbornly, I try to reach for the original, but the blurry image of the many chairs swinging left and right is beyond my grasp. I fall to the floor, hitting my head against it. The thud produced by my fall is the last thing I hear before blacking out.

Muffled voices race toward me and I find myself straining to decipher them.

"...for an ambulance!" one voice urges.

"...wouldn't allow it...how he is...appearing in the newspaper..." I hear the second voice.

"...as I say!"

"...order me! I am not your...! Send...yourself, goddamn it! Then he...your skin on a hook..."

I manage to half-open my eyes and notice I am still lying on the floor. The first thing I see, a few inches away from my face, is the awkward club-footed leg of one of my men. Strangely, I cannot remember to whom it belongs. My judgment feels slow, my memory impaired. Slowly, the voices become clearer and so does my memory: yes, Hess and Goebbels. What are these two idiots fighting over? Can't they see me lying here, motionless? I moan loudly as my stomach cramps return.

"Mein Führer, oh God, are you alright? Mein Führer?" asks Goebbels, dropping to his knees to get closer to where I lay.

"Thank Heavens! What happened?" Hess intervenes, kneeling down on my other side.

"Will you two idiots help me stand up?" I whisper, desperately searching for air. They both jump up to help me to my feet. I moan louder still, as the pain increases with every move I make. At least my dizziness is gone or so it appears, for I now see normally. Looking at my desk, I remember my last thoughts before I collapsed to the floor. Helped by my men, I strain to reach the letter I wrote to Maria and seal it in an envelope.

"Hess, take this," I say handing the envelope to him, "and the two packages over there, and put them on priority mail. Do it now."

"Yes, mein Führer!" He snaps his arm into the Nazi salute and exits the room.

"Goebbels, you are coming with me to Thierschstrasse."

"To your apartment? But can you walk to the car? Should I grab an aide? Let me grab an aide," he rambles. He rushes to the door and in a few moments re-enters the room, accompanied by a sinewy lad, red in the cheeks. With all my excruciating pain, I can still manage to notice the color in the lad's cheeks.

In twenty minutes time, with great pain and even greater effort, we enter my apartment. Prinz jumps on me and I motion with my hand at him to sit. Since my last thrashing of him, a simple gesture proves enough for him to obey my command.

I dismiss the aide, but ask Goebbels to linger on, as I cannot bear to be alone at this moment. I feel...scared.

Yes, I suppose I am afraid. Afraid of not knowing what is wrong with me and how long my affliction will go on this time. Well, I do know what is wrong with me, the eternal Jewish illness that eats me up inside, slowly but steadily, until it will get the best of me.

"Here," says Goebbels, helping me lie down on my iron-framed bed. I look at Mother's portrait, which hangs above it. I wish I could scream her name, as I do whenever I am alone and afraid. "You should rest, mein Führer."

"Send for Doctor Conti, Goebbels, he knows what to give me. I have postponed this for far too long. Use my private telephone line," I order and he obeys.

"Well, I am a doctor," he says, as soon as he puts the telephone's ear piece down, "so maybe I could help you relieve your—"

"With all of your eight university degrees, all you can do for me, Goebbels, is call for a real doctor. I doubt that having studied history, philology, and the history of art and literature made you an expert in stomach cramps and flatulence," I mock, bursting into a loud, noisy laughter. He says nothing, just quietly pets my dog. Is that sadness I see on his face? Yes, he definitely looks hurt.

"I am sorry, Goebbels, don't mind my remark. I am in pain. Plus, you should know by now how much I admire you."

What a strange, Lilliputian man. I never thought that such intelligence, sheer willpower, cleverness, and sensitivity could all blend well in such a dwarf-like being. And yet, these are also my attributes, but I will never allow anyone to see whether I can get hurt or not.

"You do?" he asks, mildly embarrassed, as if caught off guard.

"I've given you Berlin, haven't I? That should speak for itself. Never in my life have I met a man quite like you."

His face brightens, his eyes sparkle with pride. We both laugh, yet the effort intensifies my cramps. I ask Goebbels to tuck an extra pillow under my head and he does so slavishly.

"There is something, however, that I dislike about you," I continue, catching him off guard again. His face betrays fear now. He draws back and pets the dog some more. "Do you know what it is?" I ask, enjoying every second of his fearful, flushed face and visibly uncomfortable state in which I purposefully threw him.

"I am afraid not."

"And would you like to know?"

"Very much so. Then I will do anything within my power to change it."

What a great game. I should use it more often, then sit and marvel at what I discover. Yet somehow, I feel sorry for this sensitive little man and decide to end his misery.

"Your name. I hate your first name. Joseph! A Jewish name! What was your mother thinking, Goebbels? What are all mothers thinking when naming their babies after biblical characters?"

"Well, they believe it will please God; and hence, He will protect their offspring," he explains. His self-composure amazes me. If I would have been answered in a godly, pious manner, I would have jumped straight to my feet, regardless of my cramps. But no, this otherwise sensitive man speaks with no emotion.

"But you agree that it is all bloody nonsense?"

"Of course. I have been raised into a devout catholic, but those teachings no longer serve me."

"Aren't you a wise man! You outgrew the myth spread by that bloody ancient mob who took reasoning away from thousands of generations!"

"And still, myth or not, I admire the story of the Egyptian, Joseph. And since I had no say in the matter, I mean in choosing a name for myself, I accept this one as it is for a single reason only. Out of all religious names, I believe this one suits me best."

"How so?"

"Well, this Joseph was sold into slavery by his jealous brothers, but then he rose to become vizier, the second most powerful man in Egypt, next to Pharaoh," he recounts, his expression dreamy.

I smirk. "I can understand why you like his story."

He looks ill at ease. "Yes, to some extent I identify myself with him, with his story."

"You want to be a great man, I gather. Well, I can tell you that there are similarities indeed. Your determination matches no other's and it will take you, just as it took mythical Joseph, toward great heights...or depths."

This diminutive man dreams himself as the second most powerful person within the state. This means that he sees me as the Pharaoh, as the only one more capable than himself to rule. Good.

"And yet, we mustn't forget the truth," I say. "We mustn't forget that those are just stories meant to instill fear in people, in order to conquer them."

"It's true," he nods. "But, I'm afraid I had different reasons for setting those teachings aside." His expression looks pained as if he is fighting a torturous inner struggle.

For some strange reason, I find this man with his grand inner world – well, I find him quite like myself. Then, it must be true what they say, that we actually admire in others the reflection of our own selves.

"What reasons?" I ask.

"I didn't care much about the truth to begin with, never did and still don't. Except when the truth can be molded for your own benefit," he says, kneading his chin with his fingers. "Though, lately, I discovered something in me, something that the Bible with its teachings of meekness and forgiveness would have dismissed as evil."

"Yes. It is the same for me. Forgiveness is the one thing I seem to be incapable of developing in myself. I can never forgive, no matter how much I want it."

"It is only a short while ago that I finally came to terms with my discovery."

"Which is?"

"It is the thing that I thought you noticed in me and disliked. But I suppose it isn't that obvious."

"For crying out loud, what is it?"

"I hate people."

I move onto my side, propped up on one elbow. I am somewhat stunned, not by his truth, but by his courage to admit it.

"The human being is a canaille!" he shouts. His face is livid. I stare at him half-amused. "I've learned to despise the human being from the bottom of my soul! He truly makes me sick to my stomach!"

"Well, dear Goebbels, then I guess we both have stomach troubles." I sense he wants to laugh, but the transition from anger to ease, apparently to him, seems quite swift. Nevertheless, he relents, and bursts out into hearty, noisy laughter.

"Mein Führer, upon my soul! You are the first person that could ever made me laugh right in the middle of one of my angry outpourings! Incredible! No one ever succeeded in doing this!"

"And you, Goebbels, are the only person who succeeded in keeping me quiet for longer than a minute."

We both laugh, and my pain almost yields to this joyful atmosphere. I can't help but wonder though: Do I also hate people?

"The only real friend one has in the end is one's dog!" he exclaims, petting Prinz again. "I have a dog, too, you know. His name is Benno. He was also the inspiration of one of my maxims: *The more I get to know the human species, the more I care for my Benno.*"

"What made you hate it, Goebbels? The human species, what made you hate it?" I ask, pensively.

Noticing my severe expression, he follows suit, whipping his smile off. He sits quietly on the sofa and suddenly looks even smaller now in that sitting position, as if the couch had swallowed him almost entirely, leaving only his head in sight. He continues his recounting, gathering his small, white hands in his lap.

"It denied me everything I had ever hoped to get from this world. It stifled my dreams and curbed my hope." His disgust spreads throughout his features, making the deep wrinkles around his mouth all the more visible. "I've enrolled at eight of the most famous universities in Germany—nay—in the whole world by the age of twenty-four. I have a PhD. I am a doctor."

"Dr. Goebbels. It has a nice ring to it."

"That is pretty much all it got me. A nice ring to my name."

"But how so?"

"My greatest dream was to become a writer. So, I gathered my entire knowledge and determination and threw myself wholeheartedly into work. By the age of twenty-five, I had written a novel and two plays. Yet no bloody publisher and no goddamned producer would have them. They quickly dismissed me as 'untalented', 'inarticulate', and 'weak'. Their criticism left such deep scars on my soul that I never summed up the courage to write another word again."

"Surely, they were all Jews! Those scoundrels that rejected you!" My blood rushes into my head as I remember my own humiliating rejection from the academy in Vienna.

"Yes, indeed they were."

"You are not their only victim, Goebbels. We all are."

He nods.

"And then?"

"Then, I gave up writing completely and started searching for a job in the real world. I applied for a reporter's job on the *Berliner Tageblatt* newspaper, but the editor in chief, a fucking Jew, slammed the door in my face. And again, there was my foot..."

"What about it?"

"Well, it damned me forever, condemned me to be the eternal outcast. No person ever looked past this blasted deformed foot. If it was a publisher, I would be untalented; if it was a newspaper, I would be indistinctive; if it was a girl, I would be a scarecrow. Even the war rejected me, dismissing me as unfit for military service. So, slowly but surely, day after day, year after year, all the bitterness that these rejections sowed in me grew to such incredible heights that even I could no longer conquer."

"Heartbreaking. Truly."

"Not anymore. I suffer no more. My pain stopped as soon as I discovered hate. So, yes, I hate the human species from the bottom of my heart. I sincerely hate it like the plague." His uncanny insight into his own person is so astounding that I can't help but envy him.

"Sadly, your story and my story are the stories of the so many other German youths out there. With all your education... heartbreaking, simply heartbreaking."

"Yes. With all of my university degrees, knowledge, and talent, I still looked at myself in the mirror and asked: *Who am I? Who are you?* And my answer would always be: *a nobody, an absolute zero.* Then that changed. Then I met you. I was nobody until I met you. You gave meaning to my hate and practical opportunities to express it." His voice turns ingratiating again, his eyes sparkling with devotion.

"You were somebody, Goebbels, just as you are now. Maybe all these refusals were meant to happen. All these refusals sent you to me. I had fought destiny, too, with the same anger. And I had nobody to turn to, I simply had to elbow my way up all by myself."

"You have everything it takes to be king!" he blurts out, animated. "Wit, irony, humor, sarcasm, earnestness, passion! You have everything it takes to be the great tribune of the people. The coming dictator!" He looks like a puppet doll with the way he moves about the room sawing the air and dragging his deformed foot, his manipulator, and strings invisible.

"Stick with me, Goebbels, and I promise you that you shall be Germany's Joseph." He quits his trot and drops his shoulders.

"How much your words gladden me! How your confidence rubs on me! For the first time I feel that somebody understands me!"

"I do. More than you could guess. It takes one to know one," I smirk. "As to your evil...well, I believe it is justified, so you shouldn't be ashamed of it. One does what the outside world teaches one to do."

"Oh, mein Führer! As long as you are among us in good health, as long as you can give us the strength of your spirit and the power of your manliness, no evil can touch us."

"Good health..." I echo. "I am afraid this will always remain a quixotic ideal for me, a beautiful daydream." I say dejectedly, staring somewhere beyond the ceiling.

"But what bothers you? Upon my soul, I'd give an arm and a leg to take the pain away from you!"

"That wouldn't be a smart move, Goebbels. With one club-footed limb and one missing altogether, I might find no use for you, either!"

We burst into laughter again, and then sudden knocks on the door interrupt our good humor. After he lets the doctor in, I make motions for Goebbels to approach me. He squats near my bed.

"I thank you for not calling the ambulance. I heard you fighting with Hess over that."

"No need to thank me. I did what I thought best in preserving your image. A leader cannot afford to be seen as weak."

I pat him on the shoulder. "That's right. You spoke wisely. I want us to be friends. Would you like to accompany me to my mountain retreat as soon as I get better?"

"Nothing in this world would make me happier, mein Führer. Nothing."

"Good. Now go, Joseph, the doctor will take it from here."

He stands up, bows his head, and stretches his arm forward in a Nazi salute. As he labors off, I follow him with my eyes. Physically, he fails the standards imposed on my elite guards with flying colors. He looks even shorter and skinnier from the back, and not even the white suit he wears can conceal his underdeveloped physique.

"What seems to bother you, Herr Hitler?" I hear the voice of Doctor Conti bringing me back to the present.

"Capitalism bothers me, Doctor, Marxism, and the Jew, altogether."

"I am afraid I have no remedy against those," he replies gaily, coming closer, arms outstretched, to examine me.

"But I do. As for me, I have a remedy also. So, no need for further examination," I say, pushing his hands away.

He tilts his head sideways, sizing me up with a quizzical stare. "Then why am I here?"

"To administer it. You have to put me on Salvarsan right away!"

"The same old problem?"

"As old as the earth. As old as the Jew."

"I am not here to judge, you know, but why haven't you called me sooner?"

"I was busy. Plus, the pain came and went. Now it's almost a constant. The mercury did no good."

"There aren't guarantees with Salvarsan either. But..."

"But what?"

"Well, after two Wassermann tests and two negative results, you still believe—"

"Just do it. I don't pay you to think," I demand. "I wish I could replace my blood altogether! I hate my blood! I am allergic to my own goddamned blood!" He looks at me compassionately, which enrages me further. "I don't need compassion, I need a new blood! A healthy blood, free of the Jewish poison!"

"I am sorry," he says, quickly averting his look.

"Why don't you perform bloodletting on me?" I ask. No. I actually demand it and it is obvious from the tone of my voice. "I lately imagine myself slitting my wrists just to let the filth pour out of my veins!"

He throws me a strange, misanthropic look. "Bloodletting is quite damaging."

"More damaging than the Jewish poison?"

"But you don't have the—okay, I have another idea, for what is worth."

"Well?"

"Leeches."

"Leeches? How are they better than bloodletting?"

"The difference lies in their saliva. It contains over a hundred active substances that are very beneficial to one's health."

"Fascinating! Could they cure me?"

"They can't cure anything, but they can help alleviate many symptoms."

This new discovery fills me with delight and hope. "Like what?"

"Like your migraines, for example, or the skin rash. They can improve your general health condition, but don't get too excited for they cannot cure anything."

"I want them!"

The doctor scrutinizes me another couple of seconds, then

pulls out of his brown leather bag a strange apparatus, then a syringe and a vile containing a yellow powder.

"Then you'll have them," he says, while preparing the Salvarsan.

I stare through the window at the enormous snowflakes floating to earth. My thoughts fly to Maria, in hopes of relief, yet they chagrin me all the more. There really is no place for me to escape. As the dissolved yellow powder spreads through my system, I fall on my back again, arms outstretched. My cramps and headache are still present, yet the powder succeeds in slowing down my rushing thoughts, in quieting my clinging fears.

The doctor's voice sounds like those industrious swarming bees...*side-effects...nausea...risk...liver damage...death...blood poisoning...*" I want to laugh at his last two words but the beautiful, lazy feeling taking over me restrains me from doing so.

Only one single thought persists, more of a question, which rises louder and louder in my head: *Do I also hate people? Do I also use hate to muffle my pain? Do I also...*

Until, quietly, I drift off to the magnificent land of forgetfulness.

8

PUNISHMENT DOES NOT HURT

W ith my health condition improved by the yellow powder and by the five-day treatment with thirsty leeches, my strength is back again and so are my good spirits.

Only the snow of early 1927 dampens my mood. And yet even that brief dejection is eventually lifted by an unexpected visitor: Maria.

As a member of the Berchtesgaden Skating Club, it is only natural that she is part of the winter Figure Skating Championship taking place here in Munich. I, of course, attend the competition. My presence is supplemented with some of my SS bodyguards and we occupy the entire front row. *Competition* – one of my all-time favorite words. Seeing sweet Mimi competing makes me like her even more. Competing, struggling, elbowing her way up, just like a true survivor, like a true Valkyrie.

The air inside the rink is chilly. I rub my hands together to warm them up, but also in excitement. When Mimi's ice skates hit the gleaming transparent ice, throwing frozen crystals around her feet, I am transported back in time to more than thirty years ago when Johann, my childhood friend, saved me from drowning. He grew up, I heard, to become a priest. Singing in the church choir as a child, I often dreamed of becoming a priest also and spreading the word of God passionately. Many times, I imagined myself as John the Baptist, crying God's words into the wilderness. But then, Mother died. Then, I discovered who God really was—nay—who God really wasn't. Life's mocking irony never ceases to amaze me.

Maria performs beautifully and qualifies for the semi-finals, just as I expected she would. I stand up and applaud heartily, motioning for my bodyguards to follow suit. The clamor produced touches her visibly and she skates toward me, waving her hand at the cheering audience.

"I cannot believe you are here," she says, propping her hands against the glass surrounding the ice-rink. "Did you watch my entire performance?"

"I did. And Mimi, I must tell you, I never in my entire life have been so enraptured seeing a performance. You were magnificent!" My palms meet hers on the other side of the glass, as does our gaze. The clamor intensifies and I realize the audience is now applauding us. It embarrasses me and makes me realize my mistake, for in my enthusiasm I forgot I was a public person. I withdraw my hands and take a step back.

"I will be waiting for you outside in my car," I say, and with a quick nod I signal my men to follow me outside.

When she arrives at the roaring car, I jump to the back seat to be near her. As the car moves away, I look out of the corner of my eye at the beauty next to me. Maurice is uncommonly silent, looking at us – or is he looking at her – in the rearview mirror. The goddamn womanizer!

"Where are we going, Wolf?" Maria asks, stealing my attention again.

"I am taking you to my apartment so you may change, and then we will have dinner. Would you like that, sweet Mimi?" I ask, gently caressing her hand.

"Sure! I would love to see where my dear Wolfie eats and sleeps."

As she talks I glance at her, once again impressed by the transformation. Her slick hair tied back in a bun, her heavily made-up face, the knee-length strapless black velvet dress with rhinestones swirling down the front, and the glitter covering her bare skin...all make her look enchanted. I think she is no wood nymph anymore but rather a deeply sensual enchantress, playing with my senses, a woman exuding sexuality through all her pores. *Sexuality*. The thought paralyses me. The mere attachment of this word to my sweet, child-like Mimi triggers an insufferable nervousness. My hands begin to shake and I pull them from her, lest she might notice my true state of heart.

"My father would be very mad if he knew I was all alone with a man at his home," she says, as we enter my apartment. I say nothing and she continues talking, as if to shake off her obvious nervousness. "He is very old-fashioned and such a deed would surely make him punish me." Her own uneasiness somewhat helps me get over mine.

"How would he punish you?" I ask, startled by my own question. The sudden image of her father slapping her naked body gives rise to a strange excitement.

She looks at me quizzically, raising a brow.

"I don't know. He'll perhaps confine me to my room."

My excitement cools off and I follow her while she inspects my apartment. As she moves, stabs of light reflected from her dress's rhinestones dance around the room in thousands of spectacular colors.

The image takes me again to the day I was almost swallowed up by the furious Inn River. When I received, in a state near death, that fated message – the message of my great destiny lying ahead. I wonder if there is yet another message to be received, as I had learned to pay heed to these things.

"You are so quiet, Wolf," she says, while gazing at the swastika flag hanging from one of the walls. I approach her from behind, wreathing my arms around her body. "What does it mean? This strange symbol?"

"Only great things, Mimi. Just as our future together." I press my forehead against her neck. The smell of her skin is intoxicating and I breathe it in greedily. My hands itch to touch her soft, white, scented skin to squeeze it between my fingers. Instead, I pull back. "I believe you would like to change now."

"Where, here?" Her gaze moves about the room. "Well, ok. I

will change here then, but only if you promise to turn around and not look until I tell you I am ready."

"That I promise!"

I grab a chair and sit on it facing the wall. As she starts to undress, images of her naked body begin to dance in front of my closed eyes. I imagine us alone inside the big, chilly rink. She wears nothing but her ice-skates and performs complicated skating moves. She seems unaware of her nakedness, thus leaving nothing to the imagination. My blood begins to boil and I fidget on my chair. "May I look now?"

"No! I am not ready!"

I resume my daydreaming. Her budding breasts bounce as she swirls along the ice and her hair, freed by her vigorous movements, falls down her back, caressing her perfectly rounded buttocks. She spins now, pulling one of her legs above her head from behind, and then continues the movement, bending her knees, spread wide, her back bent backwards, parallel to the ice, and her arms extended in the air.

I squeeze my eyes tighter, as if straining to see every single detail of her intoxicating anatomy. My heart is throbbing and I can no longer contain myself.

"I am turning now!" I exclaim and stand up. She has already changed and I cannot help but feel disappointed.

"Could you help me fasten this button, please?" she asks, her gaze strangely inviting again. The last time I had seen this look on her was right before I lashed Prinz unconscious trying to impress her.

"Which button?" I inquire, hurrying to her side.

She points at the top back of her long blue dress. "This one. The last one." After I fasten it, I hungrily press my lips against her neck, breathing in her scent again.

"Mimi, you look ravishing. The most wonderful girl I have ever met."

My words seem to have the desired effect. She turns to face me, and wraps her slender arms around me, squeezing me close to her. Her breasts are pressing on my chest, the warmth of her hurried breaths on my skin awakens my senses, raising goosebumps all over my body. I clench then slacken my fists in an effort to keep my hands busy.

"My beautiful Mimi, I love you so much!" She blushes and looks down. Her uneasiness makes me feel courageous all of the sudden, and reaching out, I clasp her beautiful, sweet head and pull her face to mine until my eager lips reach hers. Her burning warmth radiates even stronger, her lips drowning me deeper and deeper.

"You can have me, Wolf. I am ready," she whispers into my mouth. Her words sound like magic music, like notes breaking through from an enchanted world. I slowly push her backwards, guiding her steps toward my cramped, iron-framed bed. As she lays on it, her eyes pierce mine, shooting out arrows of eagerness and passion.

"Wolf..." she whispers again, moistening her lips with her tongue.

I pause.

Annoying thoughts begin to shuffle maddeningly in my mind. The way she called me, the way I urged her to call me...Wolf...it sounds so dishonest now, so phony and fraudulent when whispered with such passion. It makes me feel I am being somebody else, a fraud hiding behind a resonant name. A name I am not worthy of. It makes me feel my true self, the true self Doctor K had seen. My true despicable self, unworthy of this beauty eager to give herself to me – eager to give herself to my fake image.

I am a goddamned fraud, wearing a goddamned mask! I shout in my head.

Suddenly, my whole being contracts in fear, my terrorizing thoughts return with tremendous speed, knocking me out of my mesmerized mood. I fall to my knees and clutch Mimi's legs in my arms, burying my face between them.

"I don't deserve you!" Digging with my fingers deeply into her skin, I repeat over and over again "I don't deserve you...I don't deserve you...I am not who you think I am...I am a fraud..."

She is fidgeting and I raise my head to look at her. Her astonished expression transforms into pity as she sees the tears in my eyes. It makes me hate myself even more, and standing up brusquely, I begin to pace the room. Mimi remains silent, looking flushed and embarrassed. I find myself unable to cope with her unnecessary guilt.

"This isn't your fault! Do you hear me? It is not your fault!"

She looks uncomfortable, if not mildly scared.

"I am sorry..." she whispers, ignoring my words. I can't stand this anymore! The guilt I feel at having tricked her into falling in love with somebody else...a strong man...her own unnecessary guilt making me hate myself even more...

I dart to the hall-stand and furiously pull out my brown leather crop.

"Here! Use it on me!" I demand, returning to her, arm outstretched to hand her the whip. "Hit me!"

"I do not feel like playing, Wolf. Please!"

"Hit me!" I demand again. She reluctantly grabs the whip and I lay down on the linoleum floor. "Hit me, Maria!" I urge her, motioning with my hand. Her eyes are wide, her pupils dilated. She stands from the bed and squats next to me, striking me gently with the whip. "Harder!" I demand. She complies and begins to hit me harder over my legs.

"Wolf?"

"All over! And harder!"

She is now lashing me over my chest, my legs and my arms. The stinging pain releases in me such a wonderful potion that I become enraptured again. My feelings of guilt, of wretchedness, of self-hatred dissipate under her punishment. My body awakens more and more with every hit Maria applies to it. She must hurt and punish the weak, despicable man on the floor. She must kill it. I moan and beg her to lash me harder and faster.

"Wolf?" Her voice is shaking more than my body. Yet I cannot preoccupy myself with her anymore, the magic fluid flowing through my veins has already transported me in that world of indescribable ecstasy.

"Go on, Mimi, please! You are not hurting me!"

The bulge in my trousers is evident and I beg her to hit it. As she hesitates, I gently grab her hand that holds the whip and hit the bulge myself. The blows are electrifying, producing an unprecedented, forceful climax. I squeeze Maria's hand, and with a last uncontrollable, loud moan, I explode inside and out in ecstatic frenzy.

My soul, mind, and body are drenched in indescribable serenity. My mind is empty, my heart is full. Yet as with everything so wonderfully pleasant, I am not permitted to retain this state longer than a few moments. With the magic quickly evaporating from my blood and the intoxicating euphoria dissipating like the morning fog under the first rays of the sun, I can hear my thoughts again...*despicable, pitiful, pathetic, laughable...*

The self-hatred returns, its strength renewed. My embarrassment and guilt paralyze my judgment. I am still squeezing Maria's hand, but I am afraid to look at her. Yet after a long maddening uncomfortable pause I do so. She is silently crying. Her expression is a kaleidoscope of contradictory emotions, changing with uncommon speed from sadness to puzzlement to anger to embarrassment and despair. She opens her hand, releasing the whip and it falls to the floor. The noise produced echoes through the scarcely-furnished room. We both look at it, terrified, as if it were the unearthed blood-stained weapon of a murderer.

"I am sorry..." I finally whisper and hug her knees again. "I don't know what came over me!"

Maria looks dismayed, her eyes searching for an explanation that could put her mind at ease. But there is none. Not even for me.

"I am sorry, too." Her face looks flushed and apologetic. "I did not know what to do..."

"Nothing bad happened! I assure you!" I say in a desperate attempt to ease my own conscience.

"Then, why does it feel so?" Her words come out in ripples.

Indeed...why does it feel so? I am sick. My poisoned blood makes my mind sick.

I can no longer stand Maria's proximity and the harrowing feelings it sends me. I call my driver and order him to take her back to her hotel.

After I see her to the car, I return to my room. For hours, I stare at the riding crop lying on the floor; until my eyes begin to play tricks on me. It seems to be laughing at me, mocking me. Hallucinating, I fall back on my bed...*sick man, the yellow powder...pervert, Jewish blood, leeches...thirsty leeches...the only answer...forever doomed...masks...leeches and masks...*

The early hours of morning find me in strange surroundings, shrieking and trembling, squatting in the corner of a hallway. A man approaches me and I rub my eyes to see who it is.

"Good morning, Herr Hitler. I knew you would return," he says calmly, extending his hand to help me stand up.

We enter the room he unlocks, and for the next few hours, I pour out my soul, baring my entire heart to Doctor K's always-eager ears.

The wretchedness in which an evil revengeful goddess immerses me for the rest of January and the greater part of February is truly unbearable. By day, I loaf about aimlessly, removed, as it feels, from my connection with my true mission. By night, I fantasize and yearn for Maria's blows, for that sensation of oblivion and ecstasy her whipping offers me. *It's horrible! It's sick! It's wonderful! I hate it! It's maddening! I love it! I don't want to stop!* I howl, my face buried in my pillow.

Then comes the tremendous shame and guilt at my own thoughts, and the horror at the state in which I have fallen. And at those times I hang my uniform on the wall in my bedroom and punch it and kick it until blood spills from my fists and toes. When the pain and exhaustion finally get to me, I lay face-up on the floor and rewind, in my mind, over and over again, the conversation I had with my doctor in January.

"It is your longing for the birth of your true self. It is your longing for freedom. Your true freedom," he says.

"What freedom?"

"The freedom from your emotional pain. You yearn to be free of the tyranny of your idealized self, which did nothing but torture you for years. Free of the defensive barriers it created within you since your early childhood. It has everything to do with your childhood traumas, as I told you before."

"It doesn't make sense! You make it sound as if I want to do those loathsome things! As if I want some freedom that in actuality do not want, for I am already free!"

"You are far from being free. And it is indeed you who are doing it. Your unconscious mind is doing it, which is the true self you have quieted many years ago." He pauses upon meeting my bewildered gaze. "Look, Herr Hitler, I feel I must repeat myself, for I still have hope that you will listen to me at last. Most parents need their children to behave in circumscribed ways in order for the child to receive their love. For a child, parental love is a matter of survival.

And as I mentioned to you before, the child forges a 'self' that he thinks will ensure parental love and approval. A self that will defend him against his parents' displeasure. Now...what you experienced through that 'loathsome' scene of masochism, as you prefer putting it, is your true self screaming to be released, to come into being. That scene allows for years of defensive barriers that support the false, idealized self to be broken through. You unconsciously seek to dissolve your self-boundaries, your defenses.

Your conscious mind cannot do that in a logical way because it is subjugated to your fake self. Thus, you are trying to do it by inflicting pain on your body in a desperate attempt to kill your fake self. And when you inflict pain on your body, your mind translates it as punishing and chasing away your fake self. That is why you achieved an erection and transcended your impotence. Because your fake self – the one always telling you to be above pleasures and vulnerability and losing control – is dead at that moment, leaving space for your natural, human self. Your deeper yearning is the longing to be known as the real you, to be reached and accepted in a safe environment, which your narcissistic, dysfunctional, preoccupied and aggressive parents were unable to provide you at a young age."

"You speak of freedom and rebirth and wonderful things!" I snap. "Then how come I want to hang myself every other second of my life since that loathsome...since that moment of weakness?"

"Again, it is the fake you that castigates you for having lost control and plagues you with suicidal thoughts. And the masochistic scene is not a state of weakness, but a sense of surrender, receptivity and sensitivity."

"And how the hell else would you call surrender, receptivity and sensitivity if not weakness?"

He smiles. "Now it is the fake, idealized you who just asked me that question."

"You are a bloody fool! A parakeet! Do you know who I am? How dare you talk to me about surrender? What are you trying to make of me? To hell with you and your Jewish mind poison!"

I ended our meeting in the usual way – by slamming the door behind me.

And now, his words reverberate in my head, as if I am somehow looking for relief in them. But there is no relief, only more despair, since not once did the bloody fool talk about my real problem — the Jewish infection. Not once did he mention the poison that spreads nonchalantly through my blood, making me act in those most unthinkable ways. All he ever mentions, repeating himself like a damn parrot, is some remote unrealistic actions of Mother and Father that he thinks damned me forever.

Ah! Where is that day? The long-ago promised day in which the world would finally have no more restrictions for me? The day that Providence vowed to grant me? How much longer must I wait for it? How much longer must I wait until I can take my revenge at last? I know not. But I do know that it will come, for every now and then, She sends me little glimpses at what is about to come.

One such glimpse I receive in late February, when some happier news reaches my eager ears and even more eager psyche: House Wachenfeld is empty and available for renting. The owner has recently passed away and his widow, now living in Buxtehude, near Hamburg, does not use the house.

I summon Maurice to drive me to Hamburg at once. He comes; accompanied by Goebbels, both looking tense and troubled. I ignore this, as I will not have anything disturb the elevated mood I though lost forever.

It is not a full year since I made the vow that the splendid, modest house on the Bavarian Alps shall one day be mine. And it came to me, it came to me by itself, as with many things in my life. My struggle is always present, always making itself known, but at the same time, I cannot deny the gifts bestowed on me by Providence. I truly am Her most spoiled darling.

"The house of my dreams will be mine by dusk," I say to my friends, while my car is speeding through the wind northward.

Goebbels' eyes burn like hot coals taken from a blazing fire. The strange, sensitive little man surely empathizes with my enthusiasm, and I smile at him warmly. But his face remains unmoved. I have seen this expression before and it always foretells misfortune. This lame little messenger from Hell isn't going to let me enjoy my cheerful mood.

"What is it, Goebbels?" I demand, half-resigned. The recent events of both my political and private life have hardened me to some extent, and I am sure I can be quite composed hearing bad information.

"Not great news, I am afraid."

"I know that already. What is it?"

He places his hand in his coat pocket and pulls out an envelope.

"Haters," he says, handing the envelope over.

I rip it out and unfold the letter within.

To The Attention of the NSDAP Headquarters:

My name is not of any importance. Yet I find it to be my utmost duty to report to you the late disgraceful deeds of your commander, Herr Adolf Hitler.

He has been seen engaging in various scandalous circumstances that would bring shame and stigma to both the Nazi Party and the entire Bavarian political world, if discovered.

Herr Adolf Hitler, under my very own eyes, seduces young, inexperienced girls, not yet of age. He just found a sixteen-year-old girl in the town of Berchtesgaden, who obviously will be his next victim. He is a pervert and a rapist.

If this deviltry does not end at once, I will send my next letter to the local newspapers.

Clenching my jaw, I crumple the damned paper between my fingers.

"Sick bastards! Calling me a rapist? I, a rapist?" I spit out the words, my eyes bulging, my forehead drenching in sweat. "Out of anything they could have slandered me with, this is what they chose? A rapist?"

"She wanted money. So, I paid her off," says Goebbels proudly, winking at me.

"Stop the bloody car!" I yell, hitting the car window with my fists. "Stop the car immediately!" Maurice drives another half mile until he can pull the car over. "Get out, Goebbels!" I order as I jump out, furiously slamming the door shut. I go 'round the car to reach him. He looks confused and apologetic.

His voice shakes as if he's just been dumped into a hogshead full of ice. "I am sorry. I thought I shouldn't bother you with such trivial things."

My words come out through clenched teeth. "I will tell you just this once, and you better get it to your head. Never again are you to do anything without my knowledge and consent. Never! Do you understand?"

He looks frozen, except for his eyes, which shoot out stabs of incandescent light. "Yes, mein Führer."

"Do you hear me? Never! Or your head will hang on a spike!"

"It will never happen again. I give you my word."

I continue to roar, my mouth close to his face. "Don't ever forget who *I* am and who *you* are!"

He shakes his head. "I will never!"

"Good! It better be!" I threaten, taking a step back to look him in the eyes.

"Upon my honor!" he insists, pounding his fist against his chest. His hands are shaking worse than mine.

I breathe in the fresh countryside air, hoping it will help me regain my composure.

"You said *she*," I resume after a few moments. "I thought the letter was sent anonymously."

"It was. But because she wanted money she made herself not all that hard to be discovered."

"For crying out loud, who is she?"

Goebbels looks uneasy, but I know it is just for show. By now, I can well differentiate between his many looks, which one is used for which purpose.

"Ida Arnold. Your driver's girlfriend."

I pause to breathe in some more air, then bend slightly forward to look at Maurice through the car's window. He does not need words from me, and immediately steps out of the car.

"If you have anything to do with this, I suggest you start running. The fastest and furthest you can," I say calmly before he could reach me. He halts, picking at his fingernails.

"I did not know anything about it, I swear it to you! I just found out a couple of hours ago and immediately put an end to it. We went, with Goebbels here, to see her. I told her I would break her legs myself if ever I would hear her name again," he blurts out.

I scrutinize him with deep gravity, eyeing him coolly for telltale signs of guilt. He seems honest, at least on the surface, with his puppy eyes begging me to forgive him.

"I shall not repeat what I have just told Goebbels. It also applies to you. Once, Maurice! Once!" I state, pointing my finger at his face.

My voice is raspy, my throat strained from the yelling. I jump back into the car and we continue our journey in complete silence. I stare through the window at the trees and the roads and the sky and wind in the only place I can be alone: my imagination.

We need better roads, longer and wider than Champs-Élysées, I tell myself, trying to keep my thoughts away from the unpleasant Ida Arnold affair. I shall build them, and soon. And I shall also design a car for my people. A car that every family can afford. Then they shall drive on my wide roads. And one day, long after I am gone, the Germans will talk about it, about what I have done for them. I want my people to call them *Hitler's roads*, and the cars *Hitler's cars*. I want my name always attached to posterity, always attached to the words of my people. I want to be seen as the father and builder of the Great Germany. Tears fall down my cheeks, burning my flesh in their fall.

Then it hits me. This was a sign. This was the sign that I needed. I have strayed from my mission, and now the Goddess of History is displeased. That's why she sent that letter. To awaken me from the grievous state into which I have fallen. To make me take the road back to my only true meaning and mission. Making Germany great again. Cleansing it of the growths poisoning her.

Once in Buxtehude, I try to persuade Lady Winter, the owner of the house, making use of my winsome character, to sell it to me instead of renting it, but she is quite intransigent. I hold no grudge, and for now, am equally happy with renting it. One day, the house will be mine, anyway. Discovering a person more stubborn than I is always good humor for my entourage, and with my anger cooled off, we laugh about the encounter on our way back to Munich.

We arrive home at the break of dawn. Even though I haven't slept a wink, I cannot rest. Somehow, I am filled with a strange energy, caught in the entangling nets of action. Goebbels and Maurice retire after they drop me at the party headquarters.

As I enter my office, the memories of my last being there are almost sufficient to trigger my stomach cramps again. But, no, I mustn't allow such stupidities to rob me of my good mood.

I approach the window and marvel at the changes the lurking spring is subtly making to the word outside. How I love and revere Nature! It has taught me everything I know, from the struggle to accepting change, to admiring beauty. I could draw and paint Spring's struggle right now and her inevitable triumph over the cold, icy claws of Winter. The artist within me shall never die, he will always surface in one way or another, this I am sure of. And the same dormant artist will tirelessly watch over the sacred culture of his ancestors, purifying it, disinfecting it, cleansing it from the filthy growths of the so-called Modern art.

This struggle of the changing seasons reminds me of Mother again. I thank the heavens in my thoughts for allowing me to keep the memory of her alive and undistorted, for I have learned to live on so little. The memory of her feels quite enough nowadays in supplanting my deep-seated need of belonging.

My mind shifts away from Mother and rests on another memory. Geli. My sweet, bubbly Geli. The way she ran away to meet me...*My sweet uncle, a celebrity! I took the matter in my own hands*. I surprise myself smiling at these thoughts. Then, swift as the wind gusts change speed in the metamorphosis of weather, my thoughts darken. I must save her from the Jew. I must rescue her from that dreadful city of Vienna, from that treacherous Sink of Inequity, before she falls prey to the devil.

The thought of that scruffy kaftan-wearer placing his filthy hands on my niece makes me sick to my stomach. Bile reaches my throat as I dart for the telephone. I unhook the ear-piece and speak into the transmitter, requesting a private line for Vienna's Mensa Academia Judaica. The simple idea of me making a call toward such a place makes my gorge rise and my blood boil.

No one answers.

I should have remembered that not everyone revolves around my wishes. It is six o'clock in the morning. I request another line, this time to my sister's home.

She answers sheepishly, on the seventh ring. I count them all, chewing on a nail.

"What are you doing sleeping at this hour?"

"Who is this?" she demands, her voice assuming.

"Your little brother, you goat."

"Adi?" A pause. "Why are you calling? It's five o'clock in the morning!"

"It's six. You should have been out of bed by now!"

"And that coming from the laziest of them all. I don't remember you ever getting out of bed before noon."

"Spare me your crap and listen! You are to quit your job immediately," I say unceremoniously.

"What? What's with this stupid nonsense at such an inappropriate hour? Are you tired of playing practical jokes on your artist-loser-friends and now you're phoning me to do so? Where did you get my number?"

"Angela, don't be stupid! I am serious. I want you to quit your job at once! You are coming to live with me on the Obersalzberg. I've got a house there." There is only silence on the line. "Angela, are you there?"

"Seriously, Adi? Because if this is another one of your—"

"Damn serious. You are to keep house for me. You will have a place to stay and a sufficient monthly income for your needs."

"But what about my children?"

"You will bring them with you, of course."

"But Angela is still in school here and so is Elfriede."

"We will think about the details later. For now, you know what you must do. Do it today!" I bark and slam the ear-piece back in its hook.

I drop into my leather armchair and close my eyes to surrender further to the pleasant sensation spreading through me. What an accomplishment it would be to save my young niece and bring her here where everything will soon be – well, the perfect reflection of myself.

Which self? I suddenly hear Doctor K's voice ringing uninvited into my head.

Ah! I grunt, annoyed. That goddamned, conceited idler infected my mind with his Jewish so-called science!

I open my eyes as to cast out his resonant voice and my gaze falls on the large, daintily-wrapped package resting on my work desk. The pink ribbon betrays its sender and I am almost startled at the thought of *her*. I untie the silky ribbon, tear off the colorful paper wrapping, and expose the contents: two beautiful white cushions embroidered with little black swastikas – and a handwritten note. I immediately recognize the writing and there is no doubt now as to who the sender is.

> *My dear Wolfie,*
>
> *I think of you all the time. It saddens me that you kept so silent after our last encounter, more than a month ago. I, as well, was a bit shaken about what came to pass between us, but that disposition left me pretty quickly once I left Munich. I miss you so much! Many times I wanted to come and visit you again, but without a plausible motive for my visit, I could not trick my father into letting me go. He saw right through me each time and became dreadfully enraged. I embroidered the cushions myself, needing to keep my hands and mind busy in your absence. Please write to me! I assure you I already forgot that little incident and hold no grudges.*
>
> *Waldfee,*
>
> *forever yours in mind and heart*

As I crinkle the paper in my hand, I realize one thing. With one single exception, I did not think of her at all for the past two days. I do know myself pretty well, at least in one respect, which is that once a day has gone by without me thinking of something or someone, I know with certainty that it is all over. The thing or person has lost any grip on me for good.

Great.

Now I am myself again. Free of the burden of feelings. I close my eyes and silently pray to the Goddess of History for pointing out, once again, the road I must take.

Yet, I still must reply to her.

But, what am I to say? Should I tell her that I am embarrassed to face her again? Should I tell her that when she dropped the whip to the linoleum floor, I realized that she was just a child and I must step back and not corrupt her sweet youth and innocence? That I might be impotent and syphilitic, hence condemning her to a life of misery? That I could never offer her the family life and the blonde, blue-eyed children she so wishes for? That my blood is corrupted and would infect my descendants for ten generations, rendering them retarded and insane?

No, no. I cannot tell her that!

What am I to tell her then?

I feel dizzy again and swirl the office chair around to sit on it. I prop my elbows against the edge of the wooden desk and sink my face into my hands, roughly rubbing my eyes with the tips of my fingers.

I rack my brain in search of answers, recounting Maria's words from the note she sent me. I could just thank her in a reply letter for the beautiful gift she has sent me without any other comments or promises. Wouldn't that be enough?

But what if she succeeds in coming to Munich? What if she runs away like Geli, just to see me? Young girls have a tendency toward such impetuous deeds. No! I could never in a million years be able to part with her while she stares me in the eyes!

I will make use of her father, then. I will tell her to listen to her father.

I jump for paper and pen, excited about my idea. She'll listen to me. She'll obey. My hands shake as I commit the words to paper.

My dear, good child,

It wasn't until I read your painfully dear letter that I realized how wrong it was of me not to write to you sooner. Before I turn to the content of your last letter, I want first to thank you for the sweet present, which took me by surprise. I was truly happy to receive this sign of your tender friendship towards me. Nothing in my flat will give me more pleasure. It will always make me think of your cheeky little face and your eyes.

As far as your personal anxieties are concerned, you can be quite sure that I sympathize with you. But you should not let it weigh down your little head with any sadness. You must just realize and believe that even if fathers often don't understand their daughters, because they have got older not only in years but in feelings, they still have the best of intentions toward them. Happy though your love makes me, I ask you, from the bottom of my heart, for our sake to go on listening to your father.

And now, my dearest treasure, all the most affectionate greetings from your Wolf, who is always thinking about you.

As I seal the envelope, running my tongue over its adherent edge, I realize I feel at peace. It is the sort of placidity you enjoy from having dealt successfully with an irksome situation. My letter is explicit and revealing, it divulges the truth of my intentions. And having dealt with the problem, I resolve to push it out of my head entirely.

As I lean back on the chair, someone knocks on my office door and opens it almost simultaneously. Irritated, I wonder, *why people do that?* Why bother knocking if they are going to enter before I grant or restrict their access?

"Missed me?" I hear a voice so familiar that it startles me. I raise my eyes as to make sure I am not mistaken and see that it is indeed him.

"Göring! Holy God Almighty! Is that really you?"

"In the flesh!" he says and we hurry toward each other, locking in a manly embrace. *That's a lot of flesh*, I think, unable to encircle him with my arms.

Hermann Göring, the air ace and one of my first loyal men. He gained the reputation of a daredevil for fighting heroically in the Great War as a pilot for the Imperial flying corps. He was awarded with the highest German decoration—*Pour le Mérite* —by the Kaiser himself. But then the bloody armistice came and rendered him, along with the other millions of fighters, a worthless tool to be dispensed with by the Diktat of Versailles, which banned military aviation as well.

But then, he met me. He marched alongside me toward Fedellenhalle on that fated November day and received several shots in the groin. I proved luckier than him that day. But the man took the bullets for me – for me and for Germany. It was the Goddess of Fate that intervened to save his life, the life of a man enormously beneficial for the Party. He managed to escape the police only by fleeing to Sweden. And now he stands before me, his large blue eyes moist with tears.

"Come in, come in!" I say, making effusive gestures. "You're still showing off your 'Blue Max', I see." I point at the decoration that hangs from his uniform's chest pocket.

He rubs his medal with his sleeve. "Ah. This! This, my friend, will be on my person to the grave."

"Of course. When did you arrive?"

"Yesterday. The amnesty allowed me to return. I haven't slept in two days." He moves heavily toward my armchair and drops himself in it with a thud.

"Look at you, Göring! You've grown so fat!" I say, squeezing his upper arm. My hand fills with his flabby flesh.

He rolls his eyes. "Tell me about it! I move like an old, fat chimpanzee. I feel like an old, fat chimpanzee! This goddamned addiction!"

"Still on morphine?"

"Still. And probably for the rest of my life. My body is my curse. Jews are my curse! For if it weren't for the bloody Jew that sold our country, I would have never been riddled with those damn bullets!"

I look at his face. It is almost unrecognizable; bloated as it is, eyes puffy, with deep, dark circles beneath. His cheeks look ready to explode. His skin is thinner and crossed with tiny broken capillaries. His eyes look small compared to his enlarged face, which looks ready to swallow them. His stomach resembles a hot-air balloon ready to take off.

"You speak truly, my dearest Göring. But rest assured, for we shall have our revenge. I am most happy you returned. I need you greatly."

His eyes are on me now, while my gaze pierces the window into the horizon.

"You have the same look the first time I met you. The same look when you spoke to us. Always reaching somewhere beyond, as if you were seeing into a world completely forbidden to the rest of us."

"Really? I never realized it."

"You sure did. It made me fall for you – hook, line and sinker. That was my first thought of you: how amazing the faraway look in that man's eyes, how magic his words. Then, I knew you were the chosen one. Chosen to avenge us all."

My friend's words bring tears to my eyes.

"You know what *my* first thoughts of you were?" I say, trying to conceal my emotions.

"Surprise me."

"I said to myself: Splendid! A war-hero with the *Pour le Mérite*—just think of that! Excellent propaganda value! And what's more, he's got plenty of money and won't cost me a penny!"

We burst into a hefty laughter; me tilting my head backwards, him clutching his bloated belly.

"And now?" he demands, wiping his sweat off his forehead.

"And now...let's see. I could use your connections. An audience with President Hindenburg wouldn't be bad for starter. Consolidating my friendship with Mussolini would be next. Then you can go ahead and secure some donations from our esteemed industrialists. I would suggest starting with Deutsche Bank," I conclude, and we burst into laughter again.

"Agreed."

"How is Carin?" I ask, remembering his sweet, beautiful Swedish wife. "Is she here with you?" His expression darkens, his eyes change into dark blue sapphires. I gaze at him for the longest time, amazed at how this otherwise brutish, caustic, scandalmonger of a man turns into a wimp at the mere speaking of his wife's name. This is what love does to a man. It weakens him. It's lucky I am not married. For me, marriage would be a disaster. For Germany, my marriage would be a disaster.

"Yes, she is," he says, then hesitates. "I am concerned, you know...she complains of chest pain much too often lately. It worries me sick."

"Have you seen a doctor?"

"What say you? We've seen a dozen. Incapable little shits. I could kill them all!" His face twists in disgust.

"I am sure you could. All you'll need to do is fart."

Uproarious laughter fills the room again and my friend seems to have by-passed the dark moment. Great. The resilience I admire. I shouldn't have dismissed him as a wimp so soon.

"Like my poor old mother used to say: *Hermann, you will either be a great man or a criminal!*"

"Well, Hermann, I really don't see any difference between the two."

"Neither do I."

Great man, criminal, or wimp – it makes no difference. My dear Göring can be any or all of those, plus a man of his word.

Within a few years, he not only succeeds in arranging for me to meet with President Hindenburg, fills the Party's coffers with Deutsche Bank's banknotes, but with those of Krupp, Thyssen, Lufthansa, BMW, Heinkel and Messerschmitt, as well.

Shaking hands with Göring proved to be a safe bet. Just as shaking hands with the Goddess of History more than three decades ago proved to be the wisest decision I have ever made.

9

ANGEL OF DEATH

S pring has finally won the battle against the long gnawing Winter. I've been watching her effort at every turn: the first stabs of warm, golden sunrays poking through the mean, dark clouds in an effort to reach the frozen earth; the slow but steady struggle to break through the ice and melt the snow; the first tiny green leaves and buds elbowing their way out of the confining branches of the torpid trees; the wet soil crying to the skies for warmth and nurturing. There is nothing in this world that deserves more reverence than Mother Nature.

I am still watching Spring's triumph in amazement, just like I did for so many years before, yet today there is a difference. Today, I stare outside through House Wachenfeld's living room window. Tears fill my eyes and I make no effort to restrain them. I do not know what moves me more, the gratitude I feel within every pore in my body for the marvelous gift bestowed on me by Providence or the euphoria enveloping me at having this bewitching spectacle of nature right in front of my eyes. Both feelings are probably stirring inside me with equal intensity, but having them at the same time feels like bliss indeed.

From now on, the breathtaking highland scenery of the Bavarian Alps will be the first thing bidding me good morning. The Watzmann, the second highest peak in Germany, is going to be my permanent companion while relishing my morning tea on the veranda. It feels as if only here can I finally breathe and think and live! Only here can I remember what I was and what I have yet to do.

If only my strength lasts; and God and Fate remain with me to the end.

Sipping my tea and staring at the mountain peaks, which have been swallowed by fog, only to re-emerge seconds later from its suffocating embrace, reminds me of my birth. My spiritual birth, that is, when in the tiny filthy room of the men's house in Vienna, I finally understood my mission, and at last discovered who I really was: the reincarnated spirit of the greatest, godliest men who walked and owned the Earth: Wotan, Rienzi, Christ.

I am reminded of *Zarathustra*, Nietzsche's Superman, who left his home at the age of thirty and went into the mountains. Like him, I have been guided here by my superior spirit. *Superman*, I say to myself and smile again. The Watzmann seems to be smiling, too. Germany, and the entire Earth, rejoice at having, at last, received a *Superman* again.

I close my eyes, take the brisk fresh air of these holy mountains into my lungs, and make a vow unto my spirit. I vow to you, Holy Spirit. I vow to you, Germany. I vow to you, Holy Mother Nature. I vow to you, righteous ancestors of this Nordic, Aryan soil. I will avenge you. I will haul all the human weeds, the bloody fungus of men eating at the flesh of Mother Nature, clean off the mankind stage. Behold. The Chalice is going to be emptying again and Man is going to be Superman again!

My hands shake, my spirit stirs. I stretch my arms wide as if to encompass the entire world within my embrace. I feel like a vessel between two worlds. I feel as if the entire energy of the Unknown traverses my whole body, then spreads out through me to the entire world. The tips of my fingers tingle and I imagine that it is the way the holy energy spreads onto the world: through my fingers. I feel as God. Indeed, I am a superman, *the* Superman. And I know that my people, my very own Übermensch, will bestrew over the entire earth. My very own Master Race will one day hold the Chalice in her righteous hand.

Spring is always the time of rebirth. This is how Nature

intended it and it affects everything around accordingly. I find myself to be no exception to this rule.

Thus, the first days of March 1927 bring with them two wonderful changes into my life.

It is on these first days of warm weather that my sister, Angela, moves in at the Berghof, as House Wachenfeld will soon be known. She brings Elfriede, her youngest daughter, leaving Geli behind to graduate high school in a couple of months. And a couple of months is all I can allow. She needs to depart that dreadful city and the sooner I take her out of there the better. There is no safer place for her than here, at her family's side, at my side.

A few days after Angela moves in the second change is revealed: the ban on my public speaking is lifted. It comes as great surprise, after two years of being condemned to silence. The reason for the removal of the ban is as surprising as the removal itself – the Government no longer thinks I am a threat.

Tiny letters in enemy newspapers corroborate this. *NSDAP is merely a reminder of the period of inflation,* says a liberal Reichstag deputy. *Hitler's star has faded into insignificance,* says yet another. Reading such accounts throw me in a whirlwind of rage and I pace the living room, violently swinging my whip. I hit my thighs and calves until the stinging pain subsides my anger, allowing me to see clearly, to sense the hidden opportunity in this.

I then realize a great thing: a man's defeat lies in the mistake of underestimating his enemy. Let them lessen me, for in doing so, they are digging their own graves.

The removal of the ban forces me to leave my dear alpine home to return to Munich.

I summon all the Party leaders to an emergency meeting the next day, and on 9 March, I am ready for my first unrestricted speech in two years.

At half-past eight, I make my entrance into the Munich's Krone Circus. Its capacity of seven thousand people proves insufficient for the flocks gathered to listen to me. Flanked by the Brownshirts, I continue toward the stage, where a lectern adorned with a red swastika flag awaits me. A band is playing marches and I recognize Hanfstaengl's creations. The beat sends shivers up and down my back and I struggle with invading tears. The loud, enthusiastic cheers, the drummers, the standards, the eagle wreaths, the outstretched arms in the Nazi salute and the trumpet blasts nearly overwhelm me.

From young men wearing windbreakers and knee socks to gentlemen in evening attire to ladies in fur coats, the crowd is a sight to behold. The spectacle is intoxicating throughout. I mount the platform and approach the lectern. A last trumpet shout reduces the entire arena to silence. I remember the tiny, spectacularly-colored gems connecting me to my destiny more than three decades ago. I remember stretching my arm to touch them and suddenly understanding what they were. They were the people gathered here. They were the spirits I was ordained to fight for. My arm jerks in a stiff Nazi salute.

"Heil Hitler!" I shout. The trumpet shouts, too.

My star is far from fading into insignificance. I am back, and I am ready.

Yet despite this triumph, an unrelenting anxiety hovers over my head. The real concern is of a different type altogether: Germany's economy seems to have stabilized. For the first time since the Great War, the Republic seems able to breathe again. With the unemployment rate dropping, people are making investments again. And while this looks good for Germany, it might prove disastrous for myself and my movement. People are reticent to change a government that seems to be efficient. The herds will vote for what they can measure, not for rabble-rousing speeches that can offer only incalculable promises.

Within a year, my insight will prove correct. Yet for now, I keep the dream alive and throw myself wholeheartedly into work. I am not to lose sight of my mission again. I am not to postpone my plans because of a mere, and possibly, illusory economic improvement. And, as I always do in times of tribulations, instead of letting myself fall prey to an unfavorable hypothesis, I plan bigger still.

It is at around this time that a personal ambition begins to crop up in my head more and more assertively: *Lebensraum.* Or how the British would translate it: Living-Space.

Without consideration of traditions and prejudices, Germany must find the courage to gather our people and their strength for an advance along the road that will lead from their present, restricted, living-space to new land and soil. This is done to free it from the danger of vanishing from the earth, or of serving others as a slave nation.

For were the great conquerors ashamed to take what wasn't theirs? Of course, they weren't. Would I be ashamed to take what should be rightfully ours, the superior race? Of course, I wouldn't. Do I think that it is the right of the stronger to conquer and subjugate the weaker? Of course, I do.

My effort to add colonies in order to enlarge Germany is not merely political. My effort stretches far beyond that. It stretches to the personal. I want to enlarge Germany itself within Europe, in search of a unity between the German folk and the land. There is a big difference, and whoever has eyes to see and ears to hear will understand. One will understand that the concept of blood and soil will not remain merely a concept.

It is indeed a great thing that my enemies underestimate me. For one day, they will look up and berate themselves for their mistake.

Sun Tzu was no fool when he said: *Let your plans be dark and impenetrable as night, and when you move, fall like a thunderbolt.* Nor was Nietzsche in saying that *the man who is by nature commanding and masterful, who is violent in deed and manner is unpredictable; he comes like faith without reason or calculation. He appears like lightning, abrupt, forceful, so dissimilar to anything else that he attracts no hatred.*

Life's irony hits me again. I am out in the open, yet I shall be heeded like a thunderbolt out of the blue.

Germany looks East. My own gaze rests on the East, on the place run by the smelly fungus, by the pestilence, by the Jew. In setting my eyes on the East, I will be taking back what is Germany's by right. A right signed in the blood spilled by my ancestors, blood that has been poisoned throughout the ages by the noxious Jew. I shall take back what has been robbed of us. Then, a world shall burn in flames.

Germany looks at Russia. My own gaze rests on Russia. A country run by the Jew. For centuries, Russia drew nourishment from this Germanic nucleus of its upper leading strata. Today, it can be regarded as almost totally exterminated and extinguished. It has been replaced by the Jew. Impossible as it is for the Russian by himself to shake off the yoke of the Jew by his own resources, it is equally impossible for the Jew to maintain the mighty empire forever. He is no element of organization, but a ferment of decomposition.

The Persian empire in the east is ripe for collapse. And the end of Jewish rule in Russia will also be the end of Russia as a state.

This is my promise. This is my vow. My Master Race will be united with its soil. It is the natural right of the German Aryan race to expand into, occupy, and exploit the lands of other countries; regardless of the populations that might inhabit it, which consist, no doubt, of sub-humans, of racially impure stock.

When the time comes, this stock I shall deport, enslave, or exterminate by starvation. Thus, the remaining surplus will feed the strongest. One being drinks the blood of another. By dying, the one furnishes food for the other. Look at the plants! Look at the animals! Look at man from the beginning of time! All have been cast onto this earth with an innate capacity for struggle.

Struggle is all there is and it is the logic of nature. If blame shall one day be sought, one should hold Mother Nature responsible for everything – if one has the courage to wrestle with her, if one has the audacity to contradict God himself.

As I wrestle with these thoughts, Maria's cheeky face pops into my head unexpectedly. The image startles me, as I did not think of her at all since sending my reply the past month.

At the same moment, my home telephone in Thierschstrasse rings. Almost immediately a disquieting feeling grabs me, and I know bad news waits for me at the other end of the line. I could dismiss my intuition, as I have done so many times before and ignore the telephone call that could put me in a bad mood. Yet experience taught me that things could go very wrong when I ignore my intuition's silent hint.

"Yes?" I inquire in the telephone mouthpiece.

"Mein Führer?"

"What is it, Hess?"

"Bad news, I'm afraid. We received a call from Berchtesgaden this morning. It's about Maria Reiter."

My heart leaps in my chest. "What about Mimi?"

"She...well, her brother-in-law called..."

"For crying out loud, Rudi! What the hell is it?"

"She tried to kill herself."

My mind strains to get around what I've just heard.

"He found her half-unconscious in the bathroom, with a clothesline slung around her neck," he continues. "Apparently, she was squeezing a letter from you in her hand."

"Is...is she okay now?"

"She is being treated for mild neck injury. But other than that, she is fine. Her brother-in-law saved her life at the last minute. He said she'll recover fully."

The image of Suzi Liptauer lying on the bathroom floor with a purple face hurtles toward me with unspeakable force. I slam the ear-piece back in its hook and plunge to the floor, clutching my stomach. Unbearable misery fills me, while bitter tears wet the linoleum floor. I am the dreadful Evil. Everything around me will be consumed by this evilness in me. I am that dreadful monster, slowly swallowing up the individual who has created it, and everything he will ever gaze upon.

I know now. I know who my only perpetual friend is. *Death*. Death was, is and always will be my only constant friend. I understand this now. That is why She always saved me. That is why She will always be around me, protecting me, guiding me.

Mother...Suzi...misery...Mimi...death...angel of death

I'm on the verge of delirium again and strain to crawl to my bed. It looks so far out of reach and the more I crawl, the further away it seems to be moving. It moves and moves, until it remains only a tiny dot, eventually swallowed by the greedy darkness.

The next day, someone is shaking me by the shoulders to wake me. It's Hess.

I am still lying on the floor. I quickly realize I permitted this embarrassing situation to continue for far too long. I also realize that I somehow allowed my balance to slip between my fingers and I must put an end to all of this at once. There is no room left for weakness now. There is room for love no longer, or for whatever that feeling was. Love makes you weak. It's a lesson I should've learned long time ago, thus avoiding exposing myself to my subordinates in such embarrassing circumstances.

I will put an end to this Berchtesgaden affair once and for all, without leaving any room for interpretations.

I ask Hess to drive me to Mimi's home. The sun has climbed to the middle of the sky and again throws its judgmental rays at me. Its light is accusing, offending, wicked. Wretched feelings take turns wrestling with my conscience: fury, then guilt, and at last, shame.

As we enter the town, I ask Hess to pull the car over.

"This was a mistake, Hess. What am I doing here?"

He says nothing, just looks at me with his serious face. I thank Heaven for having taken him with me, instead of Maurice. My tortured conscience would not be able to stand a mocking smile. Hess never smiles.

"You came to depart with Miss Reiter properly. It is a good thing, mein Führer."

"But I can't. I simply can't face her."

"What if you wouldn't have to? We came all the way here...go see her brother-in-law instead. He'll explain everything to her."

I look through the car window, pondering his words.

"This way I won't have to face her, yet she'll know I care about her enough to have come."

"That's right. And ..." He pauses.

"Yes?"

"Well, I took the liberty in comprising this," he says, taking a folded paper from his coat pocket. "That's why I came to your apartment this morning."

"What is it?" I take the paper from his hand and unfold it.

"A sworn deposition. She'll have to sign that there was never anything more than friendship between the two of you."

I sigh deeply. "Does she really have to?"

"You know she does. An affair with a minor would put an end to your political career forever if word of it ever transpired."

Hess is right. Divorcing Germany on account of an affair is out of the question.

I am well received at Mimi's brother-in-law's office, and that alone smooths out the misunderstanding I was undoubtedly expecting. I find the meeting cathartic and I breathlessly tell him about the whole Ida Arnold affair, the importance of my mission, the regret at having to sacrifice my private life for the good of the people. Yet not one word about the shameful truth. I ask the man to be kind enough to have Maria sign the deposition, and also to deliver a last gift I had brought with me: a small, dainty, gold wristwatch inscribed with her initials, and a last note. *It was never feelings that were missing, but timing. Keep this watch to forever be reminded about the safe place you shall always have in my heart. Wolf.* The man agrees meekly and before I take my leave, we both stretch our arms forward in a Nazi salute.

On the way back to Munich, I find myself analyzing the two contradictory feelings possessing me. One of them, the milder one, is sadness. Sadness mingled with regret and self-pity. How much a man of destiny must sacrifice for his greatness!

But I know that my sweet Mimi would have proved to be my undoing. The mere association with that beautiful youth would have meant, sooner or later, my political death. And this I could not possibly allow, since my political death would also mean my physical death. I would never want to carry on without politics. It took me almost three decades to realize who I am. It took Germany too much blood and sweat and humiliation to finally get a savior. And no matter how sweet her smile, how child-like the look in her eyes, or how electrifying her blows, the price for possessing these was simply too high.

I am no longer the awkward youth dreaming of killing himself for the sake of his love. Today, I am my Motherland's only hope and it is only for Her that I would consider death, ever again.

Yet how tragic it is to know I shall never hear those softly spoken, warm words coming from her little mouth. With her, my youth is gone. With her, the happy child in me has also vanished. It is the moment one grows up and learns nothing but to be a beast in the real world. The moment one's spirit begins the dreadful process of metamorphosis from its free-spirited exuberance to gloomy despondency and cold-heartedness.

The sun still pokes me with its rays, but they no longer feel judgmental, accusing, offending, and wicked. I now need their soothing warmth, just as those tall fig trees in the enchanted meadow need it.

The other feeling I ponder on considerably mellows my sadness. It is relief.

Once more, Providence saved me from oblivion; hence, from certain death. The person I am today would no longer be able to go on living, once deprived of my mission. How would I be able to face The Eternal when the time comes? What would I answer when He asks me: *What have you done for me? How have you spent the life I gave you?* What would I answer then? That I spent it loving a single person when I could have loved millions? That I was meant to deliver millions from suffering; yet I've chosen to do so for one only? I wouldn't be able to face Him.

Thus, I resolve to hold onto the latter feeling, the relief, and discard everything else at once. I am master to thousands of souls and should be able to be master of my own feelings.

I shoot a look at the sun and suddenly the words of Doctor K ring in my head: *You tell yourself, you actually demand of yourself that you should be above pleasures, you should always control your feelings, you should be able to live without close personal relationships. And what you did is...you put your feelings under a dictatorial regime.*

Oh, bloody Hell! I suppose this damned sunshine does always bring things out.

By the time we reach the outskirts of Munich it is dusk. I ask Hess to drive us to Osteria Bavaria, my favorite restaurant. I am so famished I could eat an entire cow. I love the food there. Who would have thought that a fanatic nationalist would be a fool for Italian food? I also love the restaurant's ambiance, the Italian design and decor. Each entrance has an illuminated blue glass grape bunch above it. A big Gorgonzola cheese and a Parma ham are displayed inside, with tens of bottles of Italian wine surrounding them. I hate wine, no matter its provenance, but I love the Italian cheese.

As we reach our usual table in one of the back rooms, I see that Goebbels, Hanfstaengl, Göring, and a few others are already there, caught up in a heated debate. They all stand to shake my hand.

"What's the topic here? Were you gossiping about me?"

"Of course not!" answers Goebbels as he holds the chair for me. "Hanfstaengl was trying to convince us all to believe in gypsy curses!" He lets out a mocking little laugh. Hanfstaengl's eyes narrow into a glare.

"Well, you know me. I always enjoy a good paranormal story!" I say and lift my arm to call for the waiter. "What was it about?"

"He was saying that—"

"Now, now, Goebbels, let the man speak for himself! We can't pretend he isn't here. After all, he is six-foot-four!" My companions burst into laughter, except Goebbels. I pat

Hanfstaengl on his arm. "Tell me, dear friend, what was the gypsy story about? I'm as much of a fool for these stories as I am for these foods on your plates."

"Well, I was telling our friends here," he begins, emphasizing *friends* and glaring at Goebbels, who smiles his devilish smile, "that I feel responsible for my daughter's illness."

"Yes, yes...poor child, what is she now, two?" I ask, and then whisper to the waiter to fetch me my favorite dish: grilled trout with vegetables.

"She turned three a few months ago."

"And is she just as frail?"

"She weighs no more than seventeen pounds."

"Heartbreaking...simply heartbreaking," I whisper and pat him again on his arm. "But why are you torturing yourself with guilt?"

"Because my daughter would have been a healthy child now, had I listened to the story."

"How so?"

"Well, many decades ago," he begins, wringing his hands, "an old gypsy woman told my grandfather that any member of his family whose name did not begin with 'E' would have bad luck. She said it was a curse placed on my family by a woman who worked with my grandfather at the time he was a welcome counsellor at the Coburg court. He was so terrified by the prediction that he took her words quite literally and named his son, my father, Edgar."

I lean slightly toward him. "Interesting."

"My father kept to this tradition and named me and my brothers and sister accordingly. We are, as you know, Edgar, Egon, Ernst and Erna."

"I hadn't realized that until now! That's fascinating!" My trout arrives and I begin devouring it like a mad dog attacking an animal's corpse.

"Yeah, fascinating baloney," Goebbels mutters out of the corner of his mouth.

"Go on, Hanfstaengl; don't mind our little one here. He can't stand the truth!" I look at them both, and somehow, it seems that they have exchanged facial expressions. Goebbels's face flushes bright crimson and Hanfstaengl's is animated by a mocking smile.

I love this game! I love turning people against each other! This way they will never form cliques and conspire against me! Divide et impera.

"I thought it fascinating also and followed the tradition with Egon, my son," Hanfstaengl resumes. "But then my logic got the better of me. I woke up one day thinking how ridiculous all this was. We were all healthy, me and my brothers, and I told myself that this couldn't possibly be due to our names. I suddenly felt like an idiot for holding onto such primitive thinking. Then, our daughter was born and I decided, with my wife, to break the stupid tradition."

"And you called her Hertha."

"She was such a happy, healthy-looking baby. And then, one day, she simply wasn't anymore." His last words come out distorted by his obvious grief.

"Yes, I remember her happily cooing the day I was released from prison," I say. "No obvious signs to point out that something was wrong with that adorable bundle."

"She is three now and she...she is a sad image to look at. And it's my fault. It is all my fault." His eyes well up.

"What a sad story," I whisper through the silence overhanging at our table.

"Well, forgive my hard-heartedness," Goebbels jumps in, "but I still can't accept this...superstition. Just because your daughter happens to be sick doesn't mean the gypsy story proves true or that you should reinforce your belief in it. Sometimes things like this happen without an apparent reason, without a curse that we can throw the blame on."

"You wouldn't speak in so cold and detached a manner if you had a sick child of your own," Putzi retorts.

"Well, forgive me if I have offended you," mocks Goebbels, "but you must allow me my opinions. I don't believe it and that's that. In fact, if I ever have children of my own, I will give them all names starting with 'H'. Not only out of defiance, but also as a tribute to my Führer."

"Your bootlicking disgusts me! It disgusts everyone at this

table!" sneers Putzi, and Goebbels jumps to his feet. Even standing up as he is now, Goebbels still looks shorter than Putzi, who remains in his chair.

Thanks to his clubfooted limb, Goebbels jumps on a chair so clumsily that I can no longer contain my laughter. *What is he doing? Is he going to jump on Hanfstaengl's head?*

Everyone at the table laughs as well, like well-trained dogs.

"Get down, David!" I bark at Goebbels. "You wouldn't stand a chance with Goliath here! Don't embarrass yourself."

Why the hell does this bloody Jewish Biblical tale pop into my head? Apparently, the rage possessing me when I first read it persists to this day. David, the champion of the God of Israel defeating Goliath, the embodiment of paganism. Another manipulative piece of Jewish propaganda written to enslave humanity through the use of their invented God. Bloody cursed race!

I push my plate aside, my appetite gone.

"And you are wrong, Hanfstaengl," I continue, "as not everyone at this table feels disgusted. Thank you, Goebbels, for your kind thought. We ought to get you married soon then!" I conclude and watch closely for their reaction. They exchanged facial expressions again, and I am over the edge with excitement. A wonderful game, indeed.

"If it pleases you, mein Führer, then I shall marry."

"Bootlicking," hisses Hanfstaengl.

Eager to move on to a different topic, I shift my gaze to Göring.

"Are you with us, old friend?" I ask, and grabbing a grissino, I throw it at the newspaper behind which Göring is hiding.

He folds down one corner of the paper with his forefinger to look at me.

"Barely." He looks amused, his eyes narrowed in a full-faced smile.

"What are you reading there?" I ask, curious as to what made my friend ignore our entire mystical conversation.

"*Münchener Post* and *Der Gerade Weg*. Your favorites," he answers sarcastically.

"Ah! That Poison Kitchen again! What do they say now?"

"You don't want to know."

"Don't tell me what I do or don't want to know! Go on! Read it!"

"Very well. One of the headlines runs like this: *Hitler's anti-Semitism is covering the likelihood that he is himself at least partly Jewish.*"

My muscles tense, but I go for a scoffing laugh.

"Here is another one," Göring continues, unfolding the other paper. "*Does Hitler have Mongolian blood?* It's written right above a cartoon, depicting you marrying a black woman!"

Uproarious laughter fills the back room. I struggle hard to contain myself, lest I betray my true state of mind.

"Bloody rascals! I'll sue again!"

"Oh, and listen here!" he goes on, "*Hitler's appearance is scarcely like the Nordic ideal he keeps on bragging about. His nose could not stand the scrutiny of the 'racial science' he so advocates, for it would fail his own racial test. Its attributes fit rather with the Slavic type, which was formed by intermingling after the Hun invasion of Mongols, with original Slav bloodstock. With wide base, flat bridge and a little break in its bridge that puts the end of the nose a little bit forward and higher, as opposed to the Nordic Aryan type with small bridge and small base. Look at Hitler's nose again! There could be nothing truly German about Hitler! His theories—despotic and corrupt at once—are profoundly at odds with the highest Germanic ideals of equality. To be free means the German or Nordic individual living according to his own individual judgment; he displays a passion for intellectual liberty and his own independent belief, which comes as the absolute opposite of the Asiatic-despotic conception, Adolf Hitler's conception. Even in times of war, the Germanic duke didn't have the power of life and death but was still completely indebted to the will of the people. On the other hand, Adolf Hitler explains that in his political movement there is only one will, and that is his. He never has to explain what he does, his followers have to carry out his commands without any information. The contrast between the real Nordic ideal and Hitler's cannot be expressed any more dramatically. Hitler's attitude is absolutely un-Nordic and un-Germanic. It is, racially, pure Mongolian. This 'champion of pure* blood' is not only a lying hypocrite but an aspiring German leader whose character and political ambitions are rotten to the core. Hitler is neither the right way nor the German way."

My blood boils. I grip the chair's handles until they carve deep lines into my flesh.

"Who wrote it?" I demand.

"Fritz Gerlich."

"Of course. Our most prolific poison-pen journalist."

Raising my eyes from the plate, I look at the man sitting quietly and unobtrusively on Göring's left. He stares back with an eager expression from behind his round, little spectacles.

"Yes, mein Führer?" he asks, anticipating my request.

"Do we know where he lives, Herr Himmler?"

"Certainly."

"Make him taste his own blood. Then he'll talk less about mine."

Silence swallows our table again. I find myself eager to brush away the thoughts of others as to the shape of my nose and shift my attention to my companions.

On my right side, there is the hypochondriacal Hess. His food was brought at the same time as mine, but he hasn't started eating it yet. He still wipes his fork vigorously with a cloth napkin, as if to kill all the germs supposedly clinging to it. His upbringing and life-course resembles mine the most, out of all the others. With an authoritarian tyrant for a father and a sweet, gentle, affectionate young beauty for a mother, he grew up as the embodiment of both his parents' qualities, in almost equal measure. From his father he absorbed discipline, obedience, and duty, from his mother a love of nature, music, stars, and goddesses.

And while from early childhood, I resisted my father, Hess never did. His break from his father's authority came much later with the beginning of the Great War. He was to take on the family business, his father assumed, but Rudi had other aspirations. He wanted to fight for the Fatherland, even if this meant death. And so, he did.

His courage, obedience, and quick thinking soon made him his superiors' favorite. His daring and selflessness got him a bullet in his lungs while fighting on a Romanian battlefield. Yet

Providence had other things in store for him and spared his life. The end of the war, the way the politicians saw fit to end the war, gave birth in him bitter resentment and that was the moment little Rudi grew up. The only thing that kept him from putting a bullet through his brain was his hope for a day of revenge. The same hope was also fueling me, and finally became the vehicle that brought Hess to my side.

He became an extension of my person, the voice of my conscience. Yet while I craved power to be able to exact revenge, he was content with helping me get there. While I craved authority and control, he was happy to obey me, sometimes in a dog-like fashion, which often attracted the ridicule of our entourage. He has about him an element of femininity, which doesn't seem to bother him in the least; and like all women, he craves to be possessed, ordered about, subjugated to the will of a stronger, more über male.

Hess will always prefer a shadowed corner to the limelight, that's why he makes a perfect secretary. He was also the first one to call me Führer, and possessed by jealousy, the others followed suit. Very few people have called me otherwise since I was released from prison.

And then there is the crippled Goebbels. A shrewd, smart, cunning little man, whose ambition and will power saw him through his darkest failures. In him, too, the burning desire for revenge took him from being an absolute zero—as he loves putting it—to the man who will soon have the absolute authority to inflict pain on those who inflicted pain on him. And he will spare no one and nothing.

Like Hess, he shows unwavering devotion and loyalty. Yet while Hess would never dream of pushing beyond his role of subservient disciple, Goebbels wouldn't shy away from absolute power if the chance ever presented itself. A brilliant schemer, a man who hates humanity and reveres truth only for the advantages he can gain by manipulating it. A well-defined lie is always as good as truth for this awkward dwarf-like man.

To the fat, morphine-addicted Göring, nothing seems more important than social distinction and prestige, as well as the luxuries that come with them. Unlike Hess or Goebbels, Göring is a corrupt man. *Pomp* and *pageantry* are his watchwords. His pedigree cultivated in his mind the quality all the other party members hate: arrogance. Looking at the others as his equals is simply out of the question. Yet his connections distinguish him from the rest. He will prove able to win many victories for me.

And then, of course, there is the short-sighted automaton, Heinrich Himmler. He is the kind one would tend to overlook at first glance, the kind one would quickly dismiss as the insignificant clerk, who wakes up at the same hour every morning, performs whatever duty he might happen to have in a most effective way, without delay, then goes home, kisses his wife, and carefully setting his spectacles on the night stand, resumes his sleep at an earlier hour than most – just to start a new, predictable day at the same hour the next morning. In a different setting he would prove to be just that—the insignificant clerk going quietly and conscientiously about his business, bothering no one in the process, content to have fulfilled his duty, leaving no distinguishable mark on his surroundings. Yet under my command, his gift for organization and quiet efficiency makes him an indispensable piece in the Nazi puzzle. In a sense, he truly is the embodiment of all typically German qualities: exact, efficient, organized, tidy, respectful, and conscientious.

Himmler marched on Feldherrnhalle with us on that fateful November day under the command of Röhm. When I snatched Goebbels away from Gregor Strasser, Himmler took the vacant position. Just as our ancestors chose their leader based on performance, on his capacity to prove himself worthy of the role, Himmler, too, won his place and respectability in the same fashion. Some might call him awkward, given his fascination with the occult, his inclination toward superstition, and his exaggerated passion for herbal remedies. His spartan way of life and modesty were also inherited from our Germanic ancestors.

With Himmler, I can spend days and nights talking of our

ancestors' superiority and purity, of ancient Teutonic history, of the conspiracy of the Jews that will eventually deprive our German heroes and warriors of their rights, of Charlemagne and his process of converting the Germanic tribes to Christianity by the use of armed force.

I can plan the revival of this race with Himmler, just as I can order him to exterminate another one. In both cases, his efficiency and cold-bloodedness, his ultra-methodical industrious streak and his impersonal attitude never disappoint.

Hypochondriacal Hess...crippled Goebbels...fat, morphine-addicted Göring...short-sighted automaton Himmler.

Doctor K's words ring obtrusively in my head: *'You will surround yourself with 'weird' people, people with handicaps and shortcomings, just to reinforce your own idea of superiority, of Godliness.'*

Ah! Bloody hell! I yell in my head. *What the devil possessed me to ever cross the door of that goddamn poisoner?*

I look at my companions again.

'Weird' or not, these are my most trusted men. An amalgam of qualities that, when put together, form not only the most feared Godlike strength, but also the most lethal weapon with which to be reckoned.

10

AN ANGEL DESCENDS ON MY MOUNTAIN

"You came!" Geli screams as soon as I get out of the car, then flings her arms around my neck and kisses both my cheeks. I grab her by the waist and gently push her backwards.

"I told you I would," I mumble, my face bright crimson.

"Yes, Uncle Alf, but I did not expect you to come in person! I assumed you would be sending one of your beautiful men to fetch me," she says and looks over my shoulder at Maurice. I pretend not to notice her grin.

"Nothing is more important to me than to save you from this poisoned city. Nothing! I would have walked here if I had to. No member of my family should endure the Babel of this tough city, least of all you!"

Her brown eyes fill with admiration. "You fancy yourself quite a knight, Uncle Alf, don't you?" she asks, narrowing her eyes in an arresting smile. "For I certainly feel like a princess who's just been rescued by one!" Her voice is that of a teenage girl playing at being a woman, sweet but sensual, playful yet seductive. She flings herself at me again, almost knocking me off my feet.

"You are full of animal spirits, my dearest princess," I say, pushing her gently again. "You mustn't be this open or people will take advantage of you." I open the door to my Mercedes to allow her to climb in. "What happened to your hair?" The long, dark-chocolate waves are now cropped short to her jaw.

"I cut it, after the new fashion here in Vienna. You don't like it?" she asks, toying with a strand of it.

"I love it. It makes you look...even taller, my dearest."

As she climbs in the car, I take a moment to look around. It is almost a decade and a half since I've been here last, but the painful wounds this city marked my soul with are as fresh as if they had been inflicted yesterday. I look at the cobblestone pavement under my feet and remember trotting it for hours on end, with my mind groping for meaning and tortured by endless questions. The shoes I am now wearing are quite fine, made of soft, delicate brown leather; a painful contrast to the ones Aunt Johanna gave me, the ones I wore until the holes in their soles allowed the cobblestones I am now looking at to burn the skin of my feet.

A couple of blocks to my right is the Westbahnhof Railway Station. It hasn't changed in the least, or maybe just to become even more crowded. The thought that my niece was living right next to it makes my hair stand on end. With the exception of Mother's death, there is nothing to churn my soul so viciously as the memories that weld me to this cursed train station: waiting for my godparents, who invited me here, to come for me, but never did, begging for my bread and milk coins, carrying the luggage of dirty immigrants, the kaftan wearer with disgusting long black side curls, the very noise of the train whistling for departure and leaving me behind...always behind.

"We must leave at once!" I bark as I jump on the right seat.

My chauffeur does not hear me. He is engrossed in a lively conversation with my niece. Geli wreathed her arms around his seat, her head close to his. They are laughing together. I immediately detest such familiarity.

"What is so funny?" I ask, my voice condescending. She pulls back in her seat and Maurice hurries to turn on the car's engine.

"Emil was remembering how shocked you were when I first visited you in prison. He said he never saw you being taken quite so unawares."

Is it 'Emil' now? What happened with 'Herr Maurice'?

"And then he said—" she begins, but then stops, seemingly startled by her own impetuosity.

I glare at him. "He said what?"

"He said he was taken quite unawares himself and did not expect to think of the day he met me as often as he did."

"Did he?" I ask, continuing to glare at Maurice, who purposefully avoids my look. "Don't mind this fool. He has words ready whenever a woman comes into the picture. I am sure he practices his speech at the mirror and sometimes with his dog."

She breaks into a fit of giggles.

"Why don't you marry, Maurice?" I ask. "You would do your Fatherland a service. A married man is less prone to fool around and pollute himself with race-defiling ape-women."

"What is an ape-woman?" Geli asks in a sweet, unaffected voice.

"A woman who is not of Aryan descent," I say, this time making Maurice break into giggles.

"Go on, blockhead, take us home!" I demand, slapping the back of his neck. I turn around in my seat to look at Geli. "I can't wait to show you your new home! It's befitting a princess!"

"And I can't wait to finally see it! Mother wrote to me a few times since March, and all her letters were bursting with exclamation marks! *The air here is pure health! The vista is unreal! The window looks like a postcard! The wooden verandah is out of this world! The garden below, oh, you must see the garden below! We pluck our food right out of the ground!* I swear it to you, Uncle Alf, one more letter like this and I would have given up on my graduation just to put an end to my tormenting curiosity!"

She wreathes her arms around my seat now and begins humming a lively, happy tune close to my ear. Maurice smiles. I smile. The July sun itself seems to be smiling. Ah, youth! What a contagious, intoxicating condition!

"A wonderful voice you have there," Maurice utters, mooning at her in the rearview mirror. "A nightingale!"

"You know, Emil," she says, switching between our seats again, "I sang from the time I wasn't even able to talk! Mommy said I was humming out words that didn't even exist! She said my father was especially happy whenever he heard me singing, and my song would always put him in a cheerful mood, no matter how sad or upset or tired he was."

"Or drunk..." I coo to my own ears.

"What was that, Uncle Alf?"

"Nothing princess, I was just talking to myself, like old men sometimes do."

"Nonsense!" she exclaims, getting closer to my seat again. "My teachers are old! Our landlady is old! The President is old!" I laugh, covering my rotten teeth with the palm of my hand. "But you? You are the most cheerful, enjoyable, funniest and handsomest uncle in the entire world! I won't let you say that silly word again! I wouldn't have even liked you if you were younger!" she says and laughs a bewitching laugh that makes my skin break out in goosebumps.

Just how many laughs can this creature have? She is with us for less than ten minutes and I've already counted four of them. But *cheerful, enjoyable, funniest and handsomest?* I am not that! Or am I? I don't even know. But does she really see me that way? I shake my head to cast away the strange feeling taking hold of me.

"Go on with your singing story," I demand, and avert my look, lest I might betray my emotion.

"Yes, I was Father's favorite child, mommy said."

"I bet he was very proud of his beautiful daughter," adds Maurice.

"I wouldn't know. If he was, I don't remember. He died when I was very little. I don't remember his face. I only know it from the pictures mommy showed me. How was he, Uncle? You knew him well, didn't you?"

"Better than I ever wanted," I coo again to my own ears. "Well princess, if we are to tell the truth, your father was a—" I pause to look at her. Her eager expression and puppy eyes stop me in my track. "Well, he was everything your mother told you he was," I say. *Plus, a drunkard, an abuser and a civil servant.*

"Yes, everyone talks nicely about him. I wish I could've met him," she utters dejectedly, then hugs my seat again. "But no matter, I have *you* now, Uncle!" she blurts, and tightening her grip on the seat, she lifts herself to reach for my face and lands a noisy kiss on my cheek. Ah, these kisses! They put me in a most uncomfortable, alarmed mood! I wish she would stop kissing me in front of my inferiors!

"Anyway," she continues, dropping back onto her seat, "I sang my life away, always and anywhere. The other day I was so happy to have completed my studies and taken my diploma that I sang all the way home. As I approached our apartment building, I saw one of my neighbors, Frau Braun, stopped dead in her tracks, staring at me with her mouth open. I asked if I was frightening her with my singing. *No,* she said, *I was just admiring you. You are so tall and beautiful...I hope a real man will one day make you very happy!* I burst into laughter, as I was not expecting such words and told her I never thought my happiness would lay in the hands of a man. But the thing is from that moment on I did begin to think of something else: what if I would find my happiness in a singing career? After all, singing in my truest passion!"

"That's a marvelous idea!" exclaims Maurice. "You should become a singer! Maybe an opera singer! That would do justice to your nightingale's voice!"

"That's an abhorrent idea!" I shout. "Dancing and singing is beneath a respectable girl's pursuits! I would never concede with this nonsense! You ought to be something of importance and consequence!"

"Ought I?" she asks, cynically.

"Yes. Why not a doctor? That would do you justice!" I continue and turn to look at her. She stares wistfully through the window.

"But singing is art," she resumes after a long while. "You are an artist and left your home to become one. Mommy told me. I thought the idea would please you."

"Well, it doesn't," I say. "What good did that get me? I've done nothing but humiliate myself in the process of becoming one! Did your mother also tell you that the scoundrels at the Academy rejected me? Did she also tell you that I had to sell my paintings for a loaf of bread, to keep myself from dying of hunger?"

Awful memories intensify the wretchedness with which the city has already cursed me. Why is it that we turn into our parents as we advance in age? She must regard me now as I regarded that uptight, authoritarian civil servant of a father.

"I didn't know that, Uncle Alf! I am so sorry!" Of course, she doesn't know. It was a great secret to keep. She comes near again.

"Let's not spoil this wonderful day then!" she says. "Look at the sun! Doesn't it seem to invite us to smile?"

It did, I felt it myself. Geli begins humming another happy tune and our smiles return to our faces. Then I realize that it's not the sun that goads me to smile, it is the young beauty beside me. My little ray of sunshine.

For the first couple of days, Geli gives herself over to visiting her new home and its surroundings. I follow her with my eyes everywhere and it is like watching a child discovering life for the first time. The tremendous joy she exudes, the happy, bubbly chatter, the very wonder of her youth, breathes an extraordinarily positive energy in and around me. It feels as if happiness itself made House Wachenfeld its permanent residence.

I remember my own youth, the intoxicating liberty I felt at finally getting rid of the dreadful home and school restrictions, the exhilarating joy at having, for the first time in my life, acquired the right to live and breathe freely. This butterfly romping the woods and meadows of Obersalzberg must feel exactly the same.

An early August finds me preparing for the federal elections taking place the next year, 1928. Only a few more months separate me from my most ardent goal: entering the Reichstag against Catholic and Marxist deputies. Ever again, the preparations include courting investors in the movement, mainly the leading industrialists of Germany.

While Göring and other party members use their connections to win these wealthy gentlemen over to our side, I sit down at my writing table to compose a pamphlet, which upon completion, is going to be distributed by Emil Kirdorf, the esteemed icon of Germany's industrial might, in his industrial and business circles.

But how should it sound? I wonder, while twirling the freshly sharpened pen between my fingers.

Should I let out the entire truth of my intentions and hope to be perceived as a great visionary deserving their money? Would I risk everything and come across as an inconsequential fanatic? No. I must not unmask the entire truth. If I want to cultivate their support, I must appear as one of them: reasonable, moderate, and respectable. I must refrain from bragging too much on my anti-Semitism, as it does not come across as very fashionable among these money bearers. I must instead drill on Germany's present troubles and offer practical solutions, ideals that would unite our Motherland politically and socially, thus preparing it for the future struggle of acquiring her *rightful* living space. I should also appeal to the Prussian tradition if I want to entice the north German industrialists.

In short, I must become a pen wizard as much as I am a wizard of the spoken word. I must tell them what they want to hear. But how I hate writing!

Becoming a wizard, a magician, in the absence of a crowd is tremendously difficult, for there is no immediate feedback, no eyes to tell me when I strike a chord. In the absence of the crowd, the pulse of the listeners is missing, thus rendering me uncomfortably insecure.

"The Road to Resurgence," I scribble the title down. This is good. I should think that a wealthy person, always searching for new projects in which to invest money, would immediately be attracted to this. It sounds avant-garde and full of promise, revolutionary even. I know I would want to read something called this if someone would ever want my cash.

"At a time when one part of the nation is indulging in completely unfounded optimism," I begin jotting down, *"while the other—unfortunately not the worst—has lost all courage and sees no hope whatsoever, I want to attempt to describe the present situation as I see it and point out the path which I am unshakably convinced can alone lead to salvation. Even with the most unprejudiced intentions, I cannot bring myself to view our folk's present situation as satisfactory or hopeful, or even to concede that at any time in the past ten years any signs whatsoever of*

improvement, or as one says today, an upswing, have become evident. Even in the economic sphere, so-called consolidation is either an unthinking fallacy or a deliberate lie "

The truth of the matter is that the folk's situation, the economic situation, looks hopeful for the first time after the end of the Great War. This is the plain truth, a truth that I, in my current position, cannot accept. If I were to accept it, that would mean my end. My end as a politician, my end as the leader of the Nazi Party, the end of my movement altogether. For without a disastrous social and economic situation, the herds of followers would stop flocking to my public meetings, there would be no more eager ears into which to drill the thirst for revenge and betterment.

Alas, there would be no Germany to unite under my will and ambition. There would be no Germany to save any longer. For, without her weakened, humiliated inhabitants, I would be dead. No, I cannot accept the hope Germany sees! I must continue to prophesize doom or I shall be doomed.

I suddenly remember Hanussen's words: *Affirmation pure and simple, kept free of all reasoning and all proof, is one of the surest means of making an idea enter the mind of crowds. The more concise an affirmation is, the more destitute of every appearance of proof and demonstration, the more weight it carries.*

I go over the text I had just written and underline the last sentence: *Even in the economic sphere, so-called consolidation is either an unthinking fallacy or a deliberate lie.* A simple affirmation, free of proof. Yes. Wonderful. This is how I must continue.

I grab the pen. *"Outward signs of apparent prosperity should not be allowed to—"*

"Uncle Alf!" shouts Geli as she bursts into my room. "Uncle Alfie!" she screams again, even though the astonishment on my face is bloody obvious.

"Why in the world do you do this every time, Geli?" I scold her as I jump to my feet.

"Komm! Komm! You must see this!" she demands, grabbing the pen from my hand, which she throws carelessly to the floor before pulling me after her by the arm.

"I am in the middle of something very important!" I bark.

How in God's name am I to treat this girl? My severity, my coldness, my obstinacy work well with my men, but I have no goddamn clue of how to treat a nineteen-year-old girl! If I take on the attitude I use to train my inferiors, this girl just bursts into giggles! *There is nothing quite like a young girl or seventeen or twenty, pliable as wax, whom you can mold in any manner you wish*—I always said to my fellows. But, upon my soul, this girl is even thinner than wax and she simply slips through my fingers.

"Can't you ever remember to knock on my door?"

She doesn't care to answer, but instead hauls me toward the living room.

"Komm, Uncle! You must see this! Komm!"

"You are going to give me a heart attack one day!"

"Not a chance! You are immortal, Uncle Alfie. Now hurry!"

Immortal she says. So, it is not only me that's pretty sure of it. And while I may quit this body someday, my spirit shall remain in the thoughts of my people, just like my niece pointed out: immortal. Tears invade my eyes.

"Sit there!" she commands, pointing at a chair placed against one of the living room walls. On the opposite wall, stuck between the floor-to-ceiling bookcases was a small red cloth with tiny swastikas printed on it here and there.

Next to me, her mother has also been commanded to sit and watch – for god knows what. When it comes to this marvel of nature, one does not know what to expect. I sit dutifully on the chair and smile.

"What's the big secret?" I ask my sister, who fidgets in her chair. Ah! This annoying fidgeting never left her!

I remember the morning at Dr. Bloch's office when I thought I was going to die. But it wasn't to be. I am immortal, my niece said so. The immortal man born of a mortal woman. It happened before.

"I wouldn't know," she answers. "It's been a week now since she's locked herself in here, with only the Lord above knowing whatever she's doing."

"Shush," Geli commands us again, pressing her forefinger to

her lips. "We've never done this with spectators, and I don't want you to ruin our act."

"We? Our?" I echo.

"Shhh!"

I cross my legs and prop one elbow against my knee. Clasping my jaw in my hand I look astounded at this miracle woman-child.

She sits down at the big wooden table in the middle of the living room, folding her long legs underneath her. Barefoot as she is, she looks like a poor child, a goddess, a wood fairy, all wrapped up into one. Her skirt is rolled up, revealing the soft, white skin of her thighs. Her white blouse flutters in the soft breeze blowing through the opened window and shapes around her full, round breasts, hardening her nipples. My cheeks flush at the sudden realization of my thoughts.

"Komm!" she shouts suddenly, startling me out of my train of unsuitable thoughts.

A muffled noise, like that of a bird fluttering its wings, comes from the verandah. I look through the open window as the noise becomes louder and clearer. Suddenly, a big, black, mountain jackdaw flies in through the window and lands on the table.

"Schlepp!" I hear my niece again and watch as the wild bird takes off. With a few flapping movements, it reaches the red cloth stuck to the wall, and pulls it away with its beak.

"Schlepp!" she commands again and the bird flaps above the table with the cloth still in its beak, hops to Geli and lays it on the table in front of her. Geli then extends her arm forward, bending her elbow at a 90-degrees angle, her fist clenched. The bird hops on it.

"Gut gemacht!" she says and kisses the bird on its beak, then rewards it with the pine kernels she holds in her other hand.

"Bravo!" I shout out, standing up and clapping. Frightened by my outburst, the bird takes off through the window and rests on the verandah's wood railings.

Angela follows my lead and begins clapping vigorously.

"So that's what you were doing hiding up in here!" she exclaims.

I rush to hug her. "My little bird trainer! The sunshine of this place! Marvelous! Simply marvelous! How in the world did you manage to train such a wild creature?"

Her face is like a glowing torch, like a sun that renders you motionless, its warmth spreading through your bones. It lights up the room, all the objects in it, ourselves. We can only reflect her golden light. She flashes a satisfied smile, her soul reaching out through her eyes to meet mine.

"It wasn't hard really!" she begins excitedly, straightening her legs. "You know how the birds always come at breakfast time and swoop down to steal the leftover bread crumbs off the table?"

"Sure!"

"Well, this one also came, but then stayed. No matter how much mother shooed it, it simply wouldn't go away." My sister nods in agreement. "I knew something was wrong with it and I was right. Its wing was broken. So, I took the poor bird in to mend it."

"Did you?"

"I played with it every day. Then I said to myself, why not teach it a couple of tricks to make our time pass more pleasantly?"

I burst into laughter and gently squeeze her hands into mine. I want to squeeze her to bits like I would...I remember Mimi and our first kiss under the tall fig tree. No matter how hard I try to push away the same urge invading me right now, I simply cannot.

"Of course, I did not expect it all to work out as well as it did. You know, Uncle Alf, birds are smarter than we think."

I want to tell her how a dog had been sent out to me in the same way, when I needed him most in my life, how I named him Fuchsl and how he had been stolen from me by a vicious monster of a man. But she has already wrung herself free of my hold, and hiking up the rims of her skirt began twirling around the room, singing her happy tunes. I fall back into my chair following her with my eyes, the way her body undulates, the way the muscles of her neck contract, her flowing skirt creasing in her fists and caressing her bare thighs...I want to throw myself at her bare feet and beg her to...beg her to...

My eyes fill with tears. They are tears of happiness, dismay, love and shame mingling together.

"What's happened?" she gasps worriedly, throwing herself on her knees at my feet, her arms entwining my legs.

"I don't know!" I exclaim, and breaking free from her entrapment, I storm out of the living room.

As I hurry back to my bedroom, I realize that my conduct must have come across as pretty awkward. *Why have I reacted the way I have?* Bits of truth begin to hit my conscience, but I violently push them away. No! That can't be! I refuse! *You can't go down that path again!* I admonish myself. Every cell in my body alerts me to great danger. *You will become weak again, you will lose control, and whenever you are not in control, you are as good as dead. You might as well pull out your pistol right now and blow your brains out.*

I turn on my heels and return to the living room. I will prove to myself once and for all that there is nothing to be worried about. The girl is my niece, my flesh and blood. To be fond of her is logical. To care about her in a fatherly fashion is not only allowed but also called for, and that's all there is to it.

But wasn't your mother your father's niece also? the question pops in my head as I open the living room door.

"Uncle Alf ..." she mews as she sees me. "Please, forgive me! I must have done something wrong to offend you." The look in her eyes is heartbreaking, but there is something else, a curious glint of...mischief, which I've seen before, when she was laughing with Maurice. I can't quite describe it, nor the intention behind it, as my poor experience with women always renders me impotent.

Ah! That mere word sends a violent shudder throughout my whole body.

"Don't be silly!" I say, twisting my face in a surprised way to make her believe she had it all wrong. "I just remembered something. My photographer is on his way here and he is bringing his daughter with him. How would you like to go out for a picnic?"

Her eyes widen with sheer enthusiasm. "Really?"

"Really. I know the perfect spot on the Chiemsee. It's right between the woods and the lake."

She throws her arms around my neck and presses her robust

body against mine, squashing her breasts against my chest.

"I'll be ready in no time!" she exclaims, letting go of my body to run for the door. "I'll tell mommy to put together some food, coffee and tea! And Apollinaris mineral water for you!" she shouts and winks at me on her way out.

There! What was that? What in the world goes through that little mischievous head of hers?

Muffled noises reach me from the hallway, signaling my friend's arrival. The door bursts open wide and a freshly-groomed Hoffmann enters.

He rushes to shake my hand. "Heil, my friend!"

"Heil, dear Hoffmann. I almost forgot you were coming! My mind is so preoccupied these days!" I say, shaking his hand.

"With the campaign, I suppose." Ah, the campaign! Admitting to myself that my mind was less on the campaign than on my niece is frustrating.

"That's right," I lie, and look past him at his daughter, standing in the doorway.

"Come in, my little sunshine! Aren't you coming to give Uncle Adolf a kiss?" My face flushes bright crimson as soon as the words escape my mouth.

Henny shoots an angry look at me and now I know the redness in my cheeks is embarrassingly obvious.

"Good day, Herr Hitler." She must be almost fifteen now, but her well-developed body makes her look much older. Not in a bad sense, quite the contrary. Her true Aryan genes exude from all her pores. She's taken after her father.

I am still looking at her, but I no longer see her, as my memory has already transported me back in time, when she was but a child running to encircle my knees whenever she saw me in her father's doorway. The time she refused to learn to play the piano and would only acquiesce if Uncle Adolf would come every day. For weeks in a row, I walked the road to Hoffmann's house just to play the piano with little Henny.

Then, like the spring trees that burst into bloom overnight, she wasn't little Henny any longer, but a beautiful woman in her own full bloom.

Is there anything more beautiful than a woman in full bloom?

Anything more appealing than an unspoiled young girl of fourteen, whose sweet, naive charms suffocate the air in a room, any room? I remember asking myself, upon my unsettling revelation. I thought not.

So, one evening, as I was about to leave her father's house, she struck me as magical, with the strange little laugh she gave when I said, *Good night, my little sunshine!* A laugh that said, *I am not little anymore, you silly man.* I just stood, horror struck, in the doorway. She was no longer little...my little sunshine was no longer little.

Henny, would you come give me a kiss? I had asked. Once the words were out, I wished I could have taken them back. *No, I will not give you a kiss! Good night, Herr Hitler!* she had said, turning her back to me and running up the stairs.

And now I just asked her again! The same goddamn question!

Later that night, she had passed on the details to her father, who has said: *What a foolish child! What an overactive imagination! She ought to become a writer and put that imagination to good use!* Thus, I was rescued then.

But the color in my checks right now is just as good as a statement saying, *Hoffmann, I am attracted to your daughter.*

"What brings you here, dear friend?" I ask in a pathetic attempt to get past the humiliating moment.

"This!" he says, waving a large envelope in the air.

"What is it?"

"See for yourself." I grab the envelope from his hand and rip it open. A thick set of pictures fill my hands.

"What's with this filth?" I inquire, shuffling through them. "If you're asking permission to publish them, the answer is no." They are pictures of me, taken in most awkward positions.

"That's not what I want," he says. "Remember the last time you were at my studio?"

"Uh-huh."

"Remember I was snapping you for the purpose of seeing yourself in different postures and decide which of them suit you better for when you deliver a speech?"

"Ye gods! Yes! Forgive me, it seems that my memory is giving up on me!" I eagerly scrutinize the set again. All of them show me angrily gesticulating, swishing my whip in the air or hitting my boot with it, clenching and slackening my fists, my mouth closed or opened, my eyes firing anger, passion, and purpose.

"Here, this is my favorite one," he says, pointing at the one where I am gripping at my chest with one hand, while holding my other fist above my head in a threatening stance.

"Yes, it's pretty intense. And you are one brilliant fellow, Hoffmann. Can we take some more of these?"

"Uncle Alf, I'm ready!" shouts Geli, entering the room. "Oh, I am sorry," she exclaims covering her half-opened mouth in a gesture of surprise, "I wasn't aware your company was already here!"

I venture to introduce her, but she's already darted to Henny's side and has taken her hand.

"I am Angela, the sunshine of this place!" she exclaims, giggling. Henny shoots a scoffing look at my face and I pretend I don't see it. "But you can call me Geli, everyone does! How lovely your dress is! White is my favorite color in the world! You can match it with anything! I make my own clothes, you know!" she rambles on in her usual fashion, now hugging poor Henny who looks confused by such a display of familiarity. Nonetheless, the girls take to each other immediately.

"This is Heinrich Hoffmann, my dear friend and photographer," I say. Geli quits a still-bewildered Henny and approaches her father.

"A photographer! How lovely! I am most happy to meet you!" she says and hugs him, pressing her body hard against his, in the same fashion she hugged *me* earlier. Her behavior, her manner, her open yet intricate personality grieves me as much as it fascinates me.

"How I wish I had my own camera!" she continues and I search her eyes for the mischievous look. It's not there. Only bright, sunny, warm beams of innocence shoot out of them. That makes me smile ear-to-ear.

"Well, lovely Geli, if you want it badly enough, then you will certainly have it," says Hoffmann and raises his hand to her cheek to pinch it lightly. That makes her burst into giggles again, and all of a sudden, I realize that we all share her mirth. This child of nature truly is the sunshine of the house.

"I was telling Geli we should go for a picnic together. My sister has already prepared the food hampers."

"That's a wonderful idea!" Hoffmann exclaims. "Wouldn't you agree, Henny?"

"Indeed. Let's go for it!"

"Then we must hurry, Maurice is waiting outside," he says.

"Yes, please! We mustn't keep dear Emil waiting. Let's hurry!" Geli exclaims and exits the room, much too eager for my liking, with us trotting behind her.

11

THE MOST TERRIFYING FEELING OF THEM ALL

The weather of this mid-August day proves wonderful enough for our picnic. Warm enough for the girls to sunbathe and chill enough for us to remain fully clothed and read the newspapers in a shaded spot. The forests are still mostly green, but one can sense the impatient autumn struggling to manifest itself by the barely perceptible rusty color on the leaves.

The food is also wonderful: cheese and salami sandwiches with freshly-baked crusty bread, roast chicken that melts in the mouth, poppy seed strudels and vanilla pancakes. My sister truly is an outstanding cook and her coming to live with me on the Obersalzberg brought back the dearly-missed pleasure of eating our traditional Austrian specialties.

After we eat, Maurice takes his mandolin out of the trunk of the car and begins playing it. His songs are cheerless and wistful and haunting, like those composed by a heartbroken artist for a departed lover. They work like magic for the girls, who quit their spots next to me to sit on the grass near Maurice, gazing dreamingly at him with teary eyes.

I jump to my feet and search for a spot to be alone with my thoughts. I choose a shaded spot near the lake and sitting down on the grass, I take my shoes and socks off. I try the shallow water with my fingers and dip my feet into it, paddling lazily.

Harrowing thoughts suddenly rip through my mind, leaving painful trails. Is this melancholy? Jealousy? The way she laughed with him...*dear Emil*...the way she fed bites of food to him like he was a retarded, handicapped child, the way he whispered in her ear and made her giggle, the way she is mooning at him right now, and sighs with every stroke of those cursed strings...

I grab a flat pebble and send it skimming across the surface of the water. It hops a few times before it sinks in the hungry bowels of the lake forever, creating expanding ripples. In a few seconds, the lake is placid again and I surprise myself by envying it. Pulling a handkerchief out of my pocket, I wipe my wet eyes and feet.

When I suggested going out for a picnic, I was certain I would be proving to myself that there is nothing to be worried about. No feelings harbored other than the natural feelings of tenderness an uncle has for his niece.

But now, staring at the reflection of my own grief-stricken image on the glassy surface of the placid lake, I know I was wrong. The fearsome truth on my moving reflection has finally broken free and is now glowing in the full light of my conscience.

I am falling in love with my niece.

For a few days, I find myself unable to fight this new feeling. Or maybe not unable, but unwilling. Surrounded by the peaceful serenity of my mountain retreat, by the lively meadows and glistening night sky, embraced as Geli and I are by the solitude this secluded place offers us, I tell myself there is no reason to fight it. There is no one here to see me, no political enemies, no underlings, no poison-pen journalists.

By day, we romp about the wonders of nature surrounding the house, running to the lake, where Geli always bathes with me watching her from the bank. We then take our lunch in some remote clearing, lying carelessly on the grass or on chaise-lounges, smiling at each other with our eyes, hearts and souls.

At the dinner table, where my sister, Elfriede and I sit as normal people do, on their own seats, Geli resolves to sit on my lap. Her mother always scolds her, but Geli refuses to eat otherwise, and after many failed attempts to redress this child of nature, my sister finally caves in.

And then there are those mornings when I enter her bedroom, after a long sleepless night, just to look at her while she's still asleep. As I watch her peaceful face I realize that she indeed is the sleeping beauty, with her relaxed features and the corners of her mouth slightly up-turned in a childish smile, no doubt romping some green, enchanted meadow in her dreams.

I could never let anyone watch me while I sleep, as the image of my contorted face would surely make the onlooker regard me as hideous. While my childishness seems lost forever, Geli's is still here and alive. As I stare at her, I almost feel like a thief trying to rob her of it. I realize that this is her most endearing quality, her childishness, the unspoiled wonder of youth. Couple that with a beautiful face, a soft feminine body, and the sweet smell emanating from her skin, and you have the beauty of all beauties, the goddess of all goddesses – the forbidden fruit.

Goaded by my thoughts, I approach her bed, just so I can catch the scent of my Goddess of Love. Her bare shoulders peek from under the linens. I kneel by her bed and slowly move my face near her skin, taking in a deep breath of her intoxicating scent. I pull back then and refuse to exhale. I want to keep her smell in me for as long as I possibly can. Holding my breath shoots a wonderful elixir through my veins, like some chemical spreading through my system, chasing away all worries and anxieties, all guilt and shame.

I feel like a newborn, a feeling I only experience in one other circumstance: when I hear that some bloody Jew has perished from the face of the earth.

Suddenly, Geli gives out a little laugh and stretches her arms like a lazy feline.

Startled to have awakened her, I retreat to an armchair. I wish I could draw her, the way she sleeps, to capture her innocence on paper. I look around and notice a stack of blank papers, envelops and pens. Ah! Surely, she writes letters to her friends in Vienna. Standing up, I grab a white sheet of paper and a dark charcoal pen. I begin to trace the lines of her round face, of her smiling lips, square jaw, narrow nostrils and the pointed tip of her nose.

And then, her eyes, those magnificent dark brown eyes, now closed.

I remember how she smiles with her eyes. No other person I know smiles with his or her eyes like my dear Geli. I relish the memory until another replaces it, that of my dead mother, the wretched moment I drew her sunken, jaundiced corpse.

"What are you doing?"

A shudder runs through my body as I hear Geli's voice. Yet it is not scolding, not even surprised-sounding, just calm and curious.

"I was drawing your portrait. You were sleeping so beautifully, my little sunshine."

She sits up; and as she does so, the sheets covering her body glide down, revealing her naked body. I flush bright crimson and fight the urge to run away. Unperturbed, she yawns and stretches her arms, leaving in plain sight her perfectly rounded, full breasts.

"Go on, don't stop now!" she says, and ruffling her messy hair with her fingers, she begins to pose for me. My hands shake; yet I pretend there is nothing out of ordinary happening. I begin to sketch the muscles of her neck, her long, heavy arms raised overhead, her ruffled hair, the intoxicating shape of her breasts. I move the pen in a near frenzy, as her sketched body takes shape on the paper, pausing only for brief glances at her. Each time I do so, she smiles. It is no longer the smile I saw on her sleeping face, but the one she shot at Maurice after he whispered inaudible things in her ear, on that first picnic day. The mischievous, seductive one.

"Am I sitting right? Is the light proper?" she demands, but waits not for an answer, and throwing the covers off completely, she stands up. "I want you to have me fully," she says.

Now it's not only her smile that's mischievous and seductive but her voice and words as well. The more she moves around, leaving nothing to the imagination, the more frightened I become. I bury my gaze in the drawing lest she suspect my inner turmoil and continue to draw like a madman – the full, long limbs, the roll of flesh around her waist, the furry pubic hair.

When I am done, I feel exhausted. Sweat drenches my entire body, beads form relentlessly on my forehead. I pant and heave as though a mugger had just chased me here. Then, digging deep down for courage, I raise my eyes and look at her.

She's thrown a light, summery dressing gown over her body, but left it untied. The sleeping beauty is no prude, I realize. Innocence is not her only quality.

Throwing her head back, she bursts into laughter.

"You look pained, Uncle Alf. No, rather...panicked," she says, still laughing and moving toward me. I can see the swaying of her hips through her gown, the way the silk caresses her skin, the way it takes on the round form of her breasts. She now stands in front of my seat, her hairy privates at the same level with my face.

My god! This girl has no decency! I shout in my head and jump to my feet.

A shudder rips through my body but before I can move or speak or run away, she flings herself at me, pressing herself against my body. Stiff as a board, I can still feel her hard nipples protruding from her full breasts pressed against my chest and her soft, warm stomach molding to mine. Her arms slide from my neck to my hands, which she gently pulls behind her, and then rubs them softly against her buttocks.

The feel of the thin silk gliding over my hands is strangely pleasant. While my heart pounds so rapidly I can feel the blood throbbing in my temples. She throws her head slightly backward and gives a sigh of pleasure. I clutch her buttocks hard and pull her tighter. Her face comes forward with a jolt and when she presses her perfect lips against mine, my soul swells and rejoices.

Yet my mind cringes. Hundreds of dark thoughts hurtle toward me with lightning speed: *She is your niece! You are impotent! You will infect her!*

"What a funny little game you play," I say, and gently push her back as I move away from her as quickly as I can. The break is painful.

"It isn't a game, Uncle," she says, gathering the dressing gown around her body. She looks like Mother; and now she sounds like Mother, too, with her calling me 'Uncle'.

I lift the drawing from the armchair and look at it. "Do you like it?"

She avoids my question and I know she'll not allow me to move forward. Why is that women always want something?

"I know what your feelings for me are, Uncle. I feel the same way about you."

"What goes on that silly head of yours? A funny little game you play," I repeat.

"I am not playing a game, and you should quit playing yours." Her voice is grave and serious. She's not a child anymore, but a demanding, frightening woman.

I summon the courage to look at her. How I want to tell her that she means everything to me. How I want to throw myself at her feet and beg her to love me, beg her to save me.

From what I do not really know.

"Don't you love me, Uncle Alf?" Sadness rips through my body as I gaze into her longing eyes.

"Of course, I love you, princess! You are my niece, my flesh and blood! There's no one else I love more than I love you!"

Coward! I chide myself. *You hide behind words. You tell her you worship her but hide behind "niece, and flesh and blood". You get the courage to touch her only when she sits on your lap. Hiding. Always running away and hiding. Coward! Coward!*

"You are being a child," she says, and gives a little scoffing laugh.

Her remark unnerves me a little, but I decide to let it pass unaddressed. When she grabs my hand again and presses it on her breast I swiftly turn on my heels and exit her room.

For a full day and night, I refuse to come out of my bedroom, and pace it maddeningly and almost uninterruptedly, while equally loving and detestable thoughts take turns oppressing me.

How wonderful Geli is! How frightening and terrible! I hate her! I love her!

This girl has so many sides that even my psychotherapist would fail to pinpoint them all. But I did, from the first moment I saw her on the other side of the bars at Landsberg, when she ran away from home to see me. Her moods and expressions, and the many laughs she gives in different circumstances, suddenly make me realize I have a wonder of nature on my hands. An ever-changing kaleidoscope of moods, roles and even people; her lively wit and exhilarating charm, her youthful spirit and her ability to entertain people, her highly refreshing personality, and her teasing attitude, each and all enthrall the environment and the people around her.

It is no wonder she drew Hoffmann and his daughter to her almost instantly, no wonder she bewitched our lady's man, Maurice. And the wonder of wonders, she succeeded in enslaving *me*.

I feel like prey again, trapped in the webs of a merciless spider.

Oh, but how I love her! The mere resonance of that word...*love*...repeatedly hitting my eardrums, is enough to keep me awake throughout the entire night. I keep repeating it in quiet whispers, hoping that the sound of it would finally make me realize how ridiculous it is. However, it only succeeds in realizing the exact opposite of my aim. The more I think of it, the clearer it becomes.

Once again, I had fallen prey to the most terrifying feeling of them all.

It is not half a year since I realized I had strayed from my mission, since I resolved to acknowledge love as a curse. Not half a year since I understood that, just like people's humanity, love is only a tool of man's weakness, the cruelest destroyer of his existence. Love softens you, makes you vulnerable and weak until it finally robs you of the will to fight. Love takes away from you the only feeling with which man should have been endowed: the will to survive.

If life is struggle, love should only be seen as the destroyer of that struggle, and therefore, of life itself.

Why, if after deciding to free myself from Maria and finally being myself again, free of the burden of feelings, is this happening again? Wasn't the Goddess of History stark enough in pointing the way? I am letting her down again! I am letting myself down again!

By the time dawn settles on my mountain, I resolve to do what I have always done: run away. I ran away when I left for Vienna, still in the early hours of the morning, wanting to avoid Mother's pain. I ran away from Gustl, my childhood friend, before his return to Vienna, not wanting to have to explain my second failure at the Academy. And now, I am running away again, trying to forget, trying to escape.

As I scurry away from Wachenfeld and toward the train station in Berchtesgaden, I cast a faraway look at Geli's window. A painful question pops into my head. *Am I a coward?* The realization, the startling presence of that very word makes my mind go over the question repeatedly, like a broken gramophone. Am I a coward? Am I a coward? Am I a coward?

You ran away again! I berate myself. *You are a coward; and you running away like a blushing virgin wasn't cowardice by choice! When it comes to the magic of women, you are the most cowardly of men! So yes, you are a coward!*

No matter how painful that answer feels for my ego, I suppose when it comes to feelings I am, indeed, a coward. But who needs feelings anyway? Why would *I* need feelings?

My great purpose does not need them, the course I have set for myself never included feelings; except for the love I have for the Motherland.

So, yes, I am cowering away from what does not serve me. I might be a coward, if that's the only word to describe my actions, but I am a coward by choice. And being a coward by choice no longer makes me one. Instead, it makes me cautious, selective, and in charge of myself.

The train rattles along the tracks to Munich, and the sway produced by its speed relaxes me. I feel I am slipping into darkness, as if a vortex is taking me deeper and deeper, lower and lower, to the core of the earth.

"You'll destroy her, too! Just as you destroy everything around you!" I hear the voice of Father. I strain to see him yet he is nowhere to be seen.

"I should have murdered you in your cradle!" I hear him again, his voice thundering and echoing from all over the dark empty place.

"I should have murdered *you!*" I scream back. No sooner do I utter the sentence than paralyzing lightnings strike me from all around, transporting me to another scene. Mother washes my body and tickles me with her fingers. And then, the knight, the cursed knight, castrating me! His laughter and words echo in my mind with tremendous speed. *Are you chaste? Are you chaste now?*

I jerk awake from the nightmare. Tears stream from my eyes in rivers of sadness and I gasp for air again and again.

In my speeches, and sometimes in private, I tell people that I wept only two times in my life. Once when Mother died and the other when the Great War broke out and, falling to my knees, I thanked Providence for her wonderful gift. I always meant to imply from this that, in fact, only once had I cried out of weakness, as my tears were of happiness the second time. But the truth is that I cry a lot. I cry all the time. Sometimes from sadness, but mostly from anger. The tears are a good tool to let my anger out when no other means to escape it are available.

Staring dejectedly through the window, I see Geli's face everywhere; in the grey fluffy clouds covering the sky above, in the fretting leaves blowing in the warm summer wind, in my own reflection in the train's window. I can even hear her laugh hurtling toward me from the shadowed forests I pass. It is as if Mother Nature decided to deride me, to point out how ridiculous and weak I'm being.

*Coward by choice...*these words sound like mockery now. *Cautious, selective, and in charge of myself...*these literally make me blush. Hanussen's words deride me, too: *'Facies is also associated with the suppression of all male sexual pleasure and*

embodies everything that men fear in the feminine.' Bloody star!
Bloody cowardice! Bloody women!

But then, there's also this strange feeling accompanying me
on my escape, the warm presence that made me want to escape in
the first place. It stubbornly persists in burning my spirit and
wrestling with my fear.

I am afraid to name it again, lest I be forever haunted by it.

THE SWEET TYRANNY OF YOUTH

Munich greets me with the fuss and agitation of the preparations for the coming federal elections, taking place in a few months, in May 1928. The active, driven part of me helps me succeed in attaining many seemingly impossible victories, from holding speeches a few times a day, to winning over to my side great industrialist giants.

However, it takes less than two months for the other part of me, the weak despicable one, to resurface again, and to decide to make it impossible to keep me focused on the political work.

This tug of war between my mind and heart soon takes its toll and I become physically ill. My insufferable stomach cramps and headaches return and I take to my bed. I step out only when forced by the loyalty I feel for the people who want to hear me speak; and sometimes, very rarely, to dine at the Osteria Bavaria or the Café Heck, as the food the soon-to-be Frau Hess cooks for me is horrendous.

Under the constraint of my constant stomach pain, I have to cut down my speeches, lest I plummet behind the lectern. To be seen in such a weak state would prove disastrous for my career.

By the end of October, I realize that the situation can no longer be prolonged. Something must change.

"One day, you will both be handsomely rewarded for your

loyalty," I say to Goebbels and Hess, who take turns acting as my private nurses in my Munich apartment. "Just wait and see."

"Serving you, mein Führer, is a reward in itself," replies Hess, crossing his arms over his chest, as if to emphasize the sincerity of his words. "I need nothing else."

I smile. "I believe you, Rudi. Your gesture proves your honesty. Hanussen taught me the art of reading body language. It's impressive what it reveals."

"If I may say so, your guess is wrong, mein Führer," says Goebbels with a smirk.

"Really? How so?" I ask, merely for the fun of conversing, as I already know what he is about to say.

"Well, I had my share of body language training back in my years as a student. And what I know is that the crossed-arms-on-chest gesture does not prove honesty, but rather defensiveness and anxiety, which is either driven by a lack of trust in the other person or an internal discomfort and sense of vulnerability," he declares, grinning at Hess. "It is an all-around negative attitude."

I always wondered if clasping my hands over my crotch when in company, especially before I start my speeches, would send out the same message. Being perceived as insecure and nervous would be just as disastrous as plummeting behind the lectern. I had asked Hanussen about it once and found his answer most astonishing: "*Confidence is the product of that gesture, not the cause. You should keep using it.*"

"You are not entirely wrong, I give you that," I say, pausing a moment. I hate being thwarted; truly hate it from the bottom of my soul. I feel like cracking Goebbels' skull.

"Yet it's quite easy to misperceive body language," I resume, averting my flushed face. "It all depends on the context in which one uses certain gestures. In this case, Hess used it to show his determination in his words, to prove that there is no question about his honesty. You mistook confidence for defensiveness."

"Yes, but in the—"

"What about you, Goebbels?" I ask, cutting him short. I cannot allow him to win the argument. It would be bad for discipline. I stand up from my bed and begin pacing the living room.

He sighs and sits down on my sofa, squeezing his legs together in an unnatural pose, then resting his chin on his hand with his index finger daintily touching the corner of his mouth.

"What about me?"

"Do you expect a reward?" I ask, stopping mid-step to face him.

He clears his voice, then in a wounded tone blurts, "Umm, no! Of course not!" His eyes widen. "It is deeply rewarding to look after you, mein Führer!" he adds, and then rubs his nose vigorously.

"Ha! You are lying! There! That gave you away!" I exclaim, pointing at his face.

"What do you mean it gave me away? What did? I am not lying!" he shouts.

"Yes, you are. The rubbing of your nose gave you away," I say jovially, thinking how entertaining this conversation had turned out.

"I am not lying!" he keeps repeating, as if to convince himself of it.

"Yes, yes. When you lie, your nose swells with the increased blood pressure. All that blood raised in your nose gives you a tingling sensation and you want to scratch that itch. And that's what you did! You lied, the blood flooded your nose, and you had to scratch it!" I burst into a hearty laughter that makes me bend forward and clasp my stomach. "You should see your face, Goebbels! You look as if your belt popped open and your pants fell on the floor!"

He cannot bring himself to loosen up and give us a smile. He takes everything so seriously. On the other hand, my Hesserl, who's the most serious person on planet earth, who never smiles, not even a grimace resembling a smile, is now shaking with laughter.

"Well, I am glad I made your day...both of you..." Goebbels manages to whisper.

"Plus, there were other things that gave you away! The position of your legs was a sign that you were holding something back. And that index finger on your mouth came across as unnatural, as if you were telling yourself to be quiet. Not to mention clearing your throat and that fake cough that escaped you before answering."

"But I wasn't lying. Being here with you, having the chance to look after you, the person I happen to respect the most, is really gratifying."

"Now, now, don't worry, my dearest. You will be Germany's Joseph one day. I promised you that and you know I don't take promises lightly," I reassure him, patting his shoulder.

"I am sorry...if I upset you..."

"You didn't. You made me laugh. We all are in this for some gain, whether big or small, meaningful or not, personal or not."

He stares at the floor. "That is true."

"My gain is less personal than yours," I confide. "Whatever I do, I do for our ancestors, our Motherland and her descendants. But even so, even if indeed you are in merely for personal gain, I see nothing wrong in that."

"Thank you, mein Führer, I am most relieved."

I look intently at his face trying to see his eyes, but he keeps his look averted, yet another sign of keeping things back, of untruthfulness. I want to go on telling him about it but decide against it, as my soul burns with curiosity about another issue altogether.

"Tell me, Hess. Have you spoken with her? Did she agree?"

"Not only did she agree, she is on her way here, as we speak. Maurice went to fetch her."

My heart leaps in my chest and I make every effort humanly possible to restrain from suspicious body language that could give me away. I sit at the edge of the bed with my hands resting in my lap. That should make me appear confident and relaxed.

Yet the truth is, my stomach churns from nervousness. I smile a broad smile, trying further to hide my true self.

And there is yet another truth...

I can no longer bear being separated from Geli. I can't stand the thought of her being so far away from me. I abhor the days passing in so much boredom, for insufferable boredom and despondency fill me whenever she's not around. I despise the long nights in which her sweet face, her laugh, her beautiful singing haunts my thoughts and chases sleep away.

For all that, I resolved to bring her here. Two months away is more than enough self-castigation. I must have her close, must make her a permanent resident of Munich, the city that started it all.

On my express command, a furnished room has been rented for her in Königinstrasse, not far from the English Garden. She'll be able to move in as soon as she arrives. Which is any moment now, Hess said.

A shudder runs through my body and standing up, I begin pacing the room again. To Hell with body language!

"That's wonderful!" I reply, with a quick confirming look to Hess. "I must look after her and how am I to do that if she's not here? Plus, she must have a proper future. I simply cannot deny her all the opportunities Munich has to offer! Perhaps she might choose to become, say, a doctor, and the University here is one of the best in the world! And she might want to have some fun. What can Obersalzberg offer to a girl her age?" I blather on, yet feel that the more I explain myself, the faster my true motives flare up. Excuses always proceed from a guilty conscience, so the saying goes.

"Peace and quiet," says Goebbels, even though my question was merely a rhetorical one. "And freedom."

"Freedom?"

"Yes. Teenagers demand a lot of freedom. It's probably the hormones." He smirks. "I remember that age very well."

"Well, of course, but she is *my* niece and I am hated by many. There are dangers in the streets everywhere. So, yes, she'll have freedom, but she must be protected at the same time."

"Why not bringing her mother to act as chaperone?"

"No, no! My sister should look after Geli's younger sister, and Wachenfeld."

No sooner do I finish my sentence than the door bursts open. My heart sinks as I notice Maurice is alone. *She's changed her mind!* I must sit on the bed again as the feeling that I've just been stabbed in the stomach bends me over.

Maurice lets out a little strange laugh. I look at him and his expression startles me. It is as if he's read my thoughts, as if that simple gesture of sitting down gave me away and now he knows it all. He props his booted foot on the corner of my bed, with his elbow resting on his knee.

"She's all set up and cozy. I just dropped her in Koniginstrasse. Nothing to worry about."

"I wasn't worrying." My words come out too fast. I clear my throat and straighten my back. "A task given to you, dear Maurice, is never something to worry about. You never disappoint." The flattering approach works. Taking his scrutinizing eyes and mind off me and moving them onto himself, he adopts his trademark posture, chin and chest puffed out.

"Thank you, mein Führer. I take that."

Suddenly, my stomach feels as strong as that of a child who bursts with energy and health. I want my friends gone so I can pace the room or go out for a walk without worrying about body language or what my sudden recovery could reveal. In truth, this sudden recovery does reveal so many truths that even I begin to feel alarmed.

And the most alarming truth of all is the one telling me that being alone is no longer sufficient for my happiness and completeness.

My stomach churns with anxiety as I turn the key to unlock the door to Geli's flat. Because she will be under my supervision from now on and because I need to make sure she'll be safe and protected at all times, I demanded a spare key from the landlord upon signing the lease.

Strangely, as I explain myself to…myself…an uncomfortable question pops in my head: *Is this the real reason you demanded a spare key?*

I reach in my pants pocket.

"Ah! Thank God, I thought I left it home," I whisper, looking at the gold chain with a dainty gold swastika that I now dangle before my eyes. I suddenly think of it as of a talisman, meant to keep women's magic at bay.

"Uncle Alf! You startled me!" She jumps up from the sofa and flings herself at me, wrapping her arms around my neck. I resist the urge to pull back and clasp her waist in my hands. They feel tense and clumsy, and my next words prove that my judgment is in the same category.

"You've grown fatter since last I saw you!" I say and pinch the roll of flesh around her waist. She pulls back, her smile gone, leaving only a pair of listless eyes.

"Only a bit. Is it that obvious?"

"Well, I've noticed it and we were apart for only two short months." My words continue to tumble out, even though she's no longer hugging me. She retreats to the sofa and begins to solve cross-puzzles in a newspaper. I whip my hat off and hurl it on the floor.

What the Hell is wrong with her?

"Is that the way you treat your Uncle, who's walked here just to see you?"

"*You've grown fatter?* Are those the first words you use upon seeing someone after a very long time, someone who also happens to have been painfully missing you? And since you find it fit to scold me, I might as well do it in return."

"Meaning?"

"Well, I thought that knocking on the door before entering a bedroom was a sign of respect and good breeding," she says, brandishing the newspaper in the air above her head. The silly gesture ruffles her hair, and with her angry eyes and flushed cheeks, she looks...adorable. A sudden urge to grab her in my arms and squeeze her flesh to bits sets my senses on fire.

"Had I seen in *you* that sign of good breeding, I would have probably knocked! And this isn't a bedroom!"

"Isn't it? Then what would you call a room in which you see a bed?"

I clench my jaw till my teeth hurt. "Mind your words, Geli."

"I said nothing wrong. Really, what would you call it?" she demands, standing up from the couch and approaching me, while still brandishing the newspaper in the air and in my face.

I catch a glimpse of its name, *Münchener Post.*

I slam my fist on the table. "I won't have you reading this filth! It's poison! It'll defile your foolish head!" I grab the newspaper from her hand and rip it into pieces.

"But I like it. It's captivating, with all those stories of—"

"Listen carefully, Geli. You know nothing about the world you've just stepped into. It's corrupt and treacherous. I will not have my own niece reading enemy newspapers! Do you hear me? I forbid you! Or, so help me God, I'll—"

"You'll what?" she asks, coming closer. "Huh? You'll do what? Spank me, as if I were a little girl? Whip me with that ridiculous riding crop of yours?"

My eyes widen, my blood begins to boil. Drops of sweat form on my forehead and slide down my temples to my burning cheeks. This foolish girl has no idea what she's doing.

"Stop. I forbid you to talk in this way."

"*Forbid you! Forbid you!* Is this all you'll do to me? Forbid me things?"

She is so close to me that I smell her scent. It's the natural smell of baby skin.

"Why did you bring me here, Uncle Alf?"

I can feel her breath on my face as she talks. Her eyes are lively again, but it is not listlessness or mischief that I read in them anymore. It is something new, something I've never seen before, but nevertheless recognize it through some magical sense only our hearts understand. It is something that blends anticipation with eagerness and violence.

Lust. Yes. I believe it is lust.

The hand holding the gold swastika jerks up between us.

A talisman meant to keep women's magic at bay, I keep repeating to myself.

The lustful look deserts her eyes and it's replaced by child-like wonder.

"Is this for me?" Her voice is sweet and joyful, and my fear mellows.

"Yes, princess. A welcome gift. Look on the back of it!"

She brings the gold swastika closer to her eyes. "*G.R. 18. 09. 1927.* That's almost a month ago."

"Well, yes. I many times wanted to come to Wachenfeld, but couldn't," I lie. "Do you like it?"

She turns her back to me and exclaims, "Do I like it? I'm quickly becoming obsessed with it!" She lets out a loud, crystalline laugh and extends her hands to the back of her neck, holding the chain out with her fingers. "Can you fasten it for me?"

I do so with shaky hands, then rest my gaze on her bare skin. I want to grab her and press her against my body. I want to squeeze her inside my soul, so I could always have her with me.

She turns to face me, her lustful gaze alive again. Grabbing her hand before she makes further improper moves, I say, "Dress up, princess! We are going shopping. I'm rich now. There's nothing I can't afford."

"I have clothes. I make my own, have you forgotten already?" Her mood is not as expected, but rather bored and sarcastic.

"And how will you continue to make your own clothes if you don't have fabrics? Plus, you cannot make hats, stockings and perfumes, can you?" I say with a wide grin. The incentive words seem to do the trick and I watch her metamorphosis, like a chameleonic butterfly. I don't even know if that creature exists in real life, but surely it does here, right before my eyes.

As she retreats to the small den to dress up, a feeling of uneasiness envelops me, so constricting, so vicious and noxious. If I were to go for a wild guess, I would perhaps call it...jealousy? Or perhaps...possessiveness?

Selfish! I shout in my mind. *Is not enough that you're a coward, always hiding; now you are selfish as well? Of course, it is possessive jealousy. Why would you want to share her? The myriad of enticing qualities, the charm, her soft skin and round, firm breasts – why shouldn't they be displayed just for you? Selfish! Selfish!*

"I'm ready!" Geli says, bringing me back to reality. "Do you like my dress?"

"It's too short. You look like one of those harlots in Spittelberggasse. Put on something else, Geli. And let the hem down on this one, before anybody else sees you in it." My words roll out unrestrained, fueled by that wretched feeling now possessing me.

She frowns. "But all my girlfriends in Vienna wear similar—"

"Of course!" I snap and stand up to pace the room. "Because everyone in Vienna thinks it fit to copy the whores from that Sink of Inequity! And everyone there is also going crazy with dirty sex and debauchery and female liberation! Does that mean that my beloved niece has to copy them?"

"And what is wrong with female liberation, mind you?"

"Ha! Those enemy newspapers defiled your head, I gather! What is wrong with female liberation? I tell you what is wrong! It is against the nature of things! Against the biology of the human race! The best woman is inferior to the worst man! It was a Jew who said it! What more proof do you need to believe it, when even the lowest race on this earth agrees with this?"

"So, now you agree with an ape-man, as you like to call those people, just to reinforce your distorted opinion?"

"Only with that particular one. Because he hates being what he is. He is the only Jew fit to live."

"Wonderful! Then what are women supposed to do, what are they supposed to be, according to your favorite Jew, according to you?"

"Well, since they have no value in themselves, they can only acquire an instrumental value in terms of their ability to serve men."

She bursts into laughter. "I have my own opinion on this but I shall keep it to myself."

"You do well. Now, go change!"

As she turns around, I divert my eyes to her full bottom and go red in the face. I can still feel it in my hands.

"Fear..." she whispers as she trails off. "You are afraid of us... that's why you..." Her words become indiscernible, but I can still hear her laughter.

Twenty minutes and three outfit changes later, we are walking down on Königinstrasse. With her hand on my arm, Geli looks proud. People look at us as we pass them by, on the one hand because they recognize me, on the other because the beauty at my side stuns them. Of them all, I am the most stunned, the most proud. And the feeling crossing me now is what I would describe, if ever constrained to, as happiness.

13

LIKE FATHER LIKE SON

In November 1927, I finally decide to begin my campaigning tour throughout Germany. Personal matters have long postponed it and I berate myself for this weakness. A man of genius must not have a personal life, for it is only a hindrance that slows him down. The luxury of a personal life should be granted only to mediocre men.

I convince Geli to register as a medical student at the University of Munich. This way she'll be kept busy while I'm away and preoccupied with other readings than the enemy newspapers. And since she must be protected at all times from my enemies, I put Maurice in charge of her safety. He likes her well enough to defend her, with his life, if need be.

However, to my dismay, she breaks off her studies almost as soon as she starts them. She wasn't to be a doctor, she claims, and all she wants is to sing and fall in love.

How can someone live solely for these idiotic pursuits? Indeed, how someone can live knowing they have so little to aspire to will always be an annoying mystery to me.

On the 9th, I hold my annual speech commemorating the November putsch in the Munich's Bürgerbräu Beer Hall, then set off to Chemnitz, Bochum, Ulm, Braunschweig, Weimar, Essen, Hamburg and Augsburg.

The two-month tour proves exhausting yet rewarding. Even so, I know that the movement is not yet strong enough to assert itself against the Communists in the May elections. Precious time was wasted with my incarceration, time I could have used toward furthering the goals of the movement.

My instinct and logic prove correct once more. The results of the Reichstag election on 20 May 1928 are appalling. We win only twelve seats, which is far worse than the results in 1924. Sooner will the camel pass through a needle's eye than a great man be discovered by an election. I remember laughing at Röhm and Ludendorff, and the mere thought that they might be laughing at me now is enough to bring on one of my gloomy moods.

There is a certain humiliating aspect in losing, and I can only tame myself by thinking of Providence and her plan. If I must have faith in something, then I will have it in the Goddess of Destiny. If not now, then soon. Of this, I am sure.

Yet something must be done.

Studying the reports from Thuringia, Pomerania, and Mecklenburg, which all indicate increasing unrest in rural areas, I resolve to move our propagandistic focus from the urban proletariat to the rural one. The elections were plainly obvious about our position and if not changed soon, we might as well blow our brains out right this instant than watch our prospects worsen.

Besides touring the country and speaking in public, I also decide to get more involved in the propaganda machine. Thus, I take over the position of Party Propaganda Leader and make Heinrich Himmler my deputy. With his organizational skills and quiet efficiency, I expect us to encounter no troubles at all.

It is on one of the days Himmler and I hover over a rural country map at my headquarters office that I get a most unusual visit.

"Mein Führer?" says Hess, popping his head though my office door.

"What is it, Rudi?"

"There is someone here to see you." I raise my eyes from the map to look at him.

"I don't care. Can't you see that I'm busy?"

"Yes. But I think you would like to meet them."

I straighten my back. "Them?"

He's already disappeared behind the door, only to push it wide open seconds later to allow *them* to enter.

A very tall young man, with bright blue eyes and dark hair rushes to shake my hand. The woman accompanying him, trails behind.

"Thank you for having us, Herr Hitler. It's truly an honor to finally meet you!" the lad exclaims while vigorously shaking my hand. I say nothing, just look at him blankly, expecting further clarifications for this unwanted interruption.

"This is my mother, Bridget Dowling." The woman bows her head slightly but remains silent.

"Please, forgive her," the lad continues, "she speaks very few German words."

I sigh deeply trying to mask my exasperation. "How can I help you, Herr...?"

"Hitler. William Patrick Hitler."

I poke him with a glare. "What sort of nonsense is this?" I snap. "Hess!"

"I'm your nephew. Alois's son."

"Alois?"

"Yes. Your half-brother."

"I know who Alois is!"

I drop my shoulders as I struggle to make sense of it all. I look at him and I look at his mother, who smiles a friendly smile. I motion for them to sit and order Himmler out of the office.

"Your visit astonishes me, I must say. Finding out that I have a nephew, from a brother I haven't heard in decades..." I say as I drop into my leather armchair.

"Well, that is mainly the same reason for our visit, Uncle," the lad says in broken German, rubbing his large hands together.

Hearing him call me *Uncle* is unsettling and doing so in heavily accented German triggers my temper. I...I feel ashamed. I look at the woman again and my expression must betray my thoughts, for she erases the stupid grin from her face.

"Meaning?" I demand, shifting my gaze to the lad again.

"My father disappeared. We are afraid he is dead. We came here to ask you to use your connections to find him." The woman begins to sob and to mutter words in her language.

"Please, find my dearest Alois and bring him back to me, I beg of you!" the lad translates. The woman's tears soften my embarrassment and I nod, trying to reassure her of my willingness to help.

"Tell me about my brother. The last time I saw him I was barely seven years old. He left me alone with that beast! He was a coward for sneaking off like that. He should have stayed and fought! Like I did!" I yell and hit the desk with my fist.

"Beast?"

"Yes, beast! Monster, beast, devil, call him as you will!"

The lad looks flushed, and that brings me round.

"No matter," I say, "go on, tell me! From what I gather, he's been quite a busy man!"

"Well, he met my mother in 1910 at a horse show in Dublin, her native city. It was love at first sight. He told her he was a wealthy hotelier and travelled all around Europe to study the industry."

I burst into laughter. "He never was that! I'm sure of it!"

"You're quite right. My grandfather, William, discovered that his soon-to-be son-in-law was no more than a mere waiter in the Shelbourne Hotel, and that he got that position through an employment agency in London."

I am still laughing when the woman begins to mutter again.

"Everything he said was so new and interesting that even his broken English seemed charming," the lad translates.

To empty-headed women like you, everything seems charming, I muse.

"So, what they did...they eloped to London, got married a few weeks later, and settled in Liverpool. Grandfather accused him of kidnap and tried to have him arrested. But then I was born and that put an end to their dispute."

"Nothing quite like a chubby baby to put aside differences. And now? You said he's disappeared."

"Yes. He smoothed his bed one morning and never returned. Mother couldn't bring herself to ever sleep there since his disappearance."

"He packed a small rucksack, smoothed his bed, and was gone," I whisper, possessed by harrowing memories.

"I beg your pardon?" the lad demands in his smug English.

"Well, I tell you one thing. The man isn't dead. It is one thing to be dead and quite another to be a coward."

They remain quiet, their eyes beaming with hope, mingled with confusion.

I resist their plea to accommodate them until we get word of my brother's whereabouts and urge them to return to England. Their mere presence is enough to embarrass me in front of my inferiors and friends alike. Having a relative with half his blood being foreign is deeply humiliating.

It doesn't take Himmler a complete week to track down Alois. He discovers my brother not in the cemetery under a stone plaque, of course, but in the warm clutches of a woman, his new wife. He deserted his Irish family, faked his own death, and returned to Germany to enter into a bigamous marriage, all the while supporting himself and his new harlot from the merger profit earned from selling razors. No matter how far he ran away from our loathsome old man, the imprint of the latter's disgusting character couldn't be avoided. Yet, while Father hadn't had any remorse in bringing Mother to serve to his second wife, at least this one had the decency to keep his disgusting cravings a secret.

Shame – shame – shame. Embarrassment and humiliation is all my family brings to me.

Yet there is one...only one that can always erase the deeply ingrained blemish of discomfiture and disgrace with which my family has forever cursed me.

14

FALLEN ANGEL

The time spent away from Geli doesn't bring what I was hoping it would bring. The fifty-six speeches I held throughout Germany and the overall preparation for the elections kept me busy, as well as it should have, for the second half of 1927 and until the end of spring 1928.

I was certain that the imposed space between Geli and I would make me forget all those ridiculous feelings gripping my heart.

I was wrong.

Not only did they not disappear but they have increased even more. Now, with the elections over and that heavy burden released at last, I want nothing more than to spend time with that sweet little darling.

Why is it that defeat always makes us look for the company of loved ones?

Looking at Geli now, I realize a similar harrowing fight has been within her, too. Her gaze stands as witness, burning even brighter with those terrifying thoughts nesting behind it. Her attitude stands as witness, too. For while I try to avoid her as much as my heart allows me, she sees fit to toy with my reluctance, to provoke and tantalize me.

When we are picnicking on the Chiemsee she throws off her

sandals, then snatches up the hem of her skirt and begins singing and dancing. And not for a single moment does she take her eyes off me.

She sunbathes naked alongside Henny, then runs to tell me breathlessly of how a cluster of butterflies settled on her naked flesh, tickling her and making her shiver with joy.

When I take her shopping for clothes and perfumes she ostentatiously buys a white fox fur coat, even though she knows how deeply I despise them for their smell and how I loathe the Jewish furriers whose greed will surely exterminate the most beautiful animal breeds.

And yesterday, as we were dinning at the Osteria Bavaria for her birthday, she kept complaining about the looks of the star in the western we'd just seen.

"With those looks," she says, in the most affected voice, "God knows what else he had to perform to get that part! Promise me, Uncle! Promise me that when you're powerful enough, you'll let me choose which movies are to be shown at the cinema! Promise me! For there is nothing quite as bad as having your fun of watching a movie spoiled by un ugly actor!"

Our companions laugh, but I know there is more to her statement than a simple remark made to entertain her company.

Just when I feel confident that I know this creature of many moods and mysteries, she proceeds to elude me again.

Strangely, this is the exact same thing I've heard my men gossiping about me.

"Tell me, then," I reply, "what sort of looks would please you most in a man?"

"Ah, I don't know..." she almost whispers, looking dreamingly into a faraway distance. I pull a pen from my coat pocket and begin sketching a male profile on a paper napkin.

"Would a man like this appeal to you?" She shakes her head. I draw another one, this time adding all the Aryan qualities: large, long head, high forehead, full lips, narrow high-bridged nose, strong jawline. Still she shakes her head. I draw yet another portrait, with a beard. She doesn't even look at it.

"How would you like a man to look, then, princess?" I ask again, brimming with hope. I can no longer command my facial muscles and smile ear to ear.

"Well, that's what's wonderful!" she exclaims. "You never know what he'll look like, the man you're going to love." My smile is gone. Hers just turned wicked.

I pull back in my chair and bury my face in the large mug of Apollinaris mineral water. My stomach churns with anxiety and I struggle to identify the cause of it. After a few moments, it hits me. I have lost control. The most dreaded feeling of them all, love, did not come alone, but accompanied by its' dreadful sisters: anguish, softness, losing control.

My companions continue the talk, their voices like bouncing echoes hitting my eardrums.

"But do you really want to be a singer," Henny asks, "and have to stand on the stage and be able to sing every note by heart – and then make out you're dying or something – and then, when the curtain falls, get up again and bow when the people clap?"

"Oh, yes! It's wonderful that you can have so many lives. You can be Salome and ask for the head of John the Baptist on a silver platter, just because you want to kiss John the Baptist's lips," Geli replies, stabbing me with sweet-poison arrow glances. "Or you can be a Valkyrie on the flaming rocks, or Isolde, dying of love..."

I jump to my feet, grabbing her by the arm, and drag her to and along the street.

As we enter her apartment I push her against the wall.

"What are you doing?" I scream, my fingers digging deep into the soft flesh of her arms. She says nothing, just smiles a twisted, satisfied smile.

"What are you doing to me?" I yell again, slamming her against the wall with every word.

"It is about time," she says, her words distorted. "Kiss me now!"

I will never be able to forget her expression. It was the kind you get to see only once in your lifetime. The kind rendering you powerless and confused, as if you could suddenly glimpse into the magical world beyond, that chimerical world forever eluding you, forever one step out of your reach.

"Kiss me..."

Our mouths come together and I greedy bite her perfect lips. The feeling taking over my body is just...I have never...

Ah! This isn't me! This isn't me! I scream inaudibly.

I pull back, releasing myself from Geli's grasp, but she flies at me, winding her plump, soft arms close around my neck, while pressing her voluptuous body against mine. I feel dizzy, possessed by a foreign entity that conspires with Geli to break me. Her kisses are persuasive and hard, promising the rest of her.

My heart swells, my head hurts in an exquisite, delightful way.

I let her remove my shirt in a rough manner, then watch her almost ripping her dress off. She takes my hands in hers and leads them across her shivering body. The feel of her naked flesh, the fullness of her breasts filling my hands, the smell of her hair...they all make sense. All my dreams and longing, my torment and secrets...for a fleeting moment, they make sense. But only this is permitted to me...a fleeting moment.

Disgusting old man, with foul breath! You are a degenerate! You are poisonous, infectious and defected! This softness is making a fool out of you!

The ever-present voice of my consciousness screams louder and louder, ordering me to end this at once.

Trading your mission for a kiss! Wasting your whole heart on those incestuous, perfect lips!

I break down into tears and slowly slide down her body and onto the floor.

"I can't! You are my niece!" I howl, hitting the floor with my fist. She squats and begins to caress my hair.

"Then, marry me! And I shall no longer be your niece, but your wife!"

The mere alluding to marriage is enough to erase my shame and guilt, replacing them with horror. I jump to my feet and begin to pace the room.

"Marry you? What an absurd idea! How would it have entered that silly head of yours?"

"I should like so much to become your wife..."

"Never!"

"But why?" She clumsily gathers her dress around her body. Her round, youthful face is flushed, her eyes moist, her expression embarrassed. It saddens me and I turn away.

"Why? Why? Because I can't! I am not the man to make you happy! I would only bring you misery and despair!"

"Why, Uncle, why??" Her question reverberates in my head, until the fury produced by it can no longer be contained. I rush at her, grabbing her by the shoulders and violently shake her body again.

"Because I will never be able to give you children!"

Her lips open to shout out that maddening question again, but I can't bring myself to hear it, and push her against the wall.

"Because I am infected!"

"Infected?" Her eyes blaze now, like glowing coals. Their heat burns me so badly that I need to turn away again.

"Yes! Infected! The bloody Jewish scourge! I will never be able to produce sane offspring! Only retarded, feeble and sickly ones, who in turn will carry poison in their veins and pass it on to their children! For ten bloody, cursed generations!"

"I don't understand..."

"Nor should you!"

The confusion and sadness in her eyes breaks my heart into pieces. I approach her and kiss her forehead. The smell of her... the very taste of her skin...I break down in tears again and curse my life, curse my blood, and curse Father for denying me the little happiness I could have had, the only earthly heaven that would have received me. The only sort of peace I would have ever enjoyed.

That's what you always do! Blaming somebody else for your unhappiness! Never strong enough to own your own fate! the voice in my head rings again.

As does Doctor K's: "*In your search for glory, meaning in the process of implementing your idealized self into the world, you neglected your personal life, the things that make life worth living – love, family life, creative pursuits – because all these would have made you see yourself as a mortal being, just like anyone else, thus in great danger of losing everything. You tell yourself, you actually demand of yourself that you should be above pleasures, you should always control your feelings, you should be able to live without close personal relationships. And what you did is...you put your feelings under a dictatorial regime. Yet when you realized you could not possibly measure up to these inner dictates, you started to hate and despise yourself greater still, for you perceived yourself as weak."*

"Ah!!!" I scream, pounding Geli against the wall again, "I hate you! I hate you! I hate you!" Then I furiously stumble toward the door. Behind me, distorted by tears, I hear Geli's shattered voice.

"Only the unloved and the unappreciated hate."

With her words echoing in my head, I slam the door behind me and make my way into the cold, dark, unforgiving night.

A fortnight after her birthday, Geli goes to Linz to renew her passport. I order Maurice to accompany her and to act as her chaperone while there. Not for a single moment is he to lose sight of her. I also order him to keep a journal of her whereabouts and report everything to me as soon as they return to Munich.

I give myself over to my public speeches, lest the pleasant memories of Geli's smell, perfect naked body, full breasts and lips...her very desire for me, will finally manage to break me. The clamor of beer mugs and stomping feet, the shouts of 'Heil Hitler' and the deafening noise produced by my followers' applause, resound loudly enough to quiet my other thoughts.

But then the night comes, over and over again, always finding me alone and defenseless in the face of my greatest enemy: my loving thoughts. The silence and darkness in my apartment serve to increase them further and I sometimes bury my head under my pillow in a pathetic attempt to muffle them. But they aren't coming from a dark place outside of me, they are screaming to get out from inside of me.

Ah!!! Infected again!!

So help me God, I do not know which is worse, the bloody Jewish poison spreading nonchalantly throughout my body or the cursed warm feelings of affection...of love...spreading viciously and demandingly through my mind and heart and soul. I am being cursed with the afflictions I feared the most: syphilis and love.

Syphilis and love! Syphilis and love! Damn you Jews, the rodent of nations! Damn you Geli, the poisoner of my heart! Damn you all for conspiring to the fall of your savior!!!

My internal shouting goes long into the night, until my all-too-ready delirious state grips me in its claws and forcefully throws me to the floor, shrieking and mumbling unintelligible nonsense.

After many nights of fighting and resisting, after many hours of cursing and fumigating and lashing my thighs and walls, I realize I can no longer live without Geli.

Against my will and reluctance, against my doctor's words, and against all the odds that brought me to this realization, I resolve to own it. This resolve hurts me and tramples on every struggle I had to endure throughout my entire life. I remember the better stronger me, the days I had the strength to cut the evil from the roots.

My thoughts return to that sweet little darling that lit up my life, not so long ago. Maria, sweet Mimi. I gave her away in the blink of an eye. But Geli? I cannot go on living without Geli. I do not want to go on living without Geli.

I don't want to!

Yes. That's better. I shall marry her. I shall marry her and keep it secret.

Pathetic vulnerable man! I shake my head to cast the thought away.

I must see her! I must tell her! Ah! The happiness in her eyes! The bubbly chatter and the songs she'll sing! The fuss she'll make over what dress she'll wear and what perfume and shoes!

I remember the letter she's written from Linz. Only one letter.

I dash to my small desk, pull it out, and commence re-reading it.

> *Dear Uncle Alf,*
>
> *We are so happy here! I visited my childhood friends and what a proverbial fun we had! We remembered how we sang together as children and we sang last night, all night, as if to the memory of our carefree life, long passed. Emil said he's never had so much fun since his own youth. We're both sending you greetings from Linz, the city I know for a fact you love so dearly.*
>
> *Your niece, Geli*

I approach the window to stare at a glowing morning sun. My thoughts fly to Stefanie. How I hated her for dancing! *I will not make the same mistake...* Stepping from the window, I jump into my blue suit.

Geli's landlord receives me well and promises he won't hold grudges for my decision to remove the lease on her apartment. I then proceed to rent a furnished room for her in my Thierschstrasse neighbor's house, right around the corner from my own apartment. The Vogls are long-standing friends of mine. Adolf Vogl is not only a member of the Party but also a singing teacher. This will be my gift to Geli upon her return. I will allow her to take singing lessons. I am so excited at my actions that I cannot stand still.

Again, I give myself over to my public speaking, to the meetings with my Gauleiters, to my never-ending search for new investors. I visit Frau Bruckmann, wife of the publisher, Hugo Bruckmann, and born as Princess Cantacuzène of Romania. She's always supported the Party financially. Only this once do I leave her house with jewelry worth over forty thousand Reichmarks.

Finally, on the evening of August 5th, more than one month after her departure, Geli arrives home. To her new home. I'm bursting with excitement and hit my boot with my whip to release the blasted nervousness, while pacing this newly-furnished lodging far and wide. As she climbs the stairs to her room I hear laughter and giggles and realize she's not alone. Maurice accompanies her, I recognize his guttural voice all too readily.

As they open the door, the laughter ceases. Her lively, playful expression turns as cold as death.

"Uncle Alf! I wasn't expecting to find you here. An SA man delivered us to this new address as we stepped from the train. Emil and I—"

"How dare you come up here?" I sneer, glaring at Maurice.

"Mein Führer, I—"

"I invited him," Geli says. Then, hurling the luggage she is holding onto the bed, she approaches me. She removes my whip and clasps my hands in hers. Over her shoulder, I continue to glare at a frightened Maurice.

"We are in love," she continues, squeezing my fingers.

The words sound like the noise made by the church bells on Sunday mornings. Deafeningly loud. Only gradually does the noise in my head cease and I am able to grasp them.

"Uncle Dolf? Did you hear me? We are in love and we are going to get married. Emil asked me to be his wife, and I gladly accepted. We are to—"

I push Geli aside and reach for my whip.

"Bloody traitor!" I roar, darting at Maurice. I lift my whip and begin to lash him with all the force I can muster. "How dare you going behind my back like this? Ungrateful mongrel! Get out!"

Geli screams and jumps at me to stop me. But no force on earth could stop me now. I lash a hunkering Maurice furiously until, forced by the unbearable pain and terrified by the sight of his own blood, he begins screaming as well. This display of womanish reaction to pain enrages and disgusts me. I reach for the gun I always keep on my person and swiftly pull it out of its holster. Maurice is already at the window. The noise made on loading the pistol convinces him to jump.

"Filthy rat! Coward! Traitor! Run, you bloody hussy!" I shout at the top of my lungs. Placing the firearm back in its holster, I swish the whip in the air. "Look at him! Running like a scared mouse! Do you still like him now?" I roar, as I turn around to face a shaking, weeping Geli, who is cowering at the head of the bed.

"One moment! One bloody moment do I take my eyes off you, and what happens? You want to run away with the first idiot singing in your ear!" I continue to roar, hitting the bed mattress with the whip. "Bloody Hell! You are underage! Am I to be your guardian? Am I to remove myself from important matters to guard you? I will tell everything to your mother! Just wait and see! You are an imbecile! Foolish enough to make me want to lock you away!"

"It's your fault," she dares say, cupping her nostrils and running her gloved hand upward to wipe her running nose.

"My fault? Am I to be held responsible for your stupidity? My only fault was in bringing you here in the first place!"

"You encouraged Emil, over and over again, to find a wife. *'Why don't you marry, Maurice? You would do your Fatherland a service!'*" she mocks, "*'When are you getting married, Maurice? A married man is less prone to fool around and pollute himself with race-defiling ape-women.'*" Twisting her face and thickening her voice to impersonate me, she continues to mock. "*'I promise I shall come to you for supper every evening when you're married!'*"

"Enough!" I yell and lash the mattress again. "Not with you! From all of those thronging whores, he had to pause on you! Going behind my back and betraying me like this! Ah! The swine! And you...you!" I point my whip at her face. "Did you sleep with him?"

"And what if I did?"

I fly at her, and grabbing her chin with my hand, I squeeze it hard between my fingers.

"You are to answer me at once! Did you sleep with him?"

"Yes!" She jerks her head, releasing her chin from my grasp.

I hear the church bells tolling again, the noise ready to burst my eardrums.

"No...no..." I lament and let myself slide down the side of the bed. Throwing the whip away, I clasp my face between my palms and begin to sob. "No...Geli, what have you done? You were pure and unspoiled and now...now you are just like one of..." I shake my head as if to cast away the images of that swine touching her flesh and her breasts, kissing those lips that were only mine not long ago.

"Just like one what? One of Emil's whores?"

I drop my hands to look at her smug proud face.

"No, Geli. Not a whore. A fallen angel. A mortal."

For a moment I forget who I am, forget my dreams and hopes, my sorrow and pride, and let her stare me in the eyes, as floods of tears invade them, stream from them. It is as if my entire life's sorrow, my past suffering and present tormenting have all morphed into the salty water rushing from me. She reaches to touch me, to caress my head.

"I am sorry, Uncle Alf. It pains me so deeply to see how much I've hurt you. You must forgive me..."

"You must not see him again! At least not without me being present. Please, Geli!" My hand reaches to grab hers. It's as cold as a winter blizzard. As Mother's lifeless body.

"But I can't, Uncle! I love him! Please!"

"Two years. Two short years. Then you'll come of age and be free to do as you please. But for now, I must look after you. Only me. Give me two years! It is all I am asking from you."

"No! Please!"

"You must!"

"Why? Just because you don't want me, then no one else can have me? It was your fault! I loved you! So much that I wanted to give myself to you, in mind and heart, in body, in marriage!" She raises her voice now and wrenches her hand free. "You turned me down! You abandoned me! You showed yourself to me the same way you present yourself to your men: cold, detached, arrogant, superior. I had nothing from you but scorn and rejection!"

"I want you, Geli. I just can't have you."

"Sure! Because of some mysterious affliction? I've never seen you be sick! Because you think your children will be retarded? I've never asked for children! I am young. I only wanted to enjoy myself and have fun, not to clean babies' bottoms! And I wanted to do it at your side. There is no logic in any of the pathetic reasons for your rejection!"

"My logic is the only logic. Those who don't see it are idiots."

Her gaze reveals nothing but disgust.

"Forgive me," I plead. "I meant well. I rented this place for you to surprise you. I want you to sing. The landlord is a singing teacher."

Her mouth opens in awe. "Really?"

"Really. And when you think that I wanted to ask you to—"

"Ask me what, Uncle Alfie?" she demands breathlessly, jumping off the bed to kneel beside me. She cups my face with both her hands. "Ask me what?"

I can no longer answer her question, as the feel of her gloved fingers gliding over my face gives rise to that damnable forbidden lustfulness in me.

I imagine her rising from the floor and striking me with her booted foot.

She reaches forward and presses her mouth on mine, then parts my lips with her tongue, all the while gliding those gloved hands on the bare skin of my face, neck and chest. Tears burst forth once again.

"I don't deserve you! I am a despicable human being! There is no way you could love me!" I wail, striking my forehead with my palm. "No one does! They love an image! No one will ever love that vulnerable man shrieking on the floor!"

"What man on the floor? What are you saying? You speak nonsense. I love you!" Her hands are already pulling at her coat this way and that to release her burning body.

"No. Keep your clothes on," I demand and with a swift movement, I throw myself face up on the floor.

"But—"

"I don't deserve you! I am a rat! Hit me! Here! Hit me!" I demand pointing at my calves.

"No!"

"Hit me I say!"

She kicks me with her booted foot. The blow is soft, yet powerful enough to transport me in that land of forgetfulness. I no longer look at Geli's face, lest her scorn, tears or frightened look will make this bliss go away.

"Harder!"

"But I don't want to—"

"Harder!!"

She kicks harder this time sending shivers of pleasure throughout my entire body.

"Grab that whip!" I order hoarsely and she obeys.

"Lash me! Lash me!" I scream at her and she obeys again. The louder I yell at her the harder she whips me, and the harder she whips me the more enraptured I become. The blows reward me with an electrifying pleasure, it is as if my whole skin is aflame, burning the evil inside me.

"Climb on me!" I order again. "I want you to tread upon me! Here!" I point to my chest, patting it with quick movements. She bends down to unlace her boots.

"No! Keep them on!" She climbs on my chest struggling to keep her balance. As she treads on me I snatch the whip from her hand and hit my own legs. "Press harder! And spin! Don't stop!" I urge her to spin faster until the heels of her boots tear at my shirt and the bare skin of my chest.

"Now step on my face! Say you'll kill me!"

"No!" she screams, tears bursting out of her eyes. Her crying runs through my blood, but I cannot stop.

"Say it!"

"No, Uncle! Stop!"

"Bloody hell, say it!!"

"I'll kill you."

"Damn it! Say it as if you mean it!"

"Despicable monster!" she screams, squatting and slapping my face. I see the small gold swastika she wears around her neck furiously dancing from Geli's movement. "Filthy rat! I'll kill you, you undeserving, wicked, vicious monster! Do you hear me? I'll kill you! I'll kill you! I will kill you!"

Sweat bursts from my every pore. Her angered voice, the force of her blows, the saliva dropping from her mouth onto my face made me explode in a million of ecstatic pieces. She is still slapping my face long after the mountain of erotic emotion is swept away, leaving behind the overwhelming guilt to shred me to pieces.

The abrupt return to reality is more than I can bare. Disheveled, with my shirt shredded and drenched in my shameful sweat, I grab Geli's hands and cover my face with her palms. She pulls from my grasp and stands up. Her panting, her burning cheeks, her reproachful gaze rip through me. I crawl to seize her ankles.

"I am a worm!" I sob, wetting her boots with my tears. "A filthy worm!"

I bang my fists and forehead against the floor. Geli remains unmoved, only the sound of my words echoing. Her silence makes me suddenly lucid, as if I had quit my body and now I am watching myself from a corner. The impact of the image shocks me and jumping to my feet, I reach for the door.

"Uncle Alf?" Geli's shattered voice reaches me like thunder foretelling everlasting damnation. I halt, gripping the door knob, unable to turn and face her.

"Uncle Alf?" she demands again. "Will you marry me now?"

Everlasting damnation.

These are the only words ringing in my head as I disappear behind the door, leaving the fallen angel behind, to fight in silence with her own God.

As I reach my dark, cold, shabby apartment, the harrowing wretchedness is about to swallow me entirely. I stagger to my tiny creaking table and sit, burying my face in my shaky palms.

Why? Why? What is happening to me? Surely, the cursed Jewishness in me makes me have evil desires! I shake my head violently, as if to cast to hell the evil nesting in my brain. *I must confess my evilness to her! Confess the source of it. I must make amends and hope to Providence she will forgive me!*

I reach for pen and paper and begin scribbling apologetic sentences, as confused as my own knowledge of myself. I dig deep into my mind for answers, but the more I struggle to unearth them, the further they descend. Instead, fragments of thoughts from our earlier encounter struggle to make me acknowledge them. Her fingers in dark velvet, gliding over my skin, her boots stomping on my chest, shredding my skin, her legs and soft thighs, her strained features and confused tears. Before I know it, I am enraptured again, captured in the greedy claws of my baffling passion.

My hand begins to move the pencil in language so strange, yet so familiar.

My beloved Geli,

The clock hasn't yet struck one full hour since I last saw your flushed face, and I still sense your divine smell with all my undeserving senses. If I were to tell you that I crave for your forgiveness I wouldn't be lying, and yet I would. Isn't it a curse to feel unbearably guilty over the one conduct that finally brings some closeness, happiness and oblivion? For it is only with you, little sunshine, that I felt what I often heard others raving about. I can still taste the sweet flavor of your forbidden lips, still see your quivering hand gripping the whip and lashing my bare chest, still feel your weight pressing down on my body with your pointed heels. My dearest one! The thoughts that were speeding through my mind would make even the most degraded harlot blush. I am a man of many moods, an experienced man of many secrets; yet nothing has baffled me to such an extent as the excitement that rises in me under your vicious blows and threatening words; you were so credible, my darling, and it is my desire, more so, my fantasy, to perhaps use a dagger the next time? Ah! Will there ever be a next time? Could I ever hope to be your humble slave again? Could I, in any way, make you desire to do what you just did? For the mere thought of having spoiled your covetable innocence rips my soul apart. But what am I saying? You are not innocent anymore. And having you desire to treat me thus, will save me from this ghastly shame and guilt that feast on my poor wretched soul. Could I even begin to dream that you do not already hate me or see me as less than your mighty knight who came to save you? Did I save you from the ills of that poisonous city only to show you a side of humanity that is perhaps a thousand times worse? A side of humanity that only 'til recently has been unknown and unthinkable also to me. Will you allow me, my precious angel, to keep you only for myself? The mere thought of other men, lesser men, touching you, or even

as much as looking at you, makes me live moments, hours of
unutterable agony.

I can no longer continue. Re-reading what I just written seems as surreal as the deed itself. Slowly but steadily, the ghost of delirium tightens its grip on my throat again and I surrender, this time unwillingly, to oblivion.

15

DEATH PENALTY ON THE UNBORN

I am sick. Forever sick...of myself, of my poisoned blood and thoughts. I am sick of my twisted nightmares and painful memories, of wallowing on the floor of my bedroom, of being vulnerable and...womanish...libidinous. Once again, I must become myself, free of the burden of feelings. Once again, I must take up the struggle and remember who I am, who I've always been, before the Jews poisoned my blood and made me behave like one of their victims. A glowing star showing its brilliance to the world. A warrior, a Rienzi, born to redeem my people from suffering. A savior, born of a mortal woman. The son of the Goddess of History, who entrusted me with a holy mission.

Why am I still begging for answers from an invisible deity who never replies? Aren't the answers already given? Didn't my goddesses already show me all I ever needed to know? Of course, they did. Long ago, they pointed out the enemy. It was always them, always the Jews. The degenerate apes who, in their unrelenting desire to conquer the world, poisoned the mind and blood of the strong. Those who scattered themselves all over the earth to spread their obnoxious fake religion, so as to conquer and subdue poor, gullible, unsuspecting souls. To make slaves of men! Those who spread the vicious syphilis, poisoning not only the mind but also the blood of men. And so, their work became complete.

Again, I must take up my religious and patriotic struggle to conquer the germ, the fungus that tries to destroy me, destroy us. I must raise my sword and behead the Devil.

Focusing on political matters again feels like a blessing. It feels like returning to myself at last.

Flipping through the newspapers after such a long time also feels like a blessing. The tiny letters say that against all appearances and despite the misfortune of being locked away at Landsberg, *1924 was the year that made Adolf Hitler, the politician of tomorrow.*

I have said this countless times and strongly believe that Providence waved her magic wand to have me fail and be incarcerated for a greater good, not yet known to me at that time.

But when I look back now, I realize that year's ventures were nothing but child's play compared to the great events of 1929. The enemy newspapers say—because common inconsequential journalists always feel the itch to form opinions, even in the absence of the most critical details—that without the 1929 world-wide Depression, *'Adolf Hitler would have slowly disappeared from the political scene to lick his wounds on some solitary peak of the Obersalzberg.'*

But they are only half-right. It is, more than anything, my tactical instinct in regards to politics that will bring one of the greatest successes so far.

1929 is the year Providence chooses to snatch me away from the agonizing four-year-time of provincial idleness and propel me into the grand scene of national politics.

In February, on the ninth anniversary of the founding of NSDAP, I speak to my men in the Hofbraunhaus, urging them to never lose faith and hope, and trust in the Goddess of Destiny, for she has a greater plan. I have never lost hope during the four and a half years of idleness, and am as convinced of my destiny's success as is a child of his mother's love.

By the end of the year, my name is on everyone's lips.

During these four and a half years—the time in which our economy seemed to have stabilized—I've been waiting, scrutinizing, watching, like a wild beast in the shadows, all too ready for the perfect prey. And finally, the target arrived.

It came in the shape of a debate over the reparation the Motherland was coerced into paying by the cursed Diktat of Versailles. It came in the shape of the Young Plan, which is the second re-negotiation of Germany's war debts, extending such obligation and shame by stipulating sixty years of continuous payments, through to 1988. Sixty years! If this isn't a death penalty on the unborn, then nothing is.

Ah! The shame! The humiliation! The stab in our nation's dignity!

I once more remember my Vienna years, how I agonized over the resignation of the people. Compliance! The mere sitting down to re-negotiate the conditions of that bloody diktat sends out only weakness, only compliance. We are not a complying people! We were born to fight, not to idly accept others' terms! He who does not fight with deadly weapon and does not possess the strength to plunge it with one thrust into the heart of the opponent will never be able to lead a people in the mighty battle of destiny! Compliance! If men want to live, then they are forced to kill others, not to comply!

I always said that the entire struggle for survival is a conquest of the means of existence, which in turn results in the elimination of others from these same sources of subsistence; not compliance, nor reconciliation! There cannot be reconciliation for us! There is only one way: the salvation of our people through the annihilation of our opponents!

I have no reason to wish, even in the slightest degree, that a so-called "world peace" should be preserved. One is either the hammer or the anvil. There is no middle way.

So, my course of action is something that nobody, myself included, thought possible.

After much torturous deliberation, I join the campaign against the Young Plan, led by Alfred Hugenberg—former director of the Krupp Company—the might of Germany's steel industry—who built up a press empire and controls UFA, Germany's motion picture company—a stocky little capitalist pig who succeeds in uniting a national committee, consisting of the radical Rightists to the communists on the extreme Left.

Those who know me, also know my internal agony at having to join such a loathsome throng. But, they are rich and influential, and their good reputation among the Germans will serve me well.

Alas! There comes a time when you must put aside your principles for a greater good. Having a conscience works against one's own benefit anyhow, so having to get rid of it is not only an act of shrewdness but of commendable courage as well.

By the end of this extraordinarily favorable year, with the help of the stocky swine's press empire, I indeed become a notoriety. In the months following my acceptance to the campaign against the Young Plan, not one day, not one hour passes without me being displayed in every newspaper across even the most remote of hamlets of the Motherland.

It is true what they say: Whoever rules the Press, owns the masses.

It is no wonder that by the end of this equally favorable and doomed year, the SA equals the Weimar Republic's army in manpower. *I control an army the same size of my Motherland's army.* The thought is felt throughout my body like an electric shock. Gone is the mockery, gone is the Hitler who was merely a reminder of the period of inflation. In the face of this extremely great reversal, the arrogant, snobbish and stupid rejection of the party, which was the rule only a few years ago, has been transformed into expectant hope.

And then, of course, the Great Depression settles upon us like a vengeful goddess descending from her dark celestial gardens to bury the helpless, bewildered mortals under her inexorable curse of hunger, poverty and despair. It is with unbearable sorrow and disgust that my thoughts turn to the memory of the total collapse of the German mark in November 1923, when one needed over four trillion to buy one dollar! Yes, trillions, not millions!

It is with unshakable hatred that I remember the words of that Jewish harlot, Mrs. Rothschild: "*My sons can decide if there will be war or not.*" Right there and then I vowed that one day I would make them swallow their own words.

I also remember how, in 1916, while I was cold and soiled in the trenches of the Great War, the Jewish-American press began to pour their well-practiced venom on the hard-fighting Germans, portraying them as barbarous Huns and spreading their never-ending stream of anti-German hate propaganda.

I could never forget the bloody uprising in Munich at the end of the war, when upon leaving the hospital at Pasewalk, I found my country being run by the Jewish communists who were carrying out their onslaught by taking hostages, including women, to be murdered. Or the words of Toller, the leader of the Red Army that formed in Bavaria, that "most Germans should be gassed" and who received congratulations and promises of help from Lenin personally.

Will I ever be able to forget how, during the accelerating inflation of that time, most of the Jewish businessmen were able to amass fortunes in a country brought to its knees by defeat and incredible hunger? Or how the English seized every bit of private German property and how the Americans got away with stealing all German patents to sell them to the public for a dollar apiece?

I am not a man who forgets. I am not a man who forgives.

And then, there was that dreary winter day in February, 1919, when still racked with uncertainties and worries, still recovering from my blindness, I walked the streets of Munich for days and nights, able to neither sleep nor eat because I saw my country being ripped apart, ravaged, humiliated and scorned.

That day, as I crouched to warm myself over a manhole, I witnessed a scene that will forever be etched in my memory like a bloody-thirsty mite. A middle-aged Jewess, bedecked with jewelry, was lightly walking at the arm of her escort when she passed a veteran sitting on the sidewalk. The poor wretch, shivering in his old dirty uniform, lifted his trembling hand, which held a fountain pen he was trying to sell to her for a few coins, greatly needed for his basic necessities. When she looked at him, I saw the same disgust on her face that I was so well acquainted with from my Vienna years as a beggar. Her white, genuine fur coat brushed against the soldier's hand and she violently pulled away from him, as if he were the dreadful plague.

But he wasn't the plague, he just had no legs. His only disease was the probable, infectious enthusiasm with which he threw himself into battle, so the harlot who just passed him by in disgust could bathe in splendor.

My eyes well up even now, more than ten years later, but there is no more time for softness. Only for struggle. If the fictitious Jewish God rested on the seventh day of that illusionary tale of creation, remember that I, Adolf Hitler, declare that there will be no more days for resting. Only days for reckoning.

That said, will I take advantage of the Great Depression? Of course! Will I take advantage of people's misfortune and hunger, using it as fuel in my relentless struggle to depose the Jewish Republic? Of course! I am a fighter, just as our Christ the Savior was! Never in my life have I been so well disposed and inwardly contented as I am in these days! For hard reality has opened the eyes of millions of Germans to the unprecedented swindlers, lies and betrayals of the Marxist deceivers of the people.

And I am not only happy to use the Great Depression to my advantage, but am bound to do it! Bound and destined to save my people from these traitors! Bound and destined to rescue the holy land from this pestilence of moth-eaten eagles! Bound and destined to fight against the enslavement of the German people!

So, following my old method, I once more take up the struggle and say: *Attack! Attack! Always attack! If someone says I can't possibly have another try, remember that I can attack not just one more time, but ten times over.*

By the end of 1929, it becomes clear to me that our campaign against the Young Plan will fail. The Reichstag receives it with a smashing three hundred and eighteen votes against, while the plebiscite of December 22nd goes down with less than a quarter of the total votes needed.

This feels like a tough blow, especially after such a long period of political idleness. But it also gives me the opportunity to break with the defeated gang, the pigs responsible for the plebiscite's failure. No more associations with half-hearted, bourgeois weaklings. If I am to be responsible for any failure, it must be on account of my own actions and decisions, not those of quasi-revolutionaries and stoic, would-be politicians.

And yet for the first time in the life of my movement, I can say without false modesty and invaded with relief that, thanks to the exposure the Young Plan and Hugenberg's massive publications have given me, the party is catapulted to heights never before experienced.

Gone is our reliance on small factory owners for capital. The mighty industrialists had taken their turn in supplying our party with support we only dreamed of for so many years.

My association with Hugenberg had failed only in one respect. As for the rest?

Well, they brought to my feet the cream of the crop: Fritz Thyssen, head of the Vereinigte Stahlwerke trust, one of the richest and most powerful men in Germany, and Emil Kirdorf, director of the powerful Rhenish-Westphalian Coal Syndicate. Their money brings our first real success in the regional elections of 1929. Thus, I succeed in placing into office the first Nazi provincial government minister of Thuringia, Wilhelm Frick, a man after my own heart with views sculpted after my own mind. He soon introduces Nazi prayers into schools to prepare young minds for the struggle to come.

> "The purpose of history is to teach people that life is always dominated by struggle, that race and blood are central to everything that happened in the past, present and future, and that leadership determines the fate of peoples. Central themes in the new teaching, including courage in battle, sacrifice for a greater cause, boundless admiration for the Leader and hatred of Germany's enemies, the Jews."

These are his words! These are our words! These are the movement's watchwords!

The true struggle to depose the incompetent, corrupted and treacherous republic has begun. The time will come when those responsible for Germany's collapse will laugh out of the other side of their faces. Fear will grip them. Let them know that their judgement is on the way.

The free flow of the industrialists' money does not end with the regional elections. Thanks to the generosity of Fritz Thyssen, I can now think of relocating our headquarters. The humble old building on Schellingstrasse no longer matches our growing popularity and fame. Thus, I commission the party treasurer, Franz Xavier Schwarz, to purchase *Palais Barlow*, a large, resplendent, stone-structured building located in the heart of Munich. For if we are to be identified with power and strength, with Germany's true saviors, we must make a spectacle of that power. A grandiose Wagnerian spectacle! A most lordly, majestic one that my people have never seen elsewhere! Spectacle attracts fresh warrior minds and power attracts power.

The following weeks I give myself over to transforming the mansion to my own old-fashioned taste. No traces of modern art hang in my headquarters or is found in any other personal possessions.

Modern art is the reflection of the Jewish thwarting of what once was creative genius. When the Jew produces something in the field of art, he merely bowdlerizes something already in existence or simply steals the intellectual work of others. Their whole existence is an embodied protest against the aesthetics of the true Lord's image.

He essentially lacks those qualities which are characteristic of those creative races that are the founders of civilization. No, the Jews have not the creative abilities necessary to the founding of a civilization, for in them there is not, and never has been, that spirit of idealism which is an absolute necessity in the higher development of mankind.

Therefore, the Jewish intellect will never be constructive, but always destructive. At best, it may serve as a stimulus in rare cases, but only within the meaning of the poet's lines: *The power which always wills the bad, and always works the good.*

Together with my deeply admired architect, Ludwig Troost, I immerse myself in my long-neglected, but never forgotten, artistic passion. Whenever he asks for my suggestion on a certain architectural detail or how I want a certain room or facade to look, my reply is always the same: "Big, Herr Troost, very big. The biggest and grandest you can possibly imagine. Whatever your plan is, make it bigger."

As I sketch the furniture, windows and doors to my new headquarters, I remember Stefanie and my long hours sketching our renaissance home in the heart of Vienna.

Then I remember sweet Mimi, and how wonderfully young and vibrant our home could have been. *"We will choose everything together, Mitzerl, the chairs, the paintings, the carpets! Already I can see it all: beautiful, big lounge chairs of violet plush."*

How very different it all turned out for me and how grateful I am for that! In my heart, I often thank Providence for saving me from such an empty, bleak life. A life that would have squelched my creative spirit and deprived my people of their salvation.

I design a magnificent stairwell to lead up to my office. There are few suitable words in the world that could properly define the emotions invading me whenever I enter this imperial room. My architectural dreams of long ago are finally exiting my imagination to enter the reality of our material world. I place a bust of Mussolini near my desk and on the walls hang a portrait of Frederick the Great, as well as a painting of the List Regiment's attack on Flanders from the Great War.

And then, there is the adjoining Senate Hall, where I shall receive the most illustrious minds, where plans will be conceived and orders imparted. I design the colossal table in the shape of a horseshoe and surround it with sixty red, Moroccan armchairs, the party eagle emblazoned on their backs. Busts of Bismarck and my dearest Eckart stand in the far corners. In the opposite corners, bronze tablets displaying the names of the heroes fallen in the failed putsch will command respect. The hall will install fear, reverence, admiration and awe. And when I speak, the acoustics will make my voice sound like thunder from above.

I get to hear my voice echoing and bouncing back from the walls of my office earlier than expected. Soon enough, word reaches me that some of the party members, leaders who became so on *my* delegation, are gossiping about my private life. Some go as far as complaining about it to my face. One such fool, the Gauleiter of Wuerttemberg, dares to demand of me to cease showing off "my sweetheart" in public.

Ah! The wrath possessing me! It is I, always I, who makes demands, not the other way around! Or have they already forgotten the stench of professional and political death hovering about them in my absence? The swine! I order him to vacate his offices at once. Let that send out the message that no one, not one, no matter how powerful he might think himself, is entitled to meddle in my private affaires.

And yet some help with private matters from these associates is indispensable to me. One cannot struggle alone and be declared a victor, too, when one has so many enemies. And the more my fame and popularity grow, the more enemies I make. Some are rising by default and are destined to always lurk in the background, making moves against me on the grand political chess board.

However, others are driven by more personal considerations, their actions stemming from the foulness and putrescence always present in the inferior human nature.

It is Franz Schwarz, the party treasurer, whom I commissioned with the acquisition of our new headquarters' building the previous month, who comes to my rescue when one such loathsome enemy makes himself known through a disgusting letter sent to me.

To the private attention of Adolf Hitler, Leader of the NSDAP

Dear Sir,

We've never had the opportunity to meet in person, and I beg of you to pardon my decision to write such a personal note and send it to your offices. Even though we've never met, we are somewhat connected, through the lovely lady who provided me with my life and you with your lease on your apartment. It is in that apartment that I found, lying around, a most delightfully entertaining letter, addressed to your niece. I had the privilege to have seen her person from afar on numerous occasions and heard, from my mother's apartment, her enchanting, childish laughter. Such a lovely sweetheart, isn't she?

I must confess that your words, however entertaining, disquieted me to some degree. It made me wonder if your lovely niece has already come of age or is she still clutched in the vulnerable embraces of childhood? Do forgive me, Sir, for such unwarranted thoughts, but what is a man in my position supposed to do with his findings? After all, I am a doctor, and as such, always bound to help or even save, unfortunate souls from whatever misfortune might plague them.

I believe this matter must be discussed thoroughly and in the most serious terms. You do, of course, know where to reach me if you desire to do so.

Most respectfully,
Doctor Rudolph

By the time I finish reading aloud the scum's letter, my right leg stings unbearably from the blows of my riding whip. I did not even realize how furiously I lashed myself and now I limp up and down the massive office.

"Unbelievable," Schwarz whispers almost inaudibly. I search his face for a sign of his thoughts. Does he think me a pervert, a defiler of young women's innocence? Perhaps. But his eyes do not show it, looking only slightly worried.

"Not to me," I say. "I've came across men like him by the dozen. This time, however, I must admit that I am a bit shaken."

"Of course. I would be, too."

"What must we do then?"

"Pay him off, by all means."

"My very thought, Herr Schwarz, my very thought. That's why I called upon you. Not only because you are the man handling the party's money, but because you always proved yourself a man of resolve." I pause a little to look at him again and see if my deliberate flattery proved fruitful. The modest smile on his face says it did. But there is something else in his glance, vacant a moment ago, now clouded again. An entertaining thought seems to be teasing him like a fat fly.

"Speak your mind, Herr Schwarz."

"I am thinking you should not reply to the sender of that filthy missive but use another means to retrieve your stolen letter. It is money he wants and he shall get it. But not from you, at least not to his knowledge. Otherwise, he'll be encouraged to repeat his contemptible actions."

"You speak wisely, dear friend, and just saved me from the dread of interacting with that bloody scourge. What other means are you thinking of?"

"Bernhard Stempfle."

"Father Stempfle?" I ask, halting mid-step. Why I didn't think of him? An anti-Semitic journalist in priest clothes, an unorthodox bishop without a conscience, Father Stempfle had helped me tidy up *Mein Kampf.* Among other things.

"That's right. He's partner with Herr Rehse, the famous collector of political documents."

"Famous for tearing down posters from the street billboards," I add with a smirk.

"Still, he's famous enough for our plan to work. They'll contact Doctor Rudolph, with an offer to buy your letter for their collection."

I approach the immense window and look at the early snowflakes plunging to earth. The sight of them gives birth to the never-receding fear of impending disaster; and I realize Christmas is coming.

"I like this plan," I finally say, turning away from the window. "With one exception."

Schwarz raises an eyebrow. "Oh?"

"What if they read it? My letter? What if Herr Rehse and Father Stempfle read my letter?"

"Silence can always be bought. And I am prepared to spare no expense to save your reputation, mein Führer. What's more, Herr Stempfle is your friend, is he not?"

"Friend..." I echo and look out the window again. *Father was supposed to be my friend. Maurice was supposed to be my friend. There are no friends in this world of eternal struggle, selfishness and deceit.*

"See to it," I order the treasurer, and he exits.

The deal is concluded.

In exchange, I must buy the silly collection of political documents. But no matter, the letter is in my hands again in less than a fortnight.

To my chagrin, however, this isn't an isolated incident. Another thief steals the portraits I drew of Geli. My sketching her while sleeping and when wearing naught but an untied chemise were not the only portraits stolen. No. I have drawn Geli's naked body on numerous occasions since that day, with no chemise, with no restrictions, with every anatomical part displayed and included. Those were for my eyes and hers only.

Buying such unnecessary memorabilia gives raise to questions and arguments. *"Why would our leader throw away the Party's money on such odd assets? His whims are going to ruin us! That woman! Always the woman! Why must we all suffer so much over that woman?"*

Yet the more they complain, the more obstinate I become. I begin to take Geli everywhere: the theatre, opera and shopping; to the Party rallies, cafes and restaurants; on country touring and even at the most private meetings. She always becomes bored, of course, but I must make a statement. No party member should ever forget that the National Socialist movement, their impressive-sounding positions, indeed the very bread they eat, exist because of me. And all of these could go to hell just as easily if I as much as lift a finger.

But, it seems that everything feels boring to Geli. When Vogl, her singing teacher, expresses his skepticism about her future as a Wagnerian soprano, I fire him, sever the relationship, and hire another one, Hans Streck, to give her twelve lessons a month for a hundred marks. He soon calls to inform me on her progress: *Half the time she rings up to say she can't come, and she learns very little when she does.*

She now says she should study singing in Vienna, stating that "the teachers in Germany are being unfair to her voice and talent." She's lost all interest in her career and that realization is deeply unsettling. All she really wants to do is to attend banquets where she can dance and laugh and flirt with my underlings. And because Christmas is coming, with all its' parties and gatherings, and because I resist her pleas to attend such enjoyments, she throws a tantrum several times a day, until I finally give in.

This is what happens when you lose control over a woman. She tramples all over you with her little feet, using your own vulnerability against you.

I shake my head in disgust and randomly pick one banquet invitation from the stack placed on my desk. In a full-blown

Depression, when the Germans barely have bread on their tables, eating cake and drinking wine or champagne almost feels like committing a sacrilege. But trying to explain this to Geli feels like sacrilege to *her*.

I ring her room and tell her to be ready by eight o'clock, when a car will arrive for her in front of her building.

But by the time darkness settles, I become impatient and decide to go fetch her myself. As I burst into her room, a startled Geli jumps up from the little table at which she was sitting.

"Uncle Alf!" she screams and hides her hands to her back. As I inspect her flushed face, I hear what sounds like hastily crumpling paper.

"What were you doing?" I ask, half-smiling, half-tense, as I approach her.

"Nothing!"

"Then show me your hands!"

"Why? I was just about to dress up."

"Show me your goddamn hands!" I bark, grabbing her arms and squeezing until, moaning, she lets go of the paper. My stomach becomes a burning pit as I bend to lift it.

My intuition has never betrayed me.

My dear Emil,

The postman has already brought me three letters from you, but never have I been so happy as I was over the last. Perhaps that's the reason we've had such bad experiences over the last few days. Uncle Adolf is insisting that we should wait two years. Think of it, Emil, two whole years of only being able to kiss each other now and then and always having Uschla in charge. I can only give you my love and be unconditionally faithful to you. I love you so infinitely much.

Uncle Adolf insists that I should go on with my studies. He's being fearfully nice. I'd like to give him great happiness, but I don't know how. He says our love must be kept completely secret. He has promised me we'll often see each other and also often be alone together. He's wonderful; and that's mainly thanks to Frau Hess – she was the only person who believed you really loved me...

All the best from your Geli. I'm already happy!

I let the paper fall to the floor again.

"Where are they?" I ask, clenching my teeth until my jaw hurts.

"Where are what?" Her voice is assuming, her expression defiant. No trace of embarrassment, of remorse. I slam the table with my palm.

"God damn you! His letters! Where are they? Don't make me ask you again or so help me God—"

She points at the small table's drawer.

An open letter shows itself as I pull out the drawer. Devious, conspiratorial, betraying words gnaw at me from Maurice's unmistakable writing.

Now your uncle, who knows how much influence he has over your mother, is trying to exploit her weakness with boundless cynicism. Unfortunately, we won't be in a position to fight back against this blackmail yet. He's putting obstacles in the way of our mutual happiness; although he knows that we're made for each other. The years of separation your mother is imposing on us will only bind us together more closely, because I'm always very strict with myself about thinking and behaving in a direct way, I find it hard to accept when other people don't do that. But your uncle's behavior towards you can only be interpreted as egotistic. He quite simply wants you to belong to him one day and never to anyone else. Your uncle still sees you as the 'inexperienced child' and refuses to acknowledge that in the meantime you've grown up and want to take responsibility for your own happiness. Your uncle is a force of nature. In his party they all bow down to him like slaves. I don't understand how his keen intelligence can mislead him into thinking his obstinacy and his theories about marriage can destroy our love and our willpower. He is hoping to succeed this year in changing your mind, but how little does he know your soul.

The pain ripping through me is too much to bear. It grows

and grows by the second, with every word read. It begs to get out, to materialize itself.

"Undress," I order quietly, rubbing the handle of the riding crop between my shaky fingers. She complies quietly and begins taking her clothes off. Her expression intimidates me a little, for I have never seen it before. It's always been animated by curious wonder or tears or surprise or anger. But not today. Today it is vacant, as if the lively Geli had deserted her body for some remote happier place, leaving behind an empty pile of flesh, bones and mechanical movements. But it doesn't matter. Betrayers must be punished. They must be trained obedience with violence. They must feel the pain they produced in me in the first place. They must pay back tenfold in intensity.

I order her to lie down on her bed, but do not wait for her to do so. My armed hand jerks away from my body and I begin lashing Geli's naked trembling body.

"Uncle, stop!" she cries, hurrying to the corner of the room.

"You undeserving little slut! I'll teach you obedience!" I seethe, rushing after her. I strike her again and again over her thighs and breasts and stomach. Her moans and wails reach me in ripples but I cannot stop. She glides down to the floor, raising her arms above her head to defend herself, and I lash them too. Red swollen spots emerge from her flesh, but they fail to reach me.

"Betrayer! Seducer! Whore!"

"Stop, please!" she screams again and grabbing my arm she thrusts her nails in my flesh. The shock produced by her action stops me. The sight of her tears and screams and swollen flesh shocks me. I remember Prinz and how I nearly killed him. And I remember Mimi's fingers digging into my flesh.

The whip falls from my hand and I drop to my knees. I am oblivious to how much time passes with me just staring at Geli's naked bruised body and listening to her muffled sobs. But eventually and pitifully, the pleasing feelings that had long since cursed me and her with their presence, make themselves felt again. I enjoy looking at her bruises! Her whimpers and nails still grazing my skin tingle my spine!

"Here," I say, lifting the whip from the floor and handing it to her. "Use it on me."

This time she doesn't protest. Standing up and snatching the whip from my hand she kicks me to the floor. Arrows of hate thrown out of her eyes hit me even before the whip does. The old disgusting saga begins.

When it is all over, I leave Geli's room, locking her behind.

Once at home, I discover I am not alone. The harrowing guilt returns to haunt me. To hunt me, I should rather say, as it is always present, lying in wait for me, sharpening its claws and fangs, growling, snapping and drooling, with slobber pouring from its mouth.

But she deserved it, I tell myself. *Good. I killed two birds with one stone; showed Geli who's in charge and reclaimed my self-control.*

These self-assuring thoughts are not enough, and I force myself to purge the image of my niece from my mind and desperately turn to a happier one.

It is the memory of the shy smile of the beautiful young girl I met at Hoffmann's upon visiting his new photo studio: his latest acquisition, the sixteen-year-old assistant. The image of her smile and chubby face, her flushed cheeks and trembling hand shaking mine, her blonde curls and innocent chatter. Indeed, her very bright blue eyes gazing gingerly into mine – all dance before my dreamy eyes.

She pretended she had no idea who I was, although the walls of Hoffmann's studio are bursting with my portraits and she must have had developed my pictures at least a thousand times. And so, besides her appealing youthfulness and plump beauty, that was the one thing that made her unforgettable. *This girl can keep secrets*, was my first thought of her, and the second? *She has such formidable, strong legs.*

"Herr Wolf," Hoffmann said, introducing us. "Our good little Fräulein Eva. Fräulein Eva Braun."

16

CHARACTERS IN A WESTERN

B ecause keeping Geli under lock and key is but a temporary resolution to keeping her away from Maurice, and because living in an apartment where I don't feel safe anymore is no longer an option, I decide to vacate my apartment on Thierschstrasse and move into a more spacious place, a place that would accommodate us both, plus a couple of servants.

My new need is finally fulfilled by the luxurious, nine-room flat located in Prinzregentenplatz, one of Munich's most fashionable neighborhoods and a stone's throw from the theatre Geli and I often attend. At another stone's throw is the large, majestic statue of Wagner, flanked by equally majestic trees. I often walk there when in need of solitude and sit for hours on end at the bottom of it, listening to my thoughts, to the voice I once thought lost from within me, to the master's beautiful operas ringing in my head.

At those times, I remember Linz, my friend Gustl, and I remember Father. Looking up at the imposing statue, at Wagner's dignified stony stare, I marvel at the difference from Father's smug look in the portrait Mother hung on our dining room wall.

I realize that people of little or no significance must often simulate importance to fool those who might chance to look upon them. At the same time, those individuals of great consequence look not only dignified, but at peace. They no longer need to simulate for they have already proved themselves to the world.

I've always said that life is but struggle.

Just look at people's faces, at their actions. Just look at the pleasure women take in dressing up. There is always a mixture of some trouble-making element, something treacherous – to arouse another woman's jealousy by displaying something the latter doesn't possess. Women have the talent of giving a kiss to a woman-friend and at the same time piercing her heart with a well-sharpened stiletto. The motive lies in the struggle for survival. The struggle to advance, to grab, to receive, to become, to have and finally to quench those fears. In this respect, we are no more than wild animals, no more than primitive barbarians.

I commission my architect, Paul Troost, who also decorated the Brown House, to design my furniture. Dark and massive, of course. The only bright spot of color in the house is reserved to Geli's bedroom, which I have located right next to my own. Bright pastel green on the walls, furniture with painted motifs, embroidered sheets, and on a wall, the watercolor of a Belgian landscape I painted during the quiet times in the trenches of the Great War.

She resists the idea of moving in with me, but when the time comes in November 1929, she discovers she has no voice in the matter. Frau Winter and her husband, hired as servants, help her settle in, as I am in the middle of one of my sessions with Hanussen.

Two hours later, as I prepare to see the astrologer out, I hear a quiet knock on the living room door.

"I was wondering," Geli says, popping her head through the door, "if the esteemed gentleman here would have the time and willingness for a private session with me."

Her request annoys me and I just stare unblinkingly in her direction. Conversely, she is nothing but smiles. She approaches us and lifts her arm toward Hanussen, who bows slightly to kiss her hand.

"So? What do you say, Uncle Alf?"

I don't even care what the cause of her good mood is anymore, so happy I am that she *is* in a good mood – a rare thing lately.

"These are silly things, dearest, I don't know why you would want to trouble your little head with—"

"So silly that you're in here for more than two hours. Plus, you know I am addicted to Herr Hanussen's seances."

That I do know, for she's been to his house many times and always runs back to tell me how she held her breath throughout and almost fainted with excitement when several objects in his living room began to float. I always felt somewhat constrained to allow her such entertainments, on the one hand because it quieted my guilt at having mistreated her, and on the other, because it kept her mind preoccupied with things other than her sudden outbursts of passion for my underlings.

Out of the corner of my eye, I see Hanussen nodding.

"Very well then," I say dejectedly. "If Herr Hanussen has already agreed on it, then do as you please. I'll be at Hoffmann's. Be courteous, Geli, and do not ask silly questions."

Upon my return, an hour or so later, the silence in our apartment startles me. As a rule, wherever Geli is, silence is never present. I call her name. No answer. I call again, only to hear my voice bouncing back from the empty walls.

"There you are," I say, entering the living room. "Just where I left you. Didn't you hear me calling you?" Unperturbed by my question, she remains inert in the chair, just staring blankly at the wall in front of her. As I approach her, I notice her flushed cheeks and blood-shot eyes.

"Are you drunk?" I ask, half-amused, half-incredulous. Again, she doesn't answer, just takes another sip from the glass of red wine she clasps between her palms. Now I become worried and place myself at her feet, then remove the glass from her hands.

"You know how much I hate alcohol, princess. You shouldn't be drinking."

"Unnatural death..." she finally murmurs. "Unnatural death..."

"What are you saying? What death?" She doesn't answer, just

stares blankly at the wall across from her. I stand up and shake her shoulders. "Talk to me!" The movement brings her back into the room and she looks at me.

"That man...your astrologer. He said I will die an unnatural death." She pulls a crumpled piece of paper out of her cleavage and hands it over to me.

> *One will rise, one will fall*
> *The strong beclouding the weak,*
> *A death, the saddest of 'em all*
> *With nothing natural to it.*

"I know you told me not to ask silly questions," she continues, while I reread the verses, "but it didn't matter what I was asking. It was harmless entertainment to me, until I asked him about my death. Even so, I was still laughing at him. Then, I saw his expression...grave and troubled. It was then that I understood what he had written on that paper. He looked as if he was already mourning me!"

"Don't be stupid, Geli! You really can't be so naive as to—"

"He'd written a few of them...of those notes. Then placed them in his hat and had me pick one. I picked the one you hold now, and then saw his expression. I asked to pick another one and when he refused, I became so angry that I smacked his hat from his hand. All those notes scattered on the carpet and I threw myself to the floor, hastily opening them one-by-one..." Her hands begin to shake as she mimics opening the notes, her hysteria mounting. I try to step nearer, but she suddenly spins away and shrieks, "They were all the same!"

"Geli, stop!"

"All the same! They all had those same cursed words written on them!"

I grab her shoulders and shake her again.

"Listen to me! Those words mean nothing! They were written in a riddle. Surely Hanussen did not know the answer and he quickly made up something to save his reputation."

"Right. That's why you always consult him. Because he

doesn't know the answers to your questions." She glares at me and shakes loose from my grasp.

"I never ask stupid questions like you. No one can know when one will die. Not even Hanussen. The best he can do is to approximate some probable outcomes. That's it."

A heavy silence fills the room.

Geli goes to pour another glass of wine for herself as the verses reverberate in my head like a broken gramophone.

"And how probable might this outcome be? After all, you know him best," she asks, tipping her glass and filling her mouth with wine.

"Highly unlikely. You'll die of old age, with your beautiful blonde grandchildren romping about you. Who knows? Maybe you'll be at the Obersalzberg or maybe in Linz, in a majestic renaissance-style home."

"Will those grandchildren also be yours?" She gives a mocking little laugh.

"Ha! I won't live to see it. With my constant stomach troubles, my life will be as short as a clear autumn sky. I might even have stomach cancer as we speak. Who knows? Mother died of it. I could as well follow her."

She rolls her eyes. "One cannot lament without you making way for your own desolation. It's always about you, isn't it?"

I pretend I don't hear her question.

"What an idea just came to me!" I blurt. "What if I allow you to carry a pistol? Would you like that? Would that make you feel better? Safer?"

"I don't know."

"Nobody is going to hurt you. I swear it. Nobody." I pull my pistol out of its holster. "Here. Hold it." Reluctant, she takes it from my hand and turns it on all sides.

"It's heavy," she says and chuckles.

"That's my princess! How does it feel?"

She looks up at me and grins.

The next day, I take Geli and Hoffmann's daughter, to a rifle range a few miles outside Munich. They receive weapons training, complete with practicing shooting, learning about the safety catch, plus breaking down and cleaning a Walther pistol.

The girls throw off all restraints; singing out with joy and riotous laughter, pretending to be characters in a Western. They seem oblivious to this chilly day with its red sky that screams disaster.

Only I am aware of it.

In less than two years' time, because of this day, catastrophe will strike.

17

ONLY FAITH CREATES A STATE

I t seems the sky at the end of 1929 made a pact with the World-wide Depression plaguing us this year. It is a perfect reflection of the inner turmoil trying German souls: gloomy and stormy, dark and angry. It reminds me of the sky on the day I buried Mother. And just like then, I must gather my strength once more and attack all the new opportunities that show themselves with the coming of this world-wide plague.

The Wall Street Crash hits my Motherland worse than any other country. I watch in horror how by the end of the year, more than three million people lose their jobs. They walk aimlessly through the streets, their desperate eyes fastening on another business closing its doors, and then another, and another. Pawn shops spring up like meadow flowers when the first rays of sunshine hit the snow after a long winter.

I think of my own stormy past when I had to pawn my winter coat for bread and milk.

Now, day after day, young German souls wake up to no work, no hope. Their hunger pushes them to spend their miserable time selling boot-laces, playing draughts in the hall of the Labor Exchange, hanging about urinals, opening the doors of cars, helping with crates in the market, sharing stumps of cigarette ends picked up in the gutter, as well as begging and stealing.

In one of the telephone conversations I have with Goebbels,

he tells me how entire tent colonies are choking the woods around the capital, overflowing with people who can no longer afford a roof over their heads. Just like in my youth, they fall asleep only when the winter cold can no longer be fought off and they are too tired to rub their frost-bit hands and feet.

By day, the people in these tent colonies must protect themselves against something even more frightening than the cold: other starving fellow human beings, marching toward them to steal potatoes from the fields they are now inhabiting.

And then there are the massive line-ups in front of the employment offices in almost every city, with officials playing roles in a dark, acid comedy where there is no real help to give, only illusory, politely-voiced reassurances.

And these are the lucky ones! The less lucky, more sensitive souls give up the struggle and put themselves out of action forever. As unemployment grows, so grows the suicide rate.

First come the bankers who cannot go on living with their new identity. Work defines people, as well as their status, and with the disappearance of it they are left reeling and bewildered, scrabbling for their lost meaning. Then come those from the middle class who struggled all their life to rise above mediocrity, only to be thrown back to the bottom of the social pit by a vicious, unpredictable blow.

Their deaths are deeply lamented. In fact, churches and synagogues all over the country experience an unprecedented increase in attendance, people praying and lighting candles for the departed.

But to me, their deaths mean something else.

It is the one great lesson politics alone never would have revealed. These pitiful suicides teach me that humans are not driven by basic necessities or financial interests alone. What dominates the human subconscious is the need for a spiritual reason for living, a justification of their existence.

Those suicides are not carried out because people lost their jobs or savings. They are carried out because they lost their hope.

The hope that maybe, sometime, soon enough, things would be better, things would be the same again.

And when one loses hope, one loses his soul.

And this is the greatest lesson Death teaches me. Only faith creates a state. Faith and politics mingled create the greatest power in and over the entire world.

So, I resolve to let my political adversaries make promises of financial recovery and stability to the people, while I occupy myself with giving them a reason to live. I let my opponents promise higher wages, lower prices, fewer taxes, more dividends and solid pension plans, while I become the only one promising to save their souls. The only one promising to give their lives meaning.

First comes honor, and then freedom, I roar in every speech I hold in these trying days. *And from these two: happiness, prosperity, and life. That state of things will return, which we Germans only dimly saw before the War, when individuals once more live with joy in their hearts. Life has meaning and purpose. And the close of life is not in itself an end since an endless chain of generations follow. Men will know that what we create will not sink into Hades but will pass to their children and to their children's children.*

I do not promise happiness through prosperity like the others. But I tell you this: we cannot rightfully be nationalistic and shout Deutschland, Deutschland Über Alles when millions of us are on the dole and have nothing to wear. Our souls must be dedicated without thinking of an ulterior advantage!

And you will see—we will be marching!

The more the suicide numbers and general unrest increase, the more virulent our attack on the Jewish Republic becomes. My public speeches more than triple in the first part of 1930. Posters, banners and leaflets are distributed in every corner of the country. We stage "recruiting nights" with the SA participating in lecturing, athletic events, plays, singing songs and showing the movie of the Party Rally.

But recruiting young Germans with grim prospects is not the only method we employ. To be as effective as Providence wants us to be, we must corrode the Republic from within.

With this purpose, we infiltrate almost every ministry and government office in all the main cities. To say we are involved in spying on everyone and gathering important state secrets by tapping telephone wires would be an understatement. We come as enemies! Like the wolf breaking into the sheepfold – that is how we are coming.

I make Heinrich Himmler Chief of the SS, Joseph Goebbles Chief of Propaganda, and Baldur von Schirach Reich Youth Leader. With the exacting, organized, and conscientious Himmler as head of the SS, there is nothing to worry about when it comes to my safety. With shrewd and cunning Goebbels as head of propaganda and the 'Hitler cult' he so brilliantly creates and spreads around with the force of a tornado, I become much more than a notoriety. I become Germany's Savior. This word sprinkles every newspaper and rests on everyone's lips.

Now that the most vital weapons of a leader are taken care of, what remains is weeding out our enemies, the Marxists and the Communists. I relieve Von Pfeffer from his duties as Supreme SA Leader and call back the only person ruthless enough to rule the SA and help me reach my goal, Ernst Röhm.

"No more fighting?" are his first words, upon seeing me after so many years. I shake his hand strongly while exercising my stare on him.

"No more 'no more fighting,'" I say. He gets the hint and jerks his arm forward in the Nazi salute.

Thus, the brawls and bloody street battles begin. Day after day and month after month, these battles steadily increase, until they turn into a "silent" civil war.

First is the brawl in the area of Dithmarschen, which wraps up with two SA men dead and some thirty others injured. Then come the big cities, with the numbers of deaths on each side growing quickly with each skirmish. I grieve for my own, but if one bloody 'red' dies alongside one of my men, I am as happy as a chubby child handed cotton candy.

It seems that these events finally nudge good old President von Hindenburg awake from his prolonged lethargy, whispering in his ear that his present parliamentary regime is much too incompetent. It wouldn't be a bad idea to replace it with an authoritarian presidential rule.

Ah! Democracy! Didn't I shout my throat hoarse, saying that violence can only be defeated by violence and terror by terror? Didn't I say that it is time to fight with the fist and sword?

Democracy? This is what democracy presents to the people: inflation, depression, tent colonies in the woods, proud parents sending their children to soup kitchens, suicides, unemployment and brawls in the streets.

I was born way ahead of my time.

Heinrich Brüning is the choice of the old president for the position of Chancellor. A hypocrite, advocating Christian democracy, while sharply limiting the freedom of the press soon after taking power. One hundred newspaper editions are banned every month.

But only the strongest can fight a plague as savage as the World-wide Depression and come away victorious. His choice of treatment against it is the tightening of credit and a rollback of all wage and salary increases. The result is increased unemployment —in a time when the word "unemployment" is enough to make people jump in front of trains. Needless to say, this results in him becoming highly unpopular and losing his support in the Reichstag, which rejects Brüning's measures within a month. But since the President has already decided to diminish the influence of the Reichstag, he calls for new elections.

14 September 1930 is the date set for the new elections, and since this month has always been lucky for me, I am in the highest of spirits. During the two days before the big day, we hold no less than twenty-four major demonstrations in Berlin alone.

Once again, every house, factory, fence and building are drenched in our posters, baptizing the capital in magnificent red. Party members are tasked with distributing the party newspaper door-to-door. Further tasks of promoting our movement's doctrine are given to the three thousand speakers, who recently graduated from the Nazi party speakers' school. And then, there are the mobile agitation squads, marching through the cities and rural areas shouting, waving our flags in the autumn air, and singing:

> *We are the hungry toilers,*
> *A strong courageous band,*
> *We grip our rifles firmly*
> *In sooty, callused hand.*
>
> *The Storm Troops stand at ready*
> *The racial fight to lead,*
> *Until the Jews are bleeding*
> *We know we are not freed.*

My thoughts fly back to the last elections and a shudder straightens my spine and makes me break out in goosebumps. What a loss! What defeat! 810,000 votes! Twelve seats in the Reichstag!

But I am hopeful, so very hopeful. Things have changed. The Germans have finally realized how incapable their Republic has proven to be. Young and old, poor and rich, the people, at last, have grown tired. Tired of a Republic that failed them. Tired of a Republic that no one wanted in the first place. Tired of poverty, of chaos, of burying their loved ones.

I am hopeful. Maybe 30 seats this time, and why not? Maybe even as many as 50 or 70! We deserve it! We earned it! We reinstalled hope in its rightful place—in the eyes and minds of the people!

At three o'clock in the morning, the results finally arrive. As I listen to Göring reading them aloud, I become dead silent. The tears falling down my cheeks speak in my stead.

"The Communists managed to poll 13 percent!" Göring cries. "While the Catholic Centre Party maintains its position. But, the historic breakthrough comes from the National Socialist German Workers' Party, which becomes the second strongest party in the Reich, with 18 percent of the voters, and no less than 107 seats in the Reichstag! We won! 6.4 million votes!"

All my men take turns in shaking my hand, but my gaze doesn't rest on them. It has gone somewhere faraway, as if Mother were there, smiling upon me from her holy gardens. Now, I could give her a reason to stand up to Father at last. I would have had the means to take her away from the monster. How proud she would have been! How proud and how doted upon. At long last, she would have the respect and appreciation she always deserved. I would kiss her forehead and thank her for her faith in me— because her faith in me taught me how powerful faith is, and having learned that power, I now stand as the leader of the second most powerful political party in the country.

This victory means I have just won a new weapon for our fight – seats in parliament so that one day I may be able to liberate the German people.

Do not write the word *Victory* on our banners, for today that word shall be uttered for the last time. Strike it out and replace it with a word that better suits us—*Fight*.

I can sense the Goddess of Redemption and Inexorable Retribution preparing to redress the treason of 9 November 1918.

———

Apparently for me, no victory can be celebrated for longer than a moment. The loathsome scoundrels are always close by, carefully staging their attacks on me, emulating the blitz assault of piranhas gorging themselves on their prey's flesh.

By the end of 1930, my increasing political recognition and general popularity causes me to receive a generous pile of threats, not to mention newspaper articles thrashing my name and reputation, questioning the purity of my blood, and making insulting remarks to my campaigning technique.

"The man doesn't exist; he is only the noise he makes," writes Kurt Tucholsky, the vile political satirist. Fritz Gerlich apparently hadn't learned his lesson either and continues his pathetic ranting through *Der Gerade Weg newspaper,* going as far as making apocryphal predictions about my future and that of our Motherland: *"If Hitler gains power it would lead to enmity with neighboring countries, internal totalitarianism, civil war, international war, lies, hatred, fratricide and infinite trouble."*

But nothing is more hurtful than the bite of a venomous scoundrel who also happens to be a blood relative. William Patrick Hitler, my loathsome nephew from that Irish woman, has been a thistle in my rump ever since he stepped on German soil. First, he wanted me to use my connections to find him a job; and in no time he is working at Reich Credit Bank in Berlin. But no sooner does he start his job than he begins complaining about how poorly he's being treated and that his wage is offensive. In a time when most Germans could only dream of having a stable source of income, my deplorable nephew resolves to mock my help, mock his employer, and deride the grievous economic slump and the poor clogging the streets.

Of, course, his uncle is a celebrity, so why must he suffer like a regular bread winner?

"You have a job and you can maintain yourself on your earnings," I tell him. "What more can you expect? I can't have people saying I show favoritism to my family."

Still, he doesn't relent. So to get him off my back, I secure him a post at the Opel automobile factory, for almost triple the salary.

But just like the proverb says, save a thief from the gallows and he will help hang you.

So, my relative resolves to blackmail me, when tired of his pathetic renewed attempts at milking me, I decide to cut him out.

Bloody mule! Despicable mutt! He is no better than the pig who stole my dog or the harlot who called me a rapist or the son of my former landlady. Just as cancerous cells perform only for themselves, disregarding the rest of the body, the same goes for these egotistic malignant growths of humanity. I am ashamed that one such parasite bears my name.

Upon receiving his latest letter in which he threatens to expose the story about my grandmother—the stupid story my sister cursed me with—I decide to call on the party's lawyer. I commission Hans Frank to make some confidential inquiries about my ancestry, and he sets out for Austria at once. This extortion must end once and for all. I will prove the story to be nothing but the invention of those feeble-minded women, my sister and aunt.

Then I'll know how to deal with that scum of a nephew.

It's almost Christmas when I hear back from Frank. I ask him to meet me privately at my apartment at Prinzregentenplatz the following evening.

As he enters my living room, I search for telltale signs of the knowledge he carries with him. He looks exhausted, but it's his troubled expression that gives me the chills.

"Mein Führer, the mission is complete."

"Was it a success?" I ask with a fake little laugh, a desperate attempt to conceal the bad feeling that had arisen upon seeing his face. He says nothing; just hands me a handful of worn yellow papers. I hastily scan through them, with my eyes resting on disastrous words I don't yet entirely grasp. *Alois is growing fast and strong...deeply grateful for your prompt payment...will soon be able to visit...*

I force a smile again to mask the insufferable nervousness churning in my gut.

"Herr Frank, would you mind explaining it all to me, as I neither have the patience nor do I understand this faded handwriting."

"By all means." A pause follows in which he sighs and clears his throat. "My feet first took me to Döllersheim, Waldviertel, where I visited your grandmother's grave, then to Spital. Your aunt, Theresia, was very hospitable and kind. She prepared a nice warm meal and suggested an overnight rest, to which I gladly acceded. What a sweet, gentle, woman she is!"

"Spare me the details," I say dryly, emphasizing my words with a dismissive jerk of my arm.

"Yes," he nods, embarrassed. "We stayed up chatting long into the night and she recounted a story which I found unsettling. I said I despised hearsay and without proper documentation to corroborate a story, I regarded the latter as just that...a story."

Surely Aunt Theresia gossiped with my sister and her sister about that ridiculous fairytale they pranked me with. But why use the same obsolete joke on one of my men?

"Didn't she know *I* sent you?" I ask.

"Sure did. Her hospitality was, at least in part, the result of that. Of knowing that I was sent there by you."

"Go on."

"Yes...I was saying I needed proof in order to believe her story and she said I might find the proof I need in Wetzelsdorf, near Graz. She said relatives of yours live there and they might be able to present me with such proof—"

His words become muffled sounds. The word—*Graz*—reverberates in my head ... *Graz* ... *Graz* ... *Graz* ... and I slowly drag my body to rest in an armchair.

"Are you alright, mein Führer?"

"Go on, Herr Frank. I don't have all night."

"Well, the next morning I bid goodbye to Frau Theresia, took the train, and by dusk was in Wetzelsdorf. I went straight to your relatives, where they received me just as warmly."

"I never met them."

"They are your relatives from the Raubal family."

"My niece's relatives."

"Hence yours. They recounted a similar story, but also gave me the papers you hold in your hands. They are letters exchanged between your paternal grandmother and a Jewish butcher from Graz, for whom your grandmother worked as a cook at the time she got pregnant with her son, your father. But not only letters, there are also—"

"I heard this story myself, Herr Frank. But what does a pile of old friendly correspondence prove? Nothing."

"It wasn't a friendly correspondence. At least not always. Your grandmother asked for money. She claimed her baby was of the butcher's son. What you hold in your hands is not just their correspondence; but copies of installments as well. The Jew paid a monthly allowance to your grandmother, until your father turned fourteen."

My lawyer's words burn holes in my brain and a merciless claw suddenly pierces my stomach. I stand up to pace the room as the papers begin to tremble in my hands.

"These mean nothing!" I seethe, brandishing the papers this way and that, in an effort to mask my inner storm. "I am not saying they aren't authentic; but they don't prove my father was the son of that dirt!"

"Right," Frank nods.

"Everybody got it wrong! The only thing they prove is that my grandmother was a blackmailer! She smelled the opportunity! The Jew had money, she hadn't. She got pregnant while working there and who would the local newspapers be more inclined to believe? A Jew or a fine Aryan woman? That must have been it. Simple mathematics; even for her."

"But...I just wonder...whose child it was, after all?"

"Georg Hiedler's. My real grandfather."

"But wouldn't he have married your pregnant grandmother straight away?"

"He did. Eventually. After they had enough money to do so."

"That surely is possible," he nods again, but his expression betrays no sign of his real thoughts.

"There's another possibility," I add, more so for my own gnawing thoughts than anything, "that the Jew took pity on her and decided to help the boy of a poor middle-aged woman. She was in her forties, for all I know, with no husband, no money, and no prospects. Surely, a filthy Jew giving money away so lightly is almost impossible to find, even if you'd search for one with a flashlight in full daylight. But, maybe, and just maybe, one in a million does exist."

Drops of sweat glide down my temples, and casting the

documents on the living room table, I reach for the balcony's glass door. As I open it, I greedy inhale the chilly wind storming in.

Christmas...the most baleful time of the year.

"I should like you to be my personal lawyer, Herr Frank," I say, gazing into the distance. "You will also have full authority within the party. Would you like that?"

"There is no greater aspiration for me in this world."

"Don't settle, Herr Frank. Soon I will have the power to create even grander aspirations for you."

"Mein Führer...you just made me the happiest man alive!"

"You may leave now."

"Of course. Good evening, mein Führer."

"Herr Frank?"

"Yes?"

"This meeting never happened. You will take it with you to your grave. Is that clear?"

"I swear it on my soul."

"And get rid of that filth." I point at the papers still lying on the table. He grabs them, bows, and exits my apartment.

As he takes his leave, I find myself eager for some company. The thought of being alone with myself is as unbearable as my lawyer's words.

*I am a chip off the old block...I am a chip off the old block...*I tell myself. My self-disgust is getting ready to burst, like lava spewing out of the bowels of the earth.

And thus, like a moth to the flame, I enter Geli's bedroom.

18

THE GODDESS DRAWS THE
CURTAINS

I t is not until the spring of 1931 that I fully realize what the past elections have brought me. Or better stated, what the past elections haven't brought me.

If the unexpected success scored at the polls last September catapulted me even higher on the ladder of popularity and got me closer to becoming the favorite political competitor of the German people, it also brought political stagnation.

Well, truth be told, it was not the elections that brought political stagnation, but my expectations of greater progress *following* the elections, a far grander breakthrough than the one we were already gifted by Providence.

The persistent feeling of frustration and unfulfillment forces me to reconsider my political stratagem.

Again, I must place my principles in a box and lock it with a key until the time comes to throw it into a smoldering fire. And again, I must put aside my troubled conscience, gnawing at me whenever I infringe upon my political principles. But my newly-acquired knowledge is this: you cannot bring down the corrupted system counting solely on people's votes. Not in a country with a legislation containing limitations such as *Article 48,* which states that the effective power belongs to the president and his entourage, that both the power of the Reichstag and the importance of an electoral victory is subdued to the old president's desires, and he can reduce that power however and whenever his old arse sees fit.

Thus, contrary to the unwritten law of righteousness and to a good sense expectation, it is not the German voters who hold the power to determine who will become the next chancellor, but an expired and possibly deranged Hindemburg.

Must I suck up to this character?

In a sense, but not exactly.

I must return to the old and despised method of forming alliances with those already in power, those who already suck up to the old president. This is not hard to do, as the bootlickers are even more willing and ahead of me with this idea than I am.

The first to make his intention of collusion obvious is General Kurt von Schleicher, a close advisor to the President, the turncoat who had been very instrumental in the toppling of Hermann Müller's government and the appointment of Heinrich Brüning as Chancellor. He begins by lifting the ban on the participation of Nazis in the Frontier Guard. My move is to instruct the SA to refrain from street fighting. Temporarily, that is. The communists better not sigh in relief. Nor should Schleicher, for I will never forget his words about me being a *"visionary and idol of stupidity."*

Then why—some may wonder—would he want an alliance with me?

Here's the beauty of the simple logic: with a following and manpower as epidemic as my own, only a fool would not. But there is yet another reason – a reason to which they think me oblivious. They want to sound out my intentions. They aim to groom me, so to speak, to make me one of their own, to keep me in check. *Keep your friends close, but your enemies closer* is the precept to which they abide.

But don't they know that they could never capture me? That I am an eagle with indestructible, steel-feathered wings?

No, they don't. And this was, is, and always will be my

greatest advantage over such political mediocrities. *Let your plans be dark and impenetrable as night, and when you move, strike like a thunderbolt.* This is *my* precept.

Another bootlicker seeking to renew the broken alliance with me is the stocky capitalist, Alfred Hugenberg, the loser from the Young Plan days, who I meet with in Berlin in early summer. Then follow meetings with Franz Seldte and Theodor Duesterberg, leaders of the para-military veteran association, *Steel Helmet*, General von Hammerstein-Equord, Chief of the Army command, General Kurt von Schleicher, and finally, Heinrich Brüning, the Chancellor of Germany.

All these meetings serve me well. The newspapers are afire. My followers are dazzled and encouraged, my adversaries perplexed, and my voters content. At last, the feeling of frustration and unfulfillment vanishes. My political stagnation is but a memory now, speedily fading into oblivion.

Such is the fact that the road to power has many side-alleys. The alliance with those already in power is but one of them. The other is courting leading personalities in business and in the bourgeois Center parties, who find themselves at the heart of the opposition to me. I arrange confidential conferences with these pawns, some held in solitary forest clearings in the heart of nature.

Consequently, for the majority of 1931, I tour the country up and down, from south to north to east to west, and back south again. The fatigue accumulated over so many months of intensive work finally shows its claws and I return to Munich for a day of rest.

I allow not only my body to rest, but also my mind. I realize my political struggles, my ambitions, willpower, my forever juggling people and intentions and actions deplete me of so much energy. When I gift myself periods of rest, I become more sensitive, more in tune with my human desires.

It is at such moments that I realize how much I have missed Geli. Women play a bigger role in men's lives than men are inclined to acknowledge, unless they are deprived of female companionship for a long time. The greatest gap I find—a yawning chasm—is when, during my long absences, I sit down to breakfast in the morning or to lunch or in the evening that I find I am alone, quite alone. Geli's cheerful laughter is always a joy to me and her innocent chatter a pleasure. Even when she sits next to me in silence doing crossword puzzles, I feel surrounded by good health and well-being. Her presence is enough to put me in the best of spirits. I can sit next to other young women, but they leave me completely cold. I feel nothing or they actually irritate me. But with Geli, I become cheerful and bright, and if I have listened for an hour to her perhaps silly chatter—or I have only sat next to her—then I am free of all weariness and listlessness. I can go back to work refreshed.

Such are my thoughts as I enter our apartment on the evening of 17 September 1931.

Not too long ago, hearing my key unlocking the entrance door would have made Geli run to embrace me, but now I am greeted only by a heavy silence that hangs everywhere, almost scornfully.

I find Geli on the balcony, leaning lazily over the rails, staring into the distance. I knock softly on the glass balcony door.

"Good evening, Uncle," she says, turning her head only halfway.

"Where is the girl who used to run to me and throw her arms around my neck?" I admonish. She says nothing and resumes her faraway stare.

"Didn't you see me coming?" I insist.

"I did."

"And?"

"And what?" Her coolness shoots icicles through my flesh, causing me to shudder.

"Are you having another one of your gloomy moods?"

"It's my natural state nowadays."

I roll my eyes angrily. "Come. Dress up. We are expected at

Hoffmann's belated birthday dinner. He postponed it 'til I was in town. Make it fast. We're already late," I say dryly, and turning about, go change my own clothes.

A quarter of an hour later, I find her standing near the entrance door. For some reason, this image of her propped against the wall next to the door reminds me of Blondi, my German shepherd bitch from Wachenfeld. She too, stares quietly at the door when eager to get out. I find the unwelcome thought unsettling.

But even more distressing is Geli's outfit.

"Lose the fur, my dearest. I cannot possibly be seen with a woman in white fur right in the middle of my election campaign, in the middle of a full-blown Depression, when my voters go to the polls on empty stomachs."

"As you wish, wise Uncle," she mocks.

"And that feather, please, darling. You look as if an entire family of peacocks resolved to build its nest on your head," I say, sending myself into a fit of laughter. Only the revulsion on her face puts an end to it.

We arrive at the Osteria Bavaria at half-past nine. It's long past the dinner hour and all the guests look sullen. Hoffmann and his daughter are here, as well as Goebbels with his new lover, Magda Quandt, and my personal adjutant and friend, Julius Schaub, with his wife, Wilma.

"A quiet, intimate celebration! Just as I like it!" Upon hearing my voice, all the guests stand up, the grins returning to their faces as if by magic. Hoffmann rushes toward me.

"Mein Führer! We were expecting you! Everyone here refused to eat without you!"

I take Hoffmann's hands in mine. "My dear friend, may you always be as young, healthy, happy, jovial and loyal as you were when I first met you! My very best wishes on your birthday!" His eyes well up and I clasp him in a manly embrace.

"Thank you, mein Führer! And may you achieve a greatness that history has not yet witnessed!"

"That's a certainty, Hoffmann. No need for wishes." I shake hands with the rest of the men and bow to kiss the ladies's.

The dinner itself is delectable. I even sip a few times from the rare exceptional wine my photographer always acquires from his undisclosed sources. Geli barely touches her food and when the men ask for the usual after-dinner brandy, Geli joins them in their request. I slip my hand under the table and pinch her thigh as hard as I can. This causes her to whimper and slam her fist on the table. All eyes are on us now and that scornful silence makes its presence again. I gaze at Magda, as the blood reaches my cheeks.

"They say you lost the most profitable months of your life," I suddenly hear her boyfriend say. His words come like an extended hand toward a drowning man. I knew I could count on brilliant, quick Goebbels to save me from any embarrassing situation.

"Who says that?"

"The newspapers. Carl von Ossietzky," he says as he taps the newspaper resting beside his plate.

"Read it to me," I demand, in a despairing effort to keep the fury with my niece from erupting. Goebbels complies and opens the newspaper.

"Hitler has lost many months," he begins reading, *"this whiffle-whaffle has wasted his time in inactivity, and no eternity will ever restore that lost time to him. No power in the world will ever give him back the 15th of September with the defeated parties trembling and officialdom bewildered. At that time, the hour of the German Duce had come; who would have asked whether he was acting legally or illegally? But this German Duce is a cowardly, effeminate slugabed, a petty bourgeois rebel who's grown fat, who takes it easy and does not realize when fate lays him in a pickling solution along with his laurels. This drummer pounds his tom-tom only in rear echelon...Brutus sleeps."*

His words enrage me further. He was quick to act, but uninspired in his choice of subject. I look as his lover again, who is somehow the only person at the table making me painfully self-conscious. She is very beautiful and very elegant. Her strangely intense, adoring expression almost make me stand up and leave. Why is it that women – some women – have this cursed, mysterious power over me? No breathing man could ever embarrass me thus or make me feel ashamed of myself. And if all of these weren't enough, a little Jew with side-curls and dirty clothes approaches our table.

"Fountain-pens for you, esteemed gentlemen? Or maybe silk and lace hand fans for the beautiful ladies?" the loathsome creature asks, waving his miserable objects in the air. I'm the only one glaring at him, all eyes are on me again.

"A working Jew," smirks Goebbels. "Just when you think nothing can surprise you."

"You have less than a second to get out," I hiss through clenched teeth at the progeny. "If you fail to do so, I'll squash you against the wall like a filthy green fly!"

The spawn takes off running, but it's too late for me to reclaim my poise and good spirits.

"Hoffmann, the evening is over for me. I am truly sorry to have ruined your celebration," I say and standing up, I grab Geli's hand and exit the premises, leaving behind a bewildered gathering.

Once at home, a sudden feeling of desperation overtakes me. I feel my soul crumbling under Geli's chilly silence. I berate myself for feeling so vulnerable, but somehow, when I am alone with her, my castigating thoughts become a little more bearable.

"You've changed..." I say softly, as I sit at the edge of her bed. She sits in front of the mirror, gently combing her hair. The scene reminds me of Mother. But while Mother's eyes were always full of love, Geli's expression betrays nothing. It is as if her soul deserted her body, leaving behind a cold beautiful marble statue.

"You've changed, my princess..." I insist.

"I have."

"But why?" My desperation mounts and removing myself from the bed, I kneel at her feet. "What have I done, except for loving you?"

She gives a shrill little laugh. "Love? You are incapable of love. Love means giving, understanding, yielding. All you do is take."

"You speak like a sour woman. Where is my bubbly Geli? What have you done to my carefree child romping the meadows of Obersalzberg?"

"She's dead. You saw to that." Only her lips move, producing words that are beyond all stomaching. I suddenly feel like a worm wriggling in the beak of a sparrow.

"Don't you love me anymore?" I beg. She does not respond. It is one of those moments when you know the other is trying to protect you from the pain their words would produce, and thus prefer to avoid answering. But I do want to know! I grab the back of her seat and shake it violently.

"Answer me! Don't you love me anymore?"

She finally turns to look at me. The indifference resting in her eyes paralyses me, like the scorpion's venom paralyzes its prey.

"Who could love a monster indefinitely?"

"Mind your words, Geli."

"Of course!" she yells, startling me out of my deadness. She jumps to her feet and begins walking up and down the bedroom, furiously throwing her arms about, as she continues with her yelling. "Mind your words, Geli! Change your clothes, darling, you look like a harlot! You can never go out alone, my men will accompany you! Don't make me lock you in your room again! Don't trouble your silly head with such nonsense! I forbid you to buy that fur, I hate the smell! Girlfriends? What girlfriends? Don't you have me, princess? Am I not enough for you? What singing? You ought to be a doctor, be a respectable woman! Marry you? What an absurd idea to enter that silly head of yours! I shall never marry you! I am married to Germany! I will never be able to give you children! I am infected! You want to run away with the first idiot singing in your ear! You are an imbecile! I shall tell your mother! And send you away! How would you like, dearest, to be responsible for your family going poor again? Better behave yourself. You are not to question my decisions! Hit me! Harder! Curse me! Say I'm an undeserving worm! Spread your legs wider so I could examine your—!"

"Enough!" I roar.

"Enough! Imbeciles must not talk! They must only obey their master!" she continues with her mockery. It is as if a volcano I never knew existed in her suddenly erupted, spewing hot, burning lava in my face.

"Please, Geli! All I ever wanted was to protect you...you are under my care and it is my responsibility—"

"Protect me from what? A fur coat? My girlfriends? All you ever wanted was to have a malleable empty-headed little thing always at your disposal. All you wanted was to keep me to yourself, whether you were present at my side or not. All you wanted was to mold me into a stupid creature that would satisfy all you selfish, disgusting needs."

"That's not true."

"And not even once have you questioned your actions or wondered at my needs. 'My logic is the only logic. Those who don't see it are idiots.' It's been always about you, hasn't it? This pretense of being all knowing, all generous, all fair is just a deception. And not only a deception with which you fool everyone, but a mask you yourself became oblivious to, ever since you had slaves to worship you! For if you were to take it off, you would be appalled at what you'd see! You are a bluff! A fraud!"

My stomach churns in revulsion, anger and wretchedness. It is as if I suddenly died and the otherworld is castigating me for all my sins.

"I never knew these were your feelings and it grieves me—"

"Because you never listened! You never do! Not to me, not to anyone else!"

"I've always been your friend. No other woman has ever had so many privileges. And now I get this...is this what I get in return for being your friend?"

"You have no idea what friendship is, or love, or sharing. You are the child, not me! Only children behave this selfishly. And while you can always forgive a child, you...you have no excuse! And you were right. You are infected. Your mind is infected! Rotten! Putrid!"

My mind can no longer stand the insults and darting to her side, I grab her by the throat.

"Don't you dare speak to me like this!" I seethe. She carelessly pushes my hand aside and I realize I have lost all control over her.

Beware when one no longer fears you! I hear the voice in my head.

"I dare whatever the hell I want! You have long since ceased to deserve my respect. Respect is gained, not imposed. And you took it away from me. You took everything away from me! My youth, my joyfulness, the only man I truly loved."

"I protected you from that skirt chaser! You should have thanked me then and should thank me now!"

"Because you knew better, with your unparalleled logic? Because you destroyed that man's life, just because he dared to love your...possession?"

"I destroyed no one. Maurice returned to the job he had before he met me. He is a young, handsome watchmaker, surrounded by beautiful ladies, as always. Not a bad life, is it?" I smirk. The pain in her eyes gladdens me for a moment. But when they start shedding tears, my soul kneels again.

"My princess, please. You must believe me. I did it for your own protection. He would have hurt you irreparably. And I will never allow anyone to hurt my family."

She blots away her tears with her palms. "You are so blind. So high up on your self-created pedestal that you no longer see it is *you* who hurts us the most. *You* are the real danger from which I should have been protected."

"You are upset, dearest. I shall not take your words to heart." I try to take her in my arms, but she pushes me onto the bed.

"Your so-called protection robbed me of my happiness. You could have made me happy. You could have married me. You could have let me become someone else's wife. It's all I ever wanted, all I ever asked for. But the all-powerful leader of the people said *no*. All you ever say is *no*. And no breathing creature is ever happy when locked away in a gilded cage. You took away my love, and then my innocence."

"Your innocence?" I smirk. "Don't fool yourself into thinking I don't know about your filthy little affairs with ski instructors, violin players, and even my underlings. You forget who I am. And people talk."

"I was fully aware you knew. And I couldn't care less. Any affair is better than what you have to offer. A warm caress from a stranger was always more gratifying than your...lovemaking. I'd prefer to be used for sex by any one of your underlings than have sex with the master's whip."

Her defiant glare and uncontrolled words dig holes in my flesh. I jump to my feet. This humiliation must stop or I will not answer for my actions.

"And people talk, indeed," she continues. "That's also how I found out about *your* newest conquest."

I halt mid-step. Does she really know? Who's betrayed me? Is she just bluffing?

"What conquest? Only obscenities come out of that big mouth of yours!"

"Playing stupid might work with your political opponents. But not with me. You forget I know you better than any other breathing soul?"

"You mean that little Fräulein Eva child?"

"Yes, that little Fräulein Eva child. I was a child, too...once. Just as you like it."

"Don't be silly. She is nobody. She works at Hoffmann's studio. I go there often. She's an amusing little thing. What is wrong with exchanging a few friendly words with a polite young woman working for my friend?"

"There's nothing wrong in that. But taking her to the opera, to restaurants, the cinema, and on picnics is. Sending her notes and flowers is. Taking her for rides in your Mercedes is. Especially when at those times I am either locked in my bedroom or sent packing to my mother in that secluded place."

"You are a fool. My enemies whispered these lies in your ears and you believed them. You are a giddy child and I will continue to say it until you prove yourself the opposite."

"Is that so? You remember the last Oktoberfest festival to which you refused to go, and sent me off with the Schaubs?"

"What about it?"

"We were having a marvelous time in the show-booths, on swing-boats, then eating roast chicken and drinking beer, until your photographer showed up."

"So?"

"He had that shop girl on his arm. She looked like a monkey wearing that black overcoat with long strands of fur hanging from the collar and sleeves."

"And?" I roll my eyes in exasperation.

"And your dearest photographer had the nerve to introduce us. He said she was his niece. Right then, I knew. I knew who she was."

I look away in embarrassment. "Who she was..." I echo. "Maybe they are having an affair and he was embarrassed to introduce her otherwise."

"You made a fool out of me! I am ashamed to show my face to our acquaintances! You could have at least kept your respect for me only for show! You could have forbidden your friend to take that woman with him! But I am sure now. I am sure you sent her. So careful you were with her entertaining herself. A stupid blonde shop girl can have all the fun in the world, while I rot in here!"

"There you go...a child with a child's imagination..."

"I shall be old soon...and nobody will have eyes for me. And then, at last, you will be happy."

Her distraught expression, her grief and anger make my eyes well up with bitter tears.

"I love you, Geli. I love nothing more than you in this world. Please, forgive me."

"You don't love me. You don't even love yourself. You are deceitful, revengeful and full of hate. You are so blinded by your needs and ambitions you don't even see that those around you, including me, are also people. People with needs, desires and aspirations. You took them all from me and you devour everyone around you, until nothing kind and meaningful is left in them. You are like this Prince of Darkness; forever nourishing himself with whatever is kind and good and holy in people. You deplete them of that spark called life. You are a gigantic lightless cave trapping all those who love you. For you *are* loved. But fear the day, Uncle Alf, when people will see you for who you truly are."

I remain quiet.

For the first time in my life, I don't know what to say, don't know how to react. But I do know how I feel. Just as Geli said... like a monster. A worm, a rat, a parasite feeding on cadavers. Never in my entire life have I hated myself so greatly. I want to crawl to her feet and have her punish me. I reach for my whip and gently caress Geli's leg with it. As if burned by the great fires of Hell she kicks my hand, causing the whip to fly high in the air.

"I don't feel like being whipped or ever again seeing your disgusting face in the throes of excitement while whipping you. If you need punishment, go to that little Fräulein Eva child."

"I knew you couldn't really love me. No one does."

"Ugh, please. Spare me the self-pity. I've heard it all too often."

Muted, scorned, and humiliated, I resolve to save whatever dignity I have left and exit her room. But if hers was cold and unwelcoming, mine feels like a tomb. All night I shiver with cold and self-hating thoughts. And if that weren't enough, when I do manage to fall asleep just before dawn, I dream of Father again.

So much for my day of rest.

I wake at noon, and realizing how late it is, jump out of bed and straight into my uniform. Schaub, Hoffmann, and Schreck should arrive any minute now. We are to commence the electioneering tour up north with a meeting of Gauleiters and SA leaders tomorrow in Hamburg.

Over lunch, I realize nothing has changed. While I am stricken with remorse and eager for a reconciliation, Geli's expression is unchanged. The same marble statue sits next to me, ignoring her food and my questions. I look at her in amazement, not knowing who this person is anymore. Then, she abruptly stands and retires to her bedroom.

I sigh deeply to keep my irritability at bay, for I am to be absent for a long time and would hate to part with her without mending our quarrel. Finishing my lunch, I thank Frau Winter for the exquisite pasta she made, then look out the window to see that my men have already arrived.

"I'm leaving, princess," I say, knocking on her bedroom door. On the third knock and still no response, I see myself in. She sits at her writing table, deeply immersed in writing what seems to be a letter.

"I'm on my way, Geli." Again, no response. I approach her and leaning slightly forward, I look over her shoulder, at the words on the paper.

My eyes rest on her last sentence. *When I come to Vienna—I hope very soon—we'll drive together to Semmering an—"*

"Can I help you with something?" she suddenly asks, making me draw back. She spins in her chair to face me. "I never poke my nose into your correspondence."

"Who are you writing to?"

"Just a friend."

"Is it that blasted art teacher again? Who?" Blood rushes to my temples so furiously that it feels it might erupt through my skin.

"No. Just a girlfriend."

"I thought I was clear on this. You are not allowed to go to Vienna! Never are you to see him again!"

"But why???" she yells and jumps from her chair.

"Because I said so! Because you are not to dishonor yourself! You are not to dishonor *me!*"

"He asked me to be his wife! I want to leave! I want to get married! I want to be happy! I am not happy here! I hate this house! And...I...I think I'm pregnant."

Her words are like a fatal blow to my groin. Like a dagger carving through my flesh, claiming my life. I grab her arm and twist it. "You bloody whore!" I seethe through clenched teeth. "You are just like that great-grandmother of yours! The lowest of harlots, infecting yourself with the lowest of blood! I don't even want to hear it! How dare you put such an abominable thought in my mind? Especially now! I'm on the brink of grabbing power! Pray this isn't a fact, pray my love still lasts after this or I swear it on my mother's memory, I'll—"

"You'll what? Kill me like you kill all those who are inconvenient to you?"

"Do us both a favor and do that yourself. Only death could give you back your dignity."

I squeeze her arm harder until it makes her bend and wail.

"Please, Uncle Alf, let go! You're hurting me!"

I loosen my hold and she wrenches free of my grasp. Her weeping face burns through me like that dagger twisting in my wound.

"Please, Uncle, let me go to Vienna! I shall finally be—"

"Noo!!!"

Her weeping expression switches to the marble-faced one.

"Then I will tell everybody about you! About the disgusting things you make me do! I will tell the world how the almighty savior, preaching about the holiness and dignity of marriage and conjugal life, spends his nights! Let them know that whip of yours is used not for scourging the black marketers like Jesus did, but to whip yourself in exchange for an erection! If I am a harlot, then you are no better than me. You are no goddamn Jesus!"

A swift, inescapable blow to her face throws her to the floor. I throw myself at her and raise my fist again.

"Not the belly, Uncle! Not my baby! Please! Please!"

I stop as if struck to the ground by a lightning bolt from Hell. The memory of Mother being thrown to the floor by Father's heavy blow, her very same supplicating words replay before my eyes.

*I am my father. I am that devil. I am my father...*I repeat inaudibly and feel the ghost of delirium grasping my throat again.

Only when Schreck turns on the car engine and drives off, do I feel my judgement returning to me. I don't even know how I ended up in the car. I must have run down the stairs. I find myself unable to take part in the men's conversation. Hateful feelings of bewilderment and remorse grab hold of me. Geli's words, as well as mine, reverberate in my head louder and louder, like echoes bouncing back from the walls of a deserted church.

How could I have raised my hand at her? She's the only being I love. I remember Mother's tears, her discolored flesh and bruises. I am just like him. I am Father.

My wretchedness exacerbates until it becomes almost an entity in itself, living inside me, feeding on me. It's...it's almost like a premonition. Like that feeling of pending disaster surrounding Christmas.

"I don't know why, Hoffmann," I say, turning to face my photographer, "but I have a most uneasy feeling about Geli. She was screaming and...I...I..." He leans forward to reach my seat and speaks to me almost in whispers. "Don't worry unduly, Herr Hitler. She's had these moods before and they always went away. She'll come around. You'll see." He pats me lightly on my shoulder. I seem to draw a bit of comfort from his gesture, his words, the confidence in his voice.

He might be right. After all, it's September. A good month for me.

When darkness settles in, we resolve to sleep over in Nürnberg, and then continue to Hamburg first thing in the morning.

I find the room in the Deutsches Hof Hotel a blessing. No personal objects scattered about to remind me of things. That's why I love hotels. One feels like taking a break from life and all its anxieties. The Goddess of Magical Dreamland also decides to bestow upon me a most superb, peaceful sleep. I can't quite remember the last time I had a dreamless sleep.

In the morning, I make a mental note that whenever I'm in need of a day or two of rest, I should check into a hotel, rather than go home.

The good night's rest puts me in a much better mood and by eleven the next morning, we are already on our way northwards. The mood in the car is animated and cheerful. We crack up over Schaub's silly jokes about his toes being frozen while in the trenches of the Great War. This otherwise cantankerous, always suspicious man with staring eyes, is imitating his own hobbling gait when walking. Doing it from a sitting position on the back seat of our car is even more hilarious than his jokes. I join in the mood and begin imitating Goebbels and his own limping walk.

"I guess he favors using one foot over the other!" I say. Uproarious laughter fills the car once again. Throughout this time, I look at my driver, who gazes into the car's rearview mirror with quick short movements of his head. Brows furrowed, he seems to be troubled by something.

"What is it, Schreck?"

"Not sure. But a taxi seems to have been following us for quite a while," he says. I instinctively reach for my pistol.

"Do you have your weapons on you?" I ask the other men.

"Yes!"

"Keep them at hand. We might just have to fight for our lives."

"I'm not sure that's necessary," says Schreck. "The driver keeps flashing the high beams. I think they know us and want us to pull over."

I turn to look at the taxi following us and in the passenger seat I recognize the page-boy from the hotel we've just left. He's gesturing for us to stop.

"Pull over!" I order Schreck, and as he does so, I immediately jump out of the car. The taxi stops behind us and the page-boy runs toward me.

"A man...Rudolf Hess, Herr Hitler. He's called several times after your departure. *A life and death message.* He said to phone him at the Brown House immediately."

But I barely hear the boy anymore, as I've already jumped back into my front seat and told Schreck to get every ounce he can out of the car back to the hotel.

I'm almost in a fainting-fit, as I dial the number to the Brown House from the hotel's phone booth. "Hess? Hitler here. Has something happened?"

"It's your niece. They had to break open her door. She...she's in a pool of blood. A pistol next to her."

"Oh God! How terrible!"

"The police are on the way to your flat."

"Is she still alive?" No answer comes. "Hess! On your honor

as an officer, don't lie to me! Yes or no? Is she alive or dead? Hess? Hess?"

There's no reply, just a ghastly sound like that of the wind soughing through gravestones.

Then – silence.

19

ONE WILL RISE, ONE WILL FALL

Nearly two hours later and on the verge of collapse, I finally stand in front of my apartment building. The Winters and my lawyer are quietly chatting on the front landing. They raise their eyes to look at me, and I instantly know.

I run past them, fly up the stairs and into the flat. I pause in the hallway, knowing that once I see her dead, there is no way I could ever reclaim my hope; the same hope I held onto when I returned to Linz to be at my dying Mother's side. The vain hope that reality might prove kinder than I was made to believe, that it was nothing but an exaggeration, an error, a terrible nightmare.

Advancing slowly toward Geli's bedroom, sustaining myself on the hallway walls, I see her bare, inert feet. I pause again; struck by the image of the great fires of Hell.

"It's real," I whisper, and throw myself on the floor near her.

She's resting her head on her left arm, her face downwards, her nose against the floor. Her other arm is stretched out toward the sofa, where lies the pistol. I recognize it as my 6.35mm Walther, the one I always keep at home. Her blue nightdress is soaked in blood. Near her heart there is a large, bloody wound. If not for the bluish-purple color of her skin, I would think she is just quietly sleeping or playing one of her childish mischiefs.

In a corner, her canary, Hansi, a gift of mine from the happy days, lies dead, bedded in cotton in a small box. Just as stiff.

Death has wreaked havoc all around.

Why, Geli? Why, my princess? I howl to myself, caressing her disheveled hair. *Why did you do this to me? Why did you leave me all alone? How could you? Why would you?*

But there are no more answers, no more loving, hating, castigating replies. There are no more giggles, bubbly chatter, no more songs coming from those lips. All she's left behind is a deserted body displaying all hues of death.

A fit of sobs infects me and through my tears I see the tiny gold swastika and chain sticking to her cheek. With a swift movement, I rip it off her neck. The medallion is soiled with coagulated blood, which I blot off with my uniform cuff. As the sparkling gold is fully revealed, so is the inscription on it: "*G.R. 18. 09. 1927*".

Four years, yesterday, I think, bewildered. *A talisman meant to keep women's magic at bay.* The realization of my unintentional prophecy brings back the hysterical sobbing. It also brings back *her* hysterical mumbling, her words: "*Unnatural death...unnatural death...*"

> *One will rise, one will fall*
> *The strong beclouding the weak,*
> *A death, the saddest of 'em all*
> *With nothing natural to it.*

As I lean forward and press my lips to her hair, the smell of lifelessness invades my nostrils. *No more natural smell of baby skin,* I think. It's been replaced by the stench of decay. I can no longer bear associating the grotesque images and smell with my loving niece, and standing up, I leave the room.

Schwartz trails behind me as I approach the living room sofa, and quietly speaks. "Hess, Strasser, Amann and von Schirack were here. We've been discussing the statement to be released to the press. We instructed Dresler at the Brown House to tell the newspapers that you were in deep mourning after your niece's suicide."

I hear Schwartz talking, but his words fail to trigger any judgement. I realize I just don't care. Not about the press, not about the Party, not about anything except my wretchedness. He senses this but continues with reporting every detail. That's how Schwartz is.

"We soon came to the conclusion that reporting the deed of your niece as an act of suicide was wrong. We called Dresler again to change the statement from *suicide* to *terrible accident*. But our call came in too late. He had already issued the statement to the press. I thought you should know."

I stare feverishly at the balcony. Only a few hours ago she was leaning over that railing, looking all melancholic and absent. Why haven't I listened? If only I had helped her, instead of giving in to the voice of my pride and arrogance, she would be here now, singing a merry tune.

Now, all I hear are Schwartz's tragic words.

"All those present already gave their statements," he continues. "Well, I should get going. Detective Sauer is on his way and I wouldn't want him to find me here." I turn to see him quietly exiting the living room.

"Schwartz?"

He halts mid-step. "Yes, mein Führer?"

"Why do you think she did it?" I look at him with imploring eyes, lest he confirms my most frightening conclusions. He ponders my question, my begging eyes, his answer.

"She was emotionally unstable. That's all there is to it."

I nod and he takes his leave.

For now, I want to believe his words, I *must* believe his words.

Less than a minute—or so it seemed—after Schwartz's departure, the detective knocks on my living room door. I stand up and shake his hand.

"Detective Sauer," he says. "My condolences."

I nod and invite him to sit at the table. I take my own seat in front of him.

"I was here earlier with the police doctor, Dr. Müller," he begins. "He certified that the time of your niece's death was yesterday evening and the cause of death was suicide. It was a fatal shot that penetrated through her dress above the heart. The bullet did not come out of the body but lodged in the left side of the back, above the level of her hip. It can be felt beneath the skin."

I nod again and close my eyes. I am not prepared to reconstruct the event in my mind.

"The pistol was identified as belonging to you, Herr Hitler. What do you have to say about that?"

"It is my pistol, indeed. The one I always keep in my bedroom. There have been several attempts on my life lately and I do possess several weapons."

"Did your niece also possess such weapons?"

"She did. She had two smaller pistols. One she always carried in her purse. I am hated by many and those close to me could, at any time, also be in danger through association."

"Herr Hitler, if your niece had her own pistol at her disposal, why would she shoot herself with yours?"

His question rings in my head as loud as an air raid siren. "That, I do not know. But she could have taken it very easily because she knew where it was, she knew where I kept my things."

"I see." He pauses to scrutinize me with an inquisitive gaze. I stare back, looking through him.

"Sir, I know what goes through your mind," I resume. "But I will reply to you even before you ask me that unthinkable question. Had I something to do with this, would I have done it in my own apartment? With my own pistol? In full electoral campaign? When I am on the brink of getting the most coveted position in this country? I'll say nothing more, but no one is that stupid. No one."

He contemplates my words for a moment.

"Then how do you explain the trajectory of the bullet? Entering her chest and ending up in her lower back?"

"Well, I am no expert in such things, and I—"

"One doesn't have to be," he interrupts. "Ask a child and he will tell you the gun was pointed downwards when fired. Which means the shot could not have been fired by your niece but by someone else. By someone much taller than your niece."

His insinuation disgusts me and I make no secret of it.

"Detective Sauer, as you can probably see, I am not much taller than my niece is...was. And I deeply resent your—"

"But she could have been sitting on a chair or on the floor in that fatal moment, could she not?"

"I suppose she could have, yes."

"So, what do you make of it?

"Nothing!" I raise my voice, as his suspicious gaze and insinuating questions make my stomach churn in revulsion. "She wasn't experienced with firearms. Maybe she held the pistol clumsily. Or maybe it was the blow back upon firing that had much to do to the bullet's trajectory. Much more than *I* had to do with it, I assure you." My eyes well up and I turn away in embarrassment. There is silence in the room for a moment before the detective continues.

"Well, we know the cause of your niece's death, be that self-inflicted or not. What we don't know, Herr Hitler, is the motive. Those I've already questioned said they don't really understand why she might have went off on this tangent. Do you?"

"Detective Sauer, my niece was emotionally unstable," I say, echoing Schwartz's words. "She was a student of medicine once, then she didn't like that anymore. She turned toward singing lessons. She was to take to the stage in a short while, but she didn't feel able enough. Then she asked for further studies with a professor in Vienna."

"Was she about to go to Vienna then?"

"No."

"Why not? Were you against it?"

"I wasn't at first. But then said I will agree only under the condition that her mother accompany her. She refused. So, I told her I was against her Vienna plans. She was angry about this but wasn't nervous or excited. She calmly said *good-bye* to me when I left for meetings yesterday afternoon."

"I gather you were out of the city at the time of her death?"

"I was. I slept in Nürnberg last night and found out about

what had happened to my niece only a few hours ago, and then rushed back."

"Do you have any proof of your absence?"

"Well, you can inquire at the Deutsches Haus Hotel. That's where I spent the night. Or better yet," I add, as I search through my pockets and retrieve a piece of paper. "Take a look at this." I hand the piece of paper to him.

"And this is—?"

"A speeding ticket. We were driving at almost double the legal speed and were pulled over in Ebenhausen. I wanted to get back here as fast as I could."

The detective inspects the speeding ticket, then asks if he can keep it. I nod.

"Is there anything else you would like to add, Herr Hitler?"

"Well, there is something, maybe not of very great value, but my niece previously belonged to a society that held séances. She relayed to me that at one meeting she had learned that one day she would die an unnatural death." I pause, as bitter tears well in my eyes again. "Her dying touches my emotions very deeply, Herr Sauer. She was the only one of my relatives who was close to me. And now...now this must happen to me."

"To *you*?" comes his mocking question. I remain silent. "Well, I am done here," he says. "For now." Standing up, he shakes my hand again and exits.

I do not leave my living room until Geli's body is taken to the East Cemetery an hour later. I simply cannot bear to again see her dead. Only then, do I gather the courage to enter her room. The bloodstain on the carpet is maddening. It serves, I realize, to remind me not of Geli's action, but of my own bedeviled doing.

And it's not only the bloodstain that reminds me of it, but everything in her room: her new gramophone playing her Jazz records—how severely I castigated her for listening to that! *"Only fools and degenerates listen to these songs of apes!"* Her still unused writing paper with the name Angela Raubal printed in English script in the top left corner. Her favorite magazines with the crossword puzzles written in her own handwriting. *"I won't have you reading this filth! It's poison! It'll defile your foolish head!"*

And then the photograph of Muck, her favorite German shepherd from Wachenfeld, resting on her writing desk. She implored me to bring him here to keep her company. Why haven't I done so? Why had I said *no*? *"All you ever say is 'no'. And no breathing creature is ever happy when locked away in a gilded cage."* The memory of her words makes me look at the dead canary bedded in cotton.

I cannot bear this death-ridden home any longer.

I lock the room and place the key in my pocket. The gesture triggers more bitter memories of Geli's tears and her disapproving words.

I unhook the telephone earpiece and dial Hoffmann's number. In less than half an hour Schreck is driving us to my publisher's house in St Quirin on the Tegernsee, south of Munich.

Being informed that we're coming to his house and realizing that I want to be left alone to grieve, the good Adolf Müller takes his staff and empties the house for us. But even here, the memories of Geli running to the close-by lake or dancing and singing on the front yard burn holes in my flesh.

For two nights and no less days, I pace the upper room uninterruptedly. Hoffmann repeatedly checks on me. Each time he enters the room, he carries a plate with food and the daily newspapers. The smell of meat almost makes me puke. The aspect of it make me literally swear at my photographer. It reminds me of how Geli's corpse looked and smelled.

"Go away, Hoffmann! And don't again bring me cadavers to eat!"

I spend the days contemplating and reading the newspapers. The filth pouring out from the tiny printed letters feel like a mysterious potion meant to slowly poison me. As per usual, *Münchener Post* is the worse of them all.

"A mysterious Affair: Suicide of Hitler's Niece" read the title of the front page of today's issue.

"In a flat on Prinzregentenplatz, a 23-year-old music student, a niece of Hitler's, has shot herself. For two years, the girl had been living in a furnished room in a flat on the same floor on which Hitler's flat was suited. What drove the student to kill herself is still unknown. She was Angela Raubal, the daughter of Hitler's half-sister.

On Friday 18 September, there was once again a violent quarrel between Herr Hitler and his niece. What was the reason? The vivacious 23-year-old music student, Geli, wanted to go to Vienna, she wanted to become engaged. Hitler was strongly opposed to this. The two of them had recurrent disagreements about it. After a violent scene, Hitler left his flat on the second floor of 16 Prinzregentenplatz.

On Saturday 19 September, it was reported that Fräulein Geli had been found shot in the flat with Hitler's gun in her hand. The dead woman's nose was broken, and there were other serious injuries on the body. From a letter to a female friend living in Vienna, it is clear that Fräulein Geli had the firm intention of going to Vienna. The letter was never posted. The mother of the girl, a half-sister of Herr Hitler, lives in Berchtesgaden; she was summoned to Munich. Gentlemen from the Brown House then conferred on what should be published about the motive for the suicide. It was agreed that Geli's death should be explained in terms of frustrated artistic ambitions. They also discussed the question of who, if something were to happen, should be Hitler's successor. Gregor Strasser was named. Perhaps the near future will bring light to this dark affair."

Other papers spread poison with equal intensity and hatred.

"Hitler's private life with Geli took on forms that obviously the young woman was unable to bear. Leaders of subordinate rank know so much about their top leader that Hitler is, so to speak, their hostage, and thus, unable to intervene and conduct a purge if party leaders are involved in dark affaires. There was another incident about three years ago when a young woman in Berchtesgaden committed suicide on account of Hitler. The girl *hanged herself out of fear, after accusing Hitler in a letter to her parents, as the one to be held responsible for it."*

Then, another one:

"Hitler was reported to have reproached Geli for a relationship with a music teacher of alien race."

And another one:

"She killed herself out of bitter disappointment at the nature of Hitler's private life. The murderer, usually so clever, had failed to remember in this instance that young girls very rarely commit suicide by shooting, especially in the head."

"You bloody incompetent quacks! You despicable swindlers!" I roar, tearing the newspapers to pieces.

"Your food, Herr Hitler. And no more meat!" I hear Hoffmann behind me as if in a dream.

"Mimi did not kill herself!" I shout.

"She didn't."

"Geli did not shoot herself in the head!"

"No. It was the heart she was aiming for..."

"And I am not her murderer! I am not the one who pulled the trigger!"

"Of course, you are not." His voice is reassuring and soothing. "Her Hitler, if I may – why do you read that filth? Look at what it does to you. Forgive me for saying so, but you look transfigured. And it's not your disheveled hair or growing beard that worries me. It's your gaze. I have never seen it before and it terrifies me."

I hear Hoffmann's words; and yet I don't. I would laugh at him if some part of my soul would be disposed to acknowledge mirth again.

"What if I would end it all right now?" I whisper, looking at my pistol as I pull it from its holster.

"That would go against everything you've accomplished so far," he says calmly, placing the tray with food on the floor and approaching me. "It would mean betraying your fellow-fighters, who would do anything for you. Betraying the millions who voted for you. Stealing the hope of all the German peoples. Their only hope."

I continue to toy with my pistol. "Why don't those words strike a chord anymore?"

"Because you are distressed. When my wife died, I felt as if nothing mattered anymore. I began questioning life just as you are now. But it passed. It always passes. You must now trust my words."

I remain quiet, not to ponder his words but mine: *What if I would end it all right now?*

"Plus, aren't you afraid?"

His question brings the first smirk on my face in two days. "Afraid? How can anyone be afraid of that second in which he can free himself from misery? Truly, only a fraction of a second – and then you are freed from it all – and you have quiet and eternal peace."

"Then...that would mean...do you know what you've just said?" I look at him with an inquiring gaze. "It would mean that our dear little Geli is happy now. She has quiet and eternal peace."

My eyes well up. "Yes...happy at last."

Silence overhangs us for a while, with only the sound of my feet pacing the room resounding in my ears.

"You must not place the burden of guilt on yourself," Hoffmann says, breaking the silence. "You know she always was impulsive and reckless."

"I know. These past two days I tried so hard to get rid of my guilt by condemning her. But my love was too great. My sorrow and remorse are inseparable and inerasable."

"You said condemning her... For what?"

"She revenged herself on me. She knew the scandal would cause me to lose everything. That's why she used my pistol. That's why she didn't leave a suicide note. So it would look like a murder."

"With all due respect, Herr Hitler, but to do that one must really hate—"

"And she hated me, alright. But only in these past days have I realized to what extent."

"That's terrible!"

"Think about it, Hoffmann. Exactly how much must you hate someone to take your own life, just to hurt him?"

"Very much, indeed..."

"She knew very well that nothing on this earth could hurt me more than losing her. She wanted to punish me in every conceivable way. By creating a scandal that would make me lose everything and by shattering my soul. For shattered it feels, trapped under the ground even lower than her own body."

"So sad...so very sad..."

I nod and wipe away my tears. "I must pull myself together now. Here, write..." I hand him a blank page I tear from a nearby book. "I must fight back these rascals thrashing my image."

He looks content with my resolve, pulls a pen from his pocket and scribes my spoken words.

I therefore demand that, in compliance with Clause 11 of the Press Law, you publish the following correction in your next complete edition; in the same position, in type of the same size:

1. It is untrue that I had either 'recurrent disagreements' or 'a violent quarrel' with my niece Angelika Raubal on Friday 18 September or previously.

2. It is untrue that I was 'strongly opposed' to my niece's travelling to Vienna. The truth is that I was never against the trip my niece had planned to Vienna.

3. It is untrue that my niece wanted to become engaged in Vienna or that I had some objection to my niece's engagement. The truth is that my niece, tortured by anxiety about whether she really had the talent necessary for a public appearance, wanted to go to Vienna in order to have a new assessment of her voice by a qualified voice specialist.

4. It is untrue that I left my flat on 18 September 1931 'after a violent scene'. The truth is that there was no kind of scene and no agitation of any kind when I left my flat on that day.

Munich, 21 September 1931, Adolf Hitler.

"Give that to the press, Hoffmann, and have it printed also in Völkischer Beobachter immediately."

He retires to do my bidding and I retire to my own miserable thoughts. The voice of that blasted civil servant, Father, rings obtrusively in my mind: *"You'll destroy her, too! Just as you destroy everything around you! I should have murdered you in your cradle!"* I shake my head as if to purge his voice out of my mind, but it continues to go on, louder and louder, like lightning crackling from a dark cloudy sky. *Everything around you will be consumed by that evilness in you. You are a dreadful monster, slowly swallowing up into his darkness everything you will ever gaze upon.* Then Geli's own words come: *You took everything away from me! My youth, my joyfulness, the only man I truly loved. You are the real danger from which I should have been protected!*

"Enough!" I scream. "Enough with the torture!"

I rage about the room, furiously cracking my whip, lashing the furniture and windows and my legs, while continuing to argue with the stifling air surrounding me.

"The only danger was *you*, my beloved princess! Yes, you! You stood, for four years, as a real threat between Germany and its salvation! You were the only one that could have finally destroyed me with that silliness called love! You, who almost succeeded in breaking me! Yet once again, the Goddess of History has spoken. She took you away. She sacrificed you for Germany. For my destiny."

This must be it. Yes. Now I understand.

Some of those close to me will later claim through their never-ending gossip that Geli's death changed me irremediably. That after she left me, I was never the same person again.

But they are wrong.

It wasn't Geli's death that changed me. It was her life. Her life, her heart, her laughter and songs and warm presence. Her beauty and love, indeed the jealous possessiveness she aroused in me, those were the things that changed me. They softened me. They made me a weak man; forever in danger of losing touch with his destiny, forever lured into the warm clutches of the sweet idleness that almost proved to be the end of me. The end of what I have fought for the whole of my life—my true mission.

For love makes you weak and ordinary and should be reserved to mediocre men, not to me. Love should be denied to revolutionaries and forever regarded as their nemesis, a cruel siren luring them to their deaths.

Yes...Geli's songs were hypnotizing songs of doom. Yet once again, I have been saved. Now I'm completely free, internally and externally. Now, I belong only to the German people and my mission.

On 23 September, Geli's lifeless body is taken across the border to Vienna for burial. Thanks to Franz Gürtner—the Bavarian Minister of Justice and personal friend—the corpse is released without a formal autopsy. But as misfortune would have it, I cannot attend the funeral, as I am not allowed to cross the border into Austria. I forfeited my Austrian citizenship by volunteering to fight for the Bavarian army back in 1914. And after the putsch of 1923, the Austrian government issued orders to forbid me to cross back over the frontier. So, I send Himmler and Röhm in my stead.

However, at the last moment, Franz Gürtner intervenes once again for me and obtains a twenty-four-hour visiting permit from the Austrian authorities.

The day after the funeral, I kneel at my beloved niece's grave. It is a warm, pleasant day and the scent of flowers teases my nostrils. Tears invade my eyes and once more I become weak and vulnerable and human.

"You came to Vienna at last..." I whisper, and place the funeral wreath onto the fresh, moist earth. "I hope you're seeing Mother. She'll take good care of you."

As I climb back into the car, I turn to Hoffmann.

"So... Now, let the struggle begin—the struggle which must and shall be crowned with success."

Then, I order my driver to take us back to Munich.

THE YEAR OF DECISIONS

Only the strong can lead, I repeat to myself in the weeks that follow my visit to that wretched grave in Vienna's cemetery. *Only the strong and the chosen.* This is the mantra I inaudibly shout to the heavens to keep me functional and focused.

It comes in handy when only three weeks after Geli's burial, I meet with President Hindenburg for the first time.

His physique alone commands respect and reverence. His impressive height, the massive figure, the white hair, and the uniform draped in imposing medals, intimidates me a little. And when his hard, aged features remain unmoved upon seeing me, I feel the urge to turn around and run away. *Only the strong can lead*, I hear my thoughts again. And instead of running away, I approach the living legend, shake his strong hand, and bow low.

Too low. I immediately detest my humbleness.

For a few moments I am at a loss for words. Yet my mind is rushing with tremendous speed.

A tramp meeting royalty! How did you pull this off? But what royalty? He is no royalty! And you despise the frock-coated, top-hatted, be-medaled relics of the old regime! It is your time now. The time has come to snatch this dying republic from old trembling hands and hand it over to new revolutionary ones.

I straighten my back and puff out my chest once again.

Thanks to the 1930 elections, the Nazi party is now the second strongest party in the Reich. And all thanks to me. That is why I am now standing in front of the President and his entourage. That is why they seek my support. They need me. I should behave accordingly.

The meeting does not go after either the President's plan or mine. He falls flat on extracting unwavering Nazi support from me, and I fall flat in impressing him. The words he utters upon my leaving reach my ears as gossip. *"What's with this bohemian corporal? I could probably make him Minister of Posts at the most, but never my Chancellor!"*

I vow I will make him swallow his words.

The Christmas comes, like a curse from which I will never be able to escape. I lock myself in Geli's room, the only place in the world from which I can draw a bit of comfort. Just like a flower that grows toward the sun, I am drawn along the carpet leading to Geli's room, knowing that in there nothing could ever touch me.

Locking myself in Geli's room at Christmas time becomes a lifelong habit. It is my sanctuary of redemption, the only place that soothes my fears; the only place from which I can draw my strength and rekindle the will to go on.

It is also in here that I like to read the adoring letters I often receive from tens of thousands of female supporters. It is for this segment of the population that I like to keep myself a bachelor. Their support and votes are as valuable to me as the donations coming from rich industrialists. But at the same time, the thought that marrying Geli could have saved her from her cursed fate enters my mind. I shake my head to cast it away and look at the hundreds of letters scattered over the floor.

A particular lady from Spandau, Emmie Mayer, stands out as the most loyal of all. Her letters reach me twice a week with mathematical precision.

> *How utterly unhappy I am in my married life, my dearest Adolf. My only solace comes at night, when I can finally clasp your photograph to my breast. I never stir, you know, so that you could*

rest with me undisturbed. Oh, my dearest beloved, my only, Adolf, my best beloved of my heart, king of my soul ... you are in my thoughts by day as by night, you are my only love. I live only for you, you are my homeland, I want to come home to you, you are my life, my light, my heart and soul belong only to you, oh everything is yours.

Love, my heart is so filled that my mouth overflows. Oh, my Adolf, what have you done now! You have lighted everything inside me, my body in a single glowing star. Only you have lit the flame, it still burns now, oh how it burns. Oh, Adolf, my Adolf, beloved, come—take what is yours, take everything, everything there, and the flame will glow, glow, glow for you...

Your eternally loving Emmie

This kind of adoration strengthens my will. It is the shrine that moves me forward, the altar of lost souls that, ironically, emboldens me to live on. I order Frau Winter to leave the room unchanged and to place fresh flowers in it every week. The exact same orders I dispatch to my sister at Wachenfeld. A portrait of my darling goddess now adorns a wall in my own bedroom, so she can be the last thing I see before I fall asleep. And in my coat pocket, close to my heart, her small photograph joins that of Mother's.

Bypassing Christmas unscathed, as well as welcoming the arrival of 1932, feels like redemption from the depths of my anguish. This new year is not only the year of the toughest decisions we must make, but also the year of our greatest breakthrough thus far. Never in our life as a party are we as close to power as in this fateful year. And never have we faced so many situations begging for so many decisions – life-threatening decisions for the movement. But it is exactly those decisions that bring about the unparalleled advancement.

With the beginning of the new year, the struggle for power begins to intensify also. 1932 serves us five major general elections. And since the old President's term expires in spring, Chancellor Brüning—the "Hunger Chancellor"—in an effort to secure his post and gain time for his policy of austerity to reap its fruits, proposes that Hindenburg be made President for life.

The President, as old and tired as one can be at eighty-four, consents only to a two-year extension of his term, and not without his Chancellor first putting in solid bootlicking.

However, Brüning's proposition requires an amendment to the Constitution and a two-thirds majority. For this, even more solid bootlicking is required to win over the various parties to the constitutional amendment. I am now confronted with the first perilous choice in this year of decisions.

Am I to stand for the amendment of the Constitution? That would mean denying everything I stand for, siding with the enemy, and helping to further consolidate Brüning's much-coveted position as Chancellor of Germany.

Am I to stand against the amendment of the Constitution? That would mean opposing the President, this pillar of strength and reverence, and waging an electoral campaign against him. I need not be reminded that it is not the German voters who hold the power to determine who will become the next Chancellor, but Hindenburg. One better think not twice but ten times over before offending the President.

Gregor Strasser advises me to accept the proposition, while Röhm and Goebbels balk and plead with me to run against Hindenburg.

"By all means, you must stand *for* the amendment," Strasser says, as we confer about the issue at the Kaiserhof hotel one afternoon. "The Presidency—"

"The Presidency is not the issue," Goebbels interrupts. "Brüning merely wants to strengthen his own position indefinitely."

"Then force an election, and watch how Hindenburg wins. We stand no chance; can't you see that?"

I pace up and down the hotel room, listening to their exchange of words. I turn to Röhm, who sits quietly in an armchair. "What's your say in the matter?"

"Well, I agree with Goebbels. There's no room for compromises. We are who we are."

Strasser sighs and exits the room, while Goebbels and Röhm continue to pound their opinions into my ears.

"Mein Fuhrer?" I hear Hess and turn to look at him. He has a letter in his hand and a strange grin on his face. I unfold the letter, and read it in silence.

"Brüning invites me to Berlin for fresh discussions," I finally say, thrusting the paper into my men's faces. "Now I have them in my pocket! They have recognized me as a partner in their negotiations."

Although the missive instills in me a fresh dose of confidence and enthusiasm, none of these men are aware of the torment unleashed in me. While they all speak for themselves, trying to advance their own objectives and advantages, my next decision can make me or break me in equal measure.

And there is yet another thing of which they are unaware: I am afraid. Awfully afraid. So many decades of struggle can go up in flames in a moment, and no one has as much to lose as I have.

Thus, I resolve to postpone my decision. Until I am truly ready. Until the Goddess of History speaks to me again.

Minutes become hours, hours become days, and days become weeks. But no matter for how long I stare at the majestic mountains from my wooden verandah at Wachenfeld, I hear no divine guidance whispering in my ear. For days, indeed weeks, the only voice I hear shouting in my head is my own mocking one: *Running for presidency? You? The Vienna beggar? The flea-and tick-infested tramp? The full-fledged proletarian living in men's shelters? Surely, this must be a joke! Didn't your father tell you who you were? Who are you trying to fool?"* On and on and on.

Ah! If only She would speak to me! If only She would show me a sign! I scream, day and night.

Until at last, She makes her presence felt. The sign She sends is when the Social Democrats, the very party who had so passionately opposed Hindenburg in 1925, come out in support of him.

Now, I am the only one left to represent the nationalist right wing. And now, alas, I have my decision.

Machiavellian, but correct, as Goebbels would say.

On 3 February 1932, I announce my candidacy against President Hindenburg. But to be able to run for president in Germany, I first need to be a citizen. I remember my years in Vienna, and again laugh at the irony. I am *stateless*...like the status of every disgusting Jew.

And when the NSDAP interior minister of Braunschweig appoints me government counsel for Braunschweig's consulate in Berlin, the irony strikes me again. I am not only *stateless*, but a civil servant, as well. *How proud this would have made Father*, I muse.

But at least, the appointment certificate, at last, makes me a German citizen.

Now, battle is declared. The chess game for power begins.

With the election set for 13 March, our campaign immediately starts running at full capacity. Fifty thousand gramophone records of Goebbels delivering a campaign speech are delivered across the country. A ten-minute sound film, depicting me as the coming savior of the Germans, is played in the squares of the big cities. Strident posters drench the entire country in red: *Down with the system! Power to the National Socialists!*

On 27 February I address 25,000 people at the Sportpalast, and between 1 and 11 March, I speak in Hamburg, Stettin, Breslau, Leipzig, Bad Blankenburg, Weimar, Frankfurt, Nuremberg, Stuttgart, Dortmund, Hanover. Almost half a million people in all hear my thundering voice:

"I believe in Divine Justice! I believe that it has defeated Germany because we had become faithless, and I believe that it will help us because we now once again profess our faith! I believe that the long arm of the Almighty will withdraw from those who are seeking merely alien shelter.

"We once served the Field Marshal obediently as our

Supreme Commander. We honor him and desire that the German Volk continue to see in him the leader of the great struggle. It is because this is our wish and our desire that today we view it as our duty to call out to the old Field Marshal: Venerable old man, you no longer bear the weight of Germany's future on your shoulders. You need no longer assume responsibility for us. We—the war generation—must take it on ourselves. Venerable old man, you can no longer protect those who we want to destroy. Therefore, step aside and clear the way!"

The crowd's response is as spectacular as our campaigning efforts. The men mob to shake my hand or touch my uniform; while the women scream, faint, or throw themselves at my feet, declaring their adoration or begging me to touch them, to make them mine. Now I am almost certain we will win.

Yet like an old grumbling parent who always thinks he knows better, the Goddess of Divine Justice resolves to contradict me. President Hindenburg defeats us with 18 million votes to our 11 million, but just misses out on an absolute majority with his 49.8 percent. A run-off is required.

My spells of depression soar, but I realize one quality of my character that others often complain about – intransigeance – has just come to my rescue. It is my intransigence that doesn't allow me to brood. My obstinacy that orders me to increase my attack and make it all the more violent. My stubbornness that does not allow me to accept a defeat. My uncompromising nature that forbids me, in the name of my own survival, to accept the will of others.

My will is the only will.

Such is the fact that on the very evening of our defeat, I throw myself into work. Our momentum must not be slowed down but increased. This battle is lost, but the undisputed fact is that we have risen to become the strongest party in Germany. The attack upon the front Centrists and Marxists must be renewed in the sharpest form; for if we are to be victorious, every Nazi must give his all!

And there is another fact: 11 million Germans voted for me.

For me! Again and again, I repeat this sentence in my mind, as if by repetition I will come to believe it. Well, Hanussen said this is how it all works. So, I keep repeating it, until the echo produced by it makes my enthusiasm soar.

Goebbels's propaganda genius also soars. But the President declares an "Eastern truce" from 20 March through 3 April, so he has a mere week to put that genius to work before the run-off of 10 April. The short timing requires new methods of propaganda.

One such method is chartering an aeroplane, which will enable me to attend every single mass event in the country. So, from 3 April until the elections, the Lufthansa plane takes me and my closest men to more than twenty stops in just a few days. The brilliant campaign proves every bit successful, bringing an increase in votes from 11 to 13 million. 13 million people voted for *me*!

But still, we are defeated. President Hindenburg wins the absolute majority with 53 per cent of the total votes.

"Then we haven't done enough!" I roar at my men, pacing and fumigating. "Struggle, struggle, struggle! This is the word you must repeat to yourselves before going to sleep and upon waking up! You should fear not so much for losing votes but for your lives; for if we are defeated, there is only one truth left in the end: the strongest won. And if that strongest one wasn't me, if it wasn't us, then your lives worth nothing! Our lives will serve just to serve! You will be the food of the strong! Is this what you want? To serve a Jewish Republic? To serve those who stabbed our Germans in the back? To serve the fungus? Be food for microbes? I want more of you! I want your sweat and blood! And I want it now, or else they will belong to our enemies!"

I am almost giving in under the strain of nervousness, fatigue and the fear of flying. And because state elections in Prussia, Bavaria, Württemberg and Anhalt follow on the 24th, repeated flights over Germany take me to twenty-five cities in just over a week. Whoever knows my absolute terror at flying, knows my will. We will not rest one moment and are already making decisions. A third flight over Germany has me speaking in fifty cities over the course of fifteen days. Thus, it comes as no surprise that major gains are bestowed in the 31 July Reichstag elections. We more than double our seats! The largest party in the Landtag! Never had this breakthrough happened in the entire history of Germany! We are setting a precedent and, as sure as the gardens of Olympus, we will win!

Now we have them to their knees!

By the beginning of August, I teeter toward collapse. Physically, that is. Yet my body no longer belongs to me – it belongs to Germany.

It is my realization of long ago, when in the trenches of the Great War I was saved from certain death by the all-powerful guiding hand of Providence. It was also Providence that taught me what struggle was: the father of all things, my true father.

Now, in the quiet of my Prinzregentenplatz flat, on long sleepless nights, I come to another realization. This new father can be as cruel as my natural father. For despite our phenomenal gains, despite the historical breakthrough never before seen by our Motherland, despite the parades, ceaseless mass meetings, distribution of posters and leaflets, films being played and party speakers shouting themselves hoarse, despite the votes of 13 million people, and despite my sacrifice of flying several times a day against my suffocating panic, we still do not obtain the coveted majority.

The question I always dreaded as a child reverberates in my head: *And now? What are you going to do now?*

Indeed, what am I to do now?

It soon becomes clear that the die has been cast, even before the July elections. The Goddess of Divine Justice has already played the part of the all-loving Mother in a most significant way – by sowing discord among the pillars of the establishment. We almost did the impossible to corrode it ourselves from all the sides we found vulnerable, but there is nothing quite like the decay starting to corrode from within.

President Hindenburg, already disappointed with his Chancellor for urging him to run for president under the wrong front, shows every sign that Brüning's ruling days are numbered.

Brüning's next mistake: provoking animosity between the 'industrial powers' and thus antagonising the President's own peers in the land-owning class. It goes without saying that this mistake further widens the distrust between President and Chancellor.

And then, when General von Schleicher, the closest advisor to the President, the very man who helped in appointing Brüning as Chancellor, also turns against Brüning, the fate of the present cabinet looks very grim indeed.

The final interview the soon-to-be ex-chancellor receives, from the man he helped get re-elected, lasts only two minutes. Just long enough to let Brüning go. Just long enough to decide the ultimate fate of his government, to decide *my* fate.

And without even suspecting it, just long enough to pull the plug on the already dying Weimar Republic.

The chaotic electioneering schedule, the gains and losses, and the rollercoaster of high and low emotions that come with the nerve-racking succession of decision-making moments, succeed in keeping my mind off my personal wretchedness, as well as it should. But even in the midst of a full-blown political campaign, there come the lonely, feverish nights with the haunting self-hating thoughts and equally hateful memories.

At these times I find myself falling prey again to the depths of my darkness. *I should have killed you in your cradle...hating him will only mean hating yourself...you always put others down, just so you could raise yourself...you are the real danger from which I should have been protected...I'd prefer to be used for sex by any one of your underlings than have sex with the master's whip...*

When the spells of delirium threaten to grasp me again, I run out of the flat and across the street, where sitting on the grass, I stare unblinkingly at Wagner's statue. Humming the notes of *Rienzi*, I long for solace, long for oblivion.

But there is yet another thing that brings me relief in my never-ending, secret search for solace – the cheerful laughter and round flushed cheeks of little Fräulein Eva Braun.

Whenever my nerves can no longer bear the fuss of politics, and whenever the gaze of my men is less on me and more on their own personal ascension, I run to see little Eva.

Hoffmann proves quite instrumental in keeping these meetings a secret by initiating little dinners at his house, where each time his lovely employee is invited.

"I am most happy to have received work from Herr Hoffmann," Eva says one late February evening, as we sit together at my photographer's dining table, being served the usual superb food courses.

How someone brought up in the humblest of circumstances can turn into such a fine, gentle creature is nothing short of miraculous. The elegance of not only her features but bearing, makes me stare in wide-eyed wonder.

"How so?" I demand, even though I already suspect her answer.

"Well," she says, gently propping the fork against her plate, "I met you. The person I couldn't do without." Her own words seem to embarrass her, as her cheeks glow in the color of blood.

"Don't be silly, my child. You'd be surprised at the multitude of things one can do without."

"Not everyone. Look at how your niece, Geli—"

My astonished gaze meets hers in mid-sentence. The charm suddenly dissipates and a thick, threatening smog blooms between us. I push my plate of steamed vegetables aside. Ever since I felt Geli's stiff body, the mere sight of meat is enough to make my stomach churn in disgust. But hearing her name on another's lips turns my stomach into a burning pit.

"And when you think it was my father who first heard that there was an apprenticeship open at Hoffmann Photography..." she blurts, eager to dispel the clouds. "But, if only he knew..."

"Knew what?" I ask, my teeth still clenched.

"That I would meet you. '*Some young whippersnapper who*

thinks he knows it all,' Father said when I asked him if he's heard about you. *'Better cross the road if you see him coming.'"*

I look at her blankly. *This girl is nothing but brains,* my musing sarcasm grumbles. Perfect. Just what I need. A soft uncomplicated little thing, pretty, good-natured, and stupid. For I would never be able to stand a woman who interfered in my political affairs. In my free time I want peace and quiet.

I reach to take her hands into mine and bending slightly forward, I kiss them both.

"Well, I am glad you did not cross the road."

But these are only little things. Most of the time her presence is the much-coveted ingredient I need in my otherwise lonely private life. Her silly jokes about the nuns at the catholic boarding-school where she grew up, her disdain of typing, book-keeping, domestic science, music, drawing, French, and her incessant chatter about her passions: parallel gymnastics, dancing, swimming, skating, skiing, movie magazines and novelettes, all help me loosen, and at times, even forget about the greatest tragedy of my life.

During the following months, with the election campaigning keeping me in Berlin, I often surprise myself by missing her. Yet there are other times when I curse this great weakness of mine, the always-present wish to have a female companion around. It seems to court those very tragedies I loathe.

On 1 November, in the heat of the fifth and last pre-elections of 1932, I receive a telephone call from Hoffmann.

"She shot herself with her father's pistol," he blurts out. "She's been taken to the hospital already and will recover fully," he adds, seemingly in an effort to minimize the horror he saw on my face a bit over than a year ago under similar circumstances. I ask him to come pick me up and, in less than half a day, aghast and laden with flowers, I enter the private clinic where little Eva is hospitalized.

"She was aiming at her heart," the doctor, Hoffmann's brother-in-law, replies upon my inquiry. "But the bullet lodged in the left side of the neck. Thank God she had strength left to ring me. She probably got scared seeing so much blood. I took her to the hospital at once. We were only just in time to save her life."

A deja-vu floats before my eyes...the police doctor addressing me a year ago...'*It was a fatal shot that penetrated through her dress, above the heart. The bullet did not come out of the body but lodged in the left side of the back, above the level of her hip...*'

"Was she...did she really tried to kill herself?" I ask, feeling foolish to do so.

"Without a doubt," the doctor replies with a nod, before walking away.

I turn to my photographer. "You heard it, Hoffmann. She was aiming at her heart, but the bullet lodged in the left side of the neck. What does that tell you? What should this tell everyone?"

"That the pistol's blow back alone can decide the bullet's trajectory. That Geli's death was definitely suicide."

"Precisely. I wish I could spit in Detective Sauer's face right now...for all those hurtful questions he asked me." I twist my face in disgust, and then sigh in relief, a feeling so foreign to me these days.

"It's maddening how these women decide to solve their issues," Hoffmann says, shaking his head. "Women will always be women, I guess," he concludes with a wry smile.

"Didn't I always say that they cannot be trusted with anything? That they have no value in themselves? All they do is beg for attention. The girl did this out of love for me, Hoffmann. She hasn't seen me in months and probably couldn't bear it anymore."

"I am most relieved to hear that, Herr Hitler. Lately, I have come to have a certain fondness for the little thing."

"So have I, Hoffmann. So have I."

Even though this realization is unsettling, I vow to take better care of her in future. If only to prevent her from doing something stupid again. If only to try to redress what I couldn't handle a year back. If only to prove to myself that Father was wrong when he said that I destroy everything around me. To prove that Geli was wrong calling me a *Prince of Darkness, who devours everyone around him, until nothing kind and meaningful is left in them.* If only to quiet my guilt.

To that end, and also because I am a man of his word, the attention I vowed to show Fräulein Eva soon becomes reality.

Since discretion and loyalty are the two qualities one should possess to earn a spot at my side, and because Eva has both and also a youthful, pure and genuine love for me, I decide she's earned the right to be introduced – even if only a few – to my circle of intimates. That propitious moment comes on New Year's Day, 1933, at a small party at Hanfstaengl's house in Munich. At my arm, she looks both shy and dignified. The bruise on her neck is still visible, but she proudly displays it as if she were wearing some hard-fought-for badge of honor.

We have just attended a performance of Wagner's *Meistersinger of Nürnberg* at the Munich's National Theatre. Just before dinner is served, I ask Hanfstaengl to accompany me at his piano, while I shyly hum the words of the opera just seen and already known by heart.

> *Madness! Madness!*
> *Everywhere madness!*
> *All songs and verse the world has known*
> *Show only truths our dreams have grown...*

But the wicked flicker in Hanfstaengl's eyes startles me into silence. He follows suit reciting from the same opera.

> *Driven into fight he believes he is hunting,*
> *And does not hear his own cry of pain,*
> *When he tears and stabs into his*
> *   own body,*
> *He imagines it's pleasure he'll obtain...*

Embarrassed, I return to the table. Was he trying to make a

fool out of me in front of his guests? I'll never know, but it's enough for the seed of hatred toward him to be planted. Never will I forget, never will I forgive his impudent slight.

Inevitably, the main subject of conversation over dinner is politics. For the year that just passed is decidedly marked by it; as will 1933. But because of the last elections in November, with our loss of 2 million votes, everyone is depressed. It seems that only I am able to keep my confidence and belief in our ultimate triumph. Yet, little do we know now just how very close we are to the beginning of a new era.

As we prepare to exit Hanfstaengl's apartment, I halt in the hallway, open his guest book, and write: *On the first day of the new year: this year belongs to us. I give you this in writing.*

But I should have written: *This month belongs to us.*

Just twenty-nine days after my statement, and three months short of my 44th birthday, on January 30 1933, President Hindenburg invites me to be Chancellor of Germany.

With all his ineffectual cronies as chancellors proving disappointing, he has no choice but to offer me the position I had fought and killed for the whole of my life. It is about time he showed *"this bohemian corporal"* the respect he deserves. This might be the last leap of fate he has to take for the remainder of his days.

The meeting that is just about to change the course of history is fraught with anxiety and expectation. There is no smile on the old man's face this time either, only the feeling of defeat teases his features like an irritating wasp. His persona no longer looks imposing, but broken and conquered. Unlike the first time we met, this time he offers me a chair. I sit and stand and sit again.

Also present on the Old Gentleman's face is the noticeable taint of disgust; and when he finally shakes the hand of his new Chancellor, he barely can bring himself to look at me.

In a flash, I remember all those disgusted looks I received my entire life. But no more. No more! Finally, I am blinding everyone with my light. Finally, like the stars glowing down from the Linz sky, I am showing my brilliance to the world. Finally, I am just about to step into a world with no more restrictions.

Once out of the room, my men, who've been waiting outside the door for hours, stand up. Their features are overwhelmed with anticipation. I look sternly at each and every face, prolonging their wait for as long as I can. I want to immortalize in my mind's eye, the moment of my revealing the news. But, suddenly, their expectation, as deep and fiery as my own, make me break into a smile. As the men run to embrace me and shake my hand, my tears are already obstructing my sight.

I wish I could hold onto this pleasant feeling for an eternity. I also would like it if Father were here, if only to spite him, to see his expression when I, at last, proved him wrong. And Mother and Geli, to join in my tears and dance and marvel at what I've become.

But...*dead are all Gods*, as Nietzsche would say.

Now we want the Overman to live. For Overmen we are and have proved ourselves the strongest. The struggle for power is now complete, and the era belonging to the creation of a new man begins.

So is the time of reckoning.

THE WOMEN IN HITLER'S LIFE

MARIA REITER

Hitler with Maria Reiter

Maria Reiter was the daughter of an official of the Social Democratic Party. She was born in Berchtesgaden on 23 December 1911.

She met Adolf Hitler when she was sixteen. Hitler had been strongly attracted to teenagers. "A girl of eighteen to twenty is as malleable as wax. It should be possible for a man, whoever the chosen woman may be, to stamp his own imprint on her. That's all the woman asks for," he said to his friends.

The following is from an interview Maria gave in her later years.

"We went out into the night... Hitler was about to put his arm around my shoulders and pull me toward him when the two dogs suddenly attacked each other... Hitler suddenly intervened, like a maniac he hit his dog with his riding whip... and shook him violently by the collar. He was very excited... I did not expect that he could hit his dog so brutally and ruthlessly, the dog which he had said he could not live without. Yet he beat up his most loyal companion." Maria asked him "How can you be so brutal and beat your dog like that?" He replied: "It was necessary."

"He told me that he wanted me to be his wife, to found a family with me, to have blonde children, but at the moment he had not the time to think of such things. Repeatedly Hitler spoke of his duty, his mission." Hitler told her: "When I get my new apartment you have to stay with me... forever. We will choose everything together, the paintings, the chairs, I already can see it all: beautiful, big lounge chairs of the violet plush."

Maria Reiter told her story to a German periodical, *The Stern*, in 1959. It was never fully translated into English.

"He took my hand and put it into his lap, then he took my other hand as well and pressed it (down his crotch). He put his arm around me and tenderly placed his hand on my temple, pulled my head toward his shoulder and wanted to close my eyes with his fingers. He said I should dream."

"I looked again at the wreaths," (when they visited her mother's grave), "then I started to cry because I realized that Herr Hitler was moved by something, something he didn't want to tell me. I cried more and more. Then he turned to me, took my hands, folded them, held them to his chest and pushed my head towards him. Hitler sounded serious, like a friend in dire need: 'I am not ready', he said. 'But my dear, listen, from today, I want us to address each other as *you* and I would like you to call me *Wolf*.'"

"Hitler made me romp with him like a child. He put me standing under a tall tree. He turned me to the left, to the right. 'What should I actually see here under this great fir?' I asked, amazed. 'Nothing. You should only stop to see how I made you. A gorgeous picture,' he said. 'Do you know what you are now? You are my Waldfee, my woodland fairy', he beamed. 'What makes you suddenly think that I was a forest fairy? We're not in the theatre'. 'You will understand much later, Mimi, my child!' said Hitler. He told me not to laugh at him which made me giggle even more. Then, he came up to me, grabbed me and kissed me. He kissed me for the first time wild, wild, stormy. He pulled me in and said: 'Sweet girl, now I just cannot help myself.' He wrapped his hands firmly around my neck. He kissed me. He did not know what he should do. He said: 'I like you too much. What I feel for you, everything is easy. Mimi! Kiss me!' he asked. I wanted to stop living. I was so happy. The way Hitler looked almost frightened me. He paused and then kissed me on the forehead, on the mouth, on the neck. I felt him clench his fists. I saw how he struggled with himself. 'Child', he said, 'I could crush you, now, in this moment.' I did not try to resist. "

Hitler sent her a a leather-bound copy of *Mein Kampf* for Christmas. Reiter gave him two sofa-cushions that she had embroidered. However, he did not visit her: "My whole world started tumbling down. I did not know what had happened, nothing... All sorts of pictures appeared in my mind... faces of other women and Hitler smiling at them. I did not want to go on living." Günter Peis points out: "In this depressed mood, she went to find a clothesline. One end of it she slung around her neck, the other around a door handle. Slowly, she glided to the floor. Slowly, she lost consciousness." Luckily, her brother-in-law arrived and "saved her life at the last minute."

Hitler sent a message that he was unable to see her because he was being blackmailed. According to Maria: "Hitler told my brother-in-law, that anonymous letters had been mailed to the party office saying that Hitler was having a relationship with a girl who was underage." The letter said: "Hitler seduces young, inexperienced girls. He just found a sixteen-year-old girl in Berchtesgaden who obviously will be his next victim." Hitler explained that he could not allow his relationship to "jeopardize the success of his party". The letter was sent by Ida Arnold, the girlfriend of his chauffeur, Emil Maurice, on the latter's instigation. Hitler never learned of Maurice's betrayal.

In her book, *Nazi Women*, **Cate Haste** points out:

"Hitler introduced himself to her when their paths crossed while walking their dogs. He pursued her, flirted with her, took her out on trips in his Mercedes and invited her to a meeting he was to address. She was impressed by his celebrity, and by his dress - by this time, breeches, light velour hat, riding whip and a coat held closed by a leather belt. In her later account, she recalls him taking her to dinner, feeding her cakes like a child, and touching her leg with his knee under the table. Hitler told her that she reminded him of his own mother, especially her eyes, and suggested they visit her mother's grave. There, she recalled, Hitler was overcome." Reiter later recalled: "he was moved by something he did not want to tell me... 'I am not ready yet'."

In his book, *Hitler 1889-1936*, **Ian Kershaw** points out:

"He (Hitler) was thirty-seven years of age; she was sixteen. Like his father, he preferred women much younger than himself - girls he could dominate, who would be obedient playthings but not get in the way. The two women with whom he would become most intimately associated, Geli Raubal (nineteen years younger than he was) and Eva Braun (twenty-three years younger), fitted the same model - until, that is, Geli became rebellious and wanted a level of freedom which Hitler was unwilling to permit. Though he found it easy during his twenties and early thirties to make friends with children and with women in their forties and fifties, he was nervous of being rebuffed or humiliated by women of his own age. But at thirty-seven he was old enough to treat a teenage girl as if she were a child. With Maria, once they were sufficiently relaxed in each other's company, there was nothing to stop them from making love."

But when asked about that aspect, Maria said that "his sexual tastes were too extreme".

Maria Reiter died in 1992, aged 81.

***Maria Reiter also talked to Comer Clarke, who wrote an article for the Confidential magazine; it contains the full interview, and you can read it on a following page.

GELI RAUBAL

Geli Raubal with "Uncle Alf"

Geli Raubal was the daughter of Leo Raubal and Angela Raubal (Hitler's half-sister). She was born in Linz on 4th June, 1908. When Hitler rented a house in Obersalzberg he asked his half-sister to be his housekeeper. She agreed and in July 1927 was followed by Geli. The 39 year-old Hitler soon fell in love with her and she became his constant companion at meetings, restaurants, conferences and on walks in the mountains. In 1929 Hitler took an apartment in Munich's Prinzregentenstrasse and Geli moved in with him.

Hitler told Otto Wagener: "I can sit next to young women who leave me completely cold. I feel nothing, or they actually irritate me. But a girl like the little Hoffmann or Geli - with them I become cheerful and bright, and if I have listened for an hour to their perhaps silly chatter - or I have only to sit next to them - then

I am free of all weariness and listlessness I can go back to work refreshed."

Joachim Fest, the author of *Hitler* (1973), wrote that Hitler became obsessed with Geli: "The affection Hitler felt for this pretty, superficial niece soon developed into a passionate relationship hopelessly burdened by his intolerance, his romantic ideal of womanhood and avuncular scruples."

Patrick Hitler, the son of Adolf's brother, Alois Hitler, met her during this period: "Geli looks more like a child than a girl. You couldn't call her pretty exactly, but she had great natural charm. She usually went without a hat and wore very plain clothes, pleated skirts and white blouses. No jewellery except a gold swastika given to her by Uncle Adolf, whom she called Uncle Alf." He called her *meine prinzessin - my princess.*

Hitler became infatuated with Geli Raubal and rumours soon spread that he was having an affair with his young niece. Hitler told Heinrich Hoffman: "You know, Hoffmann, I'm so concerned about Geli's future that I feel I have to watch over her. I love Geli and could marry her. Good! But you know what my viewpoint is. I want to remain single. So I retain the right to exert an influence on her circle of friends until such a time as she finds the right man. What Geli sees as compulsion is simply prudence. I want to stop her from falling into the hands of someone unsuitable."

Baldur von Schirach, leader of the Hitler Youth, said: "The girl at Hitler's side was of medium size, well developed, had dark, rather wavy hair, and lively brown eyes. A flush of embarrassment reddened the round face as she entered the room with him, and sensed the surprise caused by his appearance. I too stared at her for a long time, not because she was pretty to look at but because it was simply astonishing to see a young girl at Hitler's side when he appeared at a large gathering of people. He chatted animatedly to her, patted her hand and scarcely paused long enough for her to say anything. Punctually at eleven o'clock he stood up to leave the party with Geli, who had gradually become more animated. I had the impression Geli would have liked to stay longer. He (Hitler) followed her into millinery shops and watched patiently while she tried on all the hats and then decided on a beret. He sniffed at the sophisticated French perfumes she enquired about in a shop on the Theatinerstrasse, and if she didn't find what she wanted in a shop, he trotted after her... like a patient lamb. She exercised the sweet tyranny of youth, and he liked it, he was more cheerful, happier person."

Ernst Hanfstaengel, Hitler's good friend, suggested that Geli was willing "to submit to his peculiar tastes" and was the "one woman in his life who went some way towards curing his impotence and half making a man out of him." He went on to say "that the services she was prepared to render had the effect of making him behave like a man in love... he hovered at her elbow with a moon-calf look in his eyes in a very plausible imitation of adolescent infatuation."

Hanfstaengel believes that Geli had turned away from Hitler because of his perverted sexual desires. This idea is supported by **Wilhelm Stocker**: "She (Geli) admitted to me that at times Hitler made her do things in the privacy of her room that sickened her but when I asked her why she didn't refuse to do them she just shrugged and said that she didn't want to lose him to some woman that would do what he wanted. She was a girl that needed attention and needed it often. And she definitely wanted to remain Hitler's favourite girlfriend. She was willing to do anything to retain that status. At the beginning of 1931 I think she was worried that there might be another woman in Hitler's life because she mentioned to me several times that her uncle didn't seem to be as interested in her as he once was."

Hanfstaengel also suggests that Geli disliked Hitler's violent behaviour. In his autobiography he describes a visit to the Schwarzwälder Café: "Discussing politics as we walked through the streets after the meal, Hitler emphasised some threat against his opponents by cracking the heavy dog whip he still affected. I happened to catch a glimpse of Geli's face as he did it, and there was on it such a look of fear and contempt that I almost caught my breath. *Whips as well*, I thought, and really felt sorry for the girl. She had displayed no sign of affection for him in the restaurant and seemed bored, looking over her shoulder at the other tables, and I could not help feeling that her share in the relationship was under compulsion."

Hanfstaengel later wrote that Karl Anton Reichel told him

that Hitler had shown him a letter he had recently written to Geli: "It was couched in romantic, even anatomical terms and could only be read in the context of a farewell letter of some sort. Its most extraordinary aspect was a pornographic drawing which Reichel could only describe as a symbol of impotence. Why on earth he should have been shown this letter I cannot imagine, but he was not the man to make up such a story."

Geli began a relationship with **Emil Maurice**, Hitler's chauffeur and bodyguard. Maurice later told Nerin E. Gun, the author of *Eva Braun: Hitler's Mistress* (1969), about Geli. He testified that, "her big eyes were a poem and she had magnificent hair... people in the street would turn round to take another look at her, though people don't do that in Munich." Maurice was aware that Hitler was very interested in Geli: "He liked to show her off everywhere; he was proud of being seen in the company of such an attractive girl. He was convinced that in this way he impressed his comrades in the party."

Maurice admitted that he was "madly in love" with Geli and "I decided to become engaged to Geli... she gladly accepted my proposal". **Henriette Hoffmann**, the daughter of Hitler's photographer, believes that Geli was in love with Maurice: "He was a sensitive man, not just someone who took pride in fighting, and there was a genuine tenderness behind his affability." Geli told Henriette that she no longer wanted to be loved by Hitler and preferred her relationship with Maurice: "Being loved is boring, but to love a man, you know, to love him - that's what life is about. And when you can love and be loved at the same time, it's paradise."

Historian **Ian Kershaw** said that after Maurice's betrayal, "there was such a scene that the chauffeur feared Hitler was going to shoot him". Hitler sacked Maurice in 1931 upon discovering the affair.

Geli told **Otto Strasser** after one large argument with Hitler: "She told me that she really loved Hitler, but she couldn't bear it any longer. His jealously wasn't the worst thing. He demanded things from her that were simply disgusting. She had never dreamed that such things could happen. When I asked her to tell me, she described things I had previously encountered in my reading of Krafft-Ebing's *Psychopathia Sexualis* when I was a student."

Strasser later went into more detail about this when he was interviewed by officials of the US Officer of Strategic Studies in 1943. "Hitler made her undress... He would lie down on the floor. Then she would have to squat over his face, where he could examine her at close range and this made him very excited. When the excitement reached its peak, he demanded that she urinate on him and this gave him sexual pleasure. Geli said the whole performance was extremely disgusting to her and it gave her no gratification."

In an article titled "Hitler's Doomed Angel", historian **Ron Rosenbaum** said Hitler's sex life "took a form so bizarre and aberrational that they (women) found it, quite literally, unspeakable." On another occasion, the historian noted: "Part of the price (for knowing Hitler) was virtual confinement in a huge apartment with no company but Hitler and her pet canary, *Hansi*. Geli, too, was a bird in a gilded cage, trapped within the stony fortress with an uncle twice her age, an uncle increasingly consummated with what Hitler biographer Alan Bullock calls jealous possessiveness of her. Whatever the explicit form Hitler's affections took, it became increasingly evident that for Geli the rewards of her public celebrity could not compensate for the oppressiveness of her private confinement with Hitler. And that in the final months of her life, indeed withing days of her death, she was making desperate efforts to escape. There are those who believe that with Geli Raubal, Hitler experienced the closest he came to real love, the closest he came to emotional life of a normal person. But there are those who believe that in his relationship with Geli, Hitler expressed the true, profound deformity of his moral nature in perverse sexual practices [paraphilia] that either drove Geli to suicide or led to her murder to prevent her from talking about them."

Konrad Haiden (*Hitler: A Biography*) noted: "[The] uncle and great lover gave himself completely away. [A letter meant for Geli] expressed feelings which could be expected from a man with masochistic-coprophilic inclinations, bordering on what Havelock Ellis calls 'undinism'. The letter probably would have been repulsive to Geli if she had received it. But she never did. Hitler left the letter lying around, and it fell into the hands of his landlady's son, a certain Doctor Rudolph."

Murray Davies (*The Mirror:* 2006): "Historical evidence suggests Geli and some other Frauleins treated Hitler to golden showers, and maybe a brown or two."

Hitler insisted that Geli and her friend, Henriette Hoffmann, received weapons training. They were both encouraged to carry loaded pistols around with them and they practiced shooting on a rifle range just outside Munich; they were taught how to use a safety catch and how to clean a Walther 6.35 pistol, taking it to pieces and putting it together again. Henriette said they enjoyed this as it made them feel like characters in a Western.

On the morning of Saturday, 19th September, 1931, Geli's body was found on the floor of her room in the flat.

Henriette Hoffmann, her closest friend, believed that Geli had killed herself: "He (Hitler) fenced her life so tightly, confined her in such a narrow space that she saw no other way out. Finally she hated her uncle, she really wanted to kill him. She couldn't do that. So she killed herself, to hurt him deeply enough, to disturb him. She knew that nothing else would wound him so badly. And because he knew too, he was so desperate, he had to blame himself."

At the time of her death, Geli was 23 years old.

BIBLIOGRAPHY

- August Kubizek, *The Young Hitler I Knew: The Memoirs of Hitler's Childhood Friend* (Frontline Books, 2011)
  - Volker Ullrich, *Hitler: Ascent 1889 – 1939* (New York, Alfred A. Knopf, 2016)
  - R. H. S. Stolfi, *Hitler: Beyond Evil and Tyranny* (Prometheus Books, 2011)
  - Alan Bullock, *Hitler: A Study in Tyranny* (Harper Perennial, 1991)
  - Ian Kershaw, *Hitler 1889-1936: Hubris* (Penguin; New Ed edition, 2001)
  - Adolf Hitler, *Mein Kampf: The New Ford Translation* (Elite Minds Inc., 2009)
  - http://spartacus-educational.com
  - Hermann Rauschning, *"Hitler Speaks"* (New York: G.P. Putnam's Sons, 1940)
  - Brigitte Hamann, *Hitler's Vienna: A Portrait of the Tyrant as a Young Man* (Tauris Parke Paperbacks, 2010)
  - Edward Bulwer-Lytton, *Rienzi: The Last of the Roman Tribunes* (New York, Charles Scribner's Sons, 1902)
  - Friedrich Nietzsche, *On the Genealogy of Morals and Ecce Homo* (Vintage, Reissue edition, December 17, 1989)
  - Robert Waite, *The Psychopathic God: Adolph Hitler* (Da Capo Press, 1993)

- Joachim C. Fest, *Hitler* (Mariner Books, 2013)
- Ernst Hanfstaengl, *Hitler: The Memoir of the Nazi Insider Who Turned Against the Führer* (New York, Arcade Publishing, 1957)
- Ron Rosenbaum, *Explaining Hitler: The Search for the Origins of his Evil* (Da Capo Press, 2014)
- Arthur De Gobineau, *The Inequality of Human Races* (London, William Heinemann, 1915
- Konrad Heiden, *Der Fuehrer: Hitler's Rise to Power* (Skyhorse Publishing, 2012)
- Fritz Redlich, M. D., *Hitler: Diagnosis of a Destructive Prophet* (New York, Oxford University Press, 1998)
- Andrew Rawson, *Showcasing the Third Reich: The Nuremberg Rallies* (The History Press, 2012)
- Kurt Krueger, M. D., *I Was Hitler's Doctor* (New York, Biltmore Publishing CO. Inc., 1943)
- Jill D. Montgomery, Ph.D., Ann C. Greif, Ph.D., *MASOCHISM: The Treatment of Self-Inflicted Suffering* (Connecticut, International Universities Press, Inc., 1989)
- Christopher Isherwood, *The Berlin Stories* (New Directions, Reissue edition, September 17, 2008)
- Christopher Isherwood, *Goodbye to Berlin* (New Directions, September 27, 2012)
- William L. Shirer, *The Rise and Fall of the Third Reich: A History of Nazi Germany* (RosettaBooks, 2011)
- Edward F. Dolan, Jr., *Adolf Hitler: A Portrait in Tyranny* (New York, Dodd Mead & Company, 1981)
- Friedrich Nietzsche, *Thus Spoke Zarathustra: A Book for Everyone and Nobody* (OUP Oxford, 2008)
- Joseph Goebbels, *The Goebbels Diaries* (Penguin Books, 1984)
- David Lewis, *The Man Who Invented Hitler: The Making of the Führer* (Headline, 2004)
- Leonard L. Heston, *The Medical Case Book of Adolf Hitler: Final Diagnoses and World War II* (Wasteland Press, 2011)
- Walter Langer, *A Psychological Analysis of Adolf Hitler: His Life and Legend* (www.all-about-psychology.com, 2011)
- Mel Gordon, Erik Jan Hanussen: *Hitler's Jewish Clairvoyant*

(Feral House, 2001)

- Karen Horney, *Neurosis and Human Growth: The Struggle Towards Self-Realization* (W. W. Norton & Company, 1991)

- Arthur J. Magida, *The Nazi Séance: The Strange Story of the Jewish Psychic in Hitler's Circle* (St. Martin's Press, 2011)

- Erik Jan Hanussen, *Mindreading and Telepathy* (Translated into English and edited by Bill Palmer, 2008)

- Gustave Le Bon, *The Crowd: A Study of the Popular Mind* (Digireads.com, 2004)

- John David Morley, *Hitler's Sex: Unpublished Documents of the US-Secret Service* (OSS - 1943), (Vitolibro, 2013)

- Gustave Le Bon, *The psychology of socialism* (Forgotten Books, 2012)

- Edward Bulwer-Lytton, *The Coming Race* (Andesite Press, 1880)

- Theodor Reik, *Masochism In Modern Man* (Klempner Press, 2013)

- J. P. Holding, *Hitler's Christianity* (Tekton, 2013)

- John F. Williams, *Corporal Hitler and the Great War 1914-1918: The List Regiment* (Routledge, 2005)

- Henry Ford, *Protocols of the Learned Elders of Zion* (RiverCrest Publishing, 2011)

- Albert Speer, *Inside the Third Reich* (Simon & Schuster, 1997)

- Richard Von Krafft-Ebing, *Psychopathia Sexualis* (Arcade Publishing, 1998)

- Deborah Hayden, *Pox: Genius, Madness, And The Mysteries Of Syphilis* (Basic Books, 2003)

- J. Sydney Johns, *Hitler in Vienna, 1907-1913: Clues to the Future* (Cooper Square Press, 2002)

- Alfred Rosenberg, *The Myth of the Twentieth Century: An Evaluation of the Spiritual-Intellectual Confrontations of Our Age* (Amazon Digital Services LLC, 2009)

- Traudl Junge, *Hitler's Last Secretary: A Firsthand Account of Life with Hitler* (Arcade Publishing, 2011)

- Mark Felton, *Guarding Hitler: The Secret World of the Führer* (Naval Institute Press, 2014)

- Erich Kempka, *I Was Hitler's Chauffeur* (Pen & Sword

Books, 2011)

- Ronald Hayman, *Hitler and Geli* (Bloomsbury USA, 1998)

- Guido Knopp, *Hitler's Henchmen* (London, The History Press, 2010)

- Guido Knopp, *Hitler's Women* (Sutton Publishing, 2006)

- Douglas Botting, Ian Sayer, *Hitler and Women: The Love Life of Adolf Hitler* (London, Robinson Publishing, 2004)

- Roger Moorhouse, *Killing Hitler: The Third Reich and the Plots Against the Führer* (Vintage Digital, 2014)

- Peter Ross Range, *1924: The Year That Made Hitler* (Little, Brown and Company, 2016)

- Tacitus, *Germania* (Acheron Press, 2014)

- John Toland, *Adolf Hitler: The Definitive Biography* (Anchor, 1992)

- Bernadette Brady, *Natal Star Report: Adolf Hitler* (Starlight Software, www.zyntara.com, 2002)

- David Lewis, *The Secret Life of Adolf Hitler* (London, Heinrich Hanau Publications, 1977)

- Glenn B. Infield, *Hitler's Secret Life: The Scandalous Reality of the Führer's Private World* (London, Hamlyn Paperbacks, 1979)

- Henrik Eberle, Matthias Uhl, *The Hitler Book: The Secret Report by His Two Closest Aides* (John Murray, 2005)

- M. Hauner, *Hitler: A Chronology of his Life and Time* (Palgrave Macmillan, 2005)

- Ken Ford, *Women Close to Hitler* (KFMB, 2013)

- Adam LeBor, *Seduced By Hitler: The Choices of a Nation and the Ethics of Survival* (Barnes & Noble/Sourcebooks, 2000)

- John Lukacs, *The Hitler of History* (Vintage; 1st Vintage Books edition, 2011)

- Heinrich Hoffmann, *Hitler Was my Friend* (Burke, London, 1955)

- PROLOGUE: Roots of the Holocaust: http://www.holocaustchronicle.org/staticpages/26.html

- Roger Moorhouse, *His Struggle: Adolf Hitler in Landsberg, 1924* (Sharpe Books, 2018)

- Dorothy Hayden, *Psychological Dimensions of Masochist Surrender* (www.sextreatment.com)

ALSO BY A. G. MOGAN

- *The Secret Journals Of Adolf Hitler*: The Anointed (Volume 1)
- *The Secret Journals Of Adolf Hitler*: The Struggle (Volume 2)
- *Love on Triple W*: A Heartbreaking True Story About Love, Betrayal, and Survival
- *Humorous History*: An Illustrated Collection Of Wit & Irony From The Past
- *From Cleopatra to Hugo:* History's Most Legendary Love Affairs - Book 1
- *From Henry VIII to Lola Montez*: History's Most Legendary Love Affairs - Book 2

ABOUT THE AUTHOR

A. G. MOGAN has always loved history and the personalities that were born of bygone eras. Her interest for the world and its people fueled her passion for human analytics. She's used her knowledge to analyze people and their behavior throughout her adult career, including using her in-depth research to craft poignant biographical novels that readers eagerly devour.

When not studying great historical figures or long-lost stories from the past, she can be found at her home in Europe, enjoying the spoils of a wonderfully ordinary family life.

To learn more, please visit the author's website at
www.AGMogan.com

THANK YOU!

Thank you for purchasing this book! It means the world to me. If you enjoyed reading it, kindly leave a review on Amazon. That helps me tremendously.

Also, as a token of appreciation, you can receive my new book — **Mind Over Truth**: *An Annotated Collection of Interviews with Hitler's Closest Associates* — for free.

You can do so by subscribing to my emailing list on www.AGMogan.com

Made in the USA
San Bernardino, CA
12 November 2018